KU-476-198

THE DARKENING

SUNYA MARA

HODDER &
STOUGHTON

First published in Great Britain in 2022 by Hodder &Stoughton
An Hachette UK company

1

Copyright © Sunya Mara 2022

The right of Sunya Mara to be identified as the Author of the Work has been
asserted by her in accordance with the Copyright, Designs and Patents Act 1988.

All rights reserved. No part of this publication may be reproduced, stored
in a retrieval system, or transmitted, in any form or by any means without
the prior written permission of the publisher, nor be otherwise circulated
in any form of binding or cover other than that in which it is published and
without a similar condition being imposed on the subsequent purchaser.

All characters in this publication are fictitious and any resemblance
to real persons, living or dead, is purely coincidental.

A CIP catalogue record for this title is available from the British Library

Hardback ISBN 978 1 529 35486 7
Trade Paperback ISBN 978 1 529 35487 4
eBook ISBN 978 1 529 35488 1

Printed and bound by Clays Ltd, Elcograf S.p.A

Hodder &Stoughton policy is to use papers that are natural, renewable and
recyclable products and made from wood grown in sustainable forests.
The logging and manufacturing processes are expected to conform
to the environmental regulations of the country of origin.

Hodder &Stoughton Ltd
Carmelite House
50 Victoria Embankment
London EC4Y 0DZ

www.hodder.co.uk

THE
DARKENING

for shadows

for storms

&

for those who brave them

CHAPTER 1

If nightmares had music, they'd sound like the Storm.

Thunder like a racing heartbeat. Stinging jolts of lightning, a bombardment with neither rhythm nor mercy. And a slow, seething howl, like a beast denied its prey.

With fists of wind, the Storm bangs against the shutters, trying to crack our little house open like an egg. When it can't, it slices through our walls, finding all sorts of ways to make wood scream.

Amma's sweet, rasping voice comes from downstairs, joined by the mournful thrum of her sitar. A lullaby, one she used to sing while drying my tears. But there are some sounds that even the sweetest lullaby can't drown out.

As if the Storm heard my thoughts, the shutters slam open, letting in a blast of humid air fragrant with ozone. My mouth fills with the telltale taste of spun sugar and copper.

I go to the window, bracing the shutters, and then I make the mistake of looking up.

Before me is the Storm. It's a wall not of stone or clay, but of darkness. Like a gauzy curtain that hangs in a circle around our city, made of layers of mist and smoke and shadow, all the same color as the darkness behind my eyelids. There's no escaping it; there's no gap, and it's ten times taller than the buildings it dwarfs.

The Storm is ever squeezing tighter, swallowing street and sky inch by inch. We in the fifth ring know that we're the next to be devoured. The wilds of the seventh ring were taken long before I was born, but the farms and homes of the sixth were lost when I was a child. We live in a state of constant darkening; for years, sunlight has only reached as far as the third ring. A few years from now, perhaps it won't reach even that far. But by then, Amma's will be gone.

From the nearby watchtower, the stormbells clang a warning: *A stormsurge is coming.* I scan the street for stragglers, but I can't see from up here.

Shoving the shutters back into their warped wood frame, I cross the tiny landing and leap down the stairs, into the main room where everyone's gathered.

Her slow, dreamy song makes the clanging even more jarring, but Amma's doing her best, just as she has for the last fifty years, running this home for the cursed. Her steps have gotten slower and her back bowed, but still I'll never be able to catch up to her, to do half as much as she does.

Without skipping a note, Amma gives me a worried look that asks me to hurry. She's seated with her sitar in the center of the long room, with stormtouched in their beds on either side. Seven of them live here at Amma's, mostly children, ones who got caught by the Storm — either beasts dragged them back during a surge, or they went and touched the stormwall — and were then cursed. The Storm doesn't care how young you are or how promising your life might've been. If it manages to touch you, even just the tip of your pinky, that's it, you're cursed.

Welcome to a lifetime of stares, jeers, and—if you're really unlucky—my cooking.

I try not to draw Pa's attention as I make for the door. He leans over the youngest, drawing an ikon on her arm that'll help soothe her shivering. I'd try to get a good look at it, but the clanging of the bells tells me there isn't the time.

"Vesper," Pa warns as I pass him.

I jump at his voice, and my elbow knocks into the bowl at the edge of Gia's bed, sending half-peeled shalaj roots flying. She makes a rude gesture with her left hand—her right is a gnarled twist of wood, courtesy of the Storm.

I wince, but I can't stop to pick them up, no matter how precious food is.

Pa brushes his black hair out of his eyes—the eyes we share—and his disapproving gaze lands on me like an anvil. "Don't go out there. They'll find shelter. Don't play hero."

"Sure, Pa," I throw over my shoulder, ignoring the certainty in his eyes that I can do no good, that I'm just a child, and not even a clever one at that. The front door rattles in its frame, and I plant my feet before unlocking all three deadbolts. The wind wrenches its way in, whipping at my clothes and flinging the heavy warped-wood door open. With the wind come other things: the wail of the Storm, the bite of the cold, a curl of mist that licks at my ankles. The stormbells peal once more, and the hollow of my chest reverberates with it.

Pa calls out, "*Vesper, don't*—" but the wind steals the rest of his words as I step over the threshold.

The wind whips my hair into my face. When the Storm howls like this, with the taste of burnt sugar in the air, it's rearing up for a surge.

Violet lightning streaks through the layers of darkness, revealing the beasts within the Storm. As it flashes, it illuminates the silhouettes of a scorpion's bulbous tail, the grasping talons of some massive bird of prey, the snarl of a gargantuan hound. An inhuman eye, glittering with violet lightning, looks down at me. Its gash of a pupil widens and then swivels up as something else catches its attention.

I follow its gaze. In the dim half-light, three red streaks fly toward the stormwall. The Wardana. Our guardians, the city's first and last line of defense, armed with incredible ikonomancy, sworn to protect us all. Their thousand-and-one-feather cloaks grant them flight; their crimson uniforms gleam like beacons against the wall of blackness. A guilty thrill raises goose bumps along my skin.

The way they fly right at the Storm, prepared to fight—that's bravery. That's power. I swallow down the envy that rises like bile in my throat.

The three Wardana angle into a descent. Their trajectory brings them closer than I'd like; just two blocks over and two blocks stormward. They head to where the stormwall bulges, blackness growing like a belly distending. Another bolt of lightning illuminates the stormbeasts clawing at the storm's edge, hungering to be born. My throat goes dry. If the Wardana can't stop the stormbeasts from making it out, then we're in danger.

The Wardana fly into action with a net of woven ikons, flinging it across the bulge. The net glows with pale blue light; it's as thin as lace, as if they're holding back a boulder with a spiderweb.

The woven ikonshield holds for a heartbeat, two, three—and then, in an explosion of black cloudsmoke, a massive beast claws through, roaring with the sound of a thunderclap. It's made of the same churning black cloud as the Storm: a two-headed lion with a mane that shifts like smoke, eyes like pinpricks of lightning. Smaller beasts crawl after it, taking advantage of the momentary breach.

In midair, the Wardana draw their weapons—two spears and a smaller woven ikonshield—and attack.

Behind me, the wind slams the door against its frame, and I snap back to myself.

Farther down the street, a mossy green door swings open, and a squat woman shouts, "Quick! Come inside!"

I join my voice to hers. Two huddled figures run into the woman's home, and her door slams shut. I scan the street for any other stragglers.

Something shifts in the alley across the street, but nothing emerges. My heart pounds and moss squelches underfoot as I tread forward, meeting the hungry-flat eyes of a woman huddled against a pile of rubble. Her coarse, saffron-colored clothes are worn and torn, her overdress tattered, her shawl full of holes. Her arms tighten around a small figure—a little round-cheeked girl.

"Come on!" I wave, gesturing at the door.

She pulls her child closer. I grit my teeth. Maybe it's fear paralyzing them, but my coin's on prejudice. The superstitious don't like waltzing into a home full of stormtouched.

An inhuman scream like a thunderclap cuts through the wind, over the peals of the stormbells. An unearthly chorus follows—the calls of the lion-stormbeast's entourage, the smaller beasts that've followed it out of the Storm. The hairs on the back of my neck stand up.

"Hurry!" I shout. The child twists in her mother's arms, peeling back her shawl and meeting my eyes.

A shadow passes over me, a spear-wielding, cloak-clad shadow. The Wardana lands on our street, some six houses down—that's way too close, we have to get inside *now*—but the mother just cowers against the wall. Does she want to die? Does she want to be dragged into the Storm?

Through her mother's arms, the kid looks up at me with golden eyes. I glance over my shoulder at my footprints leading back to the door—just ten steps, and I'll be safe inside.

But if I go inside and shut the door, any harm that comes to this girl might as well be my fault. Though, if I go after them and get killed in the process, Pa'll spend the whole of the afterlife calling me moss-brained.

Well, I'm used to that.

Pushing off, I sprint toward the two of them as fast as my legs will take me. I track the Wardana out of the corner of my eye, catching flashes of blood-red leather and a pale blue glow from some kind of ikon.

The alley closes in around me, cutting off my view. The kid's mother steps in front of her little girl as if protecting her from me. "Listen, there's a safe place through that door," I say in one breath. "You can't stay out here, the beasts are too close."

Her gaze flicks down to her kid, to the scales peeking from under her sleeves. Not prejudiced, then. Just stormtouched and scared.

I soften my tone. "I promise we won't hurt you."

The mother nods, and I grip her freezing hand in mine. The girl holds tight to her mother's waist as I drag them at a run out of the alley.

I stumble to a stop at the alley's mouth, my shoes skidding on mist-moistened moss, and throw out a hand to hold them back. Across the street, Pa stands in the open door, his face a mask of terror.

A spider-shaped stormbeast click-clacks across the street between me and Pa. It's the closest I've ever been to one. Its bulbous body is made of the same substance as the Storm—black cloudsmoke that churns endlessly in whorls and loops—and its eight bulging eyes spark with violet lightning.

It stands a good two feet taller than me, making it probably the runt of the litter. But that's little comfort as it snaps its pincers, tasting the air.

It turns to me, opening its maw.

My heartbeat quickens. There's only one thing I can do. What Ma would've done.

"Go around it," I tell the woman, shoving her forward when she hesitates. "I'll distract it. Go!"

I sprint to the pile of rubble in the alley's mouth and heave up a slab the size of my head, swinging it at the beast. It bats it away with one leg and click-clacks toward me with the other seven, clumsily, drunkenly, like a baby learning to walk. A terrifying baby with eight hairy legs.

Focus, Vesper. What was all your work stealing scraps of ikonomancy for, if not this? You've practiced. You must know an ikon for this. Anything.

Anything.

Thoughts dart through my mind as I back up. I shove my hand in my pocket, finding a stub of charcoal from the fire. With a shaking hand, I draw the first ikon that comes to mind, a basic ikon for light. A flare of light flashes the second I complete the ikon.

The beast falters for just a heartbeat.

My hand shakes. An elementary ikon for fire rises in my mind's eye—but there's too much moisture in the air for it to do anything but spark. I discard a half dozen more in the space of a breath. I have nothing.

The stormbeast fills my vision with its swirling-smoke body. Pa was right. I'm no hero. There's nothing I can do. I should've stayed inside.

Its pincers snap at me, and my back hits a wall.

My knees buckle, and I slide down the wall, catching a glimpse from under the beast's midsection of the street. I let out a breath, relief expanding in my chest, as the mother and her kid reach the safety of Amma's.

But someone else steps out. Pa strides forth, armed with a pen in one hand and a kitchen knife in the other. A circular ikon glints on the blade. Everything slows.

The beast snaps at me, and my head bangs against the wall, a whoosh of displaced air kissing my throat.

Pa raises his arm and sends the knife flying.

I squeeze my eyes shut.

The beast shrieks in my face, but its scream dies into a gurgle of grinding rock.

I open my eyes. Cloudsmoke pincers tremble an inch from my face. A pale grayness spreads across its eight eyes, dulling them, as if someone upended paint over its head. The grayness radiates from a single point: where Pa's knife is embedded in its side. It reaches the tips of its pincers and the furred edges of its feet, and all is still.

I stretch out a shaking hand to the beast's skin. My fingers brush cold stone. One ikon did this?

"Vesper!" Pa yells.

I inch sideways until I'm free of the beast and break into a run to him. Pa glances up at the sky as he grabs my arm and hurries me inside.

The door shuts behind us.

I lean back against it, gasping into the silence, meeting a dozen pairs of wide eyes.

Pa squeezes his eyes shut, but his relief lasts barely a second before he wheels on me, a flush reddening his tan skin and his gray eyes glinting. "What were you thinking?"

I catch my breath. "We just saved two people, Pa."

"No, I saved three people. *You* nearly threw your life away."

My cheeks heat. "It was the right thing to do."

"If you can't even protect yourself, you've no business playing hero."

The mother and her daughter watch us, huddled together on the empty bed in the corner, clutching each other even tighter than they did outside. Their terror stokes a red-hot fury in my belly, one that melts the rest of my fear away.

Giving them as much of a smile as I can manage, I push past Amma and the stormtouched, heading into the kitchen. Four of them stare openly, but a few avert their eyes in a pretense of giving us privacy. Red-haired Jem ever so sweetly slides a finger across her throat and grins at me.

"Vesper!" Pa's thudding footsteps follow me into the kitchen.

I draw down the curtain as Pa stands with his back to me, gripping the edge of the counter. He takes a deep, shuddering breath, and his voice comes out dead quiet. "When are you going to learn?"

My stomach sinks. Wisps of my hair fly around my face and stick to my cheeks, courtesy of the humidity and the static in the air, and I work my fingers through knotted curls, buying myself a moment. I know it's not what he means, but a little rebellious voice says, "I want to learn, Pa. Teach me a few tricks, and you won't have to worry anymore."

He wheels on me, more frightening than the hairy spider baby. "Don't start. Not now. Not when your foolishness almost cost you your life."

I bite my lip. How do I make him see that ikonomancy could've saved me? I had time to write an ikon. If I'd known the one that turned the beast to stone, I could've saved myself. I wouldn't need him. "If you taught me, Pa, I promise I'd make you proud."

"Vesper—"

"Pa, I'd be dead if you didn't know ikons. If I knew ikons, knew them properly—"

"Enough." His voice booms through the kitchen.

My heart is in my throat. "Or what? You know every ikon under the Storm, Pa, and you don't do anything. If I had a third—no, a tenth—of the ikons you know—"

Pa looks at me as if I've struck him.

I pause. I've said worse than that without him giving me that look. "What?"

"We need to go."

"What? Go? Where?"

"There's no time, just go pack." He flings the mosscloth curtain aside, and everyone in the main room pretends like they weren't listening.

Amma's already on her feet, her cane thudding with each of her steps. Her white hair frizzes up out of her bun, giving her an otherworldly halo as it catches the light from the kitchen lamp. "Alcanar?"

Pa kicks aside the threadbare rug that covers the kitchen floor and raises the trapdoor beneath, climbing in. He pauses halfway into the tiny, secret room that serves as his bedroom and study, and meets Amma's eyes. "We'll be going soon, Amma."

I raise my voice. "We can't just go—Amma needs us."

Amma puts a quieting hand on my shoulder. "Why now? After seven years, why now?"

Pa clenches his jaw. "Now they know I'm alive. They'll come for me soon."

"How?" I ask. "Why?"

Pa's eyes bore into mine. "That ikon—I invented it."

His words eat up all the sound in the room, save for the pounding of my heart.

A knock comes at the door, loud as a thunderclap.

CHAPTER 2

There are three kinds of knocks that we get at Amma's Home for the Cursed.

The banging on the door isn't the first kind, the knock of someone who needs a place to stay. Nor is it the second kind, the knock of someone who needs a little food to get through the night.

This door-rattling knock is the third kind. The knock of someone out for blood.

My voice is small. "Pa?"

He's gone as pale as his face can get. Amma snaps her fingers, gesturing for him to hide.

"Coming!" Amma calls, shuffling toward the door, her cane thudding with every step. With a glance from her, the stormtouched hurry to their beds and dive under the covers.

Pa lets himself down into the dark of the secret room, then pauses, peering up at me. "*Vesper,*" Pa hisses, "*come here.*"

I press a finger to my lips and stoop to shut the trapdoor for him. A slow, cold certainty sits like a stone in my stomach.

This is my fault.

I can't let Amma handle it alone. Pa holds my gaze as I seal him into the tiny room. The back of my neck prickles as I throw the rug over the trapdoor, knowing that his dark eyes watch me through the floorboards.

Another three booming knocks. *BANG BANG BANG.*

Fifteen steps take me out of the kitchen, past the stormtouched, to Amma's side. All eyes are on the front door.

Amma turns the last lock, and the door opens a crack. Gloved fingers wrap around the edge of the door and shove it wide open. I catch the edge of the door before it can hit Amma and step in front of her, even as a chill runs down my spine.

Blood-red leather. Cloaks made of a thousand and one feathers. The Wardana.

There are three of them. One so unusually pale and cruel-lipped that he could be sculpted from ice. Another who's all slinky charm and good looks: a graceful, loose-limbed walk, tousled dark hair, a twinkle like captured sunlight in his golden eyes.

But the one in the middle is the one that stops me dead. His is a face familiar to anyone who has held a brass coin. A face with no weaknesses, a strong nose and a stronger jaw, smooth cheeks without a hint of softness, without a single leftover drop of baby fat, though he only has a few years on my seventeen.

Dalca Zabulon Illusora, the Regia's son, who will one day take her crown and have inked upon his skin the same golden full-body ikon that now marks hers. Who will one day inherit the only power that can protect us all from the Storm, a power that becomes weaker every generation.

He looks down at me with cruel eyes like shards of the sky. "Won't you invite us in?"

I don't move from the doorway. I find a smile and paste it on my lips, though words freeze in my throat. They may call themselves protectors of the city, but they're not here to protect us. All my admiration sinks into icy fear, now that their bravery and power is turned upon me.

Dalca stares, waiting. His height blocks out the street and the Storm behind him. I'm so close I can see the circular ikons etched into the red leather of his uniform, each one a mark of power. Seeing so many ikons so densely packed—and on his *clothes,* no less—is a cold reminder that ikonomancy belongs to the powerful. I have to scrape and borrow and trade to learn the shape of a single ikon, while he likely has ikonomancers draw them to tie his bootlaces or to warm his bath, or has them etched into the leather above his heart to repel the Storm's wet from sinking into his clothes and chilling his princely skin. If I could just memorize that ikon, I'd never again have to rub stinking wax into the threads of my coat.

My eyes fall to the knives at his waist. Ikons cover the handles, drawn in ink the color of old blood. They're complex ikons, ones I'll never get a chance to learn. But, for the first time in my life, my curiosity grows quiet. I don't want to be made to discover what those ikons do.

"Storm take me, you've struck her stupid." The pale one rolls his eyes, stepping forward as if he's going to force me aside. His white hair shimmers with color, reflecting the world around him. Pink where his hair meets the red of his Wardana leathers, dark silver against the black of his thousand-and-one-feather cloak, and a warm gold where the light from inside reaches him. It's clearly ikonomancy, and it's beautiful. A waste on such a sour-tempered boy.

"Move," he growls.

"Yes, of course." But I don't budge an inch, my heart pounding as my hands sweat. "What is it you want?"

Amma's cane raps my anklebone. A reminder to be cautious, to be unthreatening. I soften my voice, dropping my gaze. "It's just, the stormtouched, they can get easily upset . . ."

From behind me comes a theatrical moan of pain. That's a voice I know. Jem, my closest friend amongst the stormtouched, lets out another throaty groan. It hangs in the silence for a heartbeat, then a couple of the others follow her lead. I bite back a wince, but miraculously their charade works.

The pale Wardana pulls back, belatedly taking in the sign over the door. **AMMA'S HOME FOR THE CURSED.** His face gains a pinched, disgusted look. "You sure about this?"

"He has to be on this street." Dalca stares over my shoulder and into the house. "Go inside, Casvian."

Casvian, the pale one, sighs and steps so close his boots touch my shoes. I take an instinctive step back, and he shoves the rest of the way in.

"We have evidence of unauthorized use of ikonomancy in the area. Please stay calm"—he grimaces as Jem lets out another groan—"and as *silent* as possible. I remind you that we, the Wardana, are here to protect. Unauthorized use of ikons is extremely dangerous, and we are duty-bound to protect the public from rogue, untrained ikonomancers."

Dalca and the slinky, good-looking one enter as Casvian drones on, every word of his speech perfectly rehearsed.

"Please." Amma steps in front of me. "Come in. Whatever you need."

They see only a frail old woman, white hair tied in a tidy bun, shoulders bowed under a worn shawl, a smile framed by deep lines etched in chestnut skin, once-dark eyes filmy with age, hands trembling around the head of her cane. Amma shoots me a glance, and I read the warning in her gaze: *If they see you as an ant, be an ant. Don't give them a reason to look at you.*

"I'm so sorry," I grit through my teeth, ducking my head and stepping aside. "The stormtouched are fragile, but I'm sure you'll be careful."

Casvian pushes past us with a snort. The prince's eyes slip from my face without acknowledgment. I am too far beneath him for him to even pretend to see me. I glower at him, daring him to meet my gaze. If he has guts enough to barge into my home, he'd better have the bravery to look into my eyes as he does it.

As if he heard my thoughts, the third Wardana looks at me with a strange, studying expression in his golden eyes.

I glare back at him, and the corner of his lip twists in an expression like the distant cousin of a smile. I take in the vertical slit of his pupils and his too-sharp canines — a cat's eyes and a cat's smile — and his smile widens as he sees that I understand what he is.

Stormtouched. Like most of the people at Amma's. The only difference is that he wears blood-red and so has power.

I've only heard of one other Wardana who was cursed by the Storm. She was the hero of the fifth for a couple years, until she lost her life during a stormsurge. But she hadn't been touched by the Storm herself; she had inherited her curse from a stormtouched parent.

That was lucky for her, since it meant the curse was mild enough that she could fight. Though some say that to be stormborn is to live with a ticking clock, that the curse is merely dormant until the day that it wakes.

Perhaps he, too, is stormborn.

"I'll be careful," he promises gently. I don't fail to notice that he speaks only for himself.

Giving me a small nod, he follows the others. I shut the door behind them, folding my fingers against the wood until their trembling dies down. Crossing my arms, I turn and face the room.

The Wardana go from bed to bed, peering at every face. Looking for someone. Looking for Pa.

My heart thuds an erratic, staccato beat, and I focus on the storm-touched to keep my gaze from going to the kitchen. All I can do for Pa is make sure I don't give away his hiding place.

Casvian, the mirror-haired one, stops beside Jem and picks up the large jar of baby teeth peeking out from under her bed. He yelps, and Jem catches the jar he drops in surprise. They share a few words, too quietly for me to hear.

My gaze drops to the nearest bed, to Gia. Barely eleven. Her wooden feet stick out from under her blanket, and I tug the sheets back over them. Fat tears well up in her eyes, and I kneel beside her, wiping her cheeks with my sleeve. Her mother left her on our doorstep two years ago, after Gia touched the wall of the Storm.

I reach for Ma's locket where it hangs under my shirt, drawing strength from it. She wouldn't let anyone barge into her home.

Following in the Wardana's wake, I go to the stormtouched one by one, offering soft touches so they know I'm here. The two newcomers shrink into themselves. I give them space, swallowing down the terror that rises when I think of what they could give away. Better not to draw attention to them.

Jem grabs my hand as I pass by. She holds fast and tugs me down to the edge of her bed. "Don't do anything stupid," she hisses under her breath.

I scowl. Her curse dances across the features of her face, aging her in front of my eyes. Jem's curse is the only one I've seen like it. At the moment, she has auburn hair and the unlined face of a woman in her twenties. But by the time she goes to bed, what's left of her hair will have gone white, and she'll be wearing the wizened face of a woman dying of old age. In the morning, she'll wake up a baby. Over and over, her body fits a lifetime's worth of growing into a single day. The jar under her bed is filled with all the baby teeth she's lost.

She doesn't let go of my hand, and I'm not about to make a fuss, so I stay put and watch the Wardana.

Casvian holds a brass gadget, noting things with the air of a researcher. He's slenderer than the other two, who are built like warriors. He's clearly the ikonomancer of the group—while he draws the ikons, Dalca and the stormborn will handle the fighting.

Dalca might have the build of a Wardana fighter, but his eyes—blue as a summer sky and striking against his sun-darkened skin—are as cold and assessing as a king's. The telltale eyes of those with royal blood; the eyes of the Regias.

Though Dalca's no more than a dozen feet away, he's no more touchable than the sun. We all watch him like we're spellbound, like we have no choice.

It's not because of what he is. It isn't even because he's attractive, in a sharp, still way.

It's that he's at once the past and future of the city. In the way he walks, in the way he fills the room, there's something that says he cannot be destroyed. He's safe the way the rest of us never are.

Has he ever known fear? Has he ever felt hunger, much less feared it? Has he ever huddled with others to ward off the cold? Why would he, when he can step into the sunlight whenever he pleases?

Does he even fear the Storm? One day, he'll be Regia, with the power to fight it. Power the likes of us can never imagine.

The stormborn Wardana passes in front of me, and I tear my eyes from Dalca to watch him. He slinks through the room like a lazy cat, and the stormtouched stiffen as he passes. He smiles at them, wearing a wry grin like armor.

I commit their three faces to memory, wishing they'd speak. Yet all three of them are as silent as the grave. I wish they'd ask questions; I wish they'd ask who drew the ikon they search for. If they don't need to ask . . . that means they already know.

Casviañ heads upstairs. A few moments later, a crash sounds.

Amma shoots me a look while Jem tightens her grip, but I'm already on my feet. I shake Jem loose and jump up the stairs, taking the steps by twos.

Casvian stands on the landing by the window, precious soil and shalaj roots at his feet. He holds an empty planter box, then tosses it aside. He waves the brass gadget to and fro, scanning across the ledge where the planter stood. Scanning for ikons.

He kicks idly at the shalaj root, his dirty boots stomping on our food.

He has *no idea*—no idea how I had to save for that soil, or how precious the seeds are. So precious that there were months when I had the money to pay and no one willing to sell them to me. The fear in my blood gives way to anger.

But I bite my lip. The only thing that saves me is that he's not really looking at the planters. He wants to make a mess, provoke an outburst. If he'd looked carefully, he might've noticed the little ikons I drew in the dirt to keep the shalaj healthy. Or an ikon for enlargement, one of the few I know, repeated over and over, to help the shalaj grow a little larger than they might've on their own. It wasn't even that effective—I always thought the guy who sold it to me must've gotten the proportions wrong—but it was the best I had.

I've kept my secret from Pa for years. Years of hunting down scraps of ikonomancy from gray market peddlers and folks who failed out of Wardana training. Even with all my efforts, what little I've learnt wouldn't amount to as much as a sneeze from a first-year ikonomancer trainee. Pa had been so much more than that. Amma says they'd called him the best ikonomancer in a century. Pa doesn't speak of it, except to forbid me from learning so much as an ikon to tie my shoe.

I've worked hard to keep my secret from the best ikonomancer in a century. I'm not about to let a sneering Wardana boy discover it in a matter of minutes.

Casvian moves to the next window, where hangs a box full of saplings. He knocks that box down, scattering the dirt and saplings that will now surely die. He steps on them with cruel delight, making sure to crush each one under his heel.

"*Stop!*" I snap my jaw shut, but it's too late.

Doesn't he understand? We only get two food rations here, mine and Amma's—the stormtouched don't qualify. Our bags of mancer-made food have to stretch very, very far.

Looking down at the destroyed saplings, their thin stems broken, their tiny leaves shredded, a black fury rages through my bones. It's all I can do to listen to the little voice reminding me: *An ant, remember you're an ant.*

Casvian turns to me with a patrician crook of his eyebrow. Deliberately, he reaches behind his back and upends a third box, his eyes never leaving mine.

I shove him. I don't even remember crossing the room. *This cruel, stupid boy*—

My shove barely moves him. Under his Wardana leathers, he's as hard as stone. Casvian's thin lips curl into a dark smile. He steps close as I jerk back. "Assaulting a Wardana?" His honey-scented breath puffs against my face.

His hands encircle my wrists, grip surprisingly strong. I shove at his chest and twist, trying to break free, but he doesn't let go.

I'd thought him slender compared to the other two, but I now realize that says more about the size of the other two. He's not weak, not at all. I twist in his grasp, but there's no use—he's stronger than me.

I hope Pa can't hear.

"None of that, Casvian," a voice says from behind us. The prince walks forward, confident and steady as stone, his eyes cool and assessing. "You'll incite a riot."

Casvian doesn't loosen his grip. He doesn't look away from me. "I don't forgive an insult, Dalca."

"I haven't insulted you," I snap.

He sneers down at me. "She touched me." *That's insult enough*, his tone says.

My mouth goes dry at the disgust that pinches his face. He'd hurt me, really hurt me, with no more thought than he'd give killing a rat that found its way into his home. He doesn't see me as human.

Dalca puts a hand on his shoulder. "That's an order."

Red rises in Casvian's cheeks as his hands tighten on my wrists. I wince as my skin pinches against my bones.

They have a staring match above my head, and I've never before felt so little like a person and so much like a thing. It doesn't matter what I want, what I do, what I say. I'm little more than a toy between two bickering kids.

Casvian lets go.

I jerk back, wrapping my arms around myself.

Dalca kneels before me, and I jump back. He scoops up a mound of dirt and dumps it back in a planter.

"Leave it," I say. "It can't be fixed."

He looks at me and speaks with the full force of his certainty. "Anything can be fixed."

"Dalca . . ." Casvian seethes.

Dalca takes his time filling a planter with dirt and stomped-on shalaj. I don't bother telling him that there's no use. Anything can be fixed? What kind of life does he live? "Are there any other rooms in this place?"

It's not until his eyes meet mine that I realize he's speaking to me. "Just what you see. A small room on this floor, the bathroom, and . . . well, the attic." My room.

He gets up and dusts his hands. "Please." He gestures ahead.

I have to reach over Dalca's shoulder to pull the string that releases the ladder. He catches the ladder with one hand and climbs up. Casvian brushes past me and follows the prince up to my room. My sanctuary.

I stay put. I know what they'll see. A tiny room, with a ceiling that slopes so steeply that I haven't been able to stand up straight in there since I was twelve. A cot on the floor, covered with a threadbare blanket. Two pots collecting the rainwater that seeps through leaks in the roof, ones I've been meaning to patch. A book of fairy stories, the pages water-warped and the cover soft and faded. I only still have it because no one has the spare coin to buy it. They won't need more than a second to take it all in.

Dalca comes down first. He glances at me, then at the planters, but he heads downstairs without a word. Casvian follows. I glare at his perfect, shining hair until he descends out of my view.

Alone on the landing, surrounded by piles of dirt, I let go. My hands shake. I inhale, long and slow, until my lungs are filled, and then I breathe in some more, till my chest feels fit to bursting. Only when it hurts, when the edges of my vision start to gray, do I let it all out.

Back straight, I head down the stairs, pausing on the last step as Dalca flips a golden coin toward Amma. It slips through her knobbly fingers, clattering to the floor. "For your trouble," he says.

My gasp isn't the only one that hangs in the air. That one coin could keep all of us fed for weeks.

It must be a trap.

Dalca addresses the room. "A hundred goldens for anyone who can tell us the whereabouts of Alcanar Vale. Come to any guard post with your information, and we will make sure you're rewarded. If your information leads to his capture, you'll be relocated to the third ring."

And the trap is set.

The air is electric with anticipation. I half expect someone to blurt something out on the spot. To live in the third—some would sell out their own mothers for that. I understand now. They don't need to find Pa. They'll repeat this a half dozen times, at every house on this street, maybe in the market, maybe in an alley full of the homeless. The word will spread. Pa will be caught, one way or another.

The prince's voice lowers. "When the fugitive is captured, if it's discovered that you harbored him, or aided him in any way, you will share his fate."

Dalca's eyes flick to mine, and he holds my gaze. My heartbeat pounds in my ears. How well does he know what Pa looks like? Does he recognize my eyes?

He looks away first, then flings the door open and strides out. The other two follow him into the street.

The doorway frames a slice of the Storm. The black wall has calmed; dark clouds roll against each other in a lazy, smoke-like dance. Even the lightning streaks slower, though it still illuminates eyes, tails, claws. The Storm's beastly children prowl within her womb, watching. Waiting.

Their hungry eyes seem to watch me as I shut the door and press my forehead to the damp-warped wood, squeezing my eyes shut.

A whisper echoes in my skull, in time with my heartbeat.

It says to me, *This is your fault.*

CHAPTER 3

I draw in a breath, latch the deadbolts, and turn around.

Half the stormtouched leap from their beds, friends gravitating together. Jem perches down next to the newcomers. She gives the little girl a toothy grin, making her giggle. But as I pass them, she shoots me a tense look over the mother's head. She'll talk to the woman and figure out if we can trust her and her child.

Amma sits at the edge of the bed closest to the kitchen, her hands resting on the head of her cane. They tremble until she tightens her grip. I take her hands in mine and kneel at her feet. I rub my thumbs over her knuckles, over skin that's fragile and spotted with age. Her hands are so light in mine; they're more bone than flesh.

"Go to him," Amma murmurs, slipping free of my grip and patting the top of my head.

I lean my forehead against her knee, gathering my courage, breathing in the smell of spices that lingers on her clothes. Getting to my feet takes more energy than it should, and the kitchen might as well be a mile away. Drawing the curtain shut behind me, I kick aside the rug and knock on the trapdoor, in code: three raps, a pause, then two, a pause, then two more.

A moment passes, then comes the sound of a lock unlatching. A section of the floor pops up, and I grab the edge, hauling it open. Pa lifts himself up to sit on the floor, his legs dangling into the little room beneath.

"Did you hear?" I ask.

"I heard."

I imagine dropping down beside him, and him wrapping an arm around my shoulders, pressing a warm kiss to my forehead. Telling me it'll all be okay.

"We have to leave," he says, speaking quietly so his voice doesn't carry through into the main room. "You've seen what happens. They won't stop."

Mercifully, he doesn't say, *It's all your fault.*

"We repay Amma by making sure they don't know we've been here. Get your things."

He drops back down into his hidden room and tears papers off the walls, stuffing everything into a worn pack. His room seems even tinier than when I saw it last, fitted with a small cot that's not quite long enough to sleep on without curling up.

"Where will we go?" Amma's has been our home for years. She took us in when I was ten and is more a grandmother to me than anyone who shares my blood.

Pa looks up at me, his hands stilling on the drawstrings of his bag.

The curtain rustles as it's pushed aside, and Amma enters the kitchen. "Put that bag away," Amma says, leaning on her cane as she peers down to meet Pa's eyes. "You think a couple of pretty boys in shoulder pads scare these old bones?"

Pa shakes his head, his black hair falling into his eyes. "I can't repay your kindness like that."

"You can if I say so." Amma's wispy white eyebrows draw together as she frowns down at him.

Pa almost smiles. It's not a happy one. "They won't stop, Amma. Don't toss away your life for us." He fixes his gray eyes on me. "By the time I'm back, I want you to be packed."

Wood cuts into my palms as I grip the edge of the opening tight. "Where are you going?"

Pa glances at Amma, then gestures for me to hop down.

Amma sighs as she leaves us. "This is how they win. How they've always won."

Once the mosscloth curtain falls behind her, I let myself down. A thrill flutters in my stomach to finally be allowed in Pa's secret lair. Tucking my legs under me, I sit on the cot and face him as the sounds of Amma's sitar filter down through the dusty air.

"Your mother and I had friends once," Pa says. "Some of them are still around."

Once, when they fought in a revolution. Before Ma was lost. "They'll help?"

"Maybe. We'll see."

"I'm sorry, Pa." I fix my gaze on my hands. I can't handle seeing the disappointment in his eyes.

He sighs. When it comes, his voice is tired. "It'll be okay."

"Will it?"

Pa's face is turned away from the light. I can't make out his expression, but I watch him clip a dagger to his belt and secret pens in his sleeves. "I don't know. There's a price I can never pay. And there's something else. Something neither the Wardana nor anyone else can ever have."

I draw my knees to my chest as my heart thuds and my eyes sting. Where did I go wrong? Which of my choices led to this? Should I have left the mother and child to fend for themselves?

Pa reaches under the lone pillow at the cot's head and pulls out a familiar book. I hold my breath.

Most people who use ikonomancy do so like a child learning her letters—they memorize the alphabet and learn the words that they're taught. The truly talented mancers figure out how to combine ikons by stringing the letters of the alphabet into new words. Pa was better than them all; he created new letters, and with them a whole new language.

And his little book is where he wrote down the best of his work.

Pa scrawls something on the cover. An ikon whose shape I try to commit to memory, but even as I do, I know I won't remember the exact proportions. Before my eyes, the book shrinks to the size of my thumbnail. "Will this fit in your locket?"

I pull Ma's locket out from under my shirt. Pa tips the miniature journal into my palm. The book fits easily, nestled between a painted portrait of Ma and our family ikon engraved on the other side. Ma's painted features give me pause. She has large, furious black eyes, a strong nose, a strong jaw. The only softness in her face comes from her lips. I've always liked to think I look like her, albeit a little watered down. My nose is a little less sharp and my jaw a little less bold. My gray eyes are Pa's, but my lips are hers. I've got her softness, but not her strength. I click the locket shut and pull the chain over my head to hand it to him.

He stops me. "No, Vesp, I want you to keep it."

I meet his eyes with questions caught in my throat. "I don't want to keep it. You keep it and bring it back to me."

Pa presses my fingers closed around the locket. "Just for a little while," he says in a mild tone that gives him away. He's lying through his teeth. "For safekeeping."

I tuck the locket back under the collar of my overdress. Pa holds out his hand, and tentatively, I place my hand in his.

"In case something happens, you need to promise me that it won't fall into the Wardana's hands. If you can't keep it, burn it."

My stomach churns. "What if I read it?" That's his worst fear, isn't it? Some childish part of me wants to threaten him. *Come back to me, or else I'll do it, I'll read it.*

His expression flickers, reverting to his usual somber so fast I must've imagined the smile. "Do you know why I never wanted you to learn?"

I shake my head.

"It takes something from you. Something you can never get back. Not the magic itself, but the power. To affect the world with a word? With just a symbol? It makes men greedy. They begin to think they can rewrite fate. That they can hold the very sun in their hands."

Pa looks at our hands.

"If I had never learnt, your mother would be alive."

"Papa—"

He drops my hand, and the softness leaves his face. "If all goes well, I'll meet you at the old temple in the fourth in four hours. If not, run."

I bite the inside of my cheek and nod.

"Go now. Pack your things."

I pull myself out of the trapdoor.

"Vesper," Pa murmurs so quietly I almost miss it. "When we had you, we hoped you would be better than us."

His words are a gut punch. I've failed him. I'm not a genius like Pa.

I'm not a hero like Ma. I don't even have a quarter of Amma's kindness. I mean to apologize, but the words catch in my throat. I don't have the air in my lungs to speak them.

Pa wraps bandages around his face as if he's got a disfiguring curse—a quick disguise—and pulls on a shawl with a heavy cowl. He hops up out of the hidden room, and I follow him as he goes out into the main room.

The stormtouched are gathered around Amma, who stops playing her sitar when she sees us. A sharp note hangs in the air. Pa goes to Amma and kisses her knobby knuckles. She holds his hand tight until he pulls away.

Standing at the door are Jem and the two newcomers. Amma rises to her feet and adjusts Pa's shawl so the waxed mosscloth covers his chin. It'll ward off the damp, but more importantly, it'll keep the Storm from touching his skin if he gets caught in a stormsurge.

Amma cracks the door open. The street is full of people stretching their legs and assessing the damage. Perversely, a little gratitude hangs in the air after a stormsurge. Folks are grateful to be spared. Some get holy about it, praying to the Storm to pass them by the next time, too. Pa calls them fools.

Amma steps out with her cane, walking a few yards away as if to take in the air. A large group passes by at the same moment, carrying candles and ikonlanterns for a post-stormsurge prayer. Amma pretends to trip, and several people come to her aid.

In the middle of the commotion, Pa ducks out with the mother and her daughter. They separate quickly, and Pa slips into the crowd.

I run outside and help Amma to her feet, brushing the dirt from her clothes.

"Getting too old for this," she sighs into my ear. Over her shoulder, I watch the back of Pa's head until he melts into the distance. A dark feeling wraps its claws around my heart.

I should have said goodbye.

CHAPTER 4

In the hour after Pa leaves, between sweeping fallen soil into little piles and scrubbing the floor clean, my guilt metamorphoses into fury.

I scrub the worn-smooth wood with a single-minded focus, ignoring all other thoughts rattling in my head. If I can scrub the last of the dirt out of the floor, I can erase the last trace of Dalca and his Wardana lackeys.

I wring the rag out and pretend it's Dalca's neck. He's the target for all my fury. He gave the orders. He put a price on Pa's head. It's their fault that the stormbeast got through in the first place.

I hate that he knelt and put on the guise of someone kind, someone who wanted to help fix the problem. I hate that he thought it was fixable.

I pull one little sapling from the crack between two floorboards, its fragile neck broken and roots mangled. How would he fix this?

I grit my teeth and scrub the ikons from the inner lining of the boxes. There's so little to be salvaged from the fallen saplings and the shalaj that we'd better take that golden coin to the market soon.

Amma's gentle footsteps sound on the stairs, punctuated by the thuds of her cane. She only uses it when she has to, when her bones ache too much to do without. She stops beside me, pressing a steaming cup of sundust tea into my hands. "That's good enough, child. Drink up, get the Storm out of you."

"I'll have to get more seeds. That *stupid,* arrogant—" I stop and take a breath. "I don't know if the new sprouts are going to survive. They probably won't, but I'll try. I'll have to watch them for a few days."

As the words fall from my lips, I realize that I won't be here in a few days. In a few hours, I'll leave Amma's for good. Raising the cup, I take a long drink of the golden tea, letting the spices warm me up from inside. Who knows if it really does anything against the Storm—Amma and all the folks who wear pouches of sundust believe it wards off the Storm's curses—but the earthy, nutty flavor soothes me.

"I'll teach someone. Jem, maybe." I say. "It's not that hard, really. Anyone could do it."

"You've decided to go, then." Amma's dark eyes are soft, and a sad smile pulls at the lines of her face.

Drawing my legs in, I sit cross-legged at her feet, close enough to breathe in the scent of cardamom that always clings to her. "You heard Pa. We can't stay."

Amma peers down at me with furrowed brows. "Your father has decided he needs to go. Have you decided to follow him?"

Seeing her from this angle reminds me of being a child, of being small enough to hide in her skirts. I spent a good year hiding in her skirts, when Pa and I first came to her. I used to think Amma was as tall as a mountain. When did I start seeing her as small and frail? When did I last go to hide in her skirts, only to find that Amma came to my shoulders?

"I . . . Pa thinks I should go. Do you think . . . I could stay?" I ask, feeling it out, watching her expression. I haven't thought it through. How's she going to take care of everyone alone? Without me, she'd lose more than a pair of helping hands — she'd lose a food ration, an entire bag of mancer-made food a week. How would she feed everyone then?

"You're your own woman, Vesper. I don't see how it matters what I think."

"I want to know what you think." I squeeze her hands. "I care what you think."

"Love, as I see it, you have two possible futures. You go with your father and let him keep you safe. Or, you don't have to go with him . . ." Amma's raspy voice trails off. "You've got a home here, with me, for as long as I'm around. You could stay. There are other ways to learn ikonomancy. Don't tell me I've imagined the way you watch the Wardana fly."

A strange feeling comes over me, like a bird fluttering in the cage of my ribs. "The Wardana just about never take anyone from the fifth. And they'll know that he's my father."

"How?" she presses. "The only people who know are in this house."

"But Pa's only got me left."

"Blood isn't a leash, love. Your choice is yours."

Pa doesn't need me. Would he even want me along? What would it be like on the run with him, with no Amma as buffer against his disappointment in me?

"He can take care of himself," Amma says. She doesn't say, *The stormtouched can't.* I look at her hands, folded upon her cane. She doesn't say, *I need you.*

"He said it might be dangerous, if we stayed. Dangerous for you."

Amma smiles the danger away. "I've already said what I'm gonna say. You'll always have a place here, till the day I die. Whatever danger may come."

I jump to my feet and wrap Amma in my arms. I love her surprised laugh and her familiar, motherly scent, like cardamom and soap. She's so tiny, her bones as thin as a bird's.

"I don't want to go," I say into her silver hair. "But what's Pa going to say?"

Her voice is a low murmur, like she's telling me a secret. "Darlin', there comes a time in every woman's life where she has to decide things for herself. It's your choice, and yours alone. But remember this: you are more than just your father's daughter."

I let out a slow breath. Pa doesn't need me, and worse, I'm not sure he'd even like having me around. Amma's right. I ought to make my own choices.

I don't need him.

She pulls back, ducking her head to hide her expression from me. "I need to start dinner—"

"I'll stay," I say. "I'll tell Pa, and then I'll come back. For good."

She rests her hand on mine and squeezes once before she lets go.

Alone on the landing, I drain the last of the sundust tea. It takes me only minutes to set the room to rights and to grab my waxed mosscloth shawl from my room. I leave unpacked my two changes of clothes and book of fairy stories. They'll be here when I come back.

I bundle up and make my way out.

My fingers tingle, like they're waking up from being numb, and I wrap them around my neck. Sometimes I can feel the shadow of the choices Ma and Pa made like fingers around my throat.

My ma was a woman with a plan. She feared nothing, not the Storm, not the Regia. She spoke out when it would've been better to stay silent, decrying how little the Regia cared for us in the fifth ring. She publicly denounced what folks only whispered in private, that we of the fifth were just human buffer, another wall against the Storm if the ones of stone and ikonomancy fell.

And people listened.

The Regia's meant to protect us all from the Storm, even the poor, the tired, the cursed. That's what it means to bear the Regia's mark. When the golden ikon is tattooed onto the skin of one of the royal bloodline, the Great King grants them power, immense power. The only power that can hold back the Storm.

But for over a century, the Storm has only grown stronger—and the Regias have grown only weaker.

Ma led all those who listened in a fight against the last Regia, Prince Dalca's grandfather. Pa was always at her side, armed with ikonomancy the likes of which no one had ever seen. They overthrew the Regia. But before any real change happened, the Wardana caught her.

They gave her one last choice: death by the hangman's axe, or death by Storm. She chose the Storm.

My father chose to run, with me in tow. He's been running ever since.

So have I. I've chosen nothing for myself; I've let his fear keep me small. I'm not a fool—I know his fear has also kept me safe. Is it wrong that I want something more?

My thoughts drive me away from the edge of the fifth and toward the boundary wall that separates us from the fourth. It's only a matter of a few hundred feet, but even this little distance from the Storm relaxes the tension in my shoulders. I pull back my shawl and recognize the same easing reflected in the faces around me.

It takes me the good part of an hour to get to the white iron gates that lead from the fifth to the fourth. There are four sets of gates: the black gates to the north, the white gates to the east, the golden gates to the south, and the crimson gates to the west. The golden road is the only one that leads to the first ring, all the way to the Regia's palace. The rest of them stop at the second ring.

Amma told me there used to be a reasoning to the colors; merchants and tradespeople from the fifth once took the crimson path, farmers from the sixth ring took the white, students from every ring took the black, and the gold was for the high ringers to descend. The Wardana fly right over it all, naturally.

Guards in gray uniforms stand at either side of the gates, watching the messy queue of people intending to cross. Their chests are puffed out, their cruel eyes watching for a petty excuse to exercise their power. I suppose they've got to get their respect somehow, when everyone knows they wear gray because they failed to earn Wardana red.

Every now and then, they pull someone aside and question them. But no one needs transit papers to go up to the fourth, where the markets are. Security is tighter at the crossing into the third ring, as it's home to the Wardana headquarters, the old entertainment district, and the residences of people with more means than most, but still less than those who live in the second. I've never been higher than the fourth.

I duck my head and shuffle my way forward through the white gates, up the ash-colored stairs and into the fourth. A guard with a drooping black mustache frowns in my direction. "Hey, you!"

I jump, heart racing. Before I can say anything, he comes at me, and darts right past, seizing the arm of a sandy-haired kid behind me.

I take the rest of the stairs by twos, without looking back.

At the top of the stairs begins the Pearl Bazaar, so named for its proximity to the white gates. Stalls line the walkway, filled with merchandise meant to appeal to fifth-ringers; rolls of pre-waxed cloth, ikonlamps proclaimed to last a decade, mancer-made drying powder to sprinkle around the house to keep the damp out, amulets meant to ward off the Storm that do little other than give false hope—they sell just about every household need and then some. But there are no pearls here, and neither is there a single grain of food.

Apart from the stormtouched, most people qualify for rations to get bags of mancer-made food every month. But it's never enough. It may start out as just enough, but by the time bags move from the ikonomancer stronghold in the third, through the fourth, into the fifth, so many hands have dipped inside the bags that what's left is painfully little.

Above, the circle of sky framed by the Storm grows dark, slipping from a violent sunset red into deep dusk. I count the hours till I'm meant to meet Pa. There's still a half hour to spare, but I make my way to the meeting place, a little old shrine that sits just past the outer crush of the bazaar. Pa used to take me to it when I was small, and I trace our old steps through stall-lined streets.

The ikon-powered streetlamps of the fourth flicker on, and almost at once, tired-eyed refugees from the long-gone sixth ring and the lost streets of the fifth cluster around them. I can't blame them for wanting a little light to ward off the shadows. At night, the darkness can be absolute. Only the circle of sky saves us: the little pinpricks of starlight stave off the feeling that we're all trapped in a cave where a monster prowls, where there's no way out, where there's only the wait until it gets us.

The walkway opens up into a wide courtyard. The dome-shaped shrine sits on a raised platform in the dead center. The iridescent stone shines even in the night, reflected a hundred times in the fountain at its base. A crowd of hungry-eyed people cluster around it, waiting. Some are here for faith; others come for food.

Two brown-robed priestesses walk through the crowd, struggling under the weight of a massive, steaming pot. Another priestess with hollow cheeks rings a bell, and the hungry line up for a bowl of steaming, spiced stew. The doe-eyed priestess doing the serving throws in a kind smile free of charge.

It's as good a meeting place as any. No one will notice two more people in the crowd.

I scan every corner of the courtyard for his familiar form. No sign of Pa. I tamp down the nerves that skitter across my skin. It's fine. I'm early, he still has time.

And besides, I need a little time to come up with a way to tell him that I'm not coming. Maybe I've just got to spit it out. Be firm.

But I can almost see his eyes deadening and his lips becoming one thin line, the way he is when he's too furious for words. The memory alone shrivels up my confidence.

Someone pushes at me, trying to get me to hurry into line, and I'm jostled into the crowd of food seekers. I shove and sidestep my way out —things aren't so bad that I have to take charity. Someone else needs that stew more, I'm sure.

The only way out is into the shrine itself. The stone steps dip in the middle, worn smooth by thousands of feet over hundreds of years. In the shrine, the sounds of the outside world fall away. The walls are deeply carved in interlocking patterns, almost like simple ikons.

A woman enters and unwraps a small piece of fragrant wood. She throws it into the undying fire at the heart of the shrine. The air is sweet and dark with the smoke of burnt offerings, smoke that curls up through the oculus, reaching for the sky.

She finishes her prayers and hurries out, leaving me alone. No one really hangs around inside the shrines. Even folks with nowhere else to go wouldn't dare linger. The Great King isn't a particularly kind god. He demands respect. He is older than the Storm, after all. The Regia is his instrument, the vessel for his undying soul. One day that'll be the prince, and his cruel, angular face will be nothing more than a mask for the Great King.

I go to the fire and pull a sliver of rosewood from my pocket. I've been saving it, but now I can't remember for what. We've never needed help more than now. I throw it into the fire and ask the Great King to watch over those I love. To protect them, and to guide me.

The smoke from my offering curls toward the circular opening in the domed ceiling. The disc of sky is pure darkness, and for a moment I have a wild fear that my prayer will be heard not by the Great King, but by the Storm.

My feet find a groove in the stone floor, smoothed by the feet of those who came before me, and I trace their steps around the fire. The shrine is old, maybe as old as the city herself. The carvings on the walls frame a depiction of the Great King, a calm face in mosaic, made up of hundreds of small symbols like ikons. The carving is faint, rubbed away by the touch of thousands of hands.

Directly across from the carving is another that's almost completely gone, lost to time. I stare at the place it once was and a dark shroud falls over my vision, the shadows of the temple growing long. I shiver, blinking. There's no darkness, no long shadows — just my imagination running wild.

All that's left of the carving is eyes aglow with fire and lips twisted in a snarl. Around his shoulders are whorls and curls, like smoke—or like the dark clouds of the Storm. Pa pointed it out to me, long ago. "We should remember that the Great King has two faces. We've forgotten the old one, the wrathful one."

Few others talk about the wrathful face of the Great King. In most newer shrines, there's only the usual depiction. It's not hard to imagine why folks have let this face fade into obscurity; if the Great King we know is his kinder side, I'm pretty sure we're all collectively hoping we never have to meet the other one.

Others enter the shrine, and I leave to give them privacy.

I bite the inside of my cheek as I walk the perimeter of the courtyard, scanning the faces of those still waiting for food.

The time to meet Pa comes and goes; the minutes tick on.

He's just late. It's no reason to worry. But my palms grow clammy.

The hungry march forward, their number dwindling as each of them gets their food and finds a safe corner to devour it. The line shrinks, then halves, then thickens into a mob as the last few fight for whatever is left.

"Come back tomorrow!" a priestess shouts, as two others carry the iron pot back inside. "There's no more today!"

The priestesses disappear. The courtyard begins to empty, and Pa still hasn't shown.

A loud shout behind me. Grunts and hollers come from the leaving crowd as a couple of folks push through. From the other entrances more people pour in.

More poor souls looking for food? "You're too late!" someone shouts, no doubt thinking the same thing.

They pay no attention, scrambling across the courtyard as if something's chasing them. I back away until I hit a chilled stone wall.

A rustle of feathers from above. My stomach sinks as I clap eyes on the source: red leather under a black feather cloak. A Wardana descends, cape flung out like wings. A wild halo of dark hair. Cold blue Regia's eyes. Prince Dalca.

I pull my hood higher, sidling away, my heart pounding with mingled fury and fear. All around me, people surge to their feet.

More red, more Wardana. They enter the courtyard from all sides. My heart thuds, panic sealing my throat shut.

Prince Dalca raises a gloved hand in signal, his eyes fixed on a figure in the crowd. The Wardana surround them, not fifteen feet from me.

A hooded figure in a shabby cloak. A familiar mottled moss-green cloak. One of them yanks the hood down—and my stomach drops. *Papa.*

I push against the sea of people trying to get out of the Wardana's way, jabbing my elbow into someone's bony side and shoving my way to Pa an inch at a time, shouting, "Move!"

Pa swings his fists like a boxer, landing a punch on one Wardana's cheek. He roars, bounding back, spinning as the circle of Wardana squeeze tighter. His eyes glint with a fire I've never seen, and he wears a grin that's both wry and feral.

From his sleeve, he pulls a slip of something that he slaps against another Wardana's chest. The Wardana screams as his armor begins to rot, radiating out from where Pa slapped him. An ikon he'd prepared in advance? Another Wardana gets her arm around Pa's throat, dragging him back, and Pa reaches into his sleeve once more.

I claw my way forward as Dalca yells, "His hands!"

Pa slaps the Wardana's arm, and she lets go as her gauntlet turns to stone. Dalca steps forward as the Wardana form a tight circle around Pa.

Pa wheels around, his expression fierce and wild and alive. In the gap between two red-clad soldiers, over the heads of the terrified crowd, his eyes meet mine. He stills.

I push harder against the crowd, holding his gaze. "Hold on," I mouth.

Pa softens. It starts with his eyes going gentle, but it seeps through the rest of him until there's no fight left. He shakes his head, wearing the strangest, softest smile, before he puts his hands up in a gesture of surrender.

A scream dies in my throat as a horrible awareness comes over me. Pa's protecting me. He'd fight if it weren't for me.

Pa slumps, and the Wardana fall on him like vultures.

This is my fault.

Prince Dalca wraps chains around Pa's wrists and activates an ikon. The metal turns molten and flows over Pa's hands until it looks as though he's wearing silver gloves.

The crowd carries me backwards, murmurs washing over me.

"Who is he?"

"Hardly matters now. They'll be makin' quick work of 'im."

I pull my shawl over my head to block them out. My ears ring as the sounds of the crowd fall away, all sounds fall away, save for my breath and the beating of my heart.

Prince Dalca and another Wardana I recognize, the ikonomancer with pale hair, each grasp one of Pa's arms and take to the sky. They rise higher and higher, flying far past the prison in the fifth ring where I might have been able to bribe him free. Over the fourth ring, the distance turns them into a three-headed blotch; over the third, they're nothing more than a speck.

My foot catches, and I stumble. By the time I right myself, all signs of Pa and the Wardana have disappeared.

Pa's gone, just like that. As if he's been plucked away by the hand of the Great King, who heard my prayer and scorned it.

People jostle at me in their hurry, and lest I trip again, I tear my gaze from the sky and let them turn me around. We pour out into the main market street, and I fight my way free of the crowd.

A deep-set doorway provides a moment's shelter. I can't catch my breath. My chest is all pressure, and a high-pitched ringing in my ears drowns out all sound, save my thoughts.

Dalca took Pa, and it's my fault. Pa let himself be caught, to protect me.

It's my fault. If I'd been stronger, smarter—

I suck in a breath. Do the Wardana know that Amma shielded us? I have to warn her.

I push myself into a run, sprinting through streets until I'm gasping for air, my lungs burning, my legs aching, a stitch in my side like a dagger in the gut. I tear through dark alleys, through bustling market streets, through the white gates into the fifth, past people who yell as I hurtle into them, all the way back to the streets I know. My legs take me home.

I smell it before I see it.

Smoke, not delicate and fragrant like the fire of the shrine, but acrid and lung scorching. Belonging to a cruel fire, the kind with tongues of flame that hunger for wood and flesh.

Amma's home burns. It's one long lick of fire against black-charred bones of what were once walls.

The neighbors dump water on the buildings on either side to keep the fire from spreading. They're only worried about their own homes. No one would have helped Amma. The prejudice against the cursed would have been too much to overcome, even to save lives.

I look for familiar faces amongst the crowd.

They must have got out.

Strangers look back at me with ugly, smoke-darkened faces. A white-hot rage rushes through me. *They let this happen.*

But why? Why this? I can't understand it.

Hands reach for me as I draw closer and voices surround me, but I can't hear over the rushing of my blood.

I charge inside, covering my head, and the heat hits me like a slap. Fire-dry air steals the moisture from my mouth, my nose, my eyes. I blink again and again, but the air trembles with heat, a mirage like the inverse of the Storm. Everything smolders: the walls, the floor, the ceiling.

The beds are blackened. There are body-shaped lumps on some of them. *Sheets,* I tell myself. *It's just the sheets.*

Something crunches underfoot.

Jem's teeth, spilling from an overturned jar.

Amma's sitar, propped up in its place by the stairs.

I reach for it, and the metal strings burn my skin. A scream tears from my throat, but I don't let go.

I scream for them.

The building creaks as if it's screaming with me. The ceiling bows, threatening to fall and bury me.

The smoke makes me wheeze, and tears blur my vision. I scrub them with the back of my free hand. I have to find them, find where they're hiding.

The mosscloth curtain has burned away, and the way to the kitchen is bare.

I stop dead.

Amma's cane, blackened, with a burnt hand still attached. Huddled around her, shielded by her, are—

No.

My legs give out, my breaths coming in gasps that scrape my throat raw. A scream tears through me and comes out a sob. I can't breathe— I can't catch my breath—but that's okay, this isn't real, this can't be—

Darkness creeps into my vision from all sides.

Amma's sitar bangs against the floor, and a low note sings in the air. *Go.*

Weeping, I drag myself back on knees and elbows with Amma's sitar clutched in hand, blindly moving until the heat breaks, until a cool gust of air licks over me.

Hands pull me the rest of the way over the threshold and into the street. Icy water splashes against my face and voices speak urgently, but I can't make out the words.

I'm already falling.

CHAPTER 5

Awareness comes in small doses.

My cheek is cold and wet. It smells of the earth and decay of damp moss. The palm of my hand stings, all hot, sharp pain. The stench of smoke—wood smoke, burning hair smoke, lost family smoke—greets me as I draw in a breath.

"She's alive," a voice murmurs, muffled as if through a layer of blankets.

I open my eyes. Everything is blurry—round moons of faces and, beyond them, the blackness of the Storm—but I stagger up onto my knees, ignoring the grasping hands and murmurs of the people around me. *They didn't help Amma.*

My knees buckle as I get my feet under me, and a hand steadies my elbow. The husk of Amma's home lies before me. I shove all thoughts from my mind, forcing it clear, blank, numb.

I wrench my arm free and snarl. "Don't touch me."

They clear the way. A cough works its way out of me, a sharp-edged one that tears up my throat, followed by a dozen others. I move on leaden legs that don't seem to be mine. I'm untethered from my body, just floating, strangely and peacefully detached.

My palm throbs, still wrapped around the sitar's neck, and the pain draws me back.

My ears ring, but my vision stills, straightens, sharpens.

The Storm is pure black. No red streaks, no black cloaks, no cruel blue eyes. They're not here yet. Maybe they don't know that they missed me, that they've one more innocent to kill.

Hair rises all along my skin, from the back of my neck to my arms. Animalic dread sinks my stomach. People are watching me. Any one of them could report me. I'm out in the open.

My heart pounds, and in each heartbeat is one word: *run.*

My legs carry me toward the Storm, away from people. My toe catches on a tuft of moss, and I steady myself on the side of a building. I keep my hand to the wall as I half run, half stagger. The moss gets thicker and thicker, until it's so thick my hand sinks all the way into it. I slow to a stop.

The buildings before me jut out of the stormwall, partly devoured by inky darkness. An electric hum fills the air, and I run my tongue over my teeth, tasting the copper-and-sugar sweetness of the Storm.

I take another step and find that I'm shaking. I watch, detached, as shudders rack me, goose bumps rising on my skin.

I find myself before a tall building covered in yellow-green moss. Under my palm, the springy rotted-wood door falls open, hanging crookedly on a rusted hinge.

A little room: three walls of mossy stone and one of black storm-cloud.

The moss on the floor looks soft.

A soft thump of wood against moss.

My eyes close.

I'm gone.

I wake up with my eyes salted shut. I've spent my dreams crying, and now I'm hollow to the bone. A soft blue glow from a street ikonlight filters in through the cloudy window. Though it's the dark of nighttime, between the ikonlight and the violet lightning streaking in lazy arcs through the wall of the Storm, the room is well lit enough to see by.

I sit up and cross my legs. My hand aches, and I spread my fingers wide, watching the seven red lines branded on my palm flex and stretch. A glint of light on metal catches my eye.

Amma's sitar. It lies beside me, turned on its side.

A keening howl tears itself from me, a wordless wail, a child's cry. I muffle it with the back of my hand, and when that doesn't work, I fold myself into a tight ball with my mouth pressed into my knee. My arms wrap around me, and it hurts, how much I wish they were Amma's.

The tears slow but don't stop. I should take better care of Amma's sitar. I take off my shawl and wrap it up to keep out the damp.

My hands shake. I press them together and lock my fingers till it stops.

It takes a monumental effort to focus and take stock of myself. My clothes are wet, as is my hair. My face is taut and dry. My throat stings.

And inside me is a horrible sharp-edged thing. I can't face it.

I turn instead to face the Storm. It's a quiet darkness now. Layers of misty veils hang as insubstantial as shadows. The edge is soft; it's hard to know exactly where it begins. Five steps, maybe, and I'd be cursed. Six, and I'd be gone. I don't move.

Ma chose this darkness over death. Now it hangs quiet and innocent.

The more I stare, the more the darkness seems to expand, until it fills my vision. It calls to me. I touch Ma's locket where it hangs below my collarbone.

I curl up at the foot of the darkness; far enough that it can't touch me, but close enough that all it would take would be one stormsurge. Let it take me, if it wants.

There's nothing left for me. Nothing but a sorrow that I can barely keep at bay, one that threatens to dig its knives into me and break me.

But the Storm soothes me. Even the high ringers, who have every-thing and stomp on us like ants, even they won't be spared. The Storm will take them, just like it took Ma.

I gaze into the dark until my eyes slip closed.

A woman hums as she runs her hands through my hair. My head is on her lap, and I twist to face her. She wears a silvery veil that shrouds her features, and yet I know who she is. "Ma?"

Her voice is as soothing as her humming. "You called for me, my child."

"Has the Storm taken me, then?"

"Isn't that what you wished for?"

"Is it?" I sit up. We're on the bank of a pond so still it looks like poured silver. I bend over its edge and meet my reflection. The an-swer is there, formed by the lips I share with Ma. "No, that's not what I want."

I turn to her. She waits, her hands clasped.

"How did you do it? How did you walk into the Storm? Where'd you find your bravery?"

"It wasn't bravery, my dear. Nothing of the sort."

"What, then?"

"Fury."

Her voice is dark.

"You say they've taken everything from you. Now what?"

I shake my head.

"Will you weep?"

I scrub my eyes.

"What do they care if you weep? What use is sorrow to you?"

"Stop it, Ma."

"Will your tears bring them back?" She grabs my wrist, and I jerk back.

"Stop it!"

She hisses. "Where's your fury?"

I push at her. My fingers catch in her veil and tear it from her face.

Darkness in the shape of a person stares back at me. I jump to my feet, and so does it.

I raise my hand, and it mirrors me. It's my shadow.

What will you do? it asks.

"What can I do?"

It steps closer. *What you will.*

It pushes me and I fall back through the silvery pool, into a starless night.

I wake up with ten inches between my nose and the soft black of the Storm. My body jerks back, and I'm halfway across the room before I know what I'm doing.

I press my palms into my eyes and breathe, pushing down that sharp-edged thing inside of me, pulling forward the memory of the pale Wardana's cruel sneer, Prince Dalca's stony, untouchable face, his glinting royal-blood eyes. I welcome the anger that fills me, feeding it memories—Amma's burnt cane, Jem's teeth, Amma's voice, the sundust tea she'd make—until the sorrow no longer threatens to eat me whole.

The Storm rumbles with thunder. I turn until it's just a hint of darkness at the corner of my eye.

I get to my feet and walk the length of the room, waking up and warming up as I do. I'd noticed nothing before, hadn't bothered to look at anything but the Storm. The stripped down skeleton of an old loom stands in one corner, and the walls are notched with deep stone shelves. This must've been a manufactory of some sort, long ago. The fifth ring was once a place of smiths and weavers; a place where things were made. But, as the Storm invaded the sixth and the displaced fled to higher rings, all the old manufactories and workshops were remade into homes, often with odd quirks and strange layouts.

The fifth once had a proper jail, until that too was made into homes. Now the handful of cells in the Wardana's fifth-ring watchtower are where lawbreakers are imprisoned, for a time. For those who've committed minor crimes, freedom comes with a fee paid by their loved ones. For those who've committed worse, there's the Storm.

That's not where Prince Dalca took Pa.

The beginning of something flickers to life in me. Pa's not gone, not the way Amma and Jem and all the rest are.

I come to a round wooden lid set in the ground, half decayed, about four feet across. I lift it up and find a metal tub. It's deep enough to sit in, though I can't imagine it was built for people. In the streets, I've seen women with strong arms and red cheeks dyeing mosscloth over freestanding tubs about this size.

A layer of moss coats the bottom. There's also a wooden doll, tucked away for safekeeping by some long-lost child. I lift it up and set it aside.

Beside the tub, I unearth a faucet and a pump from under a mound of moss. The pump groans, but with a little effort, water comes out. Though it's red at first, it clears in minutes.

A small spark of desire pierces the numbness in me. I'd like to be clean, to scrub the cinder from my skin and the stench of smoke from my hair.

Most of the moss comes off easy, and I use a fistful of it to scrub the sides of the tub. Under all the moss is a circular ikon. As the cold water touches it, steam billows out and up, warming my face. I strip off my singed, smoke-gray clothes. Goose bumps rise all over my body, a little due to the chill, a lot due to the proximity of the Storm.

A hiss escapes my lips as I step in, sinking down until the level of water rises over my lips, over the tip of my nose, past the corners of my eyes.

My body tingles all over. My awareness sinks into it, as if I'm coming back to myself: my long feet and bony ankles, my smooth calves and knobby knees, the faint curves of my hips and chest, my scarred hand and my untouched one. My skin is perhaps the same brown as the prince's, but while mine is sallow from living under the Storm's shadow, his glows from the sun's kiss.

From under the water, the room is nothing but brushstrokes and pools of dark color. Fragments of light dance on the water's surface, in intersecting lines and ephemeral curls — almost like an ikon. If I rise up, what will this ikon of light do to me?

Let it change me. Let it make me as fierce as Ma, as smart as Pa. Let it kill the weakness that twists my stomach into knots.

My lungs burn, but I stay down.

Let me come out strong.

I jolt up, coughing, sucking in air to fill my lungs.

Lines of light dance across the wet skin of my chest and arms, bouncing off the water's surface. It's no ikon; there's no power in it. And yet.

I kneel before the Storm, Amma's sitar in hand. My fingers run along the strings, and I pluck out a few notes. The sitar hums in its familiar voice.

I ignore the tears that come to my eyes. The sorrow, the sharp-edged thing in me, I can't keep holding them in my throat, in my chest, in my belly. Not if I'm to leave this place and do what I must.

I press my lips to the sitar's head, where Amma used to rest her hands. With that kiss, I let the sitar have every dark thing in me, every shred of the despair that threatens to swallow me whole.

My fingers wrap around its neck, silencing it. I cast it into the Storm.

It flies through layers of darkness, going slower and gentler than it would've through air. It sings, as if ghostly hands now play it.

The Storm welcomes the sitar into its heart. With it goes my sorrow, until all that's left in me is fury.

The sky is as dark as the Storm when I return to Amma's. It takes everything I have to face the burnt-out shell of my home. A small fragile hope had lived in my heart, that perhaps my memory exaggerated, and something or someone might've been spared. With one look, that hope dies, but there's still something I need.

The first thing I do is bend over and throw up. There isn't anything in me, but my stomach threatens to unfold itself out my throat all the same. I knuckle the spit from my lips and forge forward.

Wood and other things crunch under my feet as I make my way to where the kitchen once stood. The trapdoor to Pa's room is burned open, and scraps of charred paper eddy in the wind. I let myself down and scrounge around. Almost everything is gone.

Wedged into a crack in the floor is a folded scrap of paper. On the front is my family ikon, the same one that's on Ma's locket. When I trace it with my thumb, the paper unfolds. It's a game Pa and I used to play. The words inside seem like gibberish, until I recall the code. Pa taught me it when I was eight. I'd thought it was the first lesson of many, I'd thought he'd go on to teach me ikonomancy. But it was just a way to keep me occupied. I look for little marks that tell me in which order the words should be read. Decoded, it reads *There's a bag of flour and sugar under Jem's pillow. Bring it to Amma and she'll make you sweets.*

It crumples in my fist and I let it fall.

I haul myself up out of Pa's room and go to the loose floorboard where Amma hid valuables. I half expect that scavengers have beat me to it, but when I lift the floorboard up, in a bed of ash, is Prince Dalca's gold coin. Thank the great mancers of the past for ikon-protected currency.

I pick it up and thumb the soot from the Regia's face. Sharp cheekbones, a strong nose. She has a bold face, an unyielding face, so much like her son's.

I slip it into my pocket, and then I kneel. I mean to pray for their souls to find peace in the next world, but it's been less than a day since I prayed to the Great King to protect them all. He doesn't seem to be in the mood to help.

Instead, I make them a promise. I won't join them until I've fought for them, until I've used every last drop of willpower in me.

My eyes are still closed when I hear the distant squelch of footsteps on moss. I jump to my feet and wedge myself behind the rubble, back pressed against the house next door.

A flutter of black feathers. A head of dark curls.

Prince Dalca. A boiling rage rises in me at the sight of his face, heating me from my toes to my ears. I understand what the Ma of my dreams meant. The fury drives the sorrow away, makes it small and defeatable. I hold on to it with everything I have, and I focus my rage on Dalca.

He kneels, touching the ash with the tips of his fingers.

Dalca is behind it all. If I want to save Pa, Dalca is the key. If I want vengeance for Amma and the stormtouched, Dalca's the one to pay.

I want him to hurt, like he's hurt me.

He folds his hands in prayer. It's a mockery. What does he ask, for the Great King to bless his next monstrous act? To thank the Great King for all the blood that's been spilled in his favor?

I scoot back. Dalca snaps to attention, eyes on the corner where I crouch in shadow.

I freeze, holding my breath. After a moment, Dalca touches a dial on his wrist and his cloak billows out behind him, ash and dust rising. He shoots into the air, and is gone.

CHAPTER 6

The gold coin hangs heavy in my pocket as my feet take me to the far side of the fifth, to the northeastern quadrant between the white and black roads. I need to know what happened to Pa. I need to know where he is. And I need to figure out what I'm going to do about it. I need information.

There's one place that sells information, amongst other, more unsavory, things: the gray market. It's not a proper market, not like the established stalls of the fourth's Pearl Bazaar. For one, it's much harder to find. It moves from street to street and employs tricks both ikon-powered and not to shield it from the Wardana's eyes. Those tricks also make it a good place to get swindled or be robbed and left for dead. Jem brought me here the first time and every time after that; I've never been without her.

One street looks much like another at twilight, in the hour before the street ikonlights turn on and everything is in shades of indigo. I come to the crooked street where I last saw the market—back when I had no worries beyond getting shalaj to grow—and walk its length to a dead end strewn with moss-covered boulders.

A hooded woman sits on one of them, bottle in hand. I make the three-fingered gesture Jem taught me, and she nods and points to a large boulder. Beyond it is a zigzag path through the ruins that's invisible from the street. It lets out in front of a curtain embroidered with ikons.

When I pull the curtain aside, the gray market opens to me in a crash of sound and glittering gray light. The curtain falls behind me, and I stand a little straighter, squinting into the glow. Pipe-smoke diffuses the light from a hundred gray lanterns. It lies thick in the air, casting faces in indistinct detail and disguising where exactly the market ends.

Sellers of trinkets, totems, and necessities line each side of the floor. They've set their wares out on blankets that can be wrapped up and secreted away, in case of a Wardana raid.

I tug my shawl higher over my nose, cutting some of the resin-scented smoke. Eyes follow me, taking in the singed hem of my overdress. The hawkers at the entrance of the market gesture at their wares, but I focus on searching their faces. A familiar one catches my eye: a slender face adorned with bushy white eyebrows and a white mustache of astounding luxuriousness. Avos's shrewd eyes notice my attention, and his gestures become even more extravagant.

"Come, come, anything you need, I have for you at a good price. Better than these thieves —"

Falling to a crouch before his blanket, I lower my shawl. "I need a little information."

Avos makes a theatrical shrug. "A little information, maybe I have. But maybe you want"— he drops into a whisper just as loud as his talking voice — "ikons?"

"You sold me one once," I say. "It didn't work so well."

"No? These ikons, they're a little sensitive. Maybe you missed a line, yes?"

I frown. The hairs on the back of my neck prickle, but no one's looking when I glance behind me. "In the fourth, at the old shrine, the Wardana took someone—"

He hisses, dropping the genial act. His voice goes so low I hardly make out his words over the din. "Quiet, you idiot. You don't ask about them here. The Wardana have ears everywhere. You want to get killed?"

"What?"

His eyes don't meet mine as his act resumes. "No? That's okay, maybe another day. You!" He gestures over my shoulder. "Come, I see this has captured your eye."

I rise and back away, leaving him to his customer. Avos is the only seller I've dealt with. Guess this isn't the place to expect a break for being a loyal customer.

Tugging my shawl back up, I walk on. I catch movement out of the corner of my eye, keeping pace with me. My pulse picks up.

A bark of laughter. Three women sit around a barrel, a game of tiles set up between them. Their peals of laughter reassure me and draw me close.

They quiet as I approach, though smiles still curl their lips. "Ten brass to play, dearie."

Ten brass coins? How do they have that kind of money? "I haven't come to play. I'm looking for—do you know where I can get a bit of information?"

"Why, Marva here has ears long as a hound's. She's heard just about everything, wouldn't you say, Marv?"

"Haven't heard as much as you've sniffed out, Pera, dear. A bird once took her nose for a perch," she says behind her hand, in mock whisper to me.

I bite my lip. "Well, have you heard—or, er, sniffed—anything about the incident in the fourth? At the old shrine, the Wardana took a man—"

Their faces turn to stone, shutting me out. "No, Marv, you're right, our game's full."

"Please—I'll go. Just tell me who to ask."

The long-eared one shakes her head at me. "Go home, child."

I clench my fists and turn away. The pipe smoke lies just as thick here, but there are far fewer lanterns. I shiver. This is deeper than I've ever been into the market. Jem warned me never to go past the lanterns.

I steel myself and put one foot in front of the other. Slowly, the sellers with wares on blankets vanish. People hurry past, disappearing behind doors that open at a password. Sellers of other things lurk and lounge, some playing cards, others sipping cups of sundust tea.

A doll-like woman catches my eye, sitting on the threshold of a half-open door. She wears her shawl pulled back, so all can see the beauty of her face. She pats a reddening salve into the curve of her lower lip and smiles. "Let me make you over," she calls. A face-changer. I've heard of them, but I've never had the coin or the need for more beauty, especially not the ikon-sculpted kind.

But face-changers are skilled ikonomancers. She could know something more than the others.

She beams as I approach. "I'm sorry, I'm actually looking for information."

"Oh?" Her smile dims a notch. "What sort, love?"

"There was an incident. In the fourth, at the old shrine. A man was taken by the Wardana."

Her eyes flicker over my head, and a hand lands on my shoulder. My stomach sinks.

A gruff voice — I can't tell if it's a man or a woman — speaks over me. "You don't know anything about that, do you, Carver?"

The doll-like woman bats her eyelashes. "Not in the slightest."

"You'd better tell this girl here where she ought to go."

"Oh?" She glances at me. "If you're sure. Three doors down, love. Good luck."

The hand on my shoulder tightens and guides me past her. I roll my shoulder and duck, breaking my assailant's hold, and bolt.

I sprint down the first alley I find, but a figure stands in my way. Backtracking, I hurtle down another and hit a dead end. I spin and face two hooded, shawled figures.

"Brave, but not very smart, is she?"

"Give her a break. She's never had our hospitality before."

My legs tense in preparation. There's a gap between the bigger one and the wall and I launch myself at it.

Hands grab me around the waist and haul me up. "Let me go!"

I knee them in the chest, but they don't falter in the slightest. Their back takes up my entire view; I can't see where we're going.

A rap of knuckles on wood, a creak of a door. A dark interior; I squint as we pass shadowed shelves, and make out folded bundles of — clothes?

My captor knocks again, and this time light pours out as the door opens. A hum of conversation and scattered clinks of metal. Could they be chains, like the ones Dalca put on Pa?

I'm carried over the threshold and deposited on my feet in front of some dozen people sitting around makeshift tables laid with food and drink.

They quiet, save for one man with round cheeks. "What's this?"

One of my captors lowers her hood, revealing a sharp chin and tired green eyes. "Behold. May I present Alcanar Vale's daughter."

Several of them stand to get a better look at me, and the green-eyed woman puts her arm around me and guides me to a table at one corner of the room. Without fuss, she settles into a seat and gestures at the man behind a long counter. My fists at my sides, I stand and wonder if I can make it out of here. The other one who came for me stands at the entrance; I'd have to get past them.

"You can take off your shawl." I don't catch who spoke.

Four others are seated around the table, which seems to be an old door set on a crate.

I glare back at them. Who are these people who know about Pa, about me? To my left is a small woman with a mass of gray curls and the kindly face of a grandmother, save for the long scar that runs from the edge of her eye to her jaw. At her feet is a bundle of fluff—moss, by its shades of green and blue—which she spins into yarn by rolling it between her fingers and onto a wooden spindle. The grizzled, burly man at her side takes a swig from his cup and returns, with a click and clack of needles, to knitting a roll of yarn into a length of cloth. He grins at me when I meet his eyes, revealing that one of his teeth is marked with an ikon.

Directly opposite me is a tall woman, about Pa's age, with silver-streaked dark hair that falls over her shoulders. She pulls a pair of half-moon spectacles off her nose and closes the book before her, fixing me with a frown. She's so astoundingly gorgeous—like a warrior from legend, carved in cedar and brought to life—that I get a little embarrassed just looking at her.

Beside her is a delicate-boned person with a shaved head and pink cheeks, who squints at me with the intense focus of the inebriated.

A crumpled mass of cloth, half-mended, sits in their lap. And beside them, to my right, is the green-eyed woman who dragged me here, who beams at me expectantly.

What is this? Cautiously, I pull my shawl down.

Gasps and murmurs of surprise go around the table.

The grandmother sets down her yarn and fixes her eyes on me. "You look like your momma, girl."

"Ah." The man grins, stroking his stubble. "But there's Alcanar in the way she stands."

I'd expected him to point out my eyes. I've never noticed I stand like Pa. "You know my parents?"

All but the gorgeous woman laugh. "Where d'you think you are?"

From all appearances, a bizarre knitting circle. "I didn't get a good look. Being kidnapped and all."

"Sorry about that," the green-eyed woman says. "You were going about calling all sorts of attention to yourself."

I cross my arms. "I need information."

A boy my age flits past, depositing a plate of stuffed flatbread and five dented cups on the table. My stomach growls.

"Sit. What's your name, child?"

A stool appears, and I perch on its edge. The plate of flatbread slides toward me, steaming hot and smelling of spices.

"What're yours?" I ask.

"I remember," the grandmotherly one says, with a twinkle in her eye. "Vesper, right?"

The grizzled man with the ikontooth snaps his fingers. "That's it."

The green-eyed woman smiles. "Well, then, Vesper, eat up."

I ignore the food and my stomach. "I still need that information."

"Then ask."

All my questions tumble from my lips at once. "Do you know what happened? How did they know about my father? Where did they take him? Why did they burn Amma's?"

A gruff laugh. "We don't dabble in *whys* here."

The one with the shaved head answers, a little blurrily. "The p-prince started looking for your father a year ago."

Just a year ago? The rebellion was more than a decade ago. "Why now?"

"Ah." Green Eyes raises a finger. "That's the question, isn't it?"

"We know th-they took Vale to the th-third."

That's where I have to go, then.

"Oh," Ikontooth says. "But the prince knows all the secret passageways under the city. Alcanar could be anywhere."

"Secret passageways?" I ask.

"I heard the prince used to sleep down there, in the ruins of the old city."

"Everyone's heard th-that."

"I heard it was his grandpappy who locked him down there, when he was just a wee boy."

Green Eyes butts in. "I don't think she cares about the prince's woes, do ya, girl?"

I shake my head. I couldn't care less about his so-called hardships. But everything comes back to Prince Dalca. "What happened at Amma's?"

They sober. "That's a real tragedy. Poor souls."

"We know a pale-haired man led th-them. They used ikons to get it to burn so hot so fast."

Pale-haired. That'll be Dalca's lackey. "Do you know—did anyone get out?"

Grandmother answers. "If they did, dear, they're keeping to the ground."

The uneasy quiet and the pity in their eyes say the rest. I clench my jaw and straighten my back. "So, how do we do it?"

Ikontooth chuckles, deep and humorless.

"Do what, dear?"

"Save my father."

The gorgeous woman opposite, who's been silent this whole time, crosses her arms and leans back. The others trade looks.

I bite my lip. "But you were friends."

She breaks her silence with a low, melodic voice. "We were. That's why you get an invitation in here, why your questions get answered free of charge."

The green-eyed woman adds, gently, "None of us can risk what we risked then."

Then. The revolution that I've only heard of in snatches. "What happened back then?"

"You don't know?"

"I know they made Ma walk into the Storm. That the Regia died."

The gorgeous woman gestures, and a minute later, a round of drinks clatters onto the table. A clay cup of sundust tea appears before me. I glance at the others' cups, which are full of a frothy amber liquid.

It chafes that they see me as a child, but free is free. It's not until I take a sip that the scent of cardamom hits me like a kick in the teeth. I push the cup away. "What don't I know?"

The woman at the end speaks. "Eat, child."

I take a bite of the flatbread. Warm, flaky crust around a tongue-tingling burst of spices and sweet potato.

"There was once a boy from the fourth ring," she begins, "a boy both shy and brilliant. Ikons whispered their secrets to him; great mysteries of ikonomancy unlocked themselves for him. The ikonomancers, so high up in their third-ring fortress, saw his talent and drew him into their fold."

A muffled interruption. "What? I always thought Alcanar worked his way up, same as the rest."

"Shush."

She continues. "Under the same stars, in the second ring, a girl was born with a silver spoon in her mouth. She spat it out in favor of a dream: a world without the Storm, a world reborn, where all were equal."

Green Eyes slams her cup. "That had something to do with her right bastard of a pa, that did. She was always running away. That's how she met you, isn't it, Im?"

Im, the gorgeous one, inclines her head. "When your Ma and Pa met, his cleverness and her determination coupled into something powerful."

"Beautiful couple they were, dear." The grandmotherly one smiles at me. "Of course, they had their fights, but they had sweetness too."

"More than that, they had ambition. Your mother began remaking herself in the mold of a leader, and your father turned his mind to the mystery of the Regia. He told his findings to a trusted few, having come to understand that the Regia was an imperfect vessel, unable to hold the entirety of the Great King's soul. Something was left unbound—and the Storm devoured it and grew more powerful."

I drink in everything they say with the thirst of someone who knows they'll never get another sip.

"Your mother believed she could take on the mantle of Regia. Only, there was a Regia already on the throne, and a Regia is not an easy thing to depose. Your father never meant to kill him; he thought he knew how to neutralize the mark, make the Regia just a man. That was the plan—but something went wrong, and the Regia lost his life. Your mother, wearing the golden mark, the royal ikon, went into the Storm."

"Th-that's where it all went wrong."

"Shush. It could've worked."

"Your ma walked into the Storm to capture the last piece of the Great King's soul. We waited and waited. But she never came out."

Im's eyes are dry, but sorrow radiates out from her. The grizzled man dabs at his eyes.

My throat is dry. Is this true? Pa said Ma was forced into the Storm, that it was punishment, a death sentence. Or did he? He never liked to speak of her—all that I know of Ma comes from childhood memories, of stolen scraps sewn into a patchwork story.

Ma dreamt of being Regia. That's a bigger dream than any I've ever held. A dream worth the price of walking into the Storm . . . Is there something like that for me?

She reads my expression. "Don't paint some pretty picture in your head. Their failure—fine, *our* failure—doomed us all. This Regia is weaker than the last one. The Storm's only gotten stronger."

"And you've given up?" I ask.

"We've gotten smart. A full belly's nothing to scoff at." Her eyes drop to my empty plate.

Fair enough. I push the plate away.

They can knit till the end of time if they want to, but I have to save Pa. They've told me they don't know where Pa is. That only Dalca does. He's still the key to everything. And to get to Dalca, I need to get into the third ring. "How do I get a job in the Ven?"

A snort. "Might as well ask th-the Great King—"

"Be *kind*. Remember what it's like to be young."

"I *am* young!"

Green Eyes leans in. "What are you thinking?"

I trace a water ring on the table, ignoring the bickering. "I've got to get into the third."

The woman at the end taps her book against the table, and everyone quiets. "Your father paid for our help to hide you both. There's room in a safe house for you. You'll be hidden and fed for a month, at least."

A month. "And after that, what then?"

"Live. Alcanar kept you a secret. He kept you safe."

The grizzled man clacks his needles. "He could've brought you around once in all these years — Don't shush me! It's true!"

Pitying eyes find me. "I'm sure Alcanar had his reasons, dear."

Pa kept me safe, so safe I never knew this was part of his life.

"Safe's not enough for me anymore. If you can't help me, I'll find another way." The stool scrapes against the floor as I get to my feet. "Thanks for the food."

Stroking his stubble, the man laughs. "You sound like him. She sounds like him, doesn't she?"

"Who, Pa?"

"No." Another exchange of looks.

The green-eyed woman shrugs. "It's her life to throw away."

"Tell me," I say, crossing my arms.

She answers. "There's a fellow who's trying to, ah, stir things up. Showing up with ikons and just teaching them to people; shows up with more, sometimes. Brought us a net of ikons, asked us if we could follow the design and make more."

An ikonshield? "Only the Wardana —"

"Yep." She taps her nose. "A Wardana."

"An idiot," scoffs the grandmotherly one, shaking her mass of curls.

"Do we know it's a Wardana? Could be one of th-the maintenance folks."

"Nah, none of them would risk it."

I cut in. "Where can I find him?"

Im answers. "He shows up at the edge of the gray market, by the square with the well. Usually around midnight."

"Thanks."

"Be safe. And if you change your mind about the safe house—"

I stop her. "I won't."

CHAPTER 7

They make no move to stop me as I head back the way I came, through what I can now make out to be a clothes shop. The shop's façade is old, with peeling paint. No indication that it hides a secret pub where former revolutionaries come together in a knitting circle.

I shake my head, but it's no small comfort to know warm food is just a knock away.

The air's extra muggy and cold after the warmth of the secret pub. A scrap of paper chases the wind across the street, catching on my foot. I pick it up. It's an ikon-duplicated proclamation declaring that the Regia is hard at work on a grand plan to push back the Storm. It asks all to donate any metal to the Wardana and offers a hefty ration of food in exchange.

It might be all the talk of revolution, but it strikes me as a clever way to get fifth-ringers to give up their weapons.

I wrap my shawl tight and hurry along. When I turn the last corner, he's there. A line of people wait before him, and others huddle around the edges of the small square. It's hardly a square; more like a gap between two buildings, just large enough to house a well. The one benefit is that wood slats above shield it from the Wardana's eyes.

As I watch, some of the folks hovering nearby join the line, but others seem to think better of it and leave.

I edge to the side, until I get a good view of him. He wears his hood low, and a dark shawl covers the lower half of his face — he's taking no risks with his identity. From a sack, he pulls long, flat objects wrapped in cloth and distributes them after having a word with each person who comes up to him.

I wait the good part of an hour for the line to disappear. Out of boredom, I scratch perfect circles into the wall beside me. After ten or so, a black cat slinks across the street and sits beside me, grooming itself. I kneel and offer my hand. It sniffs my fingers and, with great dignity, allows me to pet it. It's soothing.

After what feels like a few minutes, I glance back at the well, and my hand stills. He's gone. It's empty.

I step out of the shadows, fully into the square. Stupid, Vesper. Where did he go? He could've taken any one of the four paths that lead away — I've no chance. I'll have to come back tomorrow. A whole day, wasted. Dalca could be doing anything to Pa. I don't have a day to lose.

"Looking for me?"

I jump, spinning around to face the voice, and my shawl slips down to my shoulders.

He was leaning against the wall in a pose of supreme smugness, but he starts as I turn. I eye him. Jumpy guy, but that makes sense. The cat slinks between his legs, doing figure eights around his feet.

I find my voice. "I was told you might be able to help."

"I help many people with many things," he says, affecting an airy tone. His boots gleam even in the dim light. Heavy, thick-soled boots, without a scuff or a scratch on them. Those aren't the boots of an ordinary fifth-ringer. "But you—what is it you need?"

"I'm looking for a way into the third. I'll take any work."

"My specialty is more, well, taking things out of the third."

"I can pay." I flash the gold coin before slipping it back in my sleeve.

His act falls away. "Why do you want this?"

I bite my lip.

"You have to trust me with that much, at least, if I'm to help."

Your father kept you a secret. He kept you safe. Safety's not what I need. I lean close and whisper to his cloaked ear. "The prince has my father."

He straightens, like a string pulled taut. He glances over his shoulder. "Let's get somewhere a little less exposed for this talk, shall we?"

I cross my arms, studying him through narrowed eyes. How much trust are we talking?

He rolls his eyes, then digs in his pack and throws me a parcel. "Stab me with that if I give you reason not to trust me. Fair?"

Under the cloth gleams an ikon-engraved blade. I snap the cloth closed, tucking it under my arm, where it's partially concealed by my shawl. "Fair."

"Follow me."

One street over, he stops at a dead end. The cat that I'd assumed was his scampers off. Once-ornate carvings cover a wall, but time has worn them smooth in patches. He glances over his shoulder before twisting a thin piece of stone. It slides noiselessly, and for a brief second I can make out the faint trace of an ikon in the carving. A section of the wall snicks open, and he waves me through.

It's pitch-dark, but he hums as he enters behind me and shuts the door.

"Hold on." He rustles around. I unwrap the blade.

A flash of pinkish light blinds me. I blink up into the glow of an ikonlantern set on a slab of stone that comes to knee height, with other stones arrayed around it like stools.

"Take a seat." His eyes linger on the blade.

The ikonlight shines on the carved rock walls of a small alcove that could fit no more than four people. But behind him is the eerie darkness of a pathway that goes somewhere else.

"What is this?"

"A secret passageway that goes between the fourth and the fifth. Now, please sit. If you want out, you just have to turn the dial on the wall to the right, until it clicks. Got it?"

I nod, settling myself onto a seat. "How do you know this place?"

He begins untying his scarf. "Prince Dalca showed it to me."

I'm up on my feet as he pulls back his hood and reveals a pair of golden cat-slit eyes. The third Wardana who came to Amma's. I hold the blade steady on him. "What's going on here?"

He raises his hands up high. "Might not have been my best idea, giving you that."

He makes no move to get up. I inch around him, until my back hits the door. "Explain. You were there with Dalca. *I saw you.* Who are you?" Is this a trick? Is Dalca going to jump out?

His eyes crinkle. "My ma named me Izamal Dazera. But you can call me Iz. And you're Alcanar Vale's daughter."

"I know who I am." I gesture with the blade. His eyes widen as it swishes past his nose. "What's with the weapons? Is it some trick? I know you're one of Dalca's men."

"I'm not—*his man*—for Storm's sake. Can I get something out of my pocket?"

"What?"

"Just a scrap of paper, to show you why." Izamal slowly brings out and unfolds a piece of paper. It's the proclamation from the Regia. "You've seen this?"

I nod.

"Do you believe this nonsense, that the Regia has a plan?"

I shrug. "Not really."

"That's right. They have no plan. They've already given up on the fifth. And worse, they won't give us the means to defend ourselves. Do you know why?"

I open my mouth, but he doesn't seem to need my response.

"They're afraid of us. Afraid that if we even have a scrap if ikonomancy, just a smidgen of power, we'll use it against them. We'll rise up and take the third—the second, even—for ourselves. They're more worried about that than how many of us the Storm takes. If they don't give a cat's ass, then someone has to."

Izamal's eyes blaze, and he grows more impassioned with every word. I lower my blade.

"I saw you," I whisper. "I don't understand. How could you burn Amma's and then this—"

"I *didn't*. I *wouldn't*. Dalca and I flew your father to the Ven, but that's as far as I was involved."

"Where is he?"

"I don't know. Dalca and Cas—and the rest—they don't trust me, not really. I'm their token fifth-ringer; they bring me out when they need to, but they don't let me in."

I squint at him. "Are you really from the fifth?"

"I am. You might've heard of my sister—Nashira Dazera. First fifth-ringer Wardana in a decade, and stormborn to boot."

Of course I'd heard of her. Everyone in the fifth had. I'd even thought of her when I first noted Izamal's curse. But how could I know they were siblings? When people spoke of Nashira, they talked about her dimples and her cheekiness, not her golden eyes. "I saw her once. She waved as she flew past."

His gaze lands on the floor. "After she—fell, Dalca picked me out of the trainees."

"Lucky you."

I've said the wrong thing. He scowls, pinning me with those golden eyes. "Yes, lucky me. Because of her, I'm working to change things for our people. Remind me, what have you done?"

Izamal's got a strange, fiery temper, but he's not wrong. The look in his eyes makes me want to do more. "I haven't. But I will."

He softens.

"But first I'm going to save my father. Can you—will you help?"

He nods. "You want to save him from Dalca's clutches. I want to save us all from Dalca's clutches—and that'd be a lot easier with a powerful ikonomancer like Vale on our side. It seems our desires align. But there's a price."

I bite my tongue: he's wrong about Pa. Pa's not joining any more revolutions. But he doesn't need to know that. I nod and bring out the gold coin.

"Not that. Not *money*, for Storm's sake. What I mean is—you help me, and I'll help you."

"Help you with what?"

He grins. "The cause."

"I'll help you," I say. "Help me get close to Dalca—help me save my father, and I'll do whatever you ask."

He raises an eyebrow, and his eyes twinkle. "Whatever I ask."

"For the, er, cause."

"We'll figure that part out. But first—how do we get you in?" He leaps to his feet and paces back and forth. "Cleaning wouldn't get you close enough. Maybe as a trainee? But you're so scrawny. We could get you into the armory, maybe—they're always running through recruits . . ."

He taps his chin, handsome face screwed up in thought. He's so animated—it's like he's twice as alive as the rest of us. "Oh. But of course. You're Vale's daughter. You can do ikonomancy."

I don't correct him, though I have a feeling he doesn't mean the handful of paltry ikons I know. "Where can that get me? The ikonomancers take apprentices, right?" From the Ven, I could surely keep watch on Dalca.

"Yes," he says slowly, drawing out the word into a purr. "I wonder. Well. Problem one, they've seen you. Problem two. Will they take a fifth-ringer?"

"There's a face-changer in the gray market," I say, only half following his train of thought.

"Oh good, that makes things simpler." He tilts his head at me. "What if you're a third-ringer?"

"That would be nice, I'm sure."

He gives me a withering look. "Casvian won't take a fifth-ringer. He will take a third."

"I can play a part," I say. "How different can they be?"

He laughs. "You'd be surprised."

It's unreasonably late when I return to the gray market, but only a few shops have shut for the night. The face-changer sips a cup of sundust as I approach her.

"Have you ever been to the third?"

"Sure have, love."

"Can you change me? Make me look like I belong there?"

I show her the gold coin. She waves me in.

An old woman sits on a crate, working at a small loom. Her face twists into a frown as she sees me. "Another vain fool?"

"Ignore her," the face-changer says. "You can call me Carver."

A beat. "Vesper."

"Sit." She gestures, and I take a seat on the edge of a crate in front of the mirror. "Please, make yourself comfortable." Her voice is soft, girlish.

"What can you do?" I ask.

She smiles. "Anything and everything. But you don't need to trust my word. Trust your eyes. Look at me."

A girl sweet as honey, with rose-petal lips, softly blushing cheeks, a pink tinge to the tip of her nose. She looks at her hands, her movements timid and gentle, and her long dark eyelashes sweep over high, rounded cheekbones. Her dark hair falls in sweet curls, and a heavy fringe covers her forehead, drawing attention to her huge eyes. She holds herself still, her posture radiating shyness.

She looks far too innocent to belong to the fifth. Far too sweet to be capable of anything besides sipping tea and frolicking through gardens.

I wouldn't know what to do with a face like that.

Her eyes flick up to my face, and in them I see a wry intelligence. Her posture suddenly loosens, and the demure frown widens into a lazy smirk. The illusion — for that's what it was — is broken. The doll face comes alive, and suddenly a real girl stands before me. She has the same sweet features, but without the stillness and the act of shyness, the aura of innocence is gone.

It's a lesson. The doll is a mask, an act, created by careful attention to detail. Part carefully coiffed hair and meticulous face-paint, part posture and expression.

"Looking like this has a lot of uses. People underestimate me, and I can go where I like. You wouldn't believe what people are willing to tell this face." This voice is different from the one she used before.

"You mean the color." I gesture at her rose-colored lips. "And the act?"

"That's just the edge of the stormcloud, love. My art involves a lot of skill and a little ikonomancy. I wasn't born with cheeks quite so high, nor eyes so big, nor lips so" — she smacks her lips — "luscious."

She leans against a stack of crates, waiting for me to say something.

"Impressive." And a little unsettling. Who is she, really?

Who could I be?

She winks at me. "Let's take a look at you."

Carver moves to stand behind me, meeting my eyes through the mirror. She runs her hands through my hair. "Like a third-ringer, you said? We can go for the look they love so much. Unless you have any specific requests?"

I drop my gaze from her eyes to meet my own. Pa's eyes, Ma's lips. My heart twinges at the thought of the traces of them disappearing from my face. But the change will only be temporary, until I've got Pa back. He'll know how to set me right.

I shake my head.

Carver gets down to business. "You're not the type that cries over hair, are you?"

My lips quirk. Even if I was, I'm all out of tears. "No."

She pulls a pair of scissors out of a case and begins to work. I watch my hair fall. The same inky black as Ma's hair. A tiny pang of loss surprises me, makes me sick. This is the least I can sacrifice.

My hair has always been long, stretching halfway down my back. She cuts it down to a little past my shoulders and trims a few locks so they fall in my eyes.

"Now we'll change the shape of your face, just a smidgen." She goes to a crate, the only one padlocked, and undoes the lock. She brings back something bundled in cloth. "Anything you ever wished was different? The ikon will hold stronger if it's a face you can easily accept as yours, if we alter something you've already thought to change. But the flesh remembers, and the ikon will only hold so long—it's tied to your self-image."

I find myself thinking not of my face but the faces of the cursed, the past and present inhabitants of Amma's. There had been one girl, Gelsomina, who as part of her curse been given shocking beauty, beauty like a force of nature, the kind that drew our eyes and made it addicting to look at her. I'd bitten back the little demon of jealousy by reminding myself that she was cursed, that it would be a burden to look like her. Now I'm tested. How would I feel, if that face were mine?

My eyelashes could be longer, I decide. My cheeks could be fuller, softer. My nose a little sharper. I soon find something to change about each of my features.

And then I remember how Gelsomina would claw at her face each night, bloodying herself, though by morning her skin would have knitted itself back together, and she'd be as gorgeous as ever. This isn't about beauty. This is about getting what I need from the Wardana. This is about being able to get close to the prince without him recognizing me.

I shake my head. "Give me something I can use. A face with a little power."

"Leave it to me."

Within the bundle of cloth is a copper mask; a mold of a face. She sets to work, holding it in one hand, with the other drawing an ikon on the inside of the mask. Periodically she glances up at me, with the furrowed focus of an artist drawing from life.

At last, she shows me the inside. I can't make out where each ikon starts and ends; she must have looped together a dozen to create such an intricate cat's cradle of lines.

She raises the mask to my face, the ikon-lined copper filling my vision. "Don't close your eyes, and don't move."

The mask is cool on my skin. Then the coolness turns to ice. A throbbing pain begins, like a distant drumbeat, getting closer and sharper. My eyes tear up and my vision blurs. I don't move.

The pain settles into a dull buzz, as if my face had gone to sleep and is now waking up.

She pulls the mask away. "All right, give it a moment to take. Let's do your hair in the meanwhile."

I twist to look in the mirror, but she holds me still.

"You'll have a chance to take it all in at once."

At once? "What more is there?"

"The folks of the third live in the sun. It lightens their hair."

She stirs something in a bowl, seeming for a moment a potions maker right out of a storybook, and then she smooths something cold and wet onto my scalp. It smells awful. She brushes some on my eyebrows, and they start to tingle.

"It should last a good few weeks, till your hair grows." She piles my hair on top of my head and guides me to a stone basin, where she has me bend over while she pours cold water from a pitcher over my scalp and rinses out the smelly muck. A lock of my hair curls against the stone, now a touch warmer than its usual black.

A trickle of water runs down the back of my neck as she shepherds me back to my seat.

She finishes with my hair and rummages in a crate and comes back with a little pot of kohl and brush. "Close your eyes." She grips my chin with one hand, and I feel the coarse bristles along my lashes.

"You have good eyes. Thoughtful, kind ones. The kind you can just point at someone and let them talk."

She instructs me on how to apply the cosmetics, showing me how to flick the little brushes, how much kohl to apply.

Carver lets go of my chin and steps back. "Take a look."

She holds out a circle of polished silver. A girl looks back at me, who blinks when I blink, who leans forward as I lean forward. Her dark hair frames a softer face than mine; her high cheekbones slope gently instead of curving sharply; her chin is a little pointier, a little daintier. Her eyes are the same as mine, but rimmed in kohl, they're as large as an owl's. She's sweeter than I've ever been, but the look in her eyes isn't quite innocent. She looks nothing like Ma.

I turn my head this way and that, taking in the new angles. I can use this face.

"How'd I do?"

"Perfect."

Izamal-but-call-me-Iz sits on the lip of the well, petting a gray cat while another curls up at his feet.

He plays well the part of a fifth-ringer without a home, except . . . "Your boots give you away, you know."

He looks down at them, then at me. "Vesper?"

I lower my shawl and wink. "Good enough?"

His expression turns impressed. "More than. Dalca'll fall at your feet. But—" His gaze sweeps down my overdress. "Well, I figured— you don't have any other clothes, do you?"

My voice is dry. "I'm afraid they burned to a crisp. Along with everything I own and just about everyone I loved."

Izamal winces. "Right, yes—I didn't mean—I got these."

He hands me a bundle of finely spun clothing, made of something much softer than mosscloth.

I don't know what to say, so I incline my head in thanks.

"That's good. Very patrician." Izamal gives me a gentle smile. "Meet me at first light, at the white gates to the third."

CHAPTER 8

The Wardana have many outposts in the city, but the Ven—the headquarters where the bulk of ikonomancers live and work—is in the third.

"Don't gawk," Izamal says.

I gawk. To my right, a tall woman with lush curves barks a laugh, loud and joyous. Both she and her gaggle of onlookers wear purely decorative outfits—short overdresses, some sleeveless, most open to the chest, all made out of a finely spun cloth so thin that the shapes of their bodies are darkly visible. One wears a shawl barely long enough to cover her shoulders made of a silky material that changes from purple to green in the light; another wears no shawl at all, just an embroidered strip of cloth no wider than my hand tied around her waist.

The Storm could cut through their clothes in a heartbeat.

It'd cut through my new clothes, too. The softness of the cloth is a marvel, but my overdress and pants are so vulnerably thin. The wind brushes my naked cheeks, and I shiver.

I keep pace with Izamal until I see it.

A soft line runs across the stone path and angles across the front of buildings. On one side is the shadow I know; on the other is a pale gold haze of light. The place the sun touches. I inch into the light, reaching out till I catch the light on the edge of my fingertips. I snatch my hand back, but there's no pain, no nothing.

I take a step.

The sun kisses my upturned palms, and my eyes slip closed as it warms me. Gently, softly, it traces the curves of my face, sweeter than the heat from any fire. Red and gold dance beneath my eyelids, like sprites born of light and ember. A golden warmth sinks into me, and for the first time in days, I feel a little okay.

Izamal grabs my elbow and murmurs in my ear, "Vesper, darling, please remember that you're a third-ringer."

"What, they get used to this?" I shake him off and follow in his wake, taking in the beautifully vulnerable buildings. Some have balconies, as if the outside is nothing to fear, and others have delicate glass windows with no stormshutters in sight. We come to a street lined with shops, but unlike the open-air stalls I'm used to, these are fully enclosed, with delicate glass windows displaying their wares.

Two middle-aged men shout at each other, one of them standing in the door of a shop with only pastries in its window, many of them stamped perplexingly with ikons. The other man is as squat as a shalaj, and he gestures wildly with half a pastry in his hand.

I gape at him, even as Izamal pulls me along. "How much food do they have here?"

"For Storm's sake, Vesper," he says, but he looks more amused than annoyed.

I try to get ahold of myself, but I can't quite swallow the awe. "It's another world, Iz."

"Built on the backs of fifth-ringers."

The spaciousness turns sinister. No one huddles in the wide, moss-free alleys between buildings, no crowds gather around temples with their empty bowls at the ready. I grit my teeth.

Izamal's scowl lightens. "You're good? Need to go over your story?"

"It's not much of a story, Iz."

"Humor me."

"I'm the daughter of a merchant family. We're very proud to be papermakers. Mum and Da recycle old paper and make new paper out of moss. It's all very exciting."

"You know, that note of disdain is working. I don't think anyone'll ask for more."

"I hope you're right."

"I'm always right. But just in case, stick to ikonomancy. Flatter Cas if you can, he likes that."

Cas, short for Casvian, Dalca's pale-haired lackey. Flatter him?

Izamal's lips curl in an impish smile. "Sorry, kid. But you'll have to put on your best act to get Cas to agree to take you on."

I bite the inside of my cheek. He struts a half step ahead of me, shoulders wide, wearing that impish smile like a threat. A bow-lipped girl in a flowy, sleeveless dress gives him a coy once-over, and he responds with a lingering, half-lidded look. A hawk-nosed boy pauses sweeping the front step of a spice store and blushes when Izamal turns his smile on him.

I see. Izamal's weaponized his body. A half dozen innocent passersby fall prey to the combination of his good looks and the prestige the Wardana reds bestow on him. I tilt my head. It's not peacocking, not really. He's just seized what power he can.

If I don't learn from him, I waste Carver's handiwork.

I unwind my new, slinky shawl from my neck and let it drape over my shoulder. Noting the loose, flowing locks that most women—and a few men—sport, I undo my braid and let my hair hang freely. I half expect my hair to puff up and stick to my face, but the air's less humid here. I don't think Izamal's swagger will look quite so good on me, but the rest I can learn.

The Ven rises over the tops of smaller buildings. It's a gleaming sandstone fortress in the shape of a crown, the great jewel being the watchtower that juts toward the sky. I follow close behind Izamal as he strides toward a grand arch that's ornately carved with depictions of the Wardana's most valiant deeds: Wardana in flight, one single-handedly fighting hordes of beasts while others wield ikons of light that hold back the darkness. Nothing to indicate they spend their free time marching into old women's homes and burning them down.

My burnt palm smarts, and I dig my nails into it until calm falls over me.

The carvings continue into the archway. It's deep, dark, and narrow, so much so that when we come out into a large courtyard, the riot of color and sound startles me. People in red leather run through the colonnade surrounding the courtyard, disappearing into hallways; others spar against each other, and a group of three Wardana take on a massive mock stormbeast. Its wooden body has the head of a falcon and legs of a goat. Every inch of it is engraved with ikons—I've never seen such a complex working of ikonomancy.

An ikonomancer operates the beast from a seat mounted to its back, laughing as she twists a dial and the beast spits a tongue of fire at the trainees. It's incredible—I wonder how it works, what all the other dials do. Is this really all ikonomancy? Izamal gently guides me past it.

Off to one side is a white domed building, a single ikon-marked door its only ornamentation. "What's that?"

"The way to the ikonomancers' library and most secret research rooms. Only full mancers have seen the inside." Izamal gives it a wide berth. Most of the Wardana are like Izamal and Dalca, fighters who use ikons or ikon-engraved weapons and tools. But the rest are like Pa, researchers and scholars who invent new ikons or discover new applications for ikons.

"You might make it in, one day, if you survive being Casvian's trainee. But I'd wager it's not nearly as mysterious and fascinating as he makes it sound. Probably a disgusting mess inside. You should see the foul muck that mancers come up with when they're up for advancement. Last year, Cas was working on some ikon that vaporized whatever it was written on. We had to rope off a dozen rooms, or else people kept breathing it in and passing out. Smelled like rotten cabbage, on top of it all." There's an undercurrent of easy familiarity under the exasperation that gives me pause. How close is he to them, really?

My feet itch to walk over and peek inside the ikonomancers' quarters. Pa must know what secrets that building holds. I imagine him at my age, walking through those doors for the first time, in awe of the magic inside. That was a place he belonged, once. I imagine what it would be like if he and Ma had made different choices, if I could follow in his footsteps.

"Prepare yourself." Izamal glances at me as we reach the far side of the courtyard and step into the shade under the colonnade. "Just around the corner now."

I suck in a breath and hold it till my lungs burn. I draw in another, and another. I follow Iz into a hallway studded with wooden doors, leaving the sounds of the courtyard behind. The walls are all striated sandstone, layers of sienna and umber flowing like water.

Iz stops at a wooden door, no different from the dozen we've passed. He gives me a quick nod and raps twice with his knuckles. A voice calls from within, "Come in."

I straighten my back, comb my hair flat with my fingers, and paste a smile on my lips as I step inside. Meeting two pairs of eyes, my smile freezes.

Dalca Zabulon Illusora—the Regia-to-be, the man I'd most like to strangle, abductor of my father, arsonist, and murderer—sits cross-legged on the floor. His dark hair is a wild bird's nest, and his white shirt is torn and gaping at the neck, as if he can't be bothered about his appearance. The benefit of being the Regia's only child: if he were wearing a canvas sack or nothing at all, no one would dare stand in his way.

He blinks up at me, uncomprehending, until he catches sight of Izamal over my shoulder. His face breaks into a shockingly genuine grin.

A flare of fury rises in my gut. He looks innocent. He looks like he's just a boy.

"Iz!" He bounds to his feet. "What have you brought us today?"

Casvian Haveli's head is bent over a scroll he's weighed down with a dagger and an inkstand. His expression is hidden by his curtain of pale hair, now faintly gold as it reflects the warm lamplight.

"I've found Casvian a new apprentice," Iz says as Dalca holds out a hand to me.

"No." Casvian doesn't look up. I glance at Izamal, who looks like he's trying to murder Cas with his eyes alone.

"Well." Dalca gives me a quick, almost imperceptible once-over.

When his gaze reaches mine, he startles, and the smile drops off his lips. "I'm Dalca."

I swallow down the panic that rises in me. I have to trust Carver did her job. "Vesper." I twist my mouth into something that I hope looks like a smile and take his outstretched hand. Dalca blinks, his expression smoothing. His hand is rough and warm, and I pull my hand free a second too soon to be polite.

Izamal puts a hand on my shoulder. "Cas, you haven't met her. Would it kill you to even look at her? She's clever."

Cas takes me in from head to toe, his gaze lingering on my face, but he gives no indication that he recognizes me. I exhale.

"I'm not interested in your ideas of clever, Izamal." Cas turns away. "Sorry, but I only take second-ringers who have a background in ikonomancy."

"You have no idea how good anyone might be at ikonomancy unless you give them a chance, *Casvian*." Izamal drags out his name as if it's a curse word. "You don't even know if she's a second-ringer."

Cas raises an eyebrow at me. "Are you?"

"Third," I say.

Cas shrugs, as if to say, *Well, what can I do?*

"Iz," Dalca murmurs, pressing a hand to Izamal's chest as he takes a step toward Cas.

Izamal takes a breath, and his voice turns mild. "You're right, Dalca. Cas doesn't deserve an apprentice. After all, didn't I hear something about his last apprentice running away in the middle of the night?"

"I heard something of the same." Dalca keeps his voice equally mild. "I heard he was too afraid of Cas to tell him to his face. Fine boy from the second ring, old Wardana family, wasn't he?"

Iz shakes his head. "That was the one before. This last one was a girl, wasn't she?"

Dalca makes a sound of agreement. "Nice second-ring girl. Wore ribbons in her hair, face always in a book? She seemed clever. She was clever, wasn't she, Cas?"

"She was an imbecile," Cas snaps. "We don't take just anybody, Dazera. Contrary to what you might believe, ikonomancy is an art. It takes dedication and intelligence."

"I'm not an imbecile." I don't need Dalca to make my case for me. Before we got here, Iz gave me the rundown on Casvian and the opportunity we're seizing. Cas has a trainee problem: he's required to have an apprentice, but no one lasts long under his thumb. Which is fine by me. I don't need long, but I do need him to take me on.

Pa's words tumble from my throat, words that now belong to me. "I know the power of ikons. I understand what it means to be able to affect the world with just a symbol. Ikonomancy is more than art. It's power. And I respect that."

I ignore Dalca and Izamal in favor of meeting Casvian's gaze. He tosses his hair over his shoulder, puts down his pen, and leans back in his chair. "Those are just pretty words."

"There is nothing 'just' about words. Words create meaning from chaos. When you name something—let's take *arrogance* as an example—then that thing becomes something else, something that can be understood. That can be beaten."

Casvian's eyes narrow at *arrogance*. "More pretty words." He grabs something from the table and throws it to me.

I catch it on instinct. It's a red fruit, a little larger than my palm. I've only seen its kind once before.

"What words would you use to describe this?" A test.

"I know it is called a poma," I say, but that's not what he's asking. "It is the deep red of a garnet, more of a purple-red than a blood-red." I dig a thumbnail into the skin and pull. "The skin is firm, and the seeds inside are delicate, each no larger than a baby's tooth, each a deeper shade of the same red as the skin."

"Is that it?"

Dalca shifts his weight. I fight the angry flush that rises to my cheeks. "It's larger than my fist, and perhaps a pound in weight, but I'd rather weigh it than guess. And I suppose it's not uniformly red. It turns brown near where it would have connected to the stem, and there are tan spots on the bottom. The shape is loosely spherical, with a four-pronged crown at one end."

Dalca speaks. "Cas, you *do* need a trainee."

Neither Cas nor I look to him.

Cas holds up a hand with his fingers splayed. He folds one down with each word. "Color, size, weight, texture. Mediocre analyses. And you missed the obvious — taste and smell. But ikonomancy goes much further." Cas extends a hand for the poma, and I toss it over. He holds it like he's examining a large jewel. "Knowing something doesn't just mean describing it."

Cas pulls out a piece of paper and dips his pen in the ink, sketching an ikon. "This is a poma, in approximate. But at its core, ikonomancy isn't just the naming of things — it's the naming of actions applied to those things. We can ask a stone to burn, a clay pot to siphon water from the air, metal to pull a charge from the air and make light. But to ask, we must have the instinct to see beyond what a thing is."

A silence hangs in the air. Izamal rubs the back of his neck.

"No." Cas pins me with his cold gaze. "I cannot teach the mediocre."

I hate him, for good reason, and yet I'm desperate to impress him. "What about potential? You mentioned nothing of the seeds the poma holds. Each could make a new tree, and each tree could make hundreds of fruits over its life. Or the energy that a person or animal could get from eating it. What of that? What of time? This is only a poma at this moment. A week from now, it is a mass of decay. What about two, or maybe three weeks ago? When it was just a flower?"

Cas doesn't speak. My chances are slipping through my fingers.

"You're right. I've missed the obvious. Right now, it's not a poma at all. It's a test. It's a symbol for the gap between your knowledge and mine. That's brilliant. You've turned it into something that has meaning beyond its name, so that only someone half blind would be satisfied by calling it a poma."

Low laughter sounds from behind me. Dalca—Pa's jailer, Amma's murderer—laughs into a hand, his eyes shining with mirth.

Casvian looks about ready to spit acid. Holding my gaze, he bites into the not-poma's half-peeled side. "Tastes like a poma to me."

It's such a ridiculous response that I get it. There's nothing I can say to a man like Casvian Haveli.

"You're an elitist bigot—" Izamal starts, stepping closer as if he'd like to get his hands on Casvian.

Dalca cuts him off. "Cas has a right to choose his apprentice—"

Cas's lower lip is red with the poma's juice. "That's right. And I don't owe *you* anything. Should I put every forsaken low ringer on my back, just because you say so? Ikonomancy is for those who know what it means to handle it—*your sister couldn't*—"

"Enough, Cas." Dalca's voice falls like an axe, silencing Casvian and stopping Izamal in his tracks. Dalca moves between them and puts a hand to Izamal's chest, holding Iz's gaze. There's a soft, anxious sort of look in his eyes as he regards Izamal. A look of guilt. But when he speaks, his voice is a command. "You may have a right to choose, but she's answered your questions better than many a good candidate. You have no good reason to turn her down."

Dalca turns to Casvian, who glares back at him. Something passes between them. I hold my breath.

"Fine!" Cas snarls, pointing an accusing finger at me. "I'll take you on for a trial period. Come back tomorrow at dawn. If you're late, you're out. If you slack off, you're out. If you complain even once, you're out."

Hope and relief blossom in my chest. I beam at him. "Yes, sir. Thank you."

His head falls back to his work, and he waves once, sharply. "Be-gone."

I'm at the door before he can change his mind. But to my surprise, Dalca steps up beside me and swings the door open for me. "Let's leave Cas to his work, shall we?"

My shoulder brushes his chest on the way out, and I nearly jump.

"No need to be so afraid." He lets the door fall with a sigh when Izamal lags behind, hissing at Casvian. I shoot a pleading last look in Izamal's direction, willing him to hurry, to not leave me alone with Dalca, but he doesn't notice.

Dalca turns the full force of his attention on me, wearing a slightly puzzled smile. The light traces his cheekbone, his jaw, the muscles of his neck. Even this far in shadow, the sun's light finds him.

I unclench my fists and put on an act. "Thank you for speaking up for me." The words taste bitter on my tongue.

"Wait until you've had to deal with their bickering for a week, then see if you still want to thank me."

"I can deal with bickering, for the chance to learn." My voice comes out sharp, and his smile slips away.

"Of course." His demeanor turns so polite that I wonder if he was trying to flirt before. He turns to go, and something makes me speak.

"Why choose them both to be by your side, if they bicker so much?"

Dalca turns back, though for a moment I think he won't answer. "Cas's fears are the fears of the high ringers. Those who love tradition and have both the power and the responsibility to protect this city. Iz's fears are the fears of those who've lost the most, of those the Wardana most need to protect. I need both those voices by me."

If I were clever, I'd bite my tongue and stop pushing my luck. "Why don't you give fifth-ringers the means to protect themselves?"

His eyes turn assessing. "Not a popular opinion amongst third-ringers. I see why Izamal likes you."

I bite my tongue before I say something else a real third-ringer wouldn't.

Dalca crosses his arms and leans against the wall, studying me through half-lowered eyes. "You think it's such an easy fix?"

"Who'd work harder than the folks whose homes—and lives—are at stake?"

"How would you soothe the fears of those who fought in the last rebellion? Who lost loved ones at the hands of fifth-ringers? Who still risk their lives to fight the Storm?"

"Why are you so fixated on everyone's fears? What about their hopes? If you teach every fifth-ringer — or even one out of every ten — how to fight, wouldn't our chances of fighting back the Storm be that much greater?"

His lips quirk. "You're naïve."

I want to kill him. But as I clench my fist, my burnt palm stings, reminding me of the role I'm meant to play. I bow my head. "I'm sure you know better, my prince."

Whatever he's about to say is lost as Izamal slams the door open and stomps out, followed by Casvian's voice calling, "Get out!"

"I'm *already* out, you puffed-up peacock!"

A loud thump sounds as something hits the door.

Izamal runs a hand through his hair and grins at us. "Well, that went well."

I turn wide eyes upon him. "He'll still take me on? After . . ." I gesture at him.

"He won't take out his anger at me on you. No, he'll find all new reasons not to like you."

Dalca sighs, sounding about eighty years old. "Izamal . . ."

"Yes, yes, I shouldn't disparage an ikonomancer in front of their apprentice, won't happen again, Wardana's honor."

Dalca pinches the bridge of his nose. "I'm training some new recruits in a half hour. I could use a hand."

It's still an order, but well disguised. Izamal doesn't bat an eye. "You'll let me take on the big ones? Knock 'em down a peg or two?"

"They're yours." Dalca strides off, raising a hand in farewell.

"Man of my heart, you are," Izamal calls after him.

I stare at him blankly. How can he be so friendly with Dalca when I know how he really feels? Izamal winks, as if to reassure me that it's all an act. "Why don't I show you to where you'll be staying?"

Izamal leads me through a maze of sandstone hallways, across the courtyard, up two flights of stairs into the Wardana dormitories. "Used to be four trainees to a room, but there used to be far more trainees. This one looks promising."

A simple room. One side of it is already occupied, but Iz gestures at a simple bed and nightstand fitted with a basin. Above the bed is a window that overlooks the third and the lower rings beyond. This is the furthest I've ever been from the Storm.

"You've done good," Izamal murmurs, shutting the door.

"Why antagonize them?" I ask.

He shrugs. "The more I play it up, the less they think I mean to do anything about it. What did you two talk about?"

"Nothing interesting," I lie, and change the subject. "We ought to search the Ven for Pa, right, just in case? But how? It's a lot bigger up close."

"I don't think they'd keep him in the Ven."

I smooth the hem of my overdress. "Are the stories true? About Dalca and his secret passageways?"

"First off, they're not *his*. They're ancient. Paths that lead between the rings, or to the ruins of the old city underneath us. It's a maze down there. If that's where they're keeping him—Dalca and Cas—then we need to find out how they go in and out. If we follow both of them, sooner or later we'll come across something."

Follow Dalca, follow Cas. Easy enough.

"Never forget that you're playing a part." Izamal says. "You're in now—this is where your work begins. I hope you're ready."

Izamal strides back into the hall. I stare out the window, marveling at how small and dark the fifth is from here. I've dreamt of walking these halls for so long. It sickens me that this is how my dream plays out; that only once the Wardana took everything from me could I be one of them.

I trace the lines on my palm. I'll find Pa. I'll save him. And maybe I'm wrong, maybe he will want to fight back. Because the fight that he and Ma started — it's not over.

CHAPTER 9

The night offers little rest. I spend it in a too-soft bed, clutching Ma's locket, listening to the quiet of a strange place. The few times I manage to fall asleep, I wake with the echoes of stormbells in my ears. In the dark of the night, the voice of doubt whispers in my ear. *You're homeless, without a corner of the world to call your own, sneaking where you don't belong. You're a disappointment of a daughter; your father never trusted you enough to teach you his greatest power. You have one skill to your name — coaxing plants to grow. Useless, unless you can garden your father to safety.*

You can't save anybody. You've lost everyone you've ever wanted to protect.

I silence that voice. It threatens the shield that grew around me when I gave Amma's sitar to the Storm. On the other side of this shield, something lies in wait for me. It waits in the space between my heartbeats. A dark omen, like monstrous eyes looking at me from the depths of the Storm. It's a pain I won't be able to bear.

The voice calls me weak. *Who are you to stand against the will of gods and princes?*

Another voice answers. *Your parents were revolutionaries. Rebels who fought for a better future. Their bravery and brilliance are in your blood. Who but you could stand against gods and princes?*

Back and forth these voices go. I feed the second voice all my fury. I replay for it Dalca knocking at the door, the way he bought all the lives of my loved ones for a gold coin. Anger swells in me, makes me strong.

And yet it doesn't burn away that little, awful voice of doubt.

With hours to spare before dawn, I pull myself out of bed and don the trainee's clothes I've been given—a simple white shirt and a pair of black trousers. Both still nicer than fifth-ringer mosscloth.

My roommate, another ikonomancer-in-training who grimaced when I told her who I was apprenticed to, sleeps curled up on her side. Her warm brown skin is dotted with flecks of darker brown, like stars—apparently a mysterious boon from living a life under the sun.

I shut the door quietly behind me so she doesn't wake.

The Ven is a much larger place than I'd ever imagined. Once past the dormitory wing, I pass cluttered workshops and chalky-aired class-rooms, meeting rooms with city maps on the wall, training rooms with cushioned walls, and a dozen closed doors that could hold anything at all.

As a gust of wind blows past me, it brings with it the muffled sounds of scuffles and thuds that echo softly through the halls. I follow the sound and come out onto a second-story balcony that overlooks the courtyard.

Below, a half-clad Wardana fights the wooden mock beast, armed with a spear and gauntlet. His back is slick with sweat, as if he's been at this for a while already, though the sky is still dark. He's not grace-ful; I wouldn't mistake his movements for a dance, and he throws in no flourishes. But he's brutal and relentless.

He pauses his attack and moves back a few spaces, repeating his movements until he's satisfied. He does this a dozen more times, and each time he corrects himself, I expect him to fly into action and complete the drill. But he stops again and again, measuring himself against an ideal only he sees. There's nothing showy in how he moves, nothing inspired—just the proficiency that comes with years of practice.

As the light begins rise, I'm not surprised when his features resolve into Prince Dalca's.

I run my fingers across my lips, thinking. Pa was born a genius. Sometimes I think he never had to work at the small things. When I was twelve, I spent a month drawing circles, training my hand so I'd be able to draw perfect ikons when I learnt them. When Pa came across me drawing circles in the ashes from the stove, I'd braced, expecting him to reprimand me. But it meant nothing to him; it never occurred to him that others needed to practice something so basic.

But people who need to earn their skill bit by bit don't miss such things. Dalca's dangerous. I can't underestimate him.

As if he heard my thoughts, he glances up at me and beckons me down. I wave, plastering a smile on my lips. Could I get away with not going to him? But that's my feelings showing—it'd be smart of me to get closer to him.

I make my way down.

He taps his spear to his gauntlet, and in a seamless working of ikonomancy, the spear disappears as the gauntlet absorbs its mass and thickens around Dalca's forearm. "It's hard to sleep, that first night," Dalca says, drawing my attention to his face. "Bed feels different, just a little too . . ."

"Soft," I say at the same moment he says, "Hard."

A surprised moment of silence ensues that he breaks with a laugh.

I force a smile, as if our differences are something to laugh about. I have to act this part right.

I nod at his gauntlet, changing the subject. "How does it work?"

Dalca steps closer to show me. He radiates heat, and I tense up, un-nerved by his nearness.

He points to a circular dial slightly raised from the surface of the gauntlet. "This dial initiates the transformation."

Three fourths of an ikon are inscribed on it; as he turns it, the last quarter slides into place and the ikon is completed. He pulls the spear out partway to show me, before reversing the process.

Two other dials stick out of his gauntlet, and I peer at them. "And those?"

He laughs, low and amused. "You don't expect me to give up all my secrets so quick, do you?"

A real smile comes to my lips at that. Not all his secrets—just one will do. "How many secrets do you have?"

He saunters over to a pile of clothes on the ground, reaches down, and pulls on his shirt. "That's a secret, too."

"Is it a secret why you're practicing in the dead of night?"

"It's hardly the dead of night. It's almost morning."

"That's not much of an answer. Let me guess. It's because you have to be the biggest, meanest Wardana?" I'm not sure if I'm teasing him in the vague hope he'll give away something about Pa or because I get a little thrill out of the way his eyes widen in surprise and his cheeks red-den. I might be acting a part—but it's a part I'm liking.

"There are plenty who are bigger and meaner than me."

"Oh, so it's because you're playing catch-up? I don't believe that."

He looks at the ground and tugs on a leather cord that's tied around his wrist, wearing a shy little smile. "It's not that either."

"You don't have to tell me." I take a step back.

He glances up, his eyes the brightest thing around. "It's that . . . the more I practice, the more power I'll have over my fear, when the time comes."

His honesty startles me. "You mean when you fight the Storm?"

He tugs at the cord around his wrist and then makes a production of adjusting his gauntlet.

"I didn't realize."

He gives me a crooked grin. "What, that we're afraid? Maybe everyone isn't. I don't think Izamal is."

"But you are."

The Ven's ikonlights turn on, flooding the dim courtyard with golden light. Dalca blinks at me, as if remembering that I'm no one. A polite mask falls over his face and he claps me on the shoulder, like we're chums. "There's no reason to be afraid. The Regia's got it all in hand."

He gives me a princely nod and strides off.

I call after him. "I never said I was afraid."

He doesn't look back.

Fifteen minutes until dawn. The stars are hidden behind a layer of gray clouds that hang so low the border between Storm and sky is indistinct. The halls echo with the muffled sounds of people rising and preparing for the day. I make a quick circuit of the courtyard. The colonnade's columns cast shadows that stretch across the courtyard as day breaks and the sun shines through the clouds.

Casvian is nowhere to be found. I lean against the wall and yawn so hard my jaw cracks.

Just as the sky begins to lighten, a pair of doors bang open. Casvian stands frowning, the wind making a halo of his pale hair.

I step out from the shadows and wave.

His frown deepens. "Damn."

The feeling is mutual. "Good morning." I paste on the sunniest smile I can manage.

He rolls his eyes and turns on his heel so abruptly that he's halfway down a hallway before I catch up with him. His legs are long, longer than mine, and he walks without any recognition that I'm jogging to keep up with him.

Fine. He can have his petty little power play. I unclench my jaw and try to commit to memory the path we take through a series of halls that would be identical but for the patterns in the sandstone walls.

He stops at a small door and flings it open.

The light from the hall barely penetrates into a room so packed with junk that I can't make out where the walls are. And what a stunning variety of junk: bins of colored glass bulbs emptied of ikonlight, a crate of wrapped bar soaps, a grinning bestial skull the size of my torso, three leather trunks each with a dozen padlocks, and a lone red glove.

"I want this sorted by the end of the day." Casvian pulls a timepiece from a pocket, nods to himself, then turns on a heel, and walks away.

"Wait," I call to his retreating back. "Sorted how?"

"Figure it out." He raises a hand and disappears around the corner without once looking back.

I stare at the corner. Fine. He's not getting rid of me that easily. I roll up my sleeves and pull a ribbon from a pile to tie my hair up.

I dive in.

A knock sounds at the door, startling me out of the trance I've fallen into. My stomach growls. How many hours have I been here? I drop the last of the black feathers upon a heap of its brethren and stand.

Could it be Izamal? I shouldn't wish for it to be him. I've only known him for what, a day, and I'm already expecting him to rescue me the moment things get tough? My stomach turns. I'm stronger than that.

The door opens to reveal Casvian's pointed features.

"I should have mentioned that apprentices are given a break for luncheon."

"Oh. Thank you."

"It's the law." With a grimace, he peers down at the pile of feathers at my feet. "How interesting. A heap of feathers and dust. I look forward to your explanation of why those two things belong together."

I grit my teeth. Sure, tangled in some of the feathers — feathers I've been finding in every nook and cranny, as if a vulture from a book of fairy stories swanned in through a window and exploded — are tufts and strings of dust. "When I've finished, I'd be happy to explain everything. The day hasn't ended yet."

Casvian leaves without another word. I kneel and pluck a fluff of dust off a feather.

My stomach growls again, but I don't have time to take a break. I need to figure this out.

I slump against a box filled with blue stones and draw my knees close. I bury my head in my arms.

In the shelter of my body, I search for an answer.

Everything I know of ikonomancy could fit in a thimble. But what I know of Pa could fill a dozen books. I can almost taste the hints hidden in the edges of my memories, in the way Pa organized his secret room, in the detailed orders he used to give me when I went to the market for supplies, even in the way Pa prefaced every childhood story with each character's background history. Hints to the organization of Pa's mind. To how an ikonomancer thinks.

I can almost hear his voice telling me what to do.

Casvian returns when the sky is dark, looking vaguely surprised to see me. "Well?"

I jump to my feet, and a cloud of dust rises off my body. "Well. I thought about the ways I could've sorted this. By color? By size? By function? But then I thought of the poma. I thought about the names of all of these things, of what an ikon representing them might look like."

I point to one wall. "Those are things that can be used as fuel, consumed for light or heat." Cubes of wax, scraps that can be used as kindling, strips of wood, a lump of coal. "Those are things that have been used up, things that must be replenished or recycled into something new." The bin of glass bulbs, pens with broken nibs, empty jars, a crate of broken blades. "These are things that belong somewhere else, that may have been lost, that were once part of a greater whole." The lone red glove, several leather-bound books with titles like *Elementary Ikonomancy, Volume Four,* a half of a torn love letter, a half dozen boxes of odds and ends. "Those are elements, ingredients, raw materials, building blocks for something else." The feathers, rolls of beast skins, a lump of marble, a few dozen sheaves of unmarked parchment.

"And those are mysteries, things I don't dare touch until I better understand them." The three locked trunks, the skull, a music box, and a handful of objects I have no name for.

Casvian stands with his arms crossed, frowning at every inch of the room.

The silence stretches on, and I try not to fidget. "Well? Did I pass?"

"Pass?" He turns to me with a raised eyebrow. "You cleaned out a closet."

He sweeps out the door. My palms sweat.

"Tomorrow," he calls over his shoulder. "Same time."

The next day, Casvian says nothing when I show up ten minutes before dawn. He turns on a heel and marches off without waiting to see if I follow. I jog to keep up, rolling my eyes at his back. Today, I'm prepared. In my tunic pocket is a lunch of flatbread and bean paste, and I'm fortified with half a night's worth of sleep.

A lantern dangles from the crook of his arm. Why would anyone need a lantern in the Ven? Could he be taking me to the old city?

Casvian disappoints me. He unlocks a door identical to yesterday's. A plaque beside the door frame reads Experiment Room No. 8. Under it, scrawled in chalk on the wall: BEWARE—MISHAP Level 3.

Cas pushes the door open with a flourish. It sticks halfway. He puts his shoulder to it, and it slowly screeches open. A dark, tarlike substance covers every surface of the room, from the table in the center to the walls. A layer of it covers the lone lamp and the two windows, sealing them all so completely that no light, not even a faint glow, shines forth.

I understand the lantern.

The only clear spot is on the chair beside the table, an outline in the shape of a person. They must've peeled themselves from the chair and walked out, leaving their footprints in the tar on the floor.

"What happened here?"

"A small incident." Casvian speaks with a studied, too-casual nonchalance, but his cheeks are pink.

I kick at the tar. It doesn't budge. "Someone really messed up, didn't they?"

He glares at me. "Your job isn't to ask questions. It's to clean. You have till the end of the day."

"Do I get any supplies?"

Casvian points to a door at the end of the hall. "Everything you might need will be in there. Have at it." He turns to go, a pleased smile on his lips, then pauses. "Don't ask anyone for help. No one else sets foot in this room, hear me?"

"Yes, sir." It's easy to smile at him when I imagine him covered in tar, hopping out of this room. "Should I get you when I'm done?"

"I'll be in the first ring. But don't worry—I'll be back before long. We'll see how much you get done."

As he leaves, I can't help but think I should follow him. My mission is to find Pa, not to clean up tar, and Casvian knows where he is. But if I don't find the way to Pa today, then how do I explain not having tried to clean this mess? It's better to bide my time. To earn Casvian's trust enough to avoid his suspicion and give myself a real chance to find Pa.

I take a tentative step deeper into the room. The tar gives a little under my weight, but my foot leaves no imprint. It's as though the surface has hardened, but underneath is still malleable.

The door Casvian indicated opens into a well-stocked supply closet. There are tools galore: the usual, for sweeping, mopping, scraping, and polishing, and the unusual, things I've no idea what to do with. Beside a large sink is a shelf of blue-glass jars with labels that say things like DRYING POWDER, STICKING PASTE, EXTRA-SMALL WOOD SHAVINGS, RAPID DISSOLVER, VERY SHINY SEALER.

I grab a bucket, fill it with anything that looks promising, tie my hair up with the ribbon from the storage room, and get to it. With the most promising of the tools—a small flat shovel—I hack at the tar. The shovel bounces off when I hit the tar from above, but one good thwack at an angle and a dent appears in the tar. I hit the same spot again and again, until the dent is more of a cut that goes two inches deep. I wiggle the shovel's flat edge into the cut and push down on the handle, using it like a lever to pry under the tar. The tar flexes, just barely. I get to my feet and stomp on the handle.

With a crack, a two-inch piece of tar flies free. What was that, fifteen minutes? At this rate, Pa will die of old age before I'm half done with the room.

I just have to try something else. Back in the closet, I go for the jar of dissolver, pausing only to don a pair of stiff leather gloves. I've no interest in discovering what dissolved skin looks like. I unscrew the jar at arm's length, then pour a little dollop onto the tar.

The tar sizzles and smokes, belching a noxious-smelling plume into the air. I pull the front of my tunic over my mouth and nose as a slowly widening patch melts into a glossy liquid. I wouldn't go so far as to call it dissolved, but I'll take a liquid I can mop over a solid I can't budge.

In the ten seconds that it takes for me to cross the hall, grab a mop from the closet, and return, the black mass has hardened.

I'll have to be quicker.

I pour more of the dissolver onto the floor, mop at the ready. The moment the sizzling settles, I drive the mop into the liquid. Mostly the mop just smears the stuff around, but a good pint of it sticks to the mop hairs. The first push is easy, the second pull is like dragging the mop through honey, but by the third push, the mop sticks fast to the floor.

I grip the handle tight and pull as hard as I can, but it doesn't budge. I let go, and the mop stands upright, like a giant paintbrush paused in the act of coloring the room black.

It's more interesting, but Casvian probably won't see it as an improvement.

It's all right. I'm only an hour into the day. I have time.

I throw a dozen more things at it. The hours pass, and nothing works. My heart thuds in my chest, and my vision gets blurry. I wipe my face with my sleeve, giving up on the Very Shiny Sealer.

A two-foot section of the tar is now as glossy and reflective as a mirror. A girl blinks up at me. A strange girl, with shoulder-length hair and a pretty face that's been carved free of all its boldness. She looks like she's going to cry.

I spring to my feet and bound out of the room. The air in the hallway is colder and fresher.

I breathe, pressing my palms into my eyelids. What would Pa do?

But it isn't Pa that comes to me. A memory of Amma washes over me and a riptide of longing pulls me in deep.

"Let me have a look, love." Amma takes a ruined doll from my hands. I'm seven years old; my nose is too big for my face and my hair's one huge tangle. There's a boy about my age staying at Amma's, freckled, naughty, and storm-touched.

He likes taunting me, playing pranks on the pretty wooden doll Ma carved for me when I was born. The boy calls my doll weak and says he'll make armor for her out of the dark clay that collects in the streets. He's covered my doll in the sticky clay, thinking it'll wash off, but something about the polished surface of the toy makes it bind together.

We often play with the clay, calling it fairy mud, fashioning lumpy creatures and building mock-ups of our dream houses. It's the perfect toy for kids who have nothing—it's a toy that could become everything. But of course, it will never measure up to a real toy, like my doll.

Amma comes while I sit sobbing, scrubbing at my doll, succeeding only in spreading the sticky clay around. "You can't always just separate two things by force. First, you have to understand why they've gotten so attached." She runs her finger through the clay, testing it by pressing her thumb and forefinger together. "My, this mud is well stuck, isn't it? It sure has taken a liking to your little wooden girl. She's been polished with oil, hasn't she? Clay like this loves oil. It makes it even stickier. But let me show you something."

She takes me into the kitchen, wraps the doll in husks, and sticks it into the oven where a fire burns. "The trick is to ask it to change a little, to get it to want something else." She bakes the doll for a good half hour. When it comes out, she rubs the clay with a finger. It cracks off like dust, leaving my doll spotless, if slightly browner. The air fills with clay dust, and Amma smiles at me. "Look how the clay chases after the wind now."

The boy went into the Storm a few months later. I'd given my doll to him the week before, and he took her with him into the Storm. I'd cried, thinking if I'd only kept the doll, he would've stayed. I don't remember his name, but I remember he had hair the color of bronze and a gap between his front teeth that whistled when he said f-words: *forever, faraway, father, friend.*

I shake myself free of the memory, slipping out of an old sadness that fits like a favorite sweater.

I dab some dissolver on the edges of the window frame, and as soon as the sizzling starts, I force the window open. The tar makes a smacking sound as it gives, and light shines in. I go to the other window and repeat.

Two steady shafts of light beam into the room. I uncap the Very Shiny Sealer and dab it onto the tar, making a wide circle at the exact point a beam of light hits the floor. The tar turns mirrorlike, and the column of light bounces off the floor onto the wall. I trace the light's path and apply the sealer onto the wall, and then again onto the wall opposite. The light bounces onto the ceiling. Even standing on the table, I can't quite reach, so I go after the second beam of light.

The room grows as hot as an oven. Sweat sticks my tunic to my skin. I don't know how many hours of sunlight I've got left. From the closet, I grab the box of Extra-Small Wood Shavings and sprinkle the contents out onto the tar. The shavings are so fine that when a breeze comes through the open window, they rise and dance in the air. If they work like the husks Amma used, they should draw up any remaining moisture.

I dust my hands off and head out into the hall. The air is wonderfully cool. I fish my lunch out of my pocket, unwrap it, and bring it to my lips.

I chew, but the taste doesn't register.

Thing is, the sun needs time to work, an hour or two. I could wait here, like a good apprentice.

But I'm not here to be a good apprentice.

CHAPTER 10

In the Ven's courtyard, a short Wardana with the demeanor of a boulder barks orders at a handful of trainees as they pull spears from their gauntlets. "No! Pull it even and steady! Steady! Too fast—you see that weak spot? Try and stick a beast with that, and it'll snap in your face."

Dalca made it look easy, but most of the trainees pull lumpy spears that alternate between the thickness of my wrist and pinky finger. How effortless it'd looked from afar—when I watched the Wardana from Amma's, I'd imagined their spears appeared out of thin air.

She scowls at them, her hundreds of tiny braids flying as she stalks back and forth. She catches sight of me, and her frown deepens.

"You! Who are you? Where's your gauntlet?"

I raise my hands in surrender. "I'm Casvian Haveli's apprentice."

She grimaces. "Carry on, then."

Her distaste gives me an idea. I glance at where the tip of the golden palace peeks over the edge of the Ven's wall. "He asked me to go to him in the first—but he didn't tell me how to get up there."

She rolls her eyes. "Typical. Show the guards at the gate your trainee transit pass. They're used to it."

I thank her. With a thudding heart, I make my way to the golden gates that lead to the second. They're much closer to the Ven than the black gates; somehow that makes the Ven feel like it belongs to the high ringers. I'm waved through the second's gates with a warning to be out by sundown; only those who live there are allowed after nightfall.

I've no time to linger and take in the splendor of the second, where live those born to power, a place that everyone dreams of one day calling home, of earning a ring by valiant heroism or brilliant ikonomancy. I catch a few glimpses of obscene luxury: their streetlamps are crafted in the shape of birds, casting multihued ikonlight, and every house I pass is an exercise in wasteful ikonomancy, with balcony railings wrought in looping warming ikons, windowpanes decorated with ikons to repel rain and dust, ikons carved onto front steps so that a visitor will set off a chime inside.

The first ring doesn't rise up from the dead center of the second; it's offset, close to the golden road, so that it only takes me three quarters of an hour to make it to the palace gates. The guards mark my name — I tell them *Vesper Maran*, Amma's surname — on a sheet of paper and wave me through without so much as a second glance.

The palace stands before me in all its golden splendor. It's like a lick of fire rendered in faceted gemstone, a grand peaked dome surrounded by lesser domes, a curving outer wall rippling with the curves of dozens of balconies, each set with ornate windows that glint in the light of the sun.

I walk with arms tight at my sides, afraid to touch anything. I tense up whenever I pass someone, knowing they must be able to tell that I don't belong.

My feet carry me forward through the main entrance, into an atrium. An attendant in a white uniform steps up to my side. I tell her the same cover story—I'm looking for Casvian Haveli—and she bids me to follow her. I bite my cheek. I have to find my chance to slip away.

She takes me into a corridor that runs the perimeter of the palace. We pass a balcony to the left that opens out over the city, and a smaller one to the right that looks out over a stretch of tall green hedges. The palace is set in rings, just like the city. I must be in the outer ring, but the Regia and her family would live deeper inside.

The attendant leads me into a hallway where a line of apprentices and assistants stand primly, facing a pair of heavy doors. They look at me with a mix of curiosity and distaste. "New one?" a bare-shouldered girl asks. Her beauty strikes me—it's not the beauty of symmetry, but that of status: shining unbound hair and skin that glows from living under the sun. Between the luxe clothes and the haughty look—so like Casvian's—it takes no real intelligence to peg her as a second-ringer.

I nod.

"You'll want to wait here, in case your master needs anything."

Grimacing at the word *master*, I spare a glance down the hall. "We don't go inside?"

She laughs. "You don't want to be inside. Not when the Wardana and Regia's Guard meet. You'll hear enough of the yelling from out here."

I can't wait around and waste this chance to find how Dalca enters the old city. Whatever it is—a door, a tunnel, a strange stairwell—that's how I'll get to Pa. The palace is Dalca's domain; if I were him, this is where I'd hide my way into the old city.

But the palace is a large place, and I've no idea where to start. I consider prying a little information out of the apprentice who spoke to me, but her attention is fixed further down the hall.

All the apprentices quiet as six figures approach. Uniformed in sleek black leather edged in gold, each of them built like Wardana fighters. The Regia's Guard.

They're the Regia's trusted protectors and sometime advisors, but, unlike the Wardana, they never leave the high rings. From the adoration on the apprentices' faces, it's clear that they're well respected. But I always figured it was a job for folks who weren't brave enough to fight the Storm.

Their leader has pale hair and a familiar scowl. My back hits the stone wall before my mind registers that his hair is jaw-length and gray-streaked white instead of long and mirrorlike, and his face is hard instead of pointy. The resemblance is strong; it's like seeing what Casvian would look like if he spent the next two decades lifting weights.

The Regia's Guard disappear behind the door, and in seconds the apprentices are back to chatting. I slink away, making it a few steps deeper into the palace, before a call comes from the mouth of a balcony. "There he is!"

They all go to see, and I follow them out onto the balcony. Hundreds, thousands of rooftops cascade down the rings, a semicircle of the ones nearest us glinting in the sunlight. I grip the stone railing, fighting vertigo. The people of the second are half as tall as my thumb, and the people of the third no larger than ants. The fifth is just a murky shadow at the base of the colossal darkness of the stormwall. How devastatingly high the Storm stretches—even the palace reaches only a third of its height.

But that's not why she called.

A lone Wardana flies through the air, thousand-and-one-feather cloak spread like wings. I don't have to wonder who it is, because I can see the answer in the faces of the girls staring up at him. They look with hope and ambition in their eyes, hands smoothing down locks of hair that might have escaped careful styling, angling themselves at the edge of the balcony, hoping to catch the attention of the prince so that he might one day make them Regia's consort.

Dalca.

I tamp down the fury that rises in me. He flies with an easy grace, like a creature born to the sky. He's untouchable, freedom incarnate.

I dream of yanking on a string tied to his foot and snapping him out of the sky. No creature is born to the sky; even birds are born grounded. And like all birds, he too must land.

As if echoing my thoughts, Dalca begins to descend. He seems to come straight at us—the apprentices around me collectively hold their breath, even the men—and then he swerves to the right and drops down, through the open air above the hedge-walled gardens of the palace.

While they're all watching him, I slip away.

I should've asked the other apprentice how long the meeting lasts. I can't risk Casvian beating me back to the Ven. I'll search an hour, no more.

I go deeper into the palace, and the walls soon become more art than wall. From doors to arched window frames, every piece of wood is carved with scenes of endless forests or pools of water fed by great waterfalls, showing a world unbound by the Storm. Occasional skylights cast dim, dust-speckled slants of light; each step I take is either into light or into darkness.

There's an old bedtime story I only half remember, where the palace was called the House of a Thousand Doors. It was a story about the Great King's soul wandering ghostlike through the palace, opening doors and meeting the souls of the Regias of the past and future.

I don't meet any ghosts, but that doesn't mean they aren't there.

The carved faces on the walls watch me as they no doubt watched thousands before me. The weight of history is a stifling presence, as if even the air is careful with how it moves.

How small my problems must appear to the spirit of the palace. How many girls like me has it seen? How many daughters terrified of losing their fathers?

I wonder how long I'll have to wander through the palace; how many ghosts will I meet before I find the right door? More than half my time is gone, and I've made no headway at all. Maybe this is a mistake—maybe I need to have the patience to earn Cas and Dalca's trust. But I have a feeling time isn't on my side. At any moment, Dalca could choose to end Pa's life.

I turn a corner, and there he is—not a ghost, but haunting me all the same.

Dalca walks with his hands folded behind his back, cloak billowing behind him. His gaze is fixed upon the floor, expression grim. I guess the meeting didn't go well.

He moves with purpose toward a wall carved with a depiction of a grand feast in a woodland clearing. All the carved figures are fixated upon either each other or the food—except for one woman, who gazes out at us, a poma held loosely in one hand.

Dalca presses the poma. The edge of a door pops out, and Dalca wrests it open. He steps inside, and the door begins to swing shut behind him.

It can't be this easy.

I dash toward the closing door, footsteps as quiet as possible, and catch the edge of the door with my fingertips. Behind is a long hallway, brightly lit with golden ikonlight. The edge of Dalca's cloak disappears around the far corner.

I take a deep breath and go in. The hallway curves to the right and opens out into a small white-stone atrium. There are four doors, but one swings shut as I near.

I tiptoe close and press my ear to the door.

"Hello, Papa." Dalca's voice. "Let me help you sit up."

The sound of rustling. A grunt. I'm stuck on *papa*. Surely he can't be talking to Zanam Zinde; everyone knows his father died when the old Regia was assassinated. The rumors must've been wrong; after all, rumors say Pa's dead, too.

Neither Pa nor Amma ever spoke of the Regia's consort. Most people don't. He wasn't a significant man. But I suppose even insignificant men are fathers.

What happened to him, that he's locked up in this secret corner of the palace?

"I found him. He knows the secret, Papa. We just have to get it out of him . . . I think I can save Mother. Oh, don't cry, it'll be all right. I'll make it all right."

There's silence. I press closer, crushing my ear against the door, ignoring the sweetness in his voice and how it makes something in me twinge. He's talking about Pa—about getting Pa's work from him.

A lock clicks from the next door over, and I jump back. A woman in a white apron bustles out, carrying a pile of linens. She stops when she sees me.

"Who are you, dearie?"

"I'm Casvian Haveli's apprentice." The words come from me as smooth as if I'd practiced them. "He sent me to find Dalca."

She glances at the first door to the left. "Well, the prince is meeting someone. I daresay he won't want to be disturbed. Why don't you wait for him?"

She nods at the hallway I've just come down.

I think fast. "You don't need a hand with those, do you?"

She blinks down at the linens in her hands. "Could do. Come on, then."

With one last look at the door, I follow her into a room with four beds, three of which are occupied. One glance, and I understand.

They're stormtouched. As Dalca's father must be. The room couldn't look more different from Amma's, but the familiarity of it still takes me by surprise. I squeeze my eyes shut as tears brim under my eyelids. I force back the knot that works its way up my throat, swallowing down every last drop of sorrow.

"Hey, you all right?"

I open my eyes to see a man about my age or a little older, sitting cross-legged atop his sheets. He has an easy smile bordered by dimples, and a strong, handsome face. His curse is written on his skin, literally—curving lines of white hieroglyphics on skin dark as night, fading in and out like pale reeds stroking the surface of a pool.

"I'm fine."

He holds himself carefully, as if preparing for an outburst or for me to jerk away in disgust. Most of the cursed learn to be careful with themselves. It breaks my heart to see someone afraid of me in the same way.

"I just . . . I had a cousin, who was stormtouched. I lost her recently."

It's as much of the truth as I can offer. His gaze softens. The woman in white—a nurse, I realize now—dumps a pile of linens on an empty bed and points at me. "Fold these."

The man comes with me and wordlessly helps shake out the linens and fold them. "I'm Alidan, and that's Laida." He nods at a woman doing a series of stretches. She throws me a nod over her shoulder but doesn't speak. Her curse isn't outwardly apparent. Many aren't.

The third occupant is curled up in bed with the sheets pulled high over their face.

They're both uncommonly fit, in the mold of Dalca and Izamal. "You're Wardana?"

"Cursed in the line of duty." He hands me the edges of the last sheet.

"I'm sorry," I say, quietly. "No one deserves the Storm's touch."

He smiles at me, and we fold the linens in a comfortable silence for a few minutes. If I close my eyes, it's almost like being back at Amma's before everything fell apart.

Eventually, the woman in white interrupts us. "There he goes. You'd better run if you want to catch him."

I glimpse a flutter of dark cloak. "Thank you."

Alidan answers. "Come back anytime. I mean it."

I give him a smile, then chase after Dalca. The hallway is empty, the door at the end shut. I try to open it slowly, but it swings open as if of its own accord. And then I see the red-gloved hand. I follow it up to a red-clad arm, up to a pair of summer-sky eyes.

"Hello," Dalca says pleasantly, holding the door open. "Fancy meeting you here."

I'm caught. My heart pounds. "I was looking for Mancer Haveli." I glance over my shoulder, hoping the nurse didn't hear.

Dalca tilts his head. "Here?"

My face heats up. "And then I saw you."

"You saw me. And decided to follow me."

"I knew I shouldn't have the minute I walked in . . . I just wanted to thank you." I think of the girls watching him fly, hunger in their eyes.

Maybe I can get him to think I'm like them. I tilt my face up, hoping Carver's artistry works on him. "For showing me the ikondial."

Dalca looks at me so intently that I flinch and drop my gaze. Can he tell I'm lying?

"Will you look at me?" His voice is so soft.

I drag my gaze up the blood-red of his uniform to meet those piercing Regia's eyes. The force behind his eyes pulls me back to Amma's, to the moment when I first saw him this close.

"You don't like me very much, do you?"

"I like you fine," I protest, but it sounds weak even to my ears.

He tilts his head. "I know your secret."

My heart stops dead. "My secret?"

"You are no third-ringer."

"Of course I am."

He shoots me a crooked grin that says, *Oh, please.*

How much does he know? I blink stupidly at him, my mouth dry.

"You don't walk with the ease of a third-ringer. You keep pulling the edge of your overdress, as if you're used to something longer. You're fascinated by ikondials that no third-ringer would look at twice. But it's the things you say that give it away. You're a fifth-ringer."

I search his soft, curious eyes for any hint of what else he knows. Does he know whose daughter I am?

"Don't worry. I won't tell Cas."

"You . . . won't?"

"Is that so surprising?"

I can't think of anything that'd be more surprising, save maybe him breaking into a jig. "You're right that I'm from the fifth. How could I not be surprised? I know you don't care much about us."

His expression shutters, and he grows still and taut.

"Come." He takes my hand and pulls me across the lushly carpeted hall, through a pair of doors. For a moment, I'm taken in by how he smells; under the scents of leather and metal is a sweet darkness, like honeysuckle and a heady something I've never smelled before.

We come out onto a balcony. I suck in a breath. The whole city lies at our feet. The fifth seems so dim and far away, overshadowed completely by the Storm. "I care. But I have to care for more than just the fifth. Look. This is what I have to think of, this is my problem to solve." He stares straight ahead, at the Storm.

Having said enough, I bite my lip.

A vein in his jaw moves. "What would you have me do?"

Be smart, Vesper. "Nothing. It's not my place."

"Tell me," he commands, and I'm reminded that he has all the power here. "What would you have me do?"

His imperiousness does it. "It's what you've already done. Why would you burn down a home for the stormtouched? They were innocents. Their lives were already bad enough, don't you think? Without having to go—like that—"

"I'm sorry." His hands clench into fists as I scrub a wayward tear from my cheek. "You knew them?"

I've given too much away. "Everyone in my part of the fifth knew them. She—the home gave us hope."

A slow shaky breath. I meet his eyes, surprised at the wetness in them that he rapidly blinks away.

My voice is a whisper. "Why did you do it?"

He plucks at that stupid cord around his wrist. "It was my fault. But I didn't—I wouldn't—do such a thing."

"What do you mean?"

"I told my people to watch the home—there was something I was looking for. But setting a watch drew attention to the house. Others found out." He takes a long, careful breath as if steeling himself. "They set the fire."

His words pummel the air out of me.

"What others?"

Bitterness twists his lips. "The Regia's Guard."

I shake my head. What is he saying? As if from a great distance, the memory comes of what the knitting circle told me about Amma's burning: *We know a pale-haired man led them. They used ikons to get it to burn so hot so fast.*

But now, instead of Casvian, I picture the white-haired man in the sleek black of the Regia's Guard. Is this true? I wouldn't trust Dalca, but what reason would he have to lie to me? To him, I'm no one.

"Don't the Regia's Guard listen to you?"

He laughs, sharp and surprised, but there's little humor on his face. "I wish. Much would be easier if they did."

I force myself to clear my head, to remember the act, to not give away the jumble in my mind or the reason I care.

Dalca's voice is soft. "It'll be rebuilt. I'm overseeing it. A free home for any of the stormtouched."

A fire burns in my gut. "It can't be fixed just like that."

"I can't bring them back, you're right. I'll bear the responsibility for that as long as I'm here. But everything else, I can fix."

The conceit of him. My fingers dig into my palm. "Everything can be fixed?"

"It's what I must believe."

And here I was feeling sorry for him after hearing about his father, thinking we might both have loved people we couldn't help. Another minute with him, and I'll do something I regret. I turn to leave. "I have to go."

He touches my arm and murmurs to my back. "Not just yet."

I twist around.

Dalca pauses, as if transfixed by my eyes. Perhaps Carver had a point about the power of a pretty face, but it goes both ways. His looks haven't changed, but something in me has. Seeing him now . . . it's the difference between the palace at night and the palace aglow with red-gold sunlight. Suddenly I see why so many of the apprentices were entranced by him, and it has only a little to do with him being born a prince. A sense of vertigo unsettles my stomach as the blue of his eyes fills my vision. Around the dark of his pupils is a ring of palest silver, like a crown.

Dalca blinks, and the moment shatters. He pitches his voice low. "You know who I came to meet."

His father. I consider lying, but it must show on my face.

"Ah. You do." Dalca sighs, running a hand through his black hair, turning it wild. "Tell me. What should I do with you? You now know something few are allowed to learn."

"A secret for a secret," I say. I'm playing this all wrong. I should be simpering, batting my eyelashes.

"Mine is a little more valuable."

"Not to me."

He makes a considering sort of shrug. "Perhaps."

"I won't tell. I promise." I try not to scowl.

"I should trust you, when I know you don't like me?"

There's something small and fragile in his eyes. I speak to it. "I could like you."

A strange little smile comes to his lips. It turns mocking. "Could you?"

I flush. "I won't tell."

"I know you won't. Because if I hear that you've told anyone, you'll have good reason not to like me." He steps closer, so his breath caresses my face. "One of the best people I ever knew came from the fifth. For her sake, I want to trust you. And I owe Izamal a debt I can never repay. If he trusts you, so should I. And yet."

He's so close that I see his pupils grow, the dark eating up the blue of his eyes. "I don't like the way you look at me, Vesper."

Dalca steps backwards, keeping me in his view until he turns and marches away, his shoulders high and tense.

I make my way out of the palace, trying to shake off the buzzing under my skin, half relief, half something else. I can't let him unsettle me. Sure, his sweetness with his father made me sympathize, but he doesn't deserve my sympathy. I can't afford it.

My feet take me toward an archway limned by sunlight, and I find myself before a palace garden enclosed by a courtyard, rather than the palace entrance I'd been aiming for. It isn't much of a garden from my angle; a tall wall of leaves and thorns hides the rest of the garden from sight. But I get a hint of what lies beyond as a cool breeze lifts my hair off the back of my neck, enfolding me in the aroma of honeysuckle and nectar. It's the same heady fragrance I smelled on Dalca.

What grows inside? Food? Or frivolous things, like flowers that never turn to fruit? Anything could grow here; my hands tingle with the urge to try. I breathe in the scent, growing dizzy with it. How much time does Dalca spend here, that he smells of it?

A shock of pale hair startles me out of my thoughts. Casvian strides out of a shadowed opening in the hedge, shooting a furtive look over his shoulder.

I duck back as Casvian kicks the dirt, sighs, then heads off.

Gravel crunches underfoot as I tiptoe closer. The arched opening in the hedge reveals only several feet of a winding path penned in by walls of flowering bushes. The wind purrs through the leaves, blowing past me.

My feet itch to go discover what's inside. It must be something important—I'd wager my last coin that Casvian Haveli has never stopped to smell a flower.

But if Casvian finds me gone, with the room a mess, I'm done for.

I hurry out of the palace—no guard stops me on the way out—and speed through the second. I spot the Ven as the last hint of sunset fades from the circle of sky.

No one questions me as I hurry back to the room. I hold my breath as I open the door.

Cracks spiderweb across the substance, now faded to a dull gray. I poke at it with my toe, and it flakes up easily, revealing pale stone underneath. I grab the broom and dive in.

My heart pounds. With the broom, I knock the tar off the walls and sweep it all into a big pile. Fear makes me quick. I glance up every time I hear footsteps, but no Cas. Not yet.

Prying the stuff from the windows and the desk takes a good fifteen minutes. Shoving the flakes into three bags and hauling them to a trash bin takes another five. I dash back to the room and go over every corner.

It's clean.

I slump onto the chair, leaning my forehead onto the surface of the desk. As the panic recedes, my thoughts quicken. My face burns. I can't believe I let Dalca get to me. I underestimated him; I underestimated what his presence would do to me.

He knows I'm from the fifth. And after everything I said about Amma's, how long before he pieces it all together?

I wrap my arms around me. I believe him about the fire. I wish I didn't. I wish I could hate him with no reservations. I wish I didn't know that he's sweet to his father. I wish I didn't know that his eyes aren't pure blue, that there's the slimmest ring of silver around the dark of his pupils.

But even if he didn't light the fire himself, he didn't stop it from happening. Even if he dreams of saving our city, he's letting the fifth suffer right now.

And he took Pa from me.

To let myself be distracted—am I really that silly? He's not even that handsome. Am I really that weak? But if I am, so is he. There was a moment where he couldn't look away from me.

I can use that.

A sigh. "Damn."

I shoot up out of the chair, and it topples over.

Casvian stands in the doorway, regards the chair with one raised brow. I swoop down and set it right.

I throw my hands wide. "It's clean."

Casvian rolls his eyes and strides away.

I run after him. "Tomorrow, at dawn?"

He raises a hand without looking back.

CHAPTER 11

The night is half gone when Izamal and I slip out of the Ven. We walk a strange path through the third, doubling back every so often, until Izamal is satisfied we're not being followed. I rub my eyes as I follow in his wake.

"Look sharp," Izamal says.

"I'm sharp," I mutter, standing up straighter.

He throws me a grin over his shoulder. "You sure don't look it."

I scowl at his back as we enter a neatly kept shrine—all smooth angles and bright color, no stone that's been rubbed smooth by thousands of hands, no faded patches of paint—and Izamal beelines for the statue of the Great King.

He kneels before the plinth on which the statue rests. I glance around as he taps a handful of carvings. No secondary statue here; I guess in the third they have no need to beg mercy from the Great King's wrathful face.

"Are you watching?"

"Absolutely." I drag my attention to him and memorize which carvings he twists to complete the ikon. With a soft grinding sound, the base of the statue opens to darkness. Below is a tunnel.

I hesitate. "Isn't this a bit blasphemous?"

"That's why no one else uses it. Go on."

I drop down into a tunnel that's too short to stand up straight in. Izamal follows and stoops, reaching for something. As the door closes above, he ignites an ikonlantern. "It opens out a few steps ahead. I keep this lantern here, and a change of clothes there."

As promised, the tunnel widens, and I straighten up. Izamal reaches into a bundle on the ground and hands me a cloak and my old moss-cloth overdress. Moving quickly, I don both.

Izamal keeps up a steady stream of instruction as he leads the way. "This passage comes out in the fourth. There are two passages you can take to the fifth, depending on where you want to come out."

"What if I get lost?"

"You won't. Most tunnels have one entrance and one exit. Makes it hard to get lost. It also makes the tunnels hard to find: knowing one doesn't mean you can find another."

I nod at his back. "How long does this usually take?"

"As long as it takes."

I say nothing, but he must sense that I'm not impressed.

"I'm sorry, am I pulling you away from skulking around the Ven all night, hoping to just bump into the very secret passage that'll lead to your father?"

He makes it sound like I'm a simpleton, just because he found me staring at a wall. "Dalca and Casvian could go to Pa at any moment. I was looking for them."

"Darling, even they sleep. In the meantime, this makes a difference to the fifth." He gestures at the bag of weapons slung around his waist.

Iz hopes I'll take over distributing weapons to those who want them. I suppose it's a noble task, but . . . "It's just. I don't know how much time Pa has."

Izamal is quiet. "We don't know how much time anyone has. We don't know how much time you've got or I've got. But I bet the folks down in the fifth—with no means to protect themselves—I bet they've got less."

He's right, but it doesn't make me feel any better. "Sure."

He sighs and stops, turning to face me. "I want to find Alcanar, too. If you think haunting the halls will do it, let's go back." The soft ikonlight illuminates the seriousness in his golden eyes.

"No," I say. "You're right. Watching Dalca sleep won't help anyone."

His eyes crinkle in sudden humor. "Well, when you put it like that . . ."

I roll my eyes, and his laugh echoes down the tunnel.

We pop out in the fourth in a nondescript alley near the Pearl Bazaar and take an unfamiliar passage that lets us out in the fifth. I glance back as the passage seals itself. The entrance seems too obvious—a once-ornate stone arch set in a brick wall. But I suppose I've seen ruins like this a hundred times, stone sculptures from a more prosperous past that've been assimilated into modern buildings by folks who'd rather build around them than demolish them. I would never have assumed secret tunnels to be behind any of them.

"This way," Izamal says, taking off with distance-eating strides.

I match his pace through the twisting streets of the fifth, faltering only when Izamal turns onto a seemingly dead-end street and makes a three-fingered gesture at the hooded figure there.

Iz reads the question on my face as we step into the glittering ikonlight of the gray market. "Gives people a head's up that I'm here. They'll get the word out by the time we're ready to hand things out."

A shiver runs up my spine as I squint through the thick pipe smoke that hangs in the air. The street is lined with vendors—more than last time—but none of them call out to us or make any attempt to draw our attention to their wares. They're too busy conversing furiously amongst themselves.

Izamal's brow furrows.

Three women huddle with their heads pressed together, gesturing wildly, expressions tense.

Something isn't right. I catch a snippet of a conversation, just one word: "*Alcanar*—"

I stop dead. Izamal tugs at my arm. "Keep walking."

Thoughts whiz through my head, each more panicked than the last. I take a deep breath. Maybe they're talking about another Alcanar. There has to be more than one.

"— *Vale's alive*—"

I squeeze Izamal's arm. "They're talking about Pa."

"Yes, I'd gathered that," he says through clenched teeth.

A shadow peels itself from the side of a building and falls into step with us. They lower their hood, revealing a strikingly gorgeous face. Im, from the knitting circle.

She doesn't smile. "You look like you could use a cup of sundust."

In minutes, the three of us are seated at a slightly sticky table in one corner of the place I've been thinking of as a secret pub for revolutionaries-turned-knitters. Two other familiar faces—the green-eyed woman and the grizzled man with the ikon-inscribed tooth—join us, bearing steaming mugs of sundust tea. I don't touch mine.

Im murmurs. "We've tried to squash the rumors, but they're everywhere. People know your father is alive."

A knot in my stomach loosens at *your father is alive*. I hadn't realized how afraid I was that, despite all logic, Pa might already be gone.

Im shakes her head at my relief. "It's not a good sign, love."

The man speaks. "It's not good for the city to know Vale's alive, after what he did."

Green Eyes holds my gaze. "They'll demand justice."

The taste of bile fills my mouth. "But if Dalca needs Pa—"

Three sets of eyebrows rise at *Dalca*. Im speaks. "It may not be up to the prince now. The Regia's Guard—they'll have a say."

Dalca's face flashes through my mind, the tense way he said *the Regia's Guard*. The hard face of the pale-haired man in black and gold. "Who are they?"

Izamal answers. "Their leader is Ragno Haveli. Cas's father. He lost his wife in the rebellion."

"Worse," says Green Eyes. "He was a good friend of your father's once. I'd wager he holds your father responsible. A personal betrayal."

I fight the urge to jump to my feet. "What does all this mean?"

The three of them share looks. Izamal's eyes widen.

Im answers. "Ragno will push for the Trials."

"The Trials," I repeat. "It can't—that's—they haven't for years." I barely remember the last one, well over a decade ago. Pa didn't let me go. But I heard about it from other fifth-ringer kids. A Trial is how they punish those who commit crimes against the Regia. If the condemned survives three Trials, they win their freedom.

"No one wins the Trials."

"There was Iravai the Sly."

"Yeah sure, if fairy tales count."

"The thing I don't understand is where will they get the food?"

They'll hold the Trials in a grand arena in the third ring, and the streets will fill with festivities and food. Half the city will show up just to eat. I remember kids bringing back birds made of sugar — free treats, courtesy of the Regia. It makes me sick, remembering how jealous I'd been of them, and how furious I'd been with Pa for not letting me go.

That's what it'll come to. Pa will fight for his life, and the city will watch, entertained.

I get to my feet, ignoring the others. Izamal half stands with me. "It's just speculation — we don't know for sure it'll happen."

His mouth tells me kind lies, but his eyes are sure.

"I need fresh air," I say, and push past them, out onto the street.

I head away from the gray lanterns at the market's entrance, slipping through an alley that lets me out onto an empty street. I aim stormward for no reason other than wanting to be alone.

It's like I've found myself in a dance that's been going on for decades, and of all the dozens of people dancing, I'm the only one who doesn't know the steps.

All I want is to get Pa back. Izamal can want to save the fifth. I'm not so noble. I'm selfish. How much more am I supposed to lose?

Pa's not nice. He's gruff, and he's never once told me he's proud of me. But he held me when I was small, when the stormsurges still made me cry. He did that for every one of the stormtouched who needed it.

How can he deserve being put to death in this way?

I walk on and on.

If I stop, the cold will find me, so I wander through the dimly lit fifth, until the Storm blocks my path. It hangs like a curtain, cutting off the street, slicing houses on either side in two.

A lazy streak of violet lightning zigzags through the black. The Storm is watching me. It knows what's in me better than I know it myself. It tells me so, but not in words. Faintly, far more faintly than the sound of my breath, come three plucked notes. A sitar.

I step forward.

Something rustles to my right. Huddled together on the front steps of a long-abandoned house, half hidden in shadow, are two kids staring into the Storm. The elder of the two can't be a day over twelve, a pointy-nosed boy with dark feathers instead of hair, feathers that coat his neck and peek out through the holes of his tank top. He holds the end of a thin rope that snakes into the black of the Storm.

"What have you got there?"

The other urchin, a sniffly red-nosed boy with big puppy eyes and floppy puppy ears, scowls at me. "It's nothin' to you, old lady."

The rope twitches. There's something, or someone, on the other end. "Who's in there?"

"Nobody," the puppy-faced kid growls.

I scowl at the boy holding the rope. "Is he your voice?"

He stares at the ground as the line twitches again. I seize it and pull. The weight at the end of the rope is light, too light to be a child. Whatever it is fights me, but I reel it in quickly.

A little cat pounces out of the Storm, the rope tied around its neck. It seems to pull a little piece of the Storm with it, a small wisp of black cloud wraps around its body like a living coil.

I can't tell what its curse is. All I know is that it'll suffer. There's been enough suffering, all around. I'm tired of it.

I don't have it in me to watch Pa suffer at Dalca's hands. So I've got to stop it. It's that simple.

"Why would you do this?" The rope falls from my hands.

The little kid lets out a big sniffle and rubs a fist across his nose, shielding his friend. "None of your business."

The boy with feathers speaks quietly from behind him. His voice is as delicate as birdsong. "We were just . . . We wanted her to be like us."

I frown. "Why?"

The feathered boy shrugs as the other unties the cat. "Run!" the little one yells, slinging the cat under one arm and grabbing his friend's hand with the other. The cat yowls as they run back into the fifth, disappearing into the dark.

I face the Storm. It watches me back. One day, it promises, everything and everyone will belong to it. And there'll be no more pain.

I turn my back on it and retrace my steps to the gray market.

I'm surprised when I find a cloaked figure sitting on the ground at the entrance to the secret passage. His head lolls against the stone, and a lock of long dark hair escapes his hood. A small black kitten watches me from the cradle of his folded arms.

Izamal wakes with a touch to his shoulder, his pupils sharpening to slits. He relaxes when he sees it's just me. The kitten leaps to the ground and pads away, its nose in the air.

I offer him a hand and haul him up. He clutches a bag of weapons, a bag that should've been emptied. Did he wait for me instead of handing them out?

His voice is hoarse with sleep. "You okay?"

I give him a grim smile as he opens the door and we slip into the dark. "Never better."

"Bit of an odd thing to say, isn't it?"

"I suppose."

The ikonlight flares to life.

He bites a question back, but I can hear it rattling around his head. After the third time he inhales as if to speak and then thinks better of it, I take pity on him. "It's simple, for me at least," I say. "You've got to save everyone. I've just got to save my father. If there's going to be a Trial . . . all it means is that I've just got to work faster."

"We've," he says.

"What?"

"*We've* got to work faster. I'm with you, remember."

Something warm blossoms in me. Matched by guilt that rises when I remember that I've lied to Izamal about Pa's willingness to fight.

Izamal presses his ear to the door to the third.

He leans in and breathes, "Get back and wait for my signal."

"Is someone—"

He takes the ikonlight from me, presses the bag of weapons into my hands, and pushes the door open. It nearly shuts behind him, leaving me with a thin sliver of a gap to see through.

"Dalca!" Izamal says. "Fancy seeing you here."

I inch forward, pressing my eye to the gap.

"I could say the same," Dalca murmurs.

"I was visiting my mother."

Dalca's voice grows stilted, formal. "Oh. How is she?"

"Oh, you know." Izamal waves an arm. "She says you sent her a package of palace sweets."

"I—I did. Were they all right?"

"Her favorite." Izamal takes a few steps away, and Dalca follows. "Thank you."

Dalca inclines his head. He's wearing only his Wardana-issued loose white shirt and black trousers, no red in sight.

"Why're you out so late?"

Dalca hesitates, and I wonder if he was with Pa. "Lots to do."

"I can help, you know."

"I know."

"If it's about who we found, that day in the fifth—"

Dalca makes a hushing sound.

"It is, isn't it?"

"I can't tell you anything, Iz."

Izamal rears back, and I can't tell if his hurt is genuine or an act. "Sure. I'd better go—"

"It's not that I don't—I'll bring you in as soon as I can. It's just—there's a lot of pressure right now. I just have to figure out how to fix things first."

Izamal doesn't respond.

"Cas is working on something—researching a particular ikon. That's all I can say about our . . . guest."

An ikon. It's confirmation of what the knitting circle speculated. Dalca's after Pa's research, and it has something to do with the Regia's mark.

"You don't owe me, Dalca. I know where I stand."

Dalca runs his hands through his hair. "I need to do better, don't I?"

Izamal inhales. "I know you try."

Dalca scowls at the ground, and Izamal watches for a long moment. I wonder if I'm going to be trapped here all night.

"Iz . . . what do you know about Vesper?"

Izamal starts. I nearly jump. "I didn't realize she'd caught your eye." There's an edge in his tone that Dalca takes the wrong way.

"I'm sorry—are you two—never mind—"

"We're not," Iz says slowly, a glint in his eyes, "but she is very pretty."

Dalca shrugs that notion off as if either my prettiness is beside the point or he disagrees with Iz about my Carver-given looks. "There's something about her. It's as though . . . she thinks I'm not good enough."

There's a moment of surprised silence. I guess I'm not much of an actor.

Izamal's sudden, sharp laughter startles both Dalca and me.

"Oh, shut up," says Dalca as Izamal smothers his laughs.

"It's just—you've gone on and on about apprentices aiming for your bed instead of your squad—and now that there's finally an apprentice that can't be bothered with you—"

Dalca rolls his eyes. "Right. I'm either a hypocrite or the kind of simpleton who gets his head turned at the first sign of contrariness."

Izamal quiets. "You're the prince." He shrugs, as if to say, *What more is there?*

"Yes." Dalca's voice is barely a breath, and there's something strange and sardonic in his tone. "That's all that matters, isn't it?"

"You're not bad-looking, if that's what you mean. Some folks are into the gloomy thing."

Dalca huffs a laugh.

"There you go. Much better with a smile. Maybe try that on her."

"Thanks, Iz," Dalca says dryly. And then, with the distinct air of changing the subject: "You up for a bit of sparring?"

"Dalca, darling, it's past my bedtime. And shouldn't you rest up? Tomorrow's a big day."

Izamal starts walking, and Dalca falls in step.

"Tomorrow's just a friendly scrimmage, Iz. Hardly a big day."

Once their steps fade to silence, I push the door open and peek around the edge. There's no sign of them.

I run my hands down my arms, soothing the jitters under my skin as my feet take me back to the Ven. My head is one big knot. Fear for Pa, if the Trials come to be. A heady sense of triumph, that Dalca is affected by me — by Carver's work.

And something else. A quivering in my bones that tells me to be wary of Dalca. That the closer I get to power, the closer I get to being stamped out.

CHAPTER 12

The lack of sleep scratches at the corners of my eyes as I wait for Casvian. Dawn comes and goes. The Ven's courtyard grows fuller than I've ever seen it, and the air grows thick with anticipation.

I don't like it. Memories of last night, of Pa's name on strangers' lips, make my skin buzz. If something has changed between Pa and Dalca, waiting around won't help me.

On a hunch, I make for the room where Iz brought me my first time in the Ven. As I near the door, raised voices sound from within.

Tiptoeing closer, I press my ear to the door.

Casvian's voice thrums with restraint. "I'm afraid I can't help you."

Another voice, deep and smooth as honey. "I do not pretend to understand why you would cast your lot in with the Illusoras, Casvian." The second man stretches out every syllable of the name, until I get why Casvian might insist on being called Cas. "They have failed. Over and over again. Even their line is dying out."

"Careful, Father. You're awfully close to speaking treason."

A chill runs down to my fingertips. On the other side of this door is Ragno Haveli, leader of the Regia's Guard, who would have Pa face the Trials. Who had Amma's house burned. According to Dalca, at least.

"I speak of a world with a knife to its throat. I speak of seizing our last chance of hope."

"Dalca has hope."

"I know of Alcanar's work. I know you hope for some ikon to solve all our problems. Tell me, is that the wish of a child or of a man?"

Cas says nothing. I risk inching forward, straining to hear more about Pa.

Ragno sighs. "Renounce this childhood rebellion, Casvian. Enough with following the prince about like a favored lapdog, risking your life like any common Wardana."

My mouth falls open. *Any common Wardana*, he says, as if the Wardana's power is nothing. I can't wrap my mind around it. Is this how second-ringers see the world?

"As always, Father, I decline. I look dreadful in black, you must understand."

"Always playing a fool." Ragno makes a sound of disgust. "Make your choice with care. Prince Dalca's fate is written in his blood. You need not fall with him."

"I wasn't aware he was falling."

"It may not be in your books, but it is written."

The sound of a footstep sends me sprinting. I manage to get a half dozen paces down the hall before the door opens.

Ragno strides out, his eyes passing over me without note. His gray and white hair is tied back in a neat knot, leaving nothing to soften the cut of his cheekbones or the hardness of his jaw.

I wait for him to turn the corner before approaching the ajar door. I tap my knuckles on the wood with enough force to push the door further open.

Cas stands scowling at the floor. I'm surprised to see the flush reddening his cheeks. From the irritatingly polite voice he'd used, I'd never have suspected his father got to him. His eyes—ringed by dark circles—focus on my face, and he glowers. "You're late."

I fight the urge to point out that he was meant to meet me. "It seemed like there was someone in here. I thought it better to wait."

He flicks his fingers dismissively. "Fine, whatever. Come in."

The little reading room is in fantastic disarray. It's dominated by three desks pushed together, each covered in masses of paper and parchment. Light floods in from a wall of windows, and a gentle breeze comes through glass doors that lead out onto a balcony. The breeze brings with it a swell of voices, of a crowd cheering from the direction of the Ven's courtyard. This must be the *friendly scrimmage* Iz and Dalca mentioned.

"Sit." He points to a small desk in the corner.

I move a bundle of scrolls off the chair and sit in front of a massive book. He leans over me, his pale hair slipping out of the band he's tied. He draws a small mark, an ikon consisting of two concentric loops surrounded by what look like tree roots. "Look through this tome and tell me if you find this exact sign."

Cas is researching a particular ikon. Surely this isn't it—but what if it does have to do with Pa? "Just . . . find it?"

"Were you hoping for something else?"

"Well—what does it do?"

"If I knew that," he says snidely, "I wouldn't have you looking, now, would I?"

"Right." I lift the book's cover and get a waft of something that smells like dried blood. And then I can't breathe. Each page contains three ikons, albeit with them all missing small sections so as to remain deactivated. A looping scrawl to the side defines what every ikon should do. This is a feast of ikonomancy. A thrill goes through me at the thought of the power at my fingertips. I'll need every bit of power I can scrounge up—and I'm sure I can memorize at least a few of these ikons.

Casvian's ikon looks nothing like the rest. It's more rudimentary. "It's not an ikon, is it?"

"It's a proto-ikon." At my uncomprehending look, he rolls his eyes. "Proto-ikons are small, ancient symbols that ikonomancers over the years have combined into ikons. As words have roots, so do ikons."

He waves a hand in the air, as if that explains everything. He sprawls in another chair and immerses himself in shuffling a bunch of loose sheets.

The sound of distant cheering breaks over us. I glance at the balcony. "Is something happening?"

Cas scowls. "Just the monthly mating ritual of muscle-headed imbeciles."

I blink at him.

"A scrimmage between the Wardana fighters and the Regia's Guard. Helps the Guard see which of the Wardana to poach."

I think of the conversation I overheard. "You never wanted to be Regia's Guard?"

"Are we chitchatting because you've already found the proto-ikon and want to build up suspense? Or are you just wasting my time?"

I bend back over my book.

Cas huffs, and I can practically hear the crackle of steam rising from his skin.

I turn each page with care, forcing myself to focus. Maybe in here is an ikon to enlarge Pa's notebook. There could be something in there I can use; I've been fixated on finding him, but it's just as important that I figure out how to break him free once I find whatever prison he's in.

On the desk are a loose sheet of paper and a stub of a pencil, and I pull them close to me, one eye on Cas. The scratching of my pencil is impossibly loud as I carefully copy down an ikon for sticking two objects together.

Cas doesn't seem to notice, or if he does, he doesn't mind.

Most of the ikons are strange and esoteric; many don't seem to do anything by themselves but are meant to layer with other ikons. A basic ikon is the name of a thing plus an action applied to it. But the ikons in this book aren't those that would help me learn the names of things. They don't really seem to be ones that describe general actions either. They're more specific than that; they're for modulating actions.

A whole section devotes itself to ikons that increase or decrease staying power by small increments; another section details how to specify when an ikon works, like from sunrise to sunset, or while touching something with a heartbeat. It's as though I've been given a book of poetry when I don't yet know my letters.

All the ikons are unfinished. Some are easy to puzzle out, others I have no idea how to complete. But I find a few ikons that look promising: one that magnifies, one makes things double in weight—and if I can figure out what bit of the ikon signifies *double* and what signifies *weight*, I might be able to get somewhere—and one that modulates the ikon for shrinking.

A knock comes at the door. Cas barks, "What?"

The door opens a crack, and a timid voice comes from under a thatch of sandy hair. "Um, with all respect to your privacy, Mancer Haveli, you asked me to let you know if Prince Dalca was—"

"That idiot." Cas leaps to his feet and whirls out the door.

I hesitate for a heartbeat with a glance at the book, but something compels me to my feet. I have to know what Dalca's up to.

Shutting the book, I hurry after Cas.

Cas nearly sprints down the hall, his hair catching the pinks and browns of the sandstone walls. I'm half a hallway behind, but all I need to do is follow the sound.

The noise swells as I reach the second story walkway above the courtyard. Wardana and trainees lean over the railing, transfixed. Cas shoves through the crowd until they let him out in front.

I keep an eye on Cas as I apologize and sidle my way up to the railing. Below, a circle has been chalked onto the floor of the courtyard.

Ragno and Dalca face off in the dead center. On Ragno's side, flanking him, are two other fighters in black and gold.

Izamal—hair mussed and clothing covered in the fine sand that covers the courtyard floor—stands to the side, along with several others in both blood-red and black. Folks who have already fought, I'd wager, from the cuts and bruises blossoming under a layer of golden sand.

Dalca's eyes dart between his three opponents. Ragno steps back, and his two underlings dart forward.

Dalca takes one down with precision, hooking a leg under her knee and dropping her to the floor, so that her head and shoulders fall outside the circle. She's out.

In a single motion, Dalca rolls away from the second underling's attack—and right into Ragno's path. He and Ragno spar in quick movements. I don't know enough about hand-to-hand combat to understand the nuances; all I can tell is that Ragno gets pushed back just as often as Dalca does, and that neither gets a moment to catch his breath.

The remaining fighter in black grabs Dalca from behind, and Ragno lands a blow.

Dalca falls. I bite down on my cheek, my fingers like claws on the stone railing. I tamp down the wave of concern that rises in me. I don't care who wins. Both of them are Pa's enemies. *My* enemies.

Ragno throws his arms wide, basking in the appreciation that rains down on him from the Regia's Guard—and a good number of the Wardana, as well.

Dalca jumps to his feet, grinning with blood in his teeth.

The two take turns attacking. Dalca parries them, and though the sweat pours from him as he gives inch after inch of ground, the Wardana go wild for him. Instead of ensuring victory, the two-on-one showcases Dalca's ability. With Cas, Ragno had spoken of the Illusoras' weakness. But I see none now.

Dalca's foot skids back, heel touching the white chalk of the circle. He ducks one punch and blocks another with a thud of armored boot against gauntlet. Dalca trips one of his attackers, but before he can go out of bounds, Ragno pulls him back.

When Ragno knocks Dalca down again, the cheers are far more muted.

The smile slips from Ragno's face as he understands. He commands the other fighter to leave, and he does.

"Don't have him leave on my account." Dalca gets to his feet, planting himself in the sand.

"Let's make it a fair fight."

I wouldn't call it *fair*. Dalca's chest heaves with exertion, and sweat leaves tracks in the fine dust that sticks to his face. Ragno, by contrast, looks as fresh as if he were off to lunch.

Dalca lands the first hit. But Ragno beats him down.

Dalca falls.

And rises.

It's hard to watch. No one cheers. I remember Dalca's words. *Anything can be fixed.* Is it just mule-headed determination that drives him?

Cas's face is ashen.

They fight in silence. Ragno looks up first. The adoration has faded from the faces of the gathered. Unease, disapproval, anger rise in its place.

Ragno drops his staff and places a smile on his face. "Of course, none can defeat our prince."

His voice is slick as mist-moistened stone — the kind where if you lose your step, you're likely to break your skull open.

Dalca pants, sweat shining from his throat. No smile of victory — just a furrowing of his brows.

Despite his smile, Ragno's eyes are pure ice. "In fact, the prince has a grand announcement. He has found the traitor Alcanar Vale. And in six days, the Trials will begin. He is your Trialmaker."

No.

Dalca doesn't move as the noise grows deafening.

I drag my gaze up, searching the crowd. A flash of mirror-pale hair, disappearing into the mouth of a hallway. The crowd fights me as I push against bodies covered in red leather, squeezing my way through a gap until I break free.

The hallway is empty, but I sprint down it and catch a glimpse of pale hair turning the corner. Cas. Is he going to Pa?

My footsteps echo, and I slow my pace enough to muffle them. I turn the corner, but Cas is gone. The hallway meets another, and I don't know whether to turn right or left. I pick left and hurry down, but he's nowhere to be found.

I retrace my steps and go the other way, frustration heating my cheeks and palms, but I have to admit it: I've lost him.

Dejected, I return to the reading room and kick the door open.

"Cas — fix me up quick, and we'd better go —" Dalca stops. "Oh. Vesper."

I blink stupidly at him, taking in the mussed hair and the white shirt that's open to his sweat-slicked throat. He's wiped the courtyard dust from his face, but traces of it remain in his hair. He perches on the edge of a table, his jacket and gauntlet in a pile on the floor.

"Are you all right?" I ask.

"Nothing that can't be fixed," he murmurs, holding the edge of his shirt up as he draws an ikon on his ribs.

I blink carefully at a point over his left ear. "Cas just left."

He hops off the table and moves to go. Good. I might be able to follow him.

But the words bubble up out of me. "Congratulations. On being Trialmaker." Some masochistic part of me needs to see if joy lights in his eyes.

"It is a great honor," he says tonelessly, his eyes shadowed.

Surprise softens my tone. "You're not thrilled?"

He sets his mouth in a grim line. "It is a great honor," he grits out, and goes on, in a strange, angry, dead voice. "The people deserve to have their fears soothed. To see our Regia can protect us. To look at a man who was powerful enough to kill a Regia and see that he is nothing more than a rat in a maze. And this man, Vale . . . he earned his death."

I blink hard, safe only because Dalca's fixated on his hands. "He earned . . . death?"

Dalca pins me with his gaze. "You pity him?"

The look in his eyes is dangerous. "I'm sure he should pay for his crimes. But to humiliate a man before you kill him, to design theatrics so the whole city is entertained by his death . . ." I stop myself. "If the Regia wills it, I am sure it is right."

I turn my back to him, but he catches my wrist before I take a step. He looks down at his fingers with surprise, as if they moved without his permission. "I do not like it," he admits to our hands.

His hand is warm and callused, and his thumb makes small circles on the inside of my wrist. "Then why do it? Why be Trialmaker?"

Dalca stills. He doesn't move for a long moment. "I find myself doing more and more that I do not like to do," he says finally. "To do the one good thing that I must do, I find myself caught in a thousand small evils."

I squeeze his hand until he looks at me. "I hope that one thing is worth it."

"It is the only thing that matters." Our eyes lock. In the subtle movements of his lashes, the widening of his pupils, is a language that I don't want to understand. My body betrays me at his closeness: my heart thuds in a quickening drumbeat that warns me to run, my skin tingles everywhere his gaze lands, warmth pools low in my stomach. His gaze drops to my lips.

Abruptly, Dalca lets go of my hand and strides across the room, flinging the balcony doors open. He leaps up onto the sandstone ledge and turns, facing me. The wind tousles his hair, and the feathers of his cloak rustle. The air between us is thick with words unspoken, with secrets, with fury and something else.

Something that draws me to him. I fight it, but it pulls me forward one small step.

Dalca's face breaks into a strange soft smile. He takes one small step back and falls.

I hold my breath until he rises, shooting into the air.

I walk the halls, vibrating with frustration, furious every time I turn down a hallway and find no sight of either Dalca or Cas. There must be something else I can do. Sticking like glue to Cas and Dalca must eventually lead me to Pa. But how can I follow Dalca when he's likely to jump from any convenient balcony? When both of them seem to slip like phantoms through walls? I've gotten nowhere — and the noose has only tightened around Pa's neck.

Desperate, I leave the Ven and climb the golden stairs to the second. But I'm turned away at the gates, as it's too close to sundown, so, out of ideas, I return to my room.

I open the door and find Izamal sitting on my bed cross-legged, his nose in a book. He looks up when he hears the door click shut and raises an eyebrow at me.

"When did you know?" I ask.

"About the Trials? Same time you did."

"Have you found anything?"

Izamal shakes his head. "But we have six days. We'll find him."

My strength leaves me, and I want nothing more than to be alone. "You're in my room."

He makes a show of taking in the room, surprise painted on his face. "Well, look at that."

I'm not in the mood. "My roommate might come back."

He flicks a finger. "Look again."

Her side is spotlessly clean, as if she never lived here.

"She's gone to apprentice with the Regia's Guard."

I shrug that off, having had enough of the Regia's Guard for one day. Frowning, I wait for him to get up, to leave, but he seems utterly comfortable at the foot of my bed. "Can I help you?"

He pats the mattress.

I scowl and fold myself across from him, leaning against the wall.

He puts the book down on his lap, open to a faded illustration. "Have you ever heard of the kingdom of the sky?"

I roll my eyes. "I'm not in the mood, Iz."

"It's a good one," he says. "Once, in a time long before the Storm, there was an island in the sky, ruled by a king and queen who were beautiful, and noble, and just. Their happiness was complete when they had children, twins, a boy and a girl. The twins grew up happy and loved, but they always wondered: what lay below? What was there outside of their happy island kingdom?"

Izamal's voice is soothing, warm and deep. I let him spin his tale about the twins, who leap from the island to their deaths. The king and queen are maddened by their grief and build replacement children out of clay. But there's always something wrong with the clay children; they speak backwards, or kill small animals, or weep without end.

"In the end, the queen leapt from the island to go be with her children. The king stayed behind, and till the end of time, he worked on perfecting his creatures."

Izamal trails off. "I could've sworn it had a happy ending."

"That's it?" I ask.

He grins. "Sorry. We'll have to make our happy endings, I think."

I pull loose threads from the bedspread. "I haven't found the entrance. But there's the way Dalca smells—"

His eyebrows rise.

I hope the dark hides the warmth in my cheeks. "He smells like the garden in the first. I saw Cas there, too. Unless they both have a secret love of gardening, I'd wager they're hiding something there. But they kick apprentices out of the high rings at sundown."

"I'll look around."

"What if—" I cut myself off. I've discovered so little, that I don't like entertaining the idea. But: "It might not be where Pa is. What if it *is* a hiding place—but for something else?"

Izamal's voice is low, careful. "It's possible. But not likely. He's desperate. And Alcanar's just about all that's on his mind. Except . . . maybe a certain gray-eyed apprentice."

I ignore his teasing. "Pa facing the Trials means Dalca is running out of time to get whatever he's after. You saw his face when Ragno made the announcement—he wasn't pleased. I don't think Pa's given him what he wants."

His hand falls on my shoulder. "Your father won't give him what he wants. Alcanar Vale would never."

I bite my cheek. Izamal sees Pa only as a hero from stories. I don't want him to know that Pa spent most of my life hiding, that he never taught me ikonomancy. I glance at him. "Do your parents know about what you do?"

He stills. "My mother, vaguely. I try to keep her out of it. My father . . . I tell him nothing."

"You don't get along?"

A strange tenseness comes over him.

"I'm sorry. It's none of my business."

Izamal stands and paces, then pauses at the door with his hand on the knob. He turns and leans against it, watching me through half-lidded eyes. "My father isn't like yours. He had no grand ambitions, no cleverness, no anything. He was all the things that people fear about stormborn, and he liked that people were afraid of him. He liked being a monster." Izamal straightens. "He's gone. And I'm glad."

He leaves, and I gaze at the door for several long moments.

I knew he wouldn't like me prying. I hoped he'd leave if I pushed. But now that I'm alone, I wish he was with me.

I scrub my hands over my eyes. What is wrong with me? I feel thin, like a globe of blown glass; a fragile bit of shine stretched over a hollow center. My head, my heart, my stomach—everything hurts. Everything's all jumbled up together: fear and hate and fury and desire and longing and hope.

I pull Ma's locket from my shirt and tip Pa's shrunken journal onto my palm. From my pocket, I unfold my stolen papers, some blank but most covered in copied ikons.

Squinting at the miniature cover, I first carefully copy down the shrinking ikon he used. I half hope the notebook will regain its former proportions when I rub the ikon away, but it remains locket-sized.

I test the ikons I copied from Casvian's book on the loose paper, pausing every time I hear footsteps on the floorboards outside.

It takes me a large part of an hour to find a combination that does anything, and it makes the scrap of paper as large as my pillowcase. As I watch, it keeps growing, though it grows ever more slowly. I don't dare risk using that on the book. Another combination expands a sheet of paper nearly double, but when I lift it, the paper falls to ash.

Hours pass and all around me are the scattered ghosts of my failures. I try not to think about how Pa's always so certain that I'd be no good at ikonomancy. Unbidden, a memory comes of Dalca in the courtyard, rising again and again. He won't give up, and neither will I.

A bell tolls the midnight hour before I cobble together an ikon that expands the paper just enough. I wait, holding my breath, to see if there are any side effects.

A moment passes, and the paper holds.

I laugh and clap a hand over my mouth, listening for footsteps. I turn the paper over, running my fingertips along its smooth surface. No bumps, no holes, no imperfections. *Look at me now, Pa.*

I hold Pa's book with trembling hands, and carefully write the ikon on the cover. The book expands in my hands.

I wipe my palms on my blanket. Pa would hate this, but he's not here. He can yell at me after I save him.

The book crackles as I lift the cover. On the first page, I trace with a finger Pa's lilting, precise handwriting:

The Notes of Alcanar Vale.

I flip the pages slowly, taking it in. It's in code, but an easy one, similar to what Pa taught me as a child. There are pages of simple ikons, ones to meld things together, others to tear two things apart, ones to create ikonlight, ones to extinguish ikonlight . . . It goes on and on. I hope for something magnificent, something I can use not just to save Pa, but to make Dalca see me as an equal. I hope for a glimpse into Pa's mind, always so closed to me.

Deeper in the book lie Pa's experiments. Halfway through, amongst pages of theory that I struggle to understand, I find one ikon that seems promising. Pa's notes say *To uncover.*

Footsteps sound in the hall, the floorboards creaking. They stop outside my door.

I scrawl the ikon on a piece of paper, then carefully reshrink Pa's book and slip it back in my locket.

I draw the sheets up over my chin, clutching the scraps of paper in my fist. I'll have to destroy them the first chance I get.

I wait for the doorknob to turn. I'll count to a hundred, just to be safe, then enlarge the book again.

. . . Three, four, five. I have to be careful. Pa would rather I burn the book than let it fall into the wrong hands. But whose hands are the wrong hands? Dalca's, surely. Izamal's too?

. . . Twenty-one, twenty-two, twenty-three . . . I have to search the garden. Tomorrow I'll have to think of something, some excuse.

. . . Thirty-seven, thirty-eight, thirty-nine . . . Five days. I've got five days to find it.

Sleep clutches at me, drawing me down into the dark. Behind my eyelids, the last thing I see before I go is a pair of blue eyes.

CHAPTER 13

Morning sees me in the Ven scouring Casvian's book of ikons. An enormous wealth of ikonomancy is at my fingertips, but my mind is filled with thoughts of Dalca. *A thousand small evils,* he said. Those are the words of a man who feels remorse, one who has a heart. Could I talk to him? And what, convince him to let the man who murdered his grandfather go free? What killer gets a pardon just because his daughter cries?

But if I could just get him to understand . . . What Pa did doesn't represent all of who he is. There's a bigger picture. Amma said something to me once, when I found a drawing someone had done of her when she was a teenager: *In life we wear a hundred faces—the bawling infant, the happy child, the starry-eyed youth. Each face belongs to a different life.*

I didn't fully understand it then. But maybe I do now. A lifetime is made up of dozens of lives, tied together only by shared memory. Who I was when I was a baby isn't the same person I was at age ten, much less who I am now. Who Pa was in his twenties isn't the same man he is today. And I have to believe that the man he is today shouldn't have to die for the mistakes of the other man who wore his face twelve years ago.

"I must go to the palace," Casvian says, startling me out of my thoughts.

The garden. I think fast. "Should I come with you? I could work outside, in the hall. Then if I find the mark, I can bring it to you straightaway."

It's the last that convinces him. Casvian badgered me this morning to work quicker to find the meaning of the mark.

"Fine," Cas says. "But don't speak."

"I wouldn't dream of it."

I follow him silently out of the Ven, through the golden gates to the second, then to the first, and into the palace. I push aside the strange, lightheaded feeling that comes over me again at how easy it is. Jem and I used to tell ourselves stories of what the palace must be like, but we never expected to make it up here. And now I've made it twice.

Cas waves an attendant away, marching along as if he owns the place. A honeysuckle-scented breeze tousles my hair, telling me that the garden is close by. I follow Casvian as he weaves in and out of hallways, through a pair of double doors, and out into a colonnade open to the sun. A beam of sunlight warms my face, and the scent of blooms descends upon me, thick as a blanket.

The colonnade edges a courtyard that's dominated by a thick wall of living plants. Little of the shape of the gardens is visible through the hedge that encloses them.

Casvian pays no attention to the gardens; they're merely a shortcut. He strides along the colonnade to an ornately carved door and pauses, one foot over the threshold of the room. "Wait out here."

He disappears inside, the door clicking shut. I tuck the book of ikons in the crook of my arm. There are benches all along the walkway, and I'm sure Casvian meant for me to sit on one and wait. But he really was vague with what he meant by *here*. The gardens are practically *here*.

An arched opening set in the hedge wall grants a view of pink flowers. I glance over my shoulder once before slipping through.

The archway leads to an enclosure where there's evidence of new planting: practical foods, a riot of vegetables and tubers in bloom. A path stretches past them to another arch that opens into a much larger enclosure. The air here is even sweeter; on either side of the path grows a small grove of trees heavy with luscious fruit, some red as blood, some golden. It's a decadence that curdles my stomach when I see that fallen fruit has been left to rot.

Deeper still, the gardens become purely frivolous. Trees of the sort I've never seen, with black bark and leaves that glitter like diamonds. Flowers with blooms the size of my hand, in every color under the sun, filling the air with a fragrance I can almost taste. A master gardener has been at work here. Even though the garden feels wild, there's a hidden pattern to the chaos, something I can barely make out, like a song that disappears whenever I listen for it.

Is there a path to the old city hidden in a tree? Or perhaps somewhere farther along the path. Everything is strange, and yet nothing stands out as a likely candidate.

Leaves crunch underfoot, but I haven't taken a step.

Someone's here. I press myself into the shelter of the trees and watch, squinting through a gap between trunks. His back is to me as he kicks at the ground, leaves and pebbles flying, then he stalks forward, running a hand through hair with the color and shine of spilt ink. There's something familiar about the gesture. I inch forward as he turns right and disappears behind a wall of flowering plants.

The sharp edge of his jaw and the grim line of his lips name him just as well as if I'd seen Dalca's distinctive eyes. I go as fast as I dare, taking care not to step on the piles of dried leaves that line the way. The path winds like a snake, and the trees become denser, branches intertwined like plaited hair, hung with flowers of every color. I edge around each bend, expecting Dalca at each turn. His footsteps grow quieter. There's a quick, sharp sound of flying leaves and pebbles, a soft metallic clang.

Then all is silent.

My heart pounds, adrenaline turning my vision crisp and my palms sweaty. One more bend, and the path opens wide. A brown wall of thorns stands before me, so densely packed that the space it encloses is completely hidden. Its branches have been shaped by human hands to weave in an intricate pattern, braiding themselves around an arched opening. Set in the opening is a golden gate that comes up to my thigh.

Dalca is nowhere in sight. The gate swings easily, as if it's been freshly oiled. Beyond is a clearing ringed with white-barked trees crowned with dark leaves and golden flowers that hang like teardrops. In the center is a lotus-studded pond as still as glass, with two stone benches before it and a freestanding mosaic behind it. The mosaic depicts a man and woman standing with their hands pressed together, fierce expressions on their faces. I can't tell if they're about to fight or dance.

On tiptoes, I circle the pond with eyes peeled. There's no other opening in the wall of thorns; Dalca can only be behind the mosaic wall. I hold my breath and peek behind it.

Footprints remain on the clover-studded dirt, but there's no Dalca.

My breath leaves me in a single whoosh. This is it.

I've found Dalca's way to the old city.

The stone is bare on this side, but faintly grooved as if it was once carved. I adjust my grip on the book, so I can run my fingers along the cool surface. It has to be here somewhere, some mechanism like the poma in the tapestry that led to the stormtouched Wardana.

I go over every inch, over and over, until I know this wall better than any in my bedroom at Amma's. There's no mechanism, no knob, no button.

Okay. Maybe it isn't the wall. Maybe it's the golden gate. I kneel before it and inspect every curlicue and carved creature upon it, and then I twist the knob in careful measures, anticipating the click of an ikondial. Nothing happens. The hope in my chest sinks into my gut.

Dalca's disappearance—and that I've seen Casvian leaving the garden—points to this being the secret way to Pa's prison. It has to be here. Dalca's got Pa, right under my feet, and I'm not clever enough to figure it out.

I clutch the book to my chest in a white-knuckled grip, hating my inadequacies.

I go over every inch of the clearing, touching each tree trunk, each flower, the roots, the benches, and come up with nothing. Perhaps it's something before the clearing; I head out the gate and search the intricately wound branches over the opening. What am I missing? The honeyed air grows thick in my lungs, smothering me. *Where is it?*

I retrace our steps back into the winding path, gritting my teeth in frustration. I turn in a circle.

Leaves crunch behind me.

"Vesper." Dalca's eyes glint darkly, and a half smile curls his lips.

I swallow a scream.

"You shouldn't be here." He radiates calm, but there's a watchful gleam in his eyes.

"I'm sorry. I know. I'm sorry, it's just—" What do I say? "I've never known plants like these and I—I'm sorry."

Dalca closes his eyes and tilts his head back. His chest expands, and I mimic him, inhaling the dizzying scent of honeysuckle and roses, of sweet tree-ripened fruit, the soft dark smell of decay that dances underneath it all. "What do you think?"

I bite my lip. Nothing but the truth comes to mind. "It's a terrible waste. But I've never seen such a beautiful place in my life."

He laughs, eyes fluttering open. "Can beauty be a waste?"

I smile back, uncertain, a little dizzy. "I don't know. Does beauty have a point?"

Dalca smiles as if I've told a joke, but there's something dangerous in his eyes. I take a small step back. He *is* beautiful, in his own stark way. And it occurs to me that I was wrong. His beauty has a point sharp as a razor; it's a weapon, and it's working on me.

"I'll go," I say.

"Not yet." He steps closer, and I step back.

The silver ring in his eyes stretches wide as his pupils grow, the black devouring the summer-sky blue.

His voice is a caress. "Won't you scold me? Tell me to send the fruit to the children of the fifth and kill every plant that does not bear fruit, no matter how sweetly their flowers bloom?"

I shake my head.

"No?" Dalca steps forward, and I step back. "Won't you call me cruel? No, you can't take it back. You told me what you think of the Trial, and of me as Trialmaker. You know better, don't you? Won't you tell me how to punish him, this fearmonger, this traitor, this man who murdered my grandfather?"

I don't trust myself to speak, not when he simmers in a way I've never seen, like an inferno waiting for a spark.

He steps forward. "Don't move."

I stand still. The distance between us feels like a living thing.

"Your eyes," Dalca whispers to the gap between us. "How they watch me, how they judge me. I can't escape them."

His hand comes up, and my breath catches. His fingers land on my cheekbone, featherlight.

I grab his wrist and the book falls from my hands, landing with a soft thump to which neither of us pay notice.

"There's something about you, Vesper." His gaze never wavers from mine, so much so that I start to fear that Carver's ikonwork has failed, that he recognizes me from Amma's, that he knows exactly who I am.

"Won't you tell me not to kiss you?" he breathes against my lips.

I don't say a word.

Dalca presses his lips to mine, and for a moment all is still. His lips are soft and his hand is so gentle where it cups my cheek. The fragrance of the garden wraps around our shoulders like a blanket.

I jump back, touching my lips with the tips of my fingers, staring at him.

"I'm sorry." Dalca looks surprised and troubled. His hand rises, as if he would reach for me.

His fingers brush my arm as I turn away, but fear propels me out of his reach. Fear of what it means, fear of why I didn't push him away, fear of what kind of person I am.

I run.

He could catch me if he wanted, I'm sure, but I pray he doesn't want to.

My legs take me out of the palace, drawing shouts as I go, but I'm not stopped, not as I run through the second, through the gates of the third and fourth, all the way back to the fifth. It's a sense of home I run toward, but I have no home left.

It was stupid to run. I know it. A cleverer woman would have somehow used that against Dalca to find Pa. When my legs begin to ache, I walk, and walk, and walk.

The pressure has been building inside me. It feels like too much, all of a sudden. I can't think about Dalca, I can't afford to think about how soft his lips are, not when I have to save Pa, but I can't get him out of my mind. What's wrong with him? He doesn't know me, not at all. Not enough to kiss me.

What's wrong with me? Why am I thinking about him still? I can't want him. I shouldn't. Nothing can happen between us. He's the Regia's son. My parents killed his grandfather. He's planning Pa's murder. There's got to be something wrong with me. Because some part of me understands him. *To do the one good thing that I must do, I find myself caught in a thousand small evils.*

What wouldn't I do to save Pa? In the darkness of my mind, I can admit things. I'd go back to the garden. I'd kiss Dalca till his head spun. I'd find a way to twist him around my finger if I knew it would save Pa's life.

The fifth ring feels gloriously crowded compared to the first. The clamor of brass, the tinkling of glass, the smell of bodies and incense. I wander through the crowds until I get lost within them, until the curious looks at my third-ring outfit die away. A little girl chases a gap-toothed boy, laughing like a tiny hyena, till she smacks into my legs. She giggles an apology. Stones fall from her lips with every syllable, a curse. I smile at her as the boy tugs her away.

I watch them go. I wonder what shape her life will take. Her parents met, maybe fell in love, and their choices brought her into a world that despises the stormtouched. I wonder what sort of life I would have lived, had my parents made different choices. Would I have been brought up in the safety and security of the third? Would I have become a great ikonomancer like Pa?

I scrub a hand across my eyes. Fear is making a coward of me.

My legs don't want to stay still. They drive me through a ramshackle market with meager wares, past an old metalworks that's been converted to a shelter, past hundreds of tense-eyed people packed into far too small a place. There are pockets of joy: men laughing in a tiny barbershop, a green-faced mother crooning to her child. But I also skirt a fistfight between two snarling men and edge past a woman with a frying pan yelling at a horned boy to leave her house and never come back. I duck my head and try to look as inconspicuous as possible.

My hand goes to Ma's locket, my thumb tracing the familiar grooves. What would Ma do? She had ambition, but it was an ambition born out of compassion. She had bravery, to do the things no one else dared, but in doing so, she left Pa and me behind.

I suppose Dalca's mother left him, too. To become Regia, she renounced everything else. The Great King lives in her body, but she's gone. Does he miss her, like I miss Ma?

Right beside the stormwall, cast in its shadow, is a block of ruins. The skeleton of an old temple stands amongst the rubble of its roof. A casualty from the last stormsurge. The rubble will remain until the priestesses declare it curse-free and safe to touch.

I pick my way through, wanting to see the Great King. The statue of the Great King is missing an arm, but otherwise unscathed, standing alone on a pedestal. His stern face looks down at me. Ma left me to be Regia, for the Great King's power. Was it worth it?

I kick at a piece of stone and yelp at the stabbing pain in my toe. Stupid. The stone flips over, and a pair of angry stone eyes stare up at me. They must belong to the Great King's other form, the King of Wrath. And sure enough, on the other side of the temple is the remnant of another pedestal. The statue is in a hundred pieces, one of the larger shards shows a sandaled foot, another a section of robe, but it's the third that draws my attention. Clasped hands, holding a small sapling with intertwined roots. The sculptor meant for the sapling to appear to glow; two concentric circles are chiseled into the stone.

I've seen this before. It's a more detailed version of Casvian's proto-ikon. Two concentric circles, surrounding squiggles like tree roots. I laugh. It echoes, sounding more bitter with every repetition. I've found this, and not Pa. I don't even know what the mark means, or why Casvian wants it.

I know so damn little. About Ma, about Pa. About Dalca, and why he's gotten under my skin. I hate it. I hate feeling small. I hate that I couldn't find the way to the old city. I hate that Dalca caught me. I hate that I let him kiss me.

But most of all, I hate that I ran away.

Hate builds in my gut, dark and oily. The fifth's warning bells begin to toll, as if the Storm knows, as if it comes for me. Bolts of violet lightning streak through the wall of darkness, illuminating the beasts writhing within. Thunder booms, echoing hollowly through my chest.

The ringing of the bells grows louder as the other watchtowers pick up the call. The Storm has awakened.

Streaks of red stand out against the black as Wardana fly toward the

Storm. Ikonomancers work the woven ikonshield, and a lattice of blue-white ikons materializes, holding the Storm back.

And I'm in trouble. I'm within spitting distance of the stormwall, and worse, I don't know this part of the fifth—I don't know the nearest stormshelter. I dash out of the temple, stumbling over rubble, transfixed by the roiling clouds.

The Storm bulges, like a great hand reaching for me. The ikonshield bends and stretches, fighting against it. A flash of lightning illuminates a massive serpent's eye that swivels, as if it's looking for something. Another strike of lightning illuminates its body, coiling around the city. The barrier strains, the glowing ikon-lines growing thin. The wrath of the Storm and the power of the ikonomancers are equally matched.

For a moment all is hushed.

The ikonshield shatters.

The blackness of the Storm crashes into the fifth like a wave. As they fall, the clouds solidify into monsters: a giant spider, a swarm of little winged beasts, a pack of hybrid creatures with the bodies of lions, scorpion tails, and human faces.

The ikonshield rematerializes behind them, cutting off the deluge of beasts and holding back the rest of the Storm. I'd be reassured if three of the lion-beasts weren't bounding toward me. Their jaws snap, spittle flying in streaks behind them, rows of blade-sharp teeth glinting.

They're forty feet away. I have no weapon, no shelter. They bound forth faster than I can run. I grab the charcoal pencil in my pocket. I drop to my knees and pick up the first piece of rubble that I find, scrawling an ikon I copied from Casvian's book, to attach two things together. The stone flies true, but it misses the stormbeast's eyes and instead sticks to its forehead like a demented hat. The beast doesn't even slow.

Thirty feet away.

I scribble the ikon onto the ground, over and over. I manage to scrawl it three times before looking back up.

Twenty feet.

I dive into the temple. There are two doorways, each only big enough for one beast to enter at a time. Through one, I watch them come. One of the stormbeasts shrieks as its hind foot lands on one of my ikons and is held fast. But the other two bound right over my ikons.

I grab a shattered piece of wood as long as my forearm. Splinters dig into the skin of my palms. I wish I knew more ikonomancy, just a little bit more.

My heartbeat pounds in my ears. I know only this: if I must die, I won't do so cowering.

A beast bounds through the door, and I smack it with my makeshift club. It howls and retreats. It felt real as anything when I hit it, but its coat is the same shifting darkness of the Storm, cloudlike, as if I could put my hand to it and it'd pass right through.

A rustle of stone is my only warning as another claws through the far opening. I swing at it, catching a paw that snaps my club in two.

My shoulder throbs with the impact, but I hunt for another weapon as they prowl outside the temple, their claws clicking on stone with every movement.

One bolts inside and pounces, its lightning eyes on me.

I brace for the bite of teeth, the pain of my flesh tearing.

The beast screams. The pain doesn't come.

I peek through my arms, up through the shattered roof. A Wardana descends, cloak stretched wide, arm outstretched from having just thrown a spear. My stomach flips when I see his blue eyes.

The spear pins the stormbeast's shoulder, and Dalca swoops down, yanking it out and touching down into a fighting stance before me.

Another lion-beast enters the temple.

I don't break eye contact with the second beast, but my hand searches the ground for something to defend myself with. My fingers brush against wood. I lift it with shaking arms. A shattered beam, heavy enough. It'll have to do.

I raise the club as Dalca jabs his spear at the wounded beast. It jumps back, and the other beast lunges forward. Dalca bats its swipe aside with the pole of his spear, but I can tell that he's handicapped, fighting at this close range. He's only doing it to keep himself between me and them. To save me.

Dalca stabs the first stormbeast, sticking it in the leg, in the chest. It thrashes at him, and he ducks as the scorpion tail comes around. Dalca fights like he was made for it, his movements smooth as water, meeting each and every one of the beast's strikes. But even I can tell that he won't last long, not when he has to fight this close.

The second beast had hung back, watching, but with Dalca distracted, it lunges. I swing my club, connecting with the beast's muzzle with an arm-rattling thud. Its claw catches the side of my leg as it rears back. A sharp pain blossoms, but I ignore it.

Dalca stabs the beast, shoving it away from me, and its claws rake against his chest. He rolls with its momentum, sliding under it and sticking it deep through the eye.

It falls. But that was what the first beast was waiting for; it jumps on him, sinking its teeth into his shoulder. Dalca doesn't scream. But I'm close enough to hear him draw in a sharp breath.

His eyes meet mine, and his lips part. "Run."

I've done enough running. With all my power, I swing my club at the beast's head. The wood connects with the stormbeast's nose with a satisfying crunch, and it releases Dalca. He drops to his knees, ducking under its teeth, and in one fluid movement, he hefts his spear and rises to his feet, stabbing the beast through the heart.

I watch the light leave its too-human eyes. Dalca gives it a good shove, and it falls to the side, slowly, heavily, but a hairsbreadth before impact, the body dissolves into a whorl of dark cloud. The black cloud rises into the air and is sucked back into the Storm, becoming one with the darkness encircling the city. It's a dark promise: the beast will be born again, someday.

Dalca turns to me. He gasps, face shiny with sweat, chest heaving. Blood pours from his sleeve, coating his hand, dripping to the ground.

"I'm sorry," he says, before I know what to make of him, before I know what to feel. He gives me an uncertain smile and falls to his knees.

I catch him before he hits the ground, but my own hurt leg buckles under our combined weight. His head drops into the crook of my shoulder, and his breaths come fast and hot against my neck. I search his body for any lingering wisp of darkness. I've never heard of anyone getting cursed from just being touched by a stormbeast, but that might be because stormbeasts don't usually let go, not until they've dragged their prey back to the Storm. I turn to inspect my leg, and my head spins at the blood soaking my pants. At least I don't see evidence of a curse.

"I'm sorry," Dalca says again, into my neck as his shoulder spurts blood. I clamp my hand around it, trying to stifle the flow. He groans, in far worse shape than I thought. Not all his wounds are from these three beasts. How many did he fight before he came here?

"Stupid." My voice trembles. "You're an idiot. Haven't you heard of backup?"

A tiny smile quirks his lips. "You were fine backup."

That surprises a smile out of me, but it fades. "I'm sorry I ran."

He closes his eyes. "I frightened you."

My head spins. "Yes."

"I'm sorry."

"Did you mean to?"

He breathes in and out, then his eyes flutter open. "Yes."

"Why?"

The words come slow, as if he has to pull them from some dark, hidden place. "Because you frighten me."

I drink in the lines of his face, the furrow between his brows, the way his jaw moves as he bites back the other things he would say.

My heartbeat hasn't slowed, even though the stormbeast is gone. A giddy dizziness comes over me.

Dalca sighs, then pushes himself up, struggling to his feet. My hands hover, ready to help, but he shies away.

Upright, he holds a hand to me. I let him pull me up, stumbling as my head spins. My leg throbs with pain hot and sharp. His mouth moves, but I can't make out what he says over the ringing in my ears.

The edges of my vision go gray, until all I see are his frightened eyes, then even those disappear, and everything is black.

CHAPTER 14

Ma squeezes my hand. Her hair billows out behind her, and her jaw is set tight. She looks down at me once, and she's beautiful in the sun-kissed, glowing way of a memory that's been worn soft by repeat viewings.

She's half dragging me, though I try to keep up. But my legs are so small, and she's too determined, too intent on her destination.

The stormwall rises before us, black clouds pressing against the boundary like smoke under glass. I try to speak, to ask Ma where we're going, but the wind steals the words from my throat.

She doesn't slow, doesn't veer away from the stormwall, and I understand. The clouds of the Storm part for us into a tunnel, and something glows within the dark: a sapling with a braided stem, rapidly growing. I won't go. I yank my hand free, but she catches it, gripping tighter than before. I dig my feet into the ground and pry her clawlike fingers from my wrist. Ma turns to me with terror in her eyes and tears on her cheeks, just as I free myself.

She falls toward the Storm with her face frozen in a scream, and I reach for her, just as her chest splits in two and a dozen-armed storm-beast climbs out, and the thing that was Ma collapses into black cloud. The tunnel begins to close, and I try to step forward, but something pulls me back. Arms around my waist pull me high into the air, away from the Storm, the tunnel, and the glowing, twisted tree deep within.

The clouds of the Storm fall like a curtain, sealing away the tree and Ma. I twist to see who carries me and meet Dalca's eyes. A thousand emotions war in them—shades of misery, of fury, frustration, desire. A certainty works its way up my spine, filling me with a single truth: Dalca is going to let me go, and I will fall.

A shout jolts me awake. I blink up at a pale sandstone ceiling carved to look like clouds. This had better not be the afterlife. I push myself up. Pale curtains hang on all sides of the bed, and muffled voices come from behind them. Where am I?

My body aches, but it's the ache of days-old bruises, not the ache I expect. Someone's put a blanket on me, and I toss it aside. Goose bumps rise on my legs at the brush of cold air, and I touch the ikon-inscribed bandage that wraps around my thigh. It barely hurts.

What am I wearing? The dress is cut from a soft, pale fabric that wraps around my waist, but it stops high on my thighs. I flush. Who changed my clothes? Ma's locket brushes against my chest, and I grip it tight, thankful it's still there. Folded across the footboard are a pair of black pants and a long shirt. Wardana-issue. I tug them on, surprised at how familiar they already feel.

The sounds of an argument come through the curtains.

"Please, let me just—"

"I'm fine." A polite, commanding voice. Dalca. "Please, move aside."

I push the curtains to one side. It's an infirmary, and from the glimpses I get of the other inhabitants through open curtains, a Ward-ana infirmary.

Dalca strides toward the exit, pulling on a knee-length embroidered jacket over pants and a shirt similar to mine.

"Wait!" a tired-looking healer calls, holding Dalca's thousand-and-one-feather cloak.

"I'll take it to him." I pluck it out of her hands.

She shoots me a quick look—just a glint of warmth in her eyes, one that doesn't trickle down to her mouth—before she hurries to the next bed.

I step out into a hallway with the hallmark striated sandstone walls of the Ven.

Dalca's already a good fifty paces away.

"Dalca!"

He startles, whipping around. "Vesper?"

He waits for me, but his gaze keeps slipping to the floor, as if he can't quite stand to keep looking at me. *You frighten me.* My neck warms. "I—I have your cloak."

"Oh, yes. Thank you." He takes it from me and, in a single fluid motion, slings it over his shoulders and hooks the clasp. "I must go."

But he doesn't move. What do I say? What do I want from him? I search his eyes. They look just as conflicted as I feel. He opens and closes his hands, and my dream comes back to me. "I found a mark that Casvian's been looking for. A proto-ikon."

Dalca blinks, and his expression sharpens into that of a hunter. So this proto-ikon is something he's after, too—but does it have to do with Pa? "Was it in one of his books?"

"No." I bite my lip, and his eyes flick down to my mouth. A dark thrill courses through me. I have power here.

He steps closer, eyes glinting, voice soft. "Then where?"

"Will you tell me why you're looking for it?"

"Why do you want to know?" Dalca tilts his head, a shutter falling over his eyes.

I try to look innocent, helpful. "I want to help. And, truth is, I'm curious."

"You want to help?" He stretches the words out until they sound hollow.

"I want to help *you*."

He steps closer, but I hold my ground, even when his voice drops into something low and liquid. "I think you're another one who dreams of getting close to the prince."

"Not the prince." Not the man who charged into Amma's. "But you, maybe."

Surprise flashes across his features, and he takes a step back.

I'm not surprised when he wheels around. But then he stops ten feet away and looks over his shoulder, wearing something like a smile on his lips, and he says in a voice strange and soft, "Come on, then. Tell me on the way."

I walk beside him, and my body prickles all over, as if tiny sparks are dancing on my skin. I tell him of the statue in the temple, of the shattered depiction of the Great King's alter ego.

He listens with a furrowed brow, weaving through the Ven until we turn into a small hallway and come to a dead end. The words die on my lips as he goes to a bas-relief embedded in the wall, one that depicts the city surrounded by a spiral of beasts, a riot of legs, claws, tails, and eyes. A man wearing the full-body ikonmark of the Regia stands, arms spread, at the city's highest point. Golden lines of light streak from his body, holding back the Storm.

Dalca reaches into the spiral of beasts and twists the tail of a serpent. The stone moves in his hand, and he adjusts it precisely. He adjusts two more pieces of stone, and it hits me. I squint, trying to make out the incomplete ikon embedded in the bas-relief sculpture.

With a grinding sound, a section of stone slides aside, revealing an opening a little shorter and squatter than either Dalca or me.

"Go ahead. It allows one at a time."

His tone is too even. It's a challenge.

I duck inside. At once, the stone slides shut behind me, and I'm left in total darkness.

My heart thuds, faster and louder with each second that passes. He's not under my power at all. I'm under his.

The door grinds open, and I'm sick at how relieved I am to see him slide in next to me.

He pulls out an ikonlight that casts a soft blue glow, illuminating a tunnel the width of a single person. Dalca brushes past me, his jacket skimming my skin, and leads the way. The path slopes upward, so I know we're not descending into the old city. I open my mouth a half dozen times to ask where we're going, but I want him to think I trust him.

At last we come to a dead end. Dalca kneels, but I don't catch what he does before the stone slides open.

The door disappears as we step through, and we come out into a long, narrow room, dark and cool as a tomb. Pedestals line the whole length of the room, each one flanked by many-hued ikonlight sconces that flicker like molten diamonds.

Atop the pedestal before me, held upright by strings of glass as thin as spider's silk, is an elderly man's face rendered in gold. His eyes are closed, and his mustache is long and curled over a frowning mouth. Someone carved each wrinkle and whisker in astonishing detail.

There's a golden face atop every pedestal, stretching far into the distance. I shiver. Any moment now, they'll open their eyes.

The ikonlight plays across Dalca's face. "These are my ancestors. Every Regia who came before us."

He points out a man whose wrinkled skin drapes over razor-blade cheekbones. "Caerno Illusora. When he was Regia, the Storm was just a darkness on the horizon. That's how strong a bond he had with the Great King."

The pedestal under Caerno's face is carved with images, one of which is a seven-ringed city surrounded by vegetation, like a forest or maybe a jungle from a fairy story. Each pedestal is likewise carved with its Regia's story.

Dalca pulls me to a mask of an old woman with deep laugh lines. "Ayeli Amero Illusora. She championed ikonomancy like no Regia before her. The first ikonlights were made during her reign."

Dalca tells me the stories of a handful more of the Regias. I listen with half an ear, transfixed by the way his face comes alive. While I had to beg and wheedle for every scrap of Ma and Pa's story, Dalca was handed hundreds of stories, each gilded and glorious, a colossal legacy, enough to drown under. How often did he linger here, among the dead?

On one end of the room are the truly ancient Regias. "Why are they arranged in twos?"

"Long ago, there used to be two Regias, ruling at once, sharing the power of the Great King. They might have been named something else, but we don't know. We do know that those were times of conflict, of war and bloodshed. The Regia Dalcanin, my namesake, was the one who ended those decades of darkness. His brother took up arms against him, though he had neither the support of the people nor mastery of his bond with the Great King. So instead of waging a clean war, his brother poisoned the wells and set fire to the crops of those loyal to Dalcanin. When even that failed, he used his power to spread a wasting sickness that crippled the city.

"Though it broke his heart, the Regia Dalcanin fought his brother and slew him. They say a cleansing rain fell over the city then, healing what had been poisoned. Dalcanin renounced the surname he had shared with his brother and became first of the Illusoras. He bore the weight of the Great King's soul alone, as all Regias after him have done."

The Regia Dalcanin has the broad good looks of a hero, with deep-set serious eyes and strong chin. He's also much younger than the Regias before him.

"Why did they sculpt him so young?"

Dalca pauses. "These are death masks."

I wrap my arms around me. From his age and looks, he might've been Dalca's brother, no more than a decade older. Too young to die.

Dalca moves to the other end of the room, toward the more recent Regias. A step here represents years. "Do you notice anything?"

Most of the Regias have deep frown lines. Some have Dalca's brows, some his nose, one even has his lips. Then I see it as brows grow smoother, lips fuller, jaws sharper. "They're dying younger."

He nods. "And the Storm grows, and the city shrinks."

"Why?"

We stop in front of Memnon Dagian Illusora, Dalca's grandfather and the Regia my parents killed. "No one knows for sure. But I believe it might have something to do with the other Regia. When my ancestor combined both marks into one, I think something was left out, something that weakened the Regia. Maybe there's a better mark. One that means we can fight back the Storm."

My head spins. It all makes sense. The ikon Dalca and Cas are after isn't just any ikon—it's the most important one of all. The other Regia's mark must be what Pa knows. That mark is why Ma thought she could be Regia, a better Regia.

Dalca interrupts my thoughts. "There are written records from those generations, when the Regias were strong. They were not consumed by the Great King; instead the Great King bestowed his power upon each vessel as a gift. And, like a gift, the potential vessel had a choice of whether or not to accept. They described the moment of acceptance—the moment of becoming Regia—as a moment of perfect stillness. Of being perfectly empty and perfectly full, a moment when the tapestry of life unravels and reveals what's beyond, a moment of being intertwined with every living thing.

"I wonder if that's still the case. If that's the last feeling my grandfather and mother had, before the Great King came into them." He shrugs. "We'll never know. But the proto-ikon you found . . . Its secrets may save our city." The ikonlight shines on his face, and for a heartbeat he's cast in gold, frozen in a death mask. This shrine for the dead isn't just his past; it's his future.

"Dalca . . ."

Dalca smiles, and the illusion breaks. "I'm sorry. These are the burdens of a Regia. I shouldn't be putting them on you."

I don't smile back. "It's my city, too."

His smile fades, and he looks at me as though he's drinking his fill.

I shiver, hoping I don't look as vulnerable as I feel. I've forgotten the role I'm supposed to be playing.

He comes to a decision. "Let me show you something."

He leads us out of the room, into the light of the palace. He makes for the nearest balcony, swinging open a pair of glittering glass doors and crossing to the railing.

Dalca checks the fastening of his cloak, then steps so close I can feel the heat of his body. "Hold tight."

He pulls me in, my shoulder tucked against his chest and his arms around my waist, as the thousand-and-one-feather cloak wraps itself around us — and he leaps right over the railing and into the air.

A startled scream escapes my throat as we fall. His chest rumbles with a low laugh, but I can't hear much over the blood pounding in my ears.

My stomach calms as we level out. We're floating. Weightless. Wrapped up in an infinite moment. A breeze combs its fingers through my hair, but I don't dare look.

"Open your eyes," Dalca breathes into my ear.

From the cage of his arms, the city spreads out before me.

The second ring is a sprawl of ornate buildings studded with gardens. A small crowd holds lights in a post-stormsurge prayer. In the third, the Arvegna arena is busy with construction for the Trial. Around the Ven, Wardana in red buzz like bees. Hundreds of tiny twinkling lights mark the living, gathered in their toylike homes. Hundreds of little figures move through the streets, becoming crowds that flow like rivers between the matchbox-houses of the fourth and fifth.

The lights shrink to pinpricks as we rise higher and higher. We're so far up that I feel like I could hold the whole of the city in my two hands. And yet the Storm still encircles us in a cage of clouds.

I grip Dalca's waist as tight as I can, remembering my dream. This isn't a fall I'd survive. "I won't drop you," Dalca promises.

He takes us higher still, into the circle of sky, above the wall of the Storm.

I hold my breath as we pass above the last of the darkness, wondering at what lies beyond. What cities and kingdoms have we been cut off from? Are there rivers thick with waterfowl, and fields lush with crops? Are there desolate mountains shrouded in a layer of deep green forests, like in my book of fairy stories?

We rise above, and it takes me a moment to understand. To make sense of the blanket of darkness that stretches as far as the eye can see.

There's no world beyond the Storm. There's no escape, no distant refuge. There's nothing but the Storm.

The wind shrieks. Dalca murmurs into my ear, his breath warm on my skin. "I once tried to find the edge of the Storm. I flew as far as I could go . . . and still I saw nothing but the Storm. I nearly lost my way, coming back. I couldn't find it. Our home is so small a thing against all this darkness."

I press my lips to his ear. "How did you find your way?"

"I didn't. I despaired. I nearly fell in. In falling, I saw a glimpse of the palace, and that was enough. It was as if the city came to me."

Coldness sinks into my bones. Maybe we've all been cursed, all of us together, the whole city. "Did we do something to deserve this?"

The wind makes a dark halo of his hair. "I don't know. All I know is that this city is a sanctuary. Perhaps the last one. It's all we have, and the only weapon we have to defend it is a stronger Regia."

As we hang in the sky, I find the truth in my bones; what he fights for is the same as what Pa fought for. But Dalca sees the city and Storm through eyes accustomed to power, through the eyes of a prince brought up in the first ring, through the eyes of an eagle, where people are as small as ants. His empathy is the empathy of a king. Can he care for the little people, like Amma did? Does he see the people of the low rings like I do? Has he seen orphan children playing by the Storm, and cried for them?

Here in his arms, with his hope for his city echoing in my ears, it's hard to remind myself that Dalca is my enemy. I want him to know me. *My name is Vesper Vale. My father is Alcanar Vale. I want what you want.*

I can't say it.

There's good in him, more than I ever imagined. But perhaps there's a difference between being a good man and a good king.

I remember the way Casvian wrecked Amma's without a thought, the coldness in Dalca's eyes the first time I saw him. The golden coin he tossed so callously. That, too, is who he is.

His eyes are the same color as the sky behind him. I see in them a vision of another Vesper. She stands hand in hand with Dalca, in ikonomancer's garb, her eyes shining with love for him, devoted to making his dream come true, to making him great. That Vesper would live a hero's life, fighting the Storm, protecting the city. She would lose him when he became Regia, but it wouldn't be a bad life, not with the power that comes with being Regia's consort, power she could use to help the fifth.

I'd only have to renounce Pa and Ma, forget Amma and the storm-touched, forget myself. I'd only have to chain myself to a man who speaks of protecting the city but doesn't speak up when his closest friend spits bigotry, who's cruel when he's afraid, who will commit another thousand small evils before he's done the good thing he hopes to do.

Amma was wrong: blood is a leash. His leash stretches back for hundreds of years, but mine's no less tight.

"Take me back."

Dalca obeys. Wordlessly, he takes me down, the golden curves of the palace rising to meet us, twinkling ikonlights in each window, dotting the open spaces, marking the spiraling, winding path through the garden. Lit like this, from above, the garden almost looks like an ikon.

My breath catches. Just like Dalca's secret tunnel from the Ven to the palace, *the garden is an incomplete ikon.* In my mind's eye, I see Dalca kicking at the ground the first time I saw him in the garden. It wasn't out of frustration like I thought, but to connect a line made by a hedge. I hold the shape of garden in my mind, burning it into my memory.

We land on the balcony, and I free myself from Dalca's arms. He catches my hand in a loose grip and presses a kiss to my fingertips.

"I know that it's overwhelming. But we can change it. Nothing is fated."

I open my mouth, but there are a thousand things that can never be said between us. He's my enemy, and I can't face the hope in his eyes.

He lets me go, but I feel his gaze on my back long after I leave the first ring.

It doesn't matter.

I know how to get to Pa.

CHAPTER 15

From the second-story walkway, I watch as Izamal leads a team of Wardana trainees through a drill in the Ven's courtyard. Dalca is with him, and they demonstrate how Izamal guards Dalca's back as Dalca strikes at the wooden stormbeast. I duck back into the shadows, watching from where I won't be seen. I'd rather keep a little space between me and Dalca—there's no reason to risk it, now that I know where Pa is.

I found Izamal once Dalca and I had reached solid ground and parted ways. Iz heard me out about the garden and the ikon, and a plan fell into place. I wanted to go at once, but Izamal convinced me to wait a day, until he found a time when Dalca and Casvian would be otherwise occupied. We parted with the promise: *tomorrow*.

But I'm restless. Looking down at the Wardana sparring, I half wish I could fight with them. It'd siphon off some of the nervousness that buzzes up and down my legs. On the surface of the stone railing, I trace the ikon Iz showed me, careful to keep it incomplete. It'll undo the restraints that Iz reckons Pa is under—the ones I saw, that covered Pa's hands in what looked like gloves of molten silver.

A shout comes from below.

Dalca and Izamal stand as a team, taking on the trainees all at once.

Dalca's hair curls with sweat, but his moves are as precise as ever as he attacks with a blunted spear. Izamal draws my eye; he moves with liquid grace, wild and unpredictable, a style that's unteachable, original—one that couldn't be more different from Dalca's practice-honed movements. None of the trainees' attacks get through Izamal's defense.

They switch roles seamlessly, and Dalca becomes defender. He seems to double in size, the light glinting off his eyes in a way that's intimidating even from where I stand. Dalca was flawless as attacker, but it's as protector that he comes into his own. He matches every trainee blow for blow. They begin to hesitate, their attacks becoming slower and slower.

Theirs is a strange relationship. It's plain that they trust each other with their lives in combat. But how does Izamal reconcile that with going behind Dalca's back and supplying weapons to the fifth? How can Dalca respect Izamal and not do more for fifth-ringers?

The training session ends, and the Wardana disperse. Izamal murmurs something to Dalca, and he laughs with his head thrown back. I step into the light as Dalca leaves, disappearing into a far hallway.

I glance down, and Izamal's already looking up at me.

"One minute," he mouths.

He disappears down a hall. I count out the seconds. Five minutes pass before he shows up at my elbow, tucking something into his jacket. "Let's go up on the roof," he says.

A haughty white cat slinks after him; I follow them both up a steep set of stairs that goes to the Ven's roof.

We settle down at a corner with a view; to one side is the courtyard, to the other is an uninterrupted vista of the lower rings and the Storm. The Ven empties as the sky darkens and street ikonlights flicker to life.

"Are you afraid?"

I turn to Iz. "No," I lie.

His lips quirk. "So confident."

I can't match his smile, but I don't want him to see what I feel. "What's fear going to do for me now?"

His smile falls. "Brave girl."

"Don't be condescending."

"I'm not, I promise. Look, I brought you something." Izamal pulls a package from his jacket, wax paper wrapped with a length of string.

I tug the string loose, and the paper falls open to a waft of warm sugar and spices. The white cat springs out of the dark to steal the string, but my full attention is on what's inside. Delicate little pastries, some in the shape of birds, some simple rounds glazed with icing.

I've seen them in third- and second-ring shops in passing, but I'd never thought to stop and try them. Figured they weren't meant for me.

"I saw you looking," Iz says.

We sit on the roof, side by side, with the pastries between us. I bite the head off a bird and sweetness melts in my mouth. Izamal holds a round one out to me.

"Break it with me?"

I hold one edge and Izamal snaps the pastry so that it cracks open. The pale-pink filling rises up in a slow spiral, forming the ridges of petals as it swirls. When the ikon is exhausted, the filling has formed a rose stretched between two halves. A little laugh bubbles out of me. Izamal pulls his half toward him, and I cup a hand under the rose, catching it as it falls.

He shoves his half into his mouth all at once, but I take my time, taking the smallest bites I can manage. I save the rose for last; it melts on my tongue, and it's achingly sweet, tasting a little like the way Dalca's garden smells.

I like it here, in the dark, sharing sweets with Izamal. He and I are in this together, at least till we get Pa. It feels good to be able to trust him right now, to let him distract me.

"One day, I'm going to own my own little bakery in the fifth. Maybe the fourth. I'll have things like these, but even better. Cleverer ones. Sugar birds that fly or flowers where each petal's a different flavor. Little, beautiful things, that's all." He takes a bite. "I'll beg a mancer to do some ikonwork for me."

What a small, sweet dream. I rest my head against the wall, imagining Izamal dashing around a cozy little bakery, arms loaded up with trays of the most delicate pastries. He'll throw a cheeky little smile in for free with every one; I'd wager that folks would come for him as much as for the treats he sells. "You must really love to bake."

Izamal smiles at the pastry in his hand. "I wouldn't know. Never had a chance to learn."

I laugh. "What if you hate it?"

"I won't." The cat swipes the last bite of pastry from his hand, and he watches it scamper off.

I take in his bloodshot eyes, the tenseness in his shoulders, his hand clenching and unclenching on his thigh. "I'd like to see that," I say. "Izamal, is something wrong?"

"No. Nothing's wrong." He fixes his golden gaze on me. "Your turn. Tell me, Vesper. What does your 'one day' look like?"

My world's shrunk to hours. I don't have what it takes to imagine a distant future. "I'll think about it when I get there."

We're quiet for a moment. I look over, and Izamal's lips part, but no words come out, like he wants to tell me something but something is holding him back.

"Iz, are you sure you're all right?"

He gets to his feet, brushing crumbs from his lap. "I'm not. I'm frustrated. I've reached only a handful of people—and the rest are too tired and scared to do anything. I can't make them want more. I don't know what to do."

He glares down at the Wardana.

"Maybe it only takes a handful of people," I say.

He softens as he looks down at me. "Maybe. And once we have your father leading them, things will change. I know it."

Guilt turns my stomach sour. "Yes," I say, because he needs to hear it. I hope I'm wrong about Pa. It's possible that being locked away has changed his perspective. Maybe he *will* want to fight.

Izamal offers me a hand, and I let him pull me up. "You don't have to come with me," I say, "if that's—"

"You think you can handle it all by yourself? A little cocky, aren't we? You've been an apprentice for, what, two days?" he says with a grin.

"What help are you anyway?" I tease him back. "What good are big muscles and a pretty face against ikons?"

He looks delighted. "You think my face is pretty?"

I roll my eyes.

"We're doing it together." Izamal smiles, but there's something in his red-rimmed eyes.

"I admire you, you know." I keep my gaze fixed on the courtyard below. "I'm selfish. I'm just here to save my father. You're dreaming of a lot more than that."

His smile wavers. He shakes his head as if he can't speak, then shrugs.

I pull him into a hug. He stands like a statue, but after a long moment, he exhales and gently pushes me away.

We scamper off the roof, back into the Ven's hallways. Iz walks with his shoulders hunched, carrying a weight only he knows. My heart aches for him, and I want to tell him that he does have a choice. But he just told me that if that were true, he wouldn't be a Wardana or working in secret for fifth-ringers. If he had a choice, he'd be a baker.

We reach my door. "Good night."

He pauses at the threshold, a faint light from the hallway outlining him in pale blue. "May your dreams be sweet."

He leaves.

I put a chair under the doorknob before curling up in bed with Pa's notebook. I enlarge it quickly and draw out the shape of the garden from memory. I work late into the night, using Pa's notebook for reference, until I'm sure I know how to complete the garden's ikon, until I know I won't fail. I find and memorize four promising unlocking ikons, and one that turns things to dust.

I shrink the notebook and tuck it into Ma's locket, stifling a yawn.

I don't need a dream for one faraway day. I just need tomorrow.

Tomorrow I'll have Pa back. The rest can wait.

The guard at the palace gates recognizes me and waves me through with barely a glance. I make my way to the gardens, sidestepping an attendant. I walk quickly, purposefully, and take a breath only when the hedges hide me from view.

I hurry down the path. At the first bend, under a gnarled tree, Izamal waits with his lips set in a grim line.

I nod at him. I know what I'm doing.

I toe a line in the dirt between the two sides of the hedge that mark the entrance to the garden. Now that I know what to look for, it's easy to pick out the traces of previous lines. How many times has Dalca walked this way?

I draw a line through pebble-studded dirt to connect two fruit-dense trees, and another to connect a gap in a row of flowering bushes. The tricky bit is knowing which gaps to close and which to leave open. Izamal's no help; he paces in a circle until I glare at him, then stands biting the pad of his thumb, shifting his weight from foot to foot.

He inches close, hovering as I draw an arc connecting two curving hedges. "Are you sure you know what you're doing?"

I point. "Go. Wait for me by the pool."

He throws his hands up and goes. When I get to my feet, I find he's left a circular track in the dirt. Great. I smooth it out and take care to erase our steps, lest they add stray lines to the ikon.

It's harder than I'd anticipated to fit the bird's-eye view of the garden to my view from the ground. Especially when I come to a set of two thigh-high gates set four feet apart. The ikon I've got in my head tells me that there has to be an open channel here, but I can't tell which it is.

I crouch, peering closely at the one on the left. I shift to the one on the right.

There—the tiny pebbles are pressed deeper into the ground here, the dirt less compacted, as if it's been shifted often.

I open the gate on the right and pick my way through the rest of the garden, until I'm satisfied all the right lines have been connected.

I make my way to the center, erasing Izamal's steps as I go.

The golden gate creaks shut behind me, and I give it a tug to make sure. That should do it. Iz crouches by the pond's edge, jumping to his feet when I nod.

I hold my breath, turning to the mosaic wall of the two figures with their hands pressed together.

Iz reaches the mosaic first and ducks behind it. He steps back into view, shaking his head. No door.

My stomach falls. What did I miss?

I close my eyes, going over the ikon. Did I forget it? Misremember it?

I open my eyes to the little pond, still as a mirror, reflecting the mosaic. There's something fierce and almost hateful in the man's and woman's expressions, as if they're locked in a struggle. But their hands are held as if they're dancing, meeting above their heads and below their hearts.

Leaves crunch underfoot as I reach and trace the tiny tiles, feeling for anything with a little give, like the bas-relief door Dalca showed me.

The curve of their arms almost makes a circle. I get so close my nose brushes the stone. There's a gap between their hands. It's at odds with their expressions — they scowl as if yearning to engage in dance or warfare. Between their fingers is a funny bit of decoration.

I press on the tiles near their fingers, and a three-by-three section of tile pushes out. I twist it, half a turn — and what seemed like a funny decoration is now the lines of their hands, fingers touching. I press the section until it clicks into place.

I do the same to the tiles between their other hands, holding my breath before they click into place.

The rumble of stone under my fingers tells me everything I need to know, though Izamal's face as he watches the mosaic wall's backside — eyes wide, mouth agape — is a welcome confirmation.

I grin at him. This is a marvel of ikonomancy, and I figured it out. A delicious warmth fills me from toes to fingertips as I circle around.

Where the back of the mosaic once stood is now a doorway into darkness. The daylight only reaches a few feet in, revealing stone stairs heading down. "It might only let one of us in at a time," I say. "You first."

He's barely in before stone rises up from below and seals it off.

It takes me thirty seconds to redo the tiles and reopen the door. "Izamal?"

His voice rises from the darkness. "You have about ten stairs, and then they end out over open air. I'm jumping down."

That can't be a good idea. "Wait—"

Something thuds below. "There's a platform not five feet down. Jump, and I'll catch you."

I inch my way down the stairs, counting as I go. My foot hits air and I draw in a readying breath. "Don't drop me."

The fall through blackness lasts a heartbeat, then warm arms wrap around me. Izamal lets me down gently.

"Do you have an ikonlight?"

Something makes a clicking sound, and then a soft blue glow emanates from Izamal's left gauntlet, lighting his face from below.

We're on a landing about ten paces across, with another set of stairs spiraling down on the other side. An ikonlight lantern rests against the carved dark stone wall. With a turn of its ikondial, a soft white glow rises within.

I carry it aloft as I descend, Izamal on my heels. The stairs go on and on. I peer over the edge and squint, turning my ikonlight off and motioning for Izamal to do the same.

Something glows down below. It's the color of the last light before nightfall. I take the rest of the stairs by twos, and reach another landing, this one much smaller. There's only one way forward, but I grab Izamal before he steps through a stone archway and into the dim light.

An ikon marks the floor. It's complex—too complex for me to figure out in full. But there's a curve that I recognize—one for sound—and I'd wager the shirt on my back that it's an alarm.

"What is it?"

I shush him. Grabbing a mound of dirt, I sprinkle it across three separate lines, breaking the ikon.

Holding my breath, I step through a stone archway and squeeze my eyes shut.

One, two, three heartbeats—and no alarm sounds. I open my eyes.

A massive city both rises above us and extends deep into the dark below, lit by hundreds of lights that reflect the deep purple-red of the stone surrounding us. A dead city, a corpse shaped like a cocoon, fat in the middle and tapered on both ends. It's supported by enormous pillars of rock that begin far below and rise high above our heads, and some dozen walkways spiderweb out from the ruins and into the stone that surrounds us, connecting this dead city to ours.

A single shaft of daylight shines from above, through an opening in the rock. That must be where the fifth caved in, on the day Izamal's sister fell.

His face is set in a mask of concentration, and he strides ahead on a walkway that curves along the stone wall and arches out over the abyss and into the city. The city isn't well preserved. Many of the walkways end in midair, shattered by time, and the ruins of buildings and archways make for a rabbit's warren of rubble. Dalca's way—the path we're on—is one of the few that still stands unobstructed.

Somewhere in the cavern, water trickles drop by drop, each drop echoing a half dozen times, the overlapping echoes sounding altogether like the ghost of rain. I shiver, remembering the rumors that Dalca's grandfather locked him down here when Dalca was only a child.

The path doesn't fork; there's only one way to go. I take a quick gulp of air and turn my ikonlight back on before stepping out onto the thin bridge that leads into the city. Izamal's foot hits a pebble that skitters over the edge of the bridge. A splash sounds. I peer down, holding the lantern aloft.

Ripples dance out, disrupting a reflection as perfect as a mirror. There's something strange about the reflection—for a heartbeat, it seems like it's reflecting a different city, a livelier one awash in color, lit by red lanterns.

"People could live here," I murmur to Izamal as we hurry across the bridge. "The Storm can't get in here."

Izamal glances at me, eyebrow quirked. "You want to volunteer?"

The splash of water echoes, each echo overlapping, the sound rising into a ghastly choir. A chill begins in my toes and rises through the tips of my hair. "Maybe not."

"When I was a child, Nashi told me stories of the ancient city. A city protected from the elements, as safe as a mother's womb. A glorious city—at least until our ancestors dug too deep and opened the door to a place no living can enter."

The shaft of daylight goes straight down, without interruption. "Your sister fell into the water? Into the . . ."

Izamal looks away, his voice clipped. "The land of the dead."

Midway across the bridge is another ikon. I break it in the same way.

The bridge takes us to the other side, where there's a path cleared through massive mounds of broken stone and the detritus of buildings. I could stand on Izamal's shoulders and not see above the rubble. The path leads straight to the once-grand doors to a temple.

We walk inside.

The temple unfolds before us, a riot of carvings leading us through a series of archways. We come out into open space, where in the center stands a boulder of jagged rock shaped like a fist. Held within the fist, half-swallowed by the rock, is a gaunt man with a stubborn chin, a scholar's brow, and familiar gray eyes.

My stomach clenches. "Pa?"

Pa raises his head. I draw in a sharp breath as tears prick my eyes. His cheeks are hollow and unshaven, his skin sallow, but worst of all is the look in his eyes, a look that says he's lost everything, including his last shred of hope.

"No," he rasps.

I cross the distance in a heartbeat, touching his stubble-rough cheek, brushing back his hair. "I'm here to save you, Pa, I'm going to get you out."

Pa looks at me as if he's drinking in the sight, as if he expects me to disappear. "Vesp, you should've let me go. Why couldn't you listen, for once?"

His tone hits home, right into the heart of the small, disappointing child that still lives within me.

Pa looks over my shoulder at Izamal. "Who is that?"

"He's—he's helping."

Grit crunches underfoot as Izamal steps closer. "Alcanar Vale— It's an honor. We'll get you out. The fifth needs you. We're fighting back, like you did."

"No, son."

I circle the mound of rock, reaching for it.

"No! Don't touch it. It'll capture you as well."

"What is it?"

"A living prison. The more I move, the more it closes in. You can do nothing. Leave, Vesper."

"You're my father. I can't just leave you here to die."

"You're my daughter. So *listen to me*, for Storm's sake."

Pa looks down at Ma's locket. His eyes widen, a question in them: *You still have it?*

I nod.

"Don't." I hear the rest of what he doesn't say: *Don't let anyone find it.*

Gravel crunches underfoot as Izamal shifts. "Vesper, would any of your ikons work?"

Would they? Not as well as what Pa could do. "Pa, if you tell me how to break it, I could draw the ikon."

The set of his face tells me he won't give me a thing. It doesn't matter. I set to drawing the ikon that turns things to dust, but the mound of rock absorbs my charcoal stub before I've finished my first line.

"Vesper. Go. And take your fool of a friend."

Darkness falls over Izamal's expression. "I'm not a fool."

"Revolutionaries are always fools. I know your type, son. Your dreams are nothing but delusions of grandeur. You think they'll worship you as their savior? First they'll spit upon you for what you say. They'll turn you out of their homes."

Izamal flinches. His face is drawn, and his hands shake, and though his eyes are furrowed and furious, they shine with wetness.

"They already do, don't they?"

I can't stand Pa destroying Izamal's last hope. "Pa, stop it. You can help him."

"I will not. Vesper . . . Anyone can make a mistake, but only fools repeat them. Now go, before you throw your mother's last sacrifice away."

A trembling shock rings in Izamal's voice. "You would turn your back on your people?"

"I have no people. Not anymore."

"They're *suffering*. They're *dying*." Iz's fists are clenched, his arms trembling.

"And you are a fool."

Izamal punches him.

Time slows as Pa wrenches himself backwards and the rock speeds to life, nearly catching Izamal's fist before he heaves back. But the stone doesn't stop. It grows over Pa's neck, over his mouth, over his eyes that stare down at me.

I stagger back from what was once my father and is now a coffin of rock. I shove Izamal aside and reach for the rock. I'll tear Pa out with my hands.

Izamal grabs me before I can touch. *"It'll take you, too—"*

A high, piercing shriek rings through the air, cutting off the rest of his words.

"An alarm. Vesper, we have to go—" Izamal reaches for me, and I slap his hand aside. What has he done?

The alarm sets off others. Izamal's mouth moves, but no sound reaches my ears over the din that fills the air. He tugs me close by the collar of my shirt. "RUN!"

Stumbling over my own feet, I break into a run, sprinting along the thin bridge. I glance back only once, to see that Izamal isn't behind me. I shove down the worry—he'll find his own way.

A flash of blood-red turns my attention—a Wardana sprints toward me, light behind them so I can't make out their face, only that they wear no cloak. I don't recognize them by their build—but they definitely see me.

I can't go forward. I can't go back.

I look down. There's another path, a bridge, ten feet down and four feet over. Between the gap, far below, the dark water of the underworld gleams.

I jump.

My stomach rises into my throat mid-jump—my reflection doesn't appear in the water. I crash into the lower walkway, nearly sliding off, but I scramble to my feet and launch myself into a sprint. *Please*, I beg the Great King, *let this path lead out into the city above.*

A quick glance back tells me that the Wardana didn't try the jump—guess they're not so brave without a cloak. The walkway before me leads to a set of stairs. I take them by twos and threes, my breath stupidly loud, my footsteps louder, too afraid to look back, too afraid to stop.

The stairs end, and I sprint ahead through pitch-darkness until I smack into a wall, bruising my cheek. My breath comes out in quick pants, and I run my hands along the stone. Come on, come on. Don't tell me I have to complete an ikon.

My fingers brush a handle, and I yank at the door. It groans open by inches, as heavy as a slab of marble and as unwilling to move. Footfalls sound behind me.

I squeeze through the six-inch gap, scraping my other cheek, and burst into an alley, breathing in the fresh air and taking in the dark wall of the Storm above—I made it, I'm outside. I shove the door behind me with all my strength. It snaps shut, all but disappearing into the wall, and I touch my forehead to the stone, catching my breath.

The stone touching my skin rumbles, vibrations going to my teeth, as the door begins to grind open.

I jump back and stagger out of the alley, clutching the stitch in my side, running through a market street, into strange alleyways and winding side streets. I have to get away, but where can I go?

Everywhere I turn, people gape at me and turn away. The black wall of the Storm looms over me, and the hair on the back of my neck stands tall.

Without rhyme or reason, I run like a rat in a maze, getting lost in the third ring. *I've screwed up.* If only I run fast enough, maybe I'll outrun my stupidity. If I run fast enough, I'll turn back time. I don't know what to do—I don't even know what I've done. If Pa's dead—what was all this for?

My heartbeat's loud in my ears, and my thighs burn. My shoes slip on wet cobblestone, and I go down on one knee, only then feeling the raindrops hitting my cheeks, soaking my hair, chilling my skin.

I get to my feet and stagger to the alley's end. My breath comes out in sobs.

A single black feather falls before me. It twists in the wind until it's shot down by the rain, falling into a puddle. Ripples fan out from it, distorting the watery reflection of a figure in red descending from above.

I look up.

Black boots, red leather, summer-sky eyes. Descending like a bird of prey, black cloak spread out like wings. Even from here, I see the fire in his eyes, the electric gleam of hatred. A new twist in a face that's become familiar to me.

He knows.

Dalca's feet touch down three feet away. I blink away the rain that gathers on my lashes. A chill spreads through my skin, sinking deep into my bones. My legs tremble. I can make them run, but where do I go?

I just need a plan. I just need an ikon. I scrub the rain out of my eyes.

The chill seeps into my mind and makes one thing clear as ice: everything I've done has brought me here. Every choice I made was the wrong one. I am as much of a fool as Pa says.

Dalca puts a cold hand to my cheek. I flinch. He looks deep into my eyes, as if he's trying to pull something from me. "It's you," he says. "It's always been you, hasn't it? The gray-eyed girl from the home for the cursed."

What does he mean? With his thumb, he wipes away my tears. I knock his hand away. I don't want him to have my tears — I don't want to be crying — I don't want his words to worm their way through my skin, into the soft, defenseless parts of me.

"I thought you were gone. I wept for you, thinking I'd wronged you." A dark, bitter smile touches his lips. "What a fool I was. You were here all along, using me." His face is so cold, so tight with simmering rage. I see nothing of the Dalca who saved me, who said, *You frighten me.*

My voice comes out a whisper. "I only wanted to save my pa."

Dalca shakes his head. "That's the difference between us. You only want to save your *pa.*" He makes the word sound childish. "I don't have that luxury. I have to save us all."

"Why do you have him? Why do you keep him there, all alone?"

"What right have you to question me? You're a thief. We found the weapons under your bed. What were you hoping to do? Finish what your parents started? Kill my mother, like they killed my grandfather?"

I shake my head.

"Perhaps you meant to kill me. I'm an easier target, after all. I'd half fallen for you."

"I wouldn't—I didn't."

"Is that what you wanted? The Great King has set his claim on my soul, and the city will have my life. Are you one of those who hunts for my heart, for power over me?"

I drag my eyes to his. Raindrops roll down his face, down his nose, down his lips. The rain clumps his eyelashes together, and his lips tremble with either cold or fury.

"All I wanted was my father."

He laughs; it's a cold, harsh sound. "You told me that *I* wasn't doing enough. And yet you would sacrifice the city to save your father?"

I shake my head, uncomprehending. He wants something from Pa —that much I know—but that the fate of the city lies in the balance?

"What should I do with you?"

I back away. "Let me go."

Dalca holds himself rigid, fists clenched, making not a single movement to chase after me. "Go, then. But where? The Wardana are not far behind me. And behind them, the Regia's Guard. Even if I let you go, they'll find you. And you've seen what the Regia's Guard does to those who shelter their enemies."

My mouth fills with an acrid taste, and I choke on the need to get away, to run and keep running until I'm free of the everything, of the wrong choices, of the sorrow and the hope, free of the small, cruel storm inside me.

But I won't bring that harm upon anyone.

The city is blanketed in mist from the rain. Where could I go? Back to the Storm-eaten house? That's as good as giving up on Pa. How long would I have before the Regia's Guard came for me?

I can't be out of choices. I can't.

A soft footfall. I startle, the hair on my arms rising.

Dalca, a notch between his brows, lips wearing neither a smile nor a cruel twist. He holds out a hand, rain dripping from his fingertips.

"Or you could come with me."

I hesitate with my hands curled under my collarbone. He holds my gaze.

I take his hand.

Dalca tugs me close as his cloak billows wide. His arms fold around me, keeping me safe or keeping me caged. I can't tell.

We rise into the air, and he makes no promise not to drop me, not this time.

CHAPTER 16

The ground falls away. The wind whipping at my cheeks becomes dryer the higher we climb. We leave the dark and the rain behind, rising into the realm of the sun.

The light is blindingly bright. It paints the insides of my eyelids the red-orange of fire. I turn my head away, but that tucks me further against Dalca's side, and I'm pretty sure that's worse. My eyes adjust enough by the time the sandstone ring of the Ven whizzes by. Where are we going?

Dalca's jaw is squared and tense as he flies us straight to the first ring, to a balcony-studded tower that's a little set apart from the rest of the frozen-fire palace. I brace for impact as we speed toward a balcony at the very top, but Dalca pulls up with the sort of practiced dexterity that I really ought not to be so surprised by.

My legs take a moment to remember how to carry my weight, long enough for Dalca to open the glass doors that lead to the room beyond. I follow him, blinking against the darkness as my eyes adjust once again. A click sounds behind me as Dalca locks the balcony door.

"Dalca?"

"This part of the palace isn't frequently visited," he says.

By which I understand: *No one is coming to save you.*

"I'll return when I can."

"Wait—"

He strides out, an ornate door shutting behind him with a heavy thud. The doorknob—polished metal, carved to look like a tree branch—twists uselessly. It's locked. The balcony door is locked too—an empty keyhole remains. Dalca must've pocketed the key.

I press my forehead to the wood and breathe. Too much rattles around in my head. A bloodless fury makes my skin crawl. Why couldn't Pa just help us get him out, instead of defaulting to his tortured-and-disappointed-father routine? Why couldn't Izamal just keep it together for another five minutes? Why couldn't I get this right?

Under all the anger is a low chill that starts in my toes and pulls me under. I've messed up, again. I wanted to save Pa, just like I wanted to save those two fifth-ringers from the stormbeast. All my good intentions come to nothing. They're not even that good, considering. While I was focused on Pa, Izamal's been fighting for all the fifth—and who knows what kind of trouble he's in because of me.

I hope he got away. I'm surprised to find I bear him no ill will. I do wish he hadn't punched Pa, but I'm sure he wishes I'd told him the truth about the chances of Pa joining his revolution. I used him more than he used me, and regret sits like a stone in my stomach. I hope he's free. The fifth needs someone who hasn't given up on them.

And Pa—

I tell myself that Pa's alive, that the rock prison didn't suffocate him as I ran away. The Wardana will have saved him, even just so they can put on a show with the Trial. I can't let myself fall apart and weep like a little helpless child. If Pa's dead, I'll know sooner or later, and then I'll weep. Until then, I need to think.

I take stock of my prison. The room is all dark violet and deep blue, the colors of midnight. A tapestry wraps around the walls and up the domed ceiling, depicting a fairy tale forest at night, inhabited by creatures of legend. A will-o'-the-wisp, little winged fairies, a red-eyed wolf. Things to devour me in the night.

There's a plush bed. A set of overstuffed chairs. There's even a rug. None of it's remotely comforting. None of it is remotely prisonlike, either, save for the locked doors. Why such comfort? I can't believe that Dalca still harbors feelings for me, not now that he knows I've been lying to him. Let me not flatter myself—even the face Carver gave me couldn't make up for that. But then why?

Pa's worry about the locket—about his notebook—means there are things he has kept secret, that he still wants to be kept secret.

That's why I'm here. Not because Dalca's soft on me, but because he's made the same assumption Iz did—that Pa must've taught me ikonomancy, that I know the secrets of the great Alcanar Vale.

But Dalca doesn't know that Pa never trusted me enough to teach me anything. All he did was give me his notebook, and that to hide. Does it hold the knowledge Dalca wants? Pa wouldn't be worried about the notebook unless it held something of importance.

There's a long list of things Pa's asked me to do—things that I haven't done. Right at the top is to burn his notebook. I pull Ma's locket over my head, running my thumb over our family ikon etched upon it. The weight of Pa's notebook shifts inside.

I unclasp the locket and let the miniature book tumble out onto my palm. I don't know an ikon that'll burn the book, but I wager there's one written in it that'll do the job.

It hasn't escaped me that there are no writing implements in sight. For all the luxuriousness of my surroundings, there's nothing to do ikonomancy with.

There's no hearth to scoop charcoal from. No sundust or other powders to pour in the shape of an ikon. I consider my fingers. I could bite them and use blood.

It's a fairly large room, at least by fifth-ring standards. Fifteen paces take me from the door to the balcony, passing the bed and chair. I run my fingers along the tapestry wall as I pace, but on my way back, my fingers catch a groove on the wall. A clever door, meant to blend in, with a small knob covered in fabric matching the tapestry.

It opens to a bathing room; a copper tub large enough to sit in, a washbasin, and behind a partition, a water closet. Fancy. I prod around, but if they're powered by ikonomancy, it's not at this end. Perhaps they use ikons wherever the water comes from.

A bar of soap rests near the washbasin. On the stone, I draw a line using the edge of the soap, pleased to find it leaves a residue. Now that I have way to write ikons . . .

I whittle the soap bar with my nails until it's thin enough to make such fine lines. With it, I draw the ikon for enlarging on the notebook's cover. It grows to a readable size. It takes a little longer to scan it than I'd like, courtesy of having to decipher Pa's code. But only ten pages in, I find it. An ikon for combustion, a complex one where lines angle sharply toward the center, tighter and tighter, until they form a dark circle. In the margin, Pa wrote, *Much easier to use a match.*

I lower the soap, just touching the cover of the notebook. I let out a long slow breath.

Why am I hesitating? My loyalty is to Pa—right? I should get rid of it.

But if Dalca's right, if it holds the key to saving the city . . . But Dalca's idea of saving the city is to keep the Regia in power. He'd have the fifth safe, but like a parent keeps their infant from harm. Would fifth-ringers like me and Amma and Izamal—would we ever have any more power over our own lives?

It comes down to this: do I trust Dalca over Pa?

I don't.

But I drop the soap anyway. I'm not ready to destroy Pa's notebook, not just yet. I shrink it back down and wipe away the soap residue with my thumb. It's a risk, keeping it on me, even shrunken and in Ma's locket. But it's a risk I'm willing to take for now.

Tossing the soap bar from hand to hand, I make a circuit of the room.

I could see if my turns-things-to-dust ikon would work on the door—but even if it does, Storm knows what—or who—is on the other side.

The balcony is a glass door set in a grid of smaller glass panes. They glimmer like jewels, distorting the world beyond into gauzy blotches of color. Were the balconies close enough together that I could jump across? Find an unlocked room?

And then what?

I bite my lip and pace the length of the room, the soap bar sticky in my hand. I don't know what I can do.

A voice that sounds an awful lot like Pa tells me not to do anything. *You've done enough.*

I don't want to believe it. But it rings of truth.

With the soap, my hand draws coarse lines on a single pane of glass. Maybe I haven't helped anyone. Maybe it was never about helping. Maybe I am selfish—too in love with the idea that I can do something, be someone.

The outer circle closes, and the ikon is complete. The glass shrinks and pops out of its metal casing, falling into my hand.

The door bangs open. I whirl around.

Casvian Haveli. Two hot points of color on his cheekbones, a simmering something in the set of his mouth. His pale eyes drop to the glass in my hand.

He stalks forward, yanking it from me and inspecting the glass. "Rudimentary." He scowls at me. "You do know these windows are a hundred years old."

My heart's still pounding from the shock of his entrance, so much so that I can't quite wrap my mind around the fact that he's critiquing my ikonomancy.

"But I wouldn't expect you people to appreciate the work that goes into the finer arts."

I try not to rise to the bait of *you people*. "What's going on?"

That simmering something boils over. "What's going on is that Dalca's a softhearted, mossbrained *fool*—and *you* should be in *chains* in some dark little hovel in the fifth."

My teeth grind as I bite back what I want to say, because it's true that I'm not in a dark hovel. I have to be smart enough now to figure out if I'm right about why. "I'm sorry for lying to you, Cas. I was just trying to save my father."

This makes him inexplicably furious. "Oh so tragic. Should I weep for your murderer of a father?"

I tamp down the fury that rises in me. Awful rich of him, talking about having a murderer for a father. "Why are you here?"

He reaches into his sleeve and pulls out a stick of chalk. "Any ikons on you that you'd like to disclose, besides whatever you've done to your face?"

"Just this. It bears my family ikon." I pull Ma's locket off with as much nonchalance as I can bear and toss it atop the bedspread. Cas glances at it, but, as I hoped, his interest fades when he sees the symbolic ikon etched upon the metal. He makes no move to open it, and I allow myself to breathe. Pa's notes will be safe from whatever Cas intends to do to me.

With neat, practiced strokes, he draws a complicated ikon on the floor. "Step in. Hold on—are your clothes ikon-made?"

"I don't know."

He turns his back, but not before rolling his eyes. "Okay, step in."

An icy wind buffets me, chilling me, stealing my breath. My skin tingles in its wake, gently everywhere, but intensifies into a painful prickling about my lips and nose and cheeks. I grit my teeth until at last it abates, and it's as if I've been wearing a full-face scowl for ages, one that finally loosens. With the tips of my fingers, I touch my face, half expecting blood or bruiselike tenderness. There's nothing; just my face, presumably restored to its default.

My Wardana-issue clothes stay just as they were. "You can turn around."

Cas turns and squints at my face. I wait for a flash of recognition, but all I get is his disdain. "Hmm. I see why you did it."

I cross my arms. "I didn't do it to improve my looks."

He sneers, voice thick with sarcasm. "I'm sure."

"Is there anything else you needed? Or you just came by to set my face to rights and throw in an insult or two for what, fun?"

He meets my scowl with his own. "Dalca thinks you can help. But I think you're just a selfish little girl."

I bite my tongue. I don't like being seen by Casvian Haveli.

"You don't even know what's at stake, do you?"

I know what's at stake for me. I know what's at stake for the fifth. But I don't know what Cas thinks is at stake. I don't know why he tries so hard for Dalca.

I shake my head.

He blinks, caught off guard, as if he was expecting a fight. He frowns, pinches the bridge of his nose, and then, as if he already regrets what he's doing, he sighs. "Fine. Come along."

"Where?" I ask as he reaches the door.

"First rule: don't speak. Not a word. I know an ikon that'll melt your lips together. Never had a chance to use it. Always wanted to try."

I press my lips together, though I wonder about the second rule.

He opens the door and leads me through endless golden hallways with gleaming marble floors, stopping only once, when a man in a black and gold version of a Wardana uniform crosses before us. Cas pulls me back against the wall. I make no objection, once I register the gray-white hair and the family scowl. Cas waits until Ragno passes before shepherding me forward.

We approach a grand set of double doors, carved, gilded, and inset with hundreds of tiny mirrors. Cas veers to the right and takes me into a much smaller room off the side.

In this room—a wood-paneled meeting room—he works something at one of the panels, and it slides free, revealing a small space beyond. He puts a finger to his lips, and in case I didn't understand, he follows it up with a threatening gesture.

I trail him in, and he replaces the panel behind us.

Voices murmur from the other side of the wall. Light flows in from holes in the wall at about eye level—peepholes.

I peer in and swallow a gasp against the blinding light. I drag my gaze to the Regia's elevated seat, made of the bones of some ancient beast dipped in dark gold. That same dusky gold colors the floor, the walls, her seat, the folds of her dress. It's the tattoo curling across her sickly-looking skin, stretched taut over the too-prominent bones of her face and bare arms. Thousands of tiny mirrors reflect both the pale ikonlights that line the walls, so the air is thick with pinpricks of light like stars. The light drowns out everything but the Regia's eyes. She pins those eyes on a figure kneeling before her.

"You are a poor example of your blood." Her voice is doubled; a high, thin woman's voice, and underneath, a deep, sonorous one that crackles.

The figure looks up. Dalca.

"On the eve of the Trial, you lose the accused?"

My heart stops. What's happened to Pa?

Dalca answers. "He was not harmed. The Trial will proceed as planned, Regia."

I let out a slow breath, tension draining out of me.

"He was not harmed. Yet how did the circumstance arise, that such a thing was a possibility?"

Dalca stiffens. "It will not happen again."

The Regia crooks her gold-tipped finger.

A soft, pained gasp comes from Dalca as he tenses, his face twisted in agony.

"Who is this girl in your mind? Are you so weak?"

"No, Regia. She is no one."

"You conceal something."

"No. All my secrets are yours, Regia."

"You are mine. Every drop of blood in your veins, every last thought in your head, everything you are belongs to me. You were born for me, as will be your future children. Have you forgotten?"

"N-no."

"*You cannot fight me, child.*"

Dalca screams, and I press a shaking hand over my mouth. Casvian stares down into the throne room, doing nothing, saying nothing.

Dalca relaxes suddenly.

A soft keening comes from the Regia. She's limp against the golden bone chair, head sagging, limbs shaking. "This weak body . . . cannot hold me for much longer."

Dalca drags himself up onto all fours and spits. Blood spatters across a dozen tiny mirrors.

"The Trial must go on. The people must love us. That is your duty."

"Yes, Regia," Dalca says as he gets to his feet and bows.

Casvian touches my shoulder and nods at the door. We retreat.

I expect him to lead me back to my alarmingly comfortable prison, but instead Casvian stops at the garden.

"That is what he faces."

It's sickening and horrifying, and I understand better the fear that drives Dalca. I understand why he risks a thousand small evils.

"It's awful," I say.

"One day—one day soon—he'll have *that* inside him. Before that happens, we—he and I—have to fix what's broken."

Dalca's words come back to me. *Anything can be fixed.* Now I get why he holds on to that idea so strongly.

"I don't know why Dalca thinks you can help. You haven't done anything but muddle his head and make it harder."

I fear it's not a good time to bring up Pa and my wanting to save him.

"If you care about the city—if you care about Dalca—you should leave."

I bite my lip. "My father—"

"Your *father* is the reason I don't have a mother." He holds up a hand to silence me. "And my father is the reason your home—your friends—were taken from you. Frankly, yours deserves what he gets, and mine probably does too. But I'm not here to talk about fathers."

Well, I care about Pa not dying. But ever since seeing this city from above—how small and fragile it seemed—I care about saving it, too.

"You said—Dalca thinks I can help."

Cas frowns. "If you can, do it."

CHAPTER 17

Ma sits upon a throne of shadows. Her face hidden by a long veil that melts into the silvery robe that shrouds all but her thin wrists and knob-knuckled hands, both covered in burnt black scar lines.

She lifts her head, and her veil shifts, the silver of it like molten metal.

She beckons.

My body moves thickly; with great effort, one foot rises. As it falls, the shadows behind me shatter like glass, and scorching light bleeds its way in. Spiderwebs of light spread under my feet, stretching forward into the dark before me, toward Ma.

Another step and the light behind me grows blinding. Still, she beckons.

With two more steps, the edges of Ma's robe and veil catch fire. The flames rise up the cloth, burning it away.

Through the gap in her veil, Ma's summer-sky blue eye widens. A sense of wrongness catches in my throat. The ashes blow away; Ma sits on the Regia's throne in all white, her dark skin gleaming with the gold lines of the Regia's mark.

She opens her mouth, and the Great King's voice booms forth in its deep, crackling splendor. *Who are you?*

My name sticks in my throat, my tongue thick and immovable. I can make no sound at all.

A little nobody.

I touch my throat—but something's not right with my hands. I raise them. There's no color to them, no depth. I'm a shadow.

What can a little nobody do?

I move my lips, willing words out of them, but I can make no sound, not even a wheeze.

A rumbling starts behind me. My footing slips as it grows closer.

I turn. A wall of black clouds rushes forward—I brace, twisting to see Ma one last time—but the clouds crash over me before my gaze reaches her.

My body that's not a body—no flesh, no blood, just shadow—falls apart as the Storm devours it, as I become another part of infinite darkness.

I jolt awake, a thick-tongued wail on my lips. I rub the salt from my eyes and the tracks of tears from my cheeks. "I'm Vesper Vale," I whisper in a voice rough with sleep. The words hang meaningless in the air of my luxuriously appointed prison. Soft early-morning light trickles in through the glass windows.

I crack my locket open to see Ma, ignoring Pa's notebook as it tumbles onto my lap. Ma's eyes are dark brown, same as ever. If she had become Regia, like she wanted—would the Great King have burned through her, the way he does through Dalca's mother? If she had succeeded, would I have lost her just the same—to the Regia's mark instead of to the Storm?

It doesn't matter. She's gone. Seeing Dalca with the Regia got me rattled, that's all.

But there's something else. The dream reminds me that there's nothing worse than the Storm—not the Regia, not the Great King, not even betraying Pa by giving his notebook to Dalca. Stopping the Storm is everything.

If Dalca can fight the Storm with what's in the notebook, then I have to give it to him.

Decided, I tuck Pa's notebook inside the locket and get out of bed.

As quickly as I can, I clean myself in the bathing room. My hair is still shorter and lighter than it once was, but my old face meets me in the polished silver mirror. It seems a little too young, a little too naked.

Tucked into a shelf in the bathing room, beside a stack of towels softer than most fifth-ringer clothing, is a small selection of clothes. I dress in the simplest of the bunch; a pair of snug black pants and an overdress that belts around the waist. It's not till I have it on that I notice the pattern of sun and stars embroidered on the neckline and down the shoulders. The sort of frippery unheard of in the fifth.

Who am I? Am I still Vesper Vale, daughter of revolutionaries, a hopeful little screwup from the fifth ring? I don't feel like it, not wearing fine clothes, not from my plush little room in the palace, just about as far from the Storm as it's possible to be. Not when I've failed Pa, again.

A firm rap comes at the door. I slip Ma's locket under my clothes and stand. My pulse quickens as the door opens and the soft scent of honeysuckle precedes Dalca in.

The pink-gold light outlines his regal brow, traces the straight line of his nose, dips into the sharp bow of his lip. He raises his eyes to meet mine. It happens in slow motion; his dark eyelashes sweep up, his gaze tracks from the floor to my bare feet, up the length of my legs, my chest, my neck, my lips, until all of me is held captive by eyes that shine like they have drunk all the colors of dawn.

His gaze lingers on my changed face, tracing the curves of my cheeks, the line of my nose, the fullness of my lips.

I study him in turn. Dalca wears full Wardana armor, encased in a shield of blood-red. He wears the distant, polite expression of a prince, but this, too, is his armor. His hands reveal more: they tremble ever so slightly, and unthinkingly, his fingers pluck at the cord wrapped around his wrist.

I wait for him to speak. Nervous energy hangs between us, like a bridge I don't quite know how to cross.

"Are you comfortable?" he asks. "Is there anything you need?"

I glance at our surroundings. "I'm fine," I say slowly. "But I'd like to know why I'm here."

"You're safe here. Neither Ragno, nor any that wish to do you harm, will get to you here."

"I'm here for my protection?"

"And something else." His jaw works. "I ask that you speak to your father."

"About what?"

"There is something your father knows. It's the key to fixing everything."

The locket grows heavier. "What could he possibly know?"

"You saw the death masks of the Regias. You know they've been dying younger and younger. My mother, too, is dying. As the Regia weakens, the Storm strengthens. I will not let the Storm win.

"I've traced every rumor, every last whisper about what your father was researching twenty years ago. Every surviving fragment of his work, I've read. As has Casvian. He was studying the Regia's mark. I think he discovered what went wrong all those years ago, when the marks were combined into one."

Two marks. My mind goes back to the old shrine. "One for the Great King we know, one for his other, darker side?"

"Yes, perhaps. The Great King is not usually depicted with that proto-ikon, but that temple you found with the shattered statue was an ancient one, if humble. We overlooked it."

"Because you didn't think anything important could be in the fifth?"

Light glimmers in his eyes. "I was wrong."

"I don't understand how this mark would change things."

"The Regias of old weren't mere vessels. They would retain their essential selves when they became Regia. They would be joined with the Great King, minds and hearts linked in exchange for power, but back then, they kept their souls. A stronger Regia—a Regia who isn't dying—will be able to fight the Storm, like the Regias of old. We could regain the lost rings, and more. Imagine, a Storm pushed to the distant horizon."

Unbidden, an image of Dalca kneeling before the Regia comes to mind. It mingles with my dream, and I have to ask, "Dalca . . . Is this to save your mother?"

He folds in on himself. "My mother . . . When a person becomes the Regia, they forfeit themselves. It is not my mother in there, in her body. Not anymore. She has become the Regia. The Regia does not speak the way my mother did, nor does she walk the way my mother used to. She doesn't dance. She doesn't . . . Now and then, I might glimpse a shadow of my mother in the way the Regia smiles. But it is not her. My mother is long gone. I don't dream of rescuing her."

The dark, miserable expression on his face gives way as he marshals his emotions, remembering his princely mask. "It's not a sad thing," he says. "She's become something more. She's our only hope against the Storm, and I must do all I can to aid her."

I whisper, feeling like I'm picking at a scab, "And if she dies?"

A flicker of real fear shows in his eyes, but it's gone so quick I might've imagined it. "Then I'll take her place, and my children will take mine. That's what it means to be an Illusora. Our lives are on loan to us, until the city demands them back."

His words are noble, a prince's words, exactly right. But his hands ball into white-knuckled fists. I see him. A paper-thin exterior of a heroic prince, selfless, dedicated to his people. Underneath is nothing but terror; it shows itself in the dark of his eyes, in the clench of his teeth, in the way his hands are never at ease. How did I miss that his noble exterior was all an act to hide the fear beneath? For all his show of perfection, it's his flaws that help me understand him. After all, haven't I buried my sorrow the same way he hides his fear?

On his shoulders is a far greater burden than any I've held. I admire him for it. Part of me wants to draw him into my arms, to help him carry his burden, to shield him from his fear. I recognize my own selfishness: I'd make myself important at his side. I'd make his dreams my dreams. I'd trade a leash of blood for a leash of something else.

I should give him Pa's notebook, but something makes me hesitate. He wants to stop the Storm, true. But I can't be sure that he wants that more than he wants to save his mother, more than he wants to save himself.

What other small evils will he commit out of fear, for the sake of the city, for his mother's life, for his own soul? When will those small evils become big evils?

I can't do it. I can't hand it over.

I trace my left wrist with my right thumb as my pulse races. "What do you want from me?"

"The Regia's body is failing. The healers say she has months if she's blessed. Weeks if she's not. If she dies—no matter how well we prepare, and how quickly I take on the mantle—the Storm will swell. It's already moving faster than we've ever seen it—who knows how much of the city it'll take at once. And then, once I'm Regia, the Great King will take over, and I won't be able to fix anything.

"There's a very small window to save the city. I hope you can convince your father to share what he knows. For all our sakes."

I turn away, facing the wall of glass and the city beyond. The view is mostly Storm; the city only fills less than a third of the frame. I can't tell if I'm doing the right thing by keeping the notebook to myself. It's a cowardly thought, but I'd rather try to convince Pa than choose between betraying Pa and dooming Dalca.

I face him. "I'll do my best."

His eyes light up, and he gives me a soft, relieved smile. "Thank you."

Dalca holds the door open for me. I walk with him in silence, stealing glimpses out of the corner of my eye. He's told me a lot, to be sure, but there's something yet unspoken between us. He told the Regia that I'm nothing to him—and he acts as if he meant it.

It's like I've lost something I didn't know I had.

We come to a floor-to-ceiling mosaic depicting warriors in red riding on the backs of horse-sized ravens, heading deep into a dark forest.

He strokes his forefinger down the mosaic, stopping at an overgrown hedge of roses guarding a door. He presses down on the little door, and a section of the mosaic slides open to reveal a dark tunnel.

"Is it true," I ask, "did you sleep in the old city when you were a kid?"

He pauses. "The Regia—my grandfather—once led me deep in the old city. He left me there with food and water to last three days. It took me nearer six to find my way out. I didn't want him to see me as a failure, so I went back, night after night, until I had a pretty good map of it up here." He taps his temple.

"That's cruel."

"Maybe. Before he left, he told me, 'Only the best will be Regia.' That's true, isn't it? The people deserve at least that."

We walk in silence through the tunnel, down a flight of stairs. I stop him before we cross a bridge into the old city. "I'm sorry," I say. "For deceiving you."

"I understand," he says, not meeting my eyes, "It was for your father."

"The face change was so you wouldn't recognize me. I didn't intend to trick you with it." But I did. "I didn't mean to use your feelings—"

He gives me a sardonic look. "My feelings are my own business."

I look away. "Of course."

"Why bring that up?"

I flush. "I guess my feelings are my own business, too."

We cross the bridge in silence, approaching the fossil of the old city. It's eerie and silent and magnificent, but Dalca shows as little reverence as if it were his bedroom armoire. We go deep into the labyrinth of the old city, passing Wardana stationed as guards.

Before a domed building three times the size of Amma's, Dalca stops. "For the record, I like this face better."

He swoops inside, leaving me a little warm and wrong-footed. I follow him in. Part of the dome has caved in, and slabs of the ceiling lie scattered upon the semicircle of ancient stone benches before a stage. It's a theater.

On the stage, still within that fist of stone, is Pa. The stone has retreated; it encloses him up to his shoulders.

If anything, he's even more haggard, but his eyes glint with cold intelligence.

My neck warms with embarrassment, and for a moment, I can't meet his eyes. I haven't gotten him out; I've gotten caught myself, and worse, I've spent the morning debating giving his life's work over to a boy who represents everything he and Ma tried to overthrow.

"Hi, Pa."

"Oh, hello, Vesp." He matches my tone, but his eyes are bright with relief. "What have you brought me this time?"

Pa drinks in the sight of me, and I wonder how worried he must've been. My eyes prickle. "Just the prince."

"We've met." Pa's eyes go cold when he fixes them on Dalca.

"Pa . . . Dalca explained, about the mark of the Regia. About what went wrong, and about you knowing the other one, the better one."

"Oh, Vesper."

"I've flown with him above the Storm. I've seen that there's nothing else. If giving him the mark can stop the Storm, if there's the smallest chance it'll work—"

Pa shakes his head.

"There's no mark. It was a dream, and not a good one."

"Share your research, then. The ikonomancers will figure it out."

"Vesper. See what they've done with all the power at their finger-tips. You want to give them more? Will more power make them care more? Do more? Be better in any conceivable way?"

I shoot Dalca a pleading look, and though he frowns, he obligingly steps back a few paces.

"Why didn't you listen?" Pa hisses. I grit my teeth, my hands itching to shake him. How? How does he think this is a good time to scold me?

"I came to save you!"

"Who's going to save *you?*"

"Between us two," I say, gesturing at him in the prison of rock, and me standing on my own two feet, "who looks like they need saving?"

He makes an abortive movement, like he would've thrown his arms up if they'd been free. "Whenever you're ready, go ahead. Commence with the rescue."

"Do you really think there's no hope left?"

His answer shines from his downcast eyes. "I — I'm sorry. For giving you this world. For bringing you into this mess. I never wanted that for you. I wanted you to be free."

"I'm part of this world, Pa. You can't change that now."

"You're right."

"Will you give him what he wants?"

"I know him, Vesper. His kind has ruled for hundreds of years. No, I won't give him anything."

Dalca steps up. "Ragno Haveli has the Regia's ear. He's the one pushing the Trial, and if he has his way, you won't be alive tomorrow. I have very little power here — not when the people hunger for a Trial. I don't want to see you die — for Vesper's sake, and also because I think you have the key to saving us all. The Illusora blood runs in my veins, it's true, but do you think there's the slightest chance that I might be more than my blood?"

"I'd like to think that, but no, son. I don't."

"Pa—"

"I . . ." He turns a little misty, as if he might say *I love you.* "I hope you've done what I asked."

I shake my head. "Pa . . . when did you decide you'd given up?"

He looks at me with the disapproval I know so well. "It's not about giving up. I know how this ends. We can't win . . . It's fate. I've accepted it. I've made peace with it."

Dalca presses his palms into his eyes, taking a slow, measured breath. "You haven't just accepted it. You've *ensured* it."

Dalca strides away, anger in each step, but I linger for a moment, catching one last glimpse of Pa before the dark swallows him up. His head hangs low, the picture of a defeated man. And yet he's won. He'll never help Dalca. Not even for me.

We're silent on the way back, but Dalca turns on his heel once we're back in my chamber. "We'll try again, tomorrow morning."

We can try, but I know Pa. "Dalca . . . What if he doesn't change his mind?"

"Then we go to the Trial. And watch our last hope throw his life away."

CHAPTER 18

When I was eight or nine, Pa told me the history of the Arvegna arena. Of how, in times long gone, the master of the games would flood the arena for full-scale naval battles. The Arvegna was once a place where ordinary people could prove themselves and fight their way into the Wardana, or to their freedom. They would face impossible odds, and rare were the stories of victors. But by stepping into the arena, anyone — young or old, high ringer or low — could become master of their destiny, even if just for a moment.

When I was a kid, I dreamt of proving myself in the Arvegna of old, up against beasts and the finest sword dancers. I imagined the thrill of demanding my right from the Regia.

I never imagined myself as a spectator at Pa's fight, one amongst the thousands who've turned up. I'd rather be forced to go up against a hundred beasts, armed with a toothpick, than be forced to sit, powerless to do anything but watch.

Dalca has his own platform in the stands, set right above the very heart of the action. It's the best view in the Arvegna, save for one. Across the arena from his is an even larger platform, empty for now.

Dalca sits stiffly beside me on a stone bench so ornate it might as well be a throne, the folds of his white and gold cloak spilling over the sides. He holds himself carefully, conscious of the eyes watching him. "Comfortable?"

"Not remotely." When he said we could watch together, I hadn't realized it would be quite so public. Thousands upon thousands of eyes watch us, belonging to folks from all corners of the city.

I tug at the neck of my white dress. Of all the three I'd been shown, this one looked the most like armor, but I hadn't expected armor to cage me so tight.

"Dalca . . ." I stop myself for what must be the fiftieth time. I pick at the embroidery on my dress. The night had hardened Pa's resolve—pleading with him at dawn had been of as much use as begging the sun not to rise. But I've only grown more uncertain. I want to give Dalca the notebook, but how can I know that he'll keep Pa alive, once he has what he needs? How do I know that it won't be just another bad decision? I've made a lot of those lately, and each time Pa's been right. But I just can't see how Pa being punished like this helps anyone.

"Are you sure you want to be here?" Dalca asks.

"Stop asking me that."

Dalca's voice is soft. "People have survived the First Trial, you know. Many of them without half the knowledge your father possesses."

"You think Pa still has the will to fight?"

His eyes glitter in the light. "It's more difficult to give up the will to live than most people imagine."

A hush falls over the crowd. The Regia ascends the steps to her platform. Her black hair is bound at the crown of her head, emphasizing the sharpness of her cheekbones and the gauntness of her cheeks. Every inch of visible skin is covered in interlocking lines of gold. There's a mesmerizing sort of beauty to the perfect symmetry of the Regia's mark, but the overall effect isn't so much beautiful as terrifying.

Her eyes zero in on me, and it's as though I'm standing before her, not sitting dozens of feet across the arena. In her gaze is the cold fury of all things unceasing, of sunrise upon endless sunrise, a world perfectly preserved in blinding light.

I snap back to myself. The power in her eyes contrasts with the frailness of her body: her gold-tipped hands shake like weathered leaves, her skin is drawn tight across her skull, as thin as paper, and she lowers herself so gingerly into her throne that her bones might be made of glass. She looks far more fragile here than she did surrounded by the splendor of the throne room.

She raises a hand, and the people cheer in one great roar; second-ringers in all their skimpy finery in the seats nearest us, third- and fourth-ringers filling out the seats in the heart of the arena, and fifth-ringers who've gotten a special pass fill the rest.

My blood boils. This is why people love a Trial. It's not just for the plentiful food, or to enjoy the festival atmosphere, or even to see the Regia. They come to be entertained. They come to forget about the Storm. The shape of the arena amplifies their voices into a single, monstrous roar.

Below us, a maze sprawls across the floor of the arena, one made of green hedges rising ten feet tall. Tucked intermittently into nooks and corners of the hedge wall are weapons, each in an ikon-locked cage. At the heart of the maze is a golden sword impaled in an ikon-engraved pedestal. If Pa unsheathes it, he wins. The arbitrariness sickens me. This is all artifice, rhyme with no reason, just to watch Pa suffer.

The cheering grows deafening as three doors materialize in the wall surrounding the arena floor. Marked by ikons, they open to admit a familiar pale-haired man in black and gold, a waiflike woman in blue, and heavyset man in green who's accompanied by a snarling hound.

I glare down at them. "Who are they?"

"I'm afraid they're volunteers. Handpicked by Ragno. Each one of them lost something irreplaceable because of your father's actions." He points to the massive man in green with a shaved head and no neck to speak of. His dog whips its head back and forth, practically buzzing with bloodlust. It's a massive creature, nearly reaching the man's chest.

"That man's father was on the last Regia's personal guard. He was . . . my grandfather's closest friend, who died protecting him."

I bite the inside of my cheek as a secondhand guilt comes over me. I shake it off. I won't believe that Pa deserves any of this. "I suppose the dog lost someone, too."

"I'm sorry."

"No, tell me."

"That beast has spent the last three days and nights without food, with only a shirt bearing your father's scent for company." It foams at the mouth, its spittle flying as it leaps forward and its leash snaps taut.

Dalca's hand slides to point at the slender woman in blue, who stands with a bow in hand. "Her husband was stationed in the sixth ring. It flooded the day my grandfather was killed, with no Regia to hold the Storm back. Her husband saved many lives. But he lost his."

Last comes Ragno in black and gold, wielding a scythe as tall as he is. "Ragno Haveli. He was once close friends with your father. When his wife died during the chaos, he felt that your father's act was a personal betrayal."

"I know who he is." Amma's blood is on his hands.

A pause. "Yes."

"When's his Trial? Or do you not punish murderers if they only kill fifth-ringers?" I snap.

"I agree with you. But that's not how it works." I can't handle the sympathy in his eyes.

I scowl down at the three hunters below. They've each faced a tragedy and come out of it ready to inflict another. But where does it end? If Pa falls at their hands, won't I feel the same kind of bloodthirst? Won't I want revenge?

"This is wrong. Isn't there another way?"

"What would you do? Never give anyone justice? Forgive the guilty and let the wronged suffer?" There's a challenge in his eyes. Would I forgive Ragno?

Never.

He touches the back of my hand with his fingertips. "Vesper . . . I want him alive, too. But nothing will make your father innocent."

My chest feels tight, and I swallow the acid fear that bubbles up in my throat.

"They volunteered out of pure hate?"

"The one who catches your father will be granted a reward from the Regia."

A violent hunger gleams in their eyes, without exception. Can Pa really face them and win? It's not just that they're strong; it's that they think they're right. Pa doesn't.

He hid himself away for years out of fear, but also out of guilt and grief. Won't that cripple him as much as how out of practice he is? For the last twelve years, his kind of fight has been the kind fought with words.

Against three highly motivated hunters — four if we include the dog — each spoiling for his blood . . . I don't like his odds. My nails dig deeper into my leg, and my dress's embroidery tears with little pops.

The maze is dense, the golden sword deep inside. How can he out-run them all long enough to find it?

He can't. It's impossible. My hands shake.

I touch Ma's locket at my throat, where it's hidden by my dress. If I gave this to Dalca, could he stop it? Or would I lose both Pa and his work in one poor move?

Dalca's hands grip the edges of his armrest, his knuckles pale.

The roar of the crowd peaks. Pa enters the arena, looking impossibly small. I rise out of my seat, my heart thudding. He squints up at the sun, raising his roped hands to block the light.

The crowd's divided. At least half of them scream, jumping to their feet, certain he's a traitor. They want a good show, capped by a satisfying death. But the other half is silent, unmoving in their seats. Wearing heavier shawls, coarser overcoats. The people of the low rings, who see themselves in him.

Dalca, too, watches the crowd.

The three hunters — the man in green with his hound, the woman in blue with her bow, and Ragno Haveli in black with his scythe — salute first the Regia, and then Dalca. Dalca gives them a nod.

The Regia looks up at the circle of sky, perfectly blue. She waits a long moment, until the golden sun peeks over the edge of the black stormwall. Her hand makes the smallest of gestures, and a horn blows.

Pa takes off into the maze. The hunters look to the Regia, waiting for their signal. I grit my teeth. Pa's being given only so much of a head start as to keep the game entertaining.

He runs as fast as he can, barreling into hedges and springing off instead of taking precious seconds to navigate around corners. His hands being tied makes him ungainly. He needs a weapon to cut the rope if he's going to have a chance.

A second horn blows. The hound and the man in green charge into the maze, tearing up the ground as they go. The slender woman slings her bow onto her back and starts climbing a hedge. She pulls herself over the edge and takes off, sprinting along the top. Under different circumstances, I'd be impressed at her cleverness.

Ragno bides his time, scythe resting against his shoulder, wandering into the maze with all the urgency of taking an afternoon stroll.

The woman has the best vantage point. She finds Pa first, just as he turns the corner to see an axe embedded in the top of a stone pedestal, in an ikon-locked cage. In one movement, she nocks her bow and releases arrow after arrow toward Pa. The first one clips his shoulder and Pa drops into a roll, so that the second one hits the ground instead of his neck.

Blood blossoms on Pa's shoulder. My heart pounds as if I'm down there with him.

"Dalca—" I start, touching Ma's locket. "If you were in my place —if you had to choose between your mother and the city—the whole city, down to every last fifth-ringer—what would you do?"

Dalca's gaze bores into the side of my face, but I keep my eyes on the arena. I need to know if he'd put his mother first. If this is about fear—or if I can trust him to make things better, for all of us.

I ask, "Could you give up your mother?"

Pa uses the blood seeping from his shoulder as ink. With it he draws something on his palm and thrusts his hand into the hedge right below the woman.

The hedge bulges. Within seconds, the branches thicken, leaves widening and twisting as a square section of hedge shoots up into the sky. The woman stumbles, her feet caught. She falls, landing with a crack on her back. Pa holds the axe to her neck.

I recoil, reflexively raising a hand to shield my eyes. Is this my father? It's one thing to hear about a Regia falling at his hands; it's another to see him ready to take a life.

Pa lowers the axe and takes precious minutes of his time to draw another ikon to bind her into the hedge. I exhale, shakily. I knew Pa wasn't a murderer. Can't they see?

The man in green traces Pa's path, his wild-eyed hound tugging him forward. As Pa hacks the rope from his hands, they close in.

Freed, Pa runs deep into the maze, but as long as his shoulder drips a trail of blood, there's no place he can go that the hound can't follow.

He knows this. Pa doubles back into a dead end. With his axe, he hacks at the ground. He's setting a trap. For the first time, the buzzing in my veins is from excitement instead of fear. Maybe he can do this. Dalca's right—winning the First Trial isn't unheard of.

Pa works as though he's done this a million times. It reminds me that he had a whole other life, one I know little of. One where he was more than a quiet ikonomancer in a home for the cursed.

The hound's tongue wags as it gets a taste of Pa's blood on the air. Its muscles ripple under its coat as it bounds closer and closer to Pa. His owner's arms bulge with the effort of keeping him under control. Both man and beast hurtle through the maze, feet thundering, howling at the thrill of the hunt.

They turn the corner and have Pa in their sights. His back is to them—he's still hacking at the ground. The beast snarls, the crowd screams, and Pa spins, rolling out of the way, and the beast's claws swipe his calf instead of his chest.

Pa scrambles out of the roll, stiffly getting to his feet. His body may remember how to fight, but it's been a long twelve years since he was in prime condition. He staggers backwards, and the beast pounces.

The crowd hushes. I look through my fingers.

The beast is caught in the ikon Pa carved into the ground. The dirt rises over it like the petals of a flower snapping shut, and then it sinks into the ground, flattening out. The hound's trapped, buried with only the tip of its snout poking free, just enough for it to breathe. The crowd roars.

The man in green, however, is less impressed. He'd let go of the leash when the hound pounced, saving himself.

Pa holds the axe in a two-handed grip, keeping the blade pointed at his opponent. The man swats it away as if his arm is made of steel instead of flesh and bone.

Beside me, Dalca hisses. I grab his hand tight, and he squeezes back with callused fingers.

Pa tries the hedge-growing ikon again. The man in green tears the vines with his bare hands, a snarl twisting his features. It won't slow him down for more than a few minutes.

But a minute is all Pa needed to finish scrawling an urgent ikon.

The ikon flares skyward in a tower of fire. The flames spread in a perfect ring—five paces across and twice as tall as the hunter. He breaks free of the branches, but as he takes a step toward the flames, the ring shrinks. He takes another, and the ring shrinks again, flames now threatening to lick at his clothes. It's a cage of fire—and the man's safe only so long as he stays put. He throws his head back and releases a furious bellow that echoes through the arena.

Pa backs out of the flaming corner of the maze without waiting to see if the hunter will find a way out.

With his shoulder and leg bleeding, Pa half runs, half limps through the maze. He uses the long handle of his axe as a walking stick to propel himself forward.

He's zeroing in on the center of the maze.

The last hunter, Ragno Haveli, closes in.

Pa hurries, no longer stopping to set traps. He runs through the maze, forced to double back three, four times as he hits dead ends. Pa moves faster and faster, his actions frantic, his focus gone. He's afraid.

"Dalca—"

"I know. He'll make it. He has to."

A chant rises from the crowd.

I can't make it out. "What are they saying?"

"*Ragno the Reaper*. It was his name in the Wardana."

What kind of mercy can you hope for from a man called that?

Pa turns the last corner—the heart of the maze stands before him. Only a long corridor separates him from victory.

He is halfway down the corridor when Ragno turns the corner. Pa stops in his tracks, as if he can feel Ragno's eyes on him. It's the reaction of prey to a predator.

The crowd quiets as Ragno shifts his scythe. "Put your weapon up, Alcanar."

"Rags, I'm sorry." Pa raises his axe partway from the ground, but it's clear he's not prepared to fight. "I'm sorry, for everything."

He's making his last amends, preparing for Ragno to take his life. I make a decision.

"Dalca—*can you stop this?*"

"I—if I did, if I took this from them, the city would turn against me."

"Would you do it if I had a way to give you Pa's work?"

He leans in. "Do you mean it?"

Below, Ragno shakes his head and says, "The time for apologies is long gone."

Pa raises his axe in time, but this is no match of equals. Ragno toys with him. A cut here, a shallow stab there—he may be the Reaper, but there's no mercy in the sort of death he offers. He makes sure Pa knows that each further minute of his life is a gift granted by him. I lose count of how many times Ragno could have killed my father.

I touch Dalca's cheek. "Tell me first: would you put your mother over the city?"

His eyes dart across my face, trying to understand. "I . . ."

Pa staggers backwards, tripping and falling. He's within feet of the golden sword and his freedom, but it's only a cruel ploy to give him hope. Ragno means to strike him down inches from victory.

There's no time. "I have his notebook. I'll give it to you."

Pa struggles to raise his axe, to point it toward Ragno, but on the ground he has no leverage. No hope. Ragno speaks to Pa, but his voice is too soft to hear, even with the Arvegna's acoustics.

Dalca gives me a long look and then jolts into action, leaping to his feet. "HALT!"

Pa freezes and scans the stadium. He stops when he sees me beside Dalca. He meets my eyes and then, very deliberately, he shakes his head.

With his eyes on me, Pa lowers the point of his axe. He can give up his life, but I can't let him.

Ragno has his scythe to Pa's throat. He makes as if to release Pa.

The arena erupts in boos and hisses.

Ragno looks to the Regia, who gestures him to continue.

"Please, Dalca." My hands tremble as I open Ma's locket and the shrunken notebook falls out onto my lap. "This is it."

Dalca leaps from the platform, his white-feather cloak flung wide. I rise to my feet as he falls, Pa's notebook clutched in my hand. He has

no weapon as he speeds toward Ragno, but he pulls the golden sword
from the pedestal and matches blows with Ragno.

"That's enough!" he shouts, voice magnified by the arena.

The boos only get louder, until the Regia raises a hand.

All eyes go to her. The Regia's crackling Great King voice seems to
come from everywhere. "The prince is wise to not end our fun so soon.
Let there be a Second Trial."

The crowd can't tell if they like that or not. Ragno lowers his scythe.

Dalca hands the golden sword to Pa, who collapses on his back
with it in hand, chest heaving.

Dalca bows, and when he rises, his gaze finds mine and holds tight.

CHAPTER 19

It starts in low in the stands, a rumbling that grows into a roar. People leap down from their seats, dropping onto the Arvegna's floor. Others follow in their wake, loud and angry.

Dalca gestures, and ikons appear in the wall around the arena. Wardana spill out and surround him and Pa in a human shield. Ragno hoists his scythe, refusing their assistance.

I follow Dalca and Pa's progress — two dark-haired heads bobbing in a sea of blood-red — until they disappear into the depths of the Arvegna and the doors seal up behind them.

"Vesper."

Casvian, clad in a pale, glittering swath of fabric that leaves a shoulder bare — his festive wear, I figure — appears behind me. Next to him, in his Wardana reds, is Izamal. He shoots me a speaking glance over Cas's shoulder. *Careful. Don't give me away.*

They reveal another secret passage that lets us out at the Ven. My mind's reeling too much to pay close attention to where we go, until we come to a stop. A door shuts behind us.

A cramped little reading room, already strewn with sheafs of paper.

Casvian frowns at me. Distantly, I notice that he's painted gold around his eyes. It looks nice.

Izamal clears his throat. "Dalca's on his way."

"The Regia will have summoned him." Casvian glares, and I understand that my actions might've cost Dalca even more than he said. "Did you beg? Did he do this for you?"

I hold out my fist. The muscles of my arm tingle from gripping too tight, and my fingers are slow to unfold. Pa's notebook rests in the palm of my scarred hand. "This is why he did it."

A half dozen expressions flash across Casvian's face. Ire fades to confusion fades to comprehension, with a few stops in between, ending in a gleaming-eyed hunger.

He reaches for it. I flinch, snapping my hand back. It takes me a second to shake the feeling that I'm betraying Pa, to let it fall into Casvian's waiting hands.

"Astounding," Cas murmurs, producing a nub of chalk from some fold of his glittering ensemble and neatly drawing an expanding ikon on the notebook's cover.

This isn't about betraying or not betraying Pa. It didn't come down to a choice between Pa and Dalca. That wasn't it at all. It wasn't even about saving Pa—though I'm more than relieved that Pa'll live at least another day. It came down to a choice between hope and fear. The slimmest shard of hope that we might be able to fight back the Storm against the teeth-clenching fear that we're one poor choice away from condemning us all to a future even worse than the present. I'm not ready to give up hope.

"By the Great King," Casvian murmurs to himself as Izamal peers at the book upside down.

I trace the burnt lines on my hand. It has to be the right choice. So why am I more afraid than I've ever been?

The door opens, and our heads swivel. Dalca walks in, his eyes locking on to mine. His fingers fall away from the cord around his wrist. "Let's get to work."

We settle in. My fingers itch, but Casvian hoards the book.

Izamal stretches.

The thing unsaid between Dalca and me—an electric stillness that draws us together, but only so far—has grown larger in the hour since I've handed over Pa's work. Cas bends over the notebook, so close the tips of his hair brush the pages. Izamal flips through another book and stretches his legs out, nudging Cas, who retaliates by stomping on my foot.

I bite back my yelp and draw my feet up.

"In the name of the King," Casvian mutters, "what absurd code is this?"

"Oh." I've forgotten that the notebook is written in code. "I can show you."

"I don't need help from an *apprentice*," Cas hisses, "for Storm's sake, I'm a master ikonomancer—"

"Cas," Dalca snaps.

I shrug, unoffended. I'm starting to understand that insulting is Cas's default state.

"I can figure it out," Cas mutters, but only out of habit, as he turns to me with Pa's notes in hand.

"Get over yourself for once, for Storm's sake," Izamal interrupts, slamming down his book. "It won't kill you to learn something from a fifth-ringer."

Cas freezes.

I sigh. Izamal's turned it into a fight.

"No, it won't," Cas says silkily. "But tell me, when did you know she was a fifth-ringer?"

"It doesn't take a genius to figure it out. Alcanar Vale was hiding in the fifth. He'd have his daughter with him."

Cas's eyes narrow, and I jump in. "I'm sorry," I say to Izamal, "for deceiving you about being a third-ringer. And everything. I—"

"*Was only trying to save my traitor father*, yes, I think we've heard," says Cas nastily in a high-pitched voice.

I clench my jaw and scrawl out the key for the code on a paper I shove in Cas's face as I jump up, my chair screeching back. "Here's the key. Good luck."

I shove out the door, stomping into the hall. The warm, dry air wraps around me like a blanket, and the anger fades.

Footsteps follow me. "I accept your apology," Izamal calls.

I tense. "I meant it. I am sorry, for everything."

"I know." His golden eyes are steady, seemingly calm, but there's something else there. "You seem to have landed on your feet."

He's angry. Is he accusing me of something? I drag him into an empty room filled with dust motes and training mats. "I thought they'd throw me in the fifth's prison, to be honest. I think it's because Dalca wanted me to talk to Pa."

Iz shakes his head. "He keeps you in the palace, he sits you by him in front of the whole city. How do you think this ends?"

I scowl. "I don't know what you mean."

"Don't think he cares for you, for any of us. He's afraid for his own skin."

"This isn't about feelings, Iz."

"Isn't it?" A wry grin splits his face, but doesn't meet his eyes. "Just— don't make the same mistake Nashi did."

Nashi? What does his sister have to do with anything? "What do you mean?"

"He fell for her, too. But Nashi was nursing a little crush on an ikonomancer, a girl from the fourth. She thought he was a good man, so she turned him down gentle. A few days later, she fell."

"Iz —"

His voice is hard. "Don't tell me he's a good man."

"I wasn't going to. Are — are you sure it wasn't —"

"Of course no Wardana will say it wasn't an accident." He looks skyward, as if I'm being obtuse, as if the truth is obvious.

It reminds me of Dalca. *You're naïve.* Am I? "Don't worry about me. My heart's not on the table. I'm helping Dalca because our goals align. Even if he just wants to save his skin — even if he just wants to save his mother — if he succeeds, that still means the Storm gets pushed back."

Iz's seriousness disappears under a familiar, smiling expression. A mask I'd never realized he was wearing. He claps me on the back. "Okay, okay. Just making sure. I am glad you aren't rotting in a cell."

"How'd you get away, anyway?"

"Doubled back, pretended I heard the alarm and was there to help. Shockingly useful, the uniform." He plucks at his blood-red lapel. "Had to cut down on trips to the fifth, though."

"I'm sorry."

"Enough of that. It's behind us now."

"What about the —" I make a fist and raise it.

His eyebrows rise and lips twitch. "If you're right, maybe this saves the fifth. If you're wrong, I need to keep an eye on him. Just in case."

Izamal crosses his arms, but his handsome face is arranged to say, *I'm mildly amused.* It's funny, in a way, how alike he and Dalca are. Both wear masks to hide their desperation. But where Dalca's fueled by fear, Izamal's driven by a dark rage. I don't know which is more dangerous.

"What?" he asks.

I shake my head. "Let's get back."

I open the door and go in, Iz on my heels.

Dalca gives Cas a speaking glance. Cas lets out a dramatic sigh and hands the notebook to me, without a word.

"Vesper," Dalca says pleasantly, "would you be so kind as to help?"

With an eye on Dalca and Casvian—in case Cas makes a lunge for it—I settle into a chair. I crack Pa's notebook open, holding my breath. It's different, this time—there's no listening for footsteps in the hall, no propping a chair under the doorknob, nothing but Pa's thoughts and me.

Sure, Dalca's breathing down my neck, I'm stuck in the middle of round two of Iz and Cas's legroom territorial dispute, and every so often a little voice reminds me that I'm on the verge of being an orphan, but there's only so much despair a person can take. I decide to enjoy the little things, like Pa's loopy handwriting and the little asides he writes about the people in his life.

Casvian Haveli, light of my life, disagrees with my enjoyment. "Here." He yanks the book from my hands. "You should start here. That's where the code changes." He flips forward to a sheaf of slightly darker papers. The words are all gibberish. Readable, ordinary words, but arranged carefully to make absolutely no sense. Familiar marks line the edge of the pages. It's not the same code as in the early sections— it's a little more complex—but I think I can work it out.

"Are you going to let me do this my way?" I say, not to Casvian, but to Dalca, who sits with his head resting on folded arms.

"Cas is smarter than he looks," Dalca says with a tired grin. Casvian scowls. "That said, do what you need to do. He's just here to help. We all are."

"Thank you." I tug the notebook out of Casvian's vise grip.

"What am I, decoration?"

"Yes, dear," Izamal says. "Just sit there and look pretty."

Cas gives him a withering look. "If this is a waste of time—"

"I'll find it. Just give me a moment."

At first glance, it's a looping, paranoid mess, until I figure out the structure underneath. My name makes an appearance as the key for one section; a sentimental touch that makes my eyes prickle. All those years of watching Pa, hoping he'd let me in to his inner world, pay off here. It takes me several hours to unravel Pa's code.

I make my face still, to keep from letting on that I've figured it out. Slowly, laboriously, I decode it in my head, glancing up at the others every so often. Casvian's lost in his own research into some of the new ikons the ikonomancers have gleaned from Pa's journal, and Izamal copies down ikons, with his tongue peeking out of the corner of his mouth. He's not very good; every so often, something starts smoking under his fingers and he hurries to correct it. Dalca has succumbed to his exhaustion. His long legs dangle over his armrest, the rest of his body folded into a position that makes my neck hurt just looking at him.

The pages Casvian pointed out are mottled and wrinkled, covered in careless watermarks. Pa kept a detailed account of his hunt for the mark, albeit a meandering one, his theories dotted with his hopes, his ideas, and his fears.

The Regia is more than a ruler, more than a figurehead, more than a leader: the Regia must be a source of balance. The question is, a balance between what? Good and evil? Man and animal? Order and chaos? Our Regia is no source of goodness. All I can guarantee is that he is, indeed, a man.

I skim ahead.

The people love her. In her eyes I see the depth of her passion for them. I don't dare compare that passion to her love for me, for I fear I won't like what I find. I know her. She is courageous and kind, but she is no fool. She knows what we're up against, and she knows how to give them hope. She knows how to use them. I do not doubt that she would make a good leader. Why does becoming a leader mean she must also become the Regia?

Ma. He's talking about Ma. He never spoke of her, not to me. Reading about her is like walking through an old, familiar home and finding a new door.

Ma, a just and fair woman who wanted to become the Regia. Kind and courageous. Who walked into the Storm and was lost.

"What are you doing?" Casvian says.

"Looking for a clue."

"Looked like you were reading."

"I *am* reading. How else do you expect me to find a clue?" For pages Pa goes on, outlining what amounts to a treason plot. Unless the Regia gives Pa a pardon, this is damning. I mean, Pa's already in a tough spot, but what if I'm facing a future where we save the Regia only so she's hale and hearty for Pa's execution?

Casvian's eyes darken, something vicious drawing to the surface. "I may not have as *extensive* a catalogue of inventions as your father, but I am rather inventive in my own right. I know an inversion ikon, which, when applied to a man's arm, will turn his skin inside out. I know a rather inoffensive warming ikon, which, when applied to a man's tongue, will cook him from the inside."

It's a strange talent he has; every time I learn something new about Casvian, I like him even less. "I don't think threatening me will solve any of our problems."

"Perhaps not." He bites back whatever else he was going to say and stares at the parchment in front of him, unseeing. Dalca's words about Ragno Haveli's wife come back to me.

He's shown better restraint than I would've, if our positions were switched. "I'm sorry," I say to my hands. "For what my father did to yours. For your mother—"

Casvian stands abruptly, two spots of color staining his cheeks. "If you're so sorry, figure it out. I'm going for a walk." He kicks Dalca's ankle on the way out. Dalca startles awake as the door thuds shut.

He scrubs a hand over his face. "What've I missed?"

"Nothing," I say, ignoring his bedhead for the seriousness in his eyes. "Dalca . . . Could you pardon my father? If this works?"

He sits up straight. "I don't have that power. But if everyone learns that Alcanar Vale saved them, I'm sure the Regia could be convinced. You have my word that I'll do everything I can."

I hold his gaze until I begin to believe him.

"Have you found anything?" Dalca asks. I trace the watermarks, following dips and wrinkles in the paper with a finger. I believe what I told Iz, that helping Dalca helps us all. Izamal won't need a revolution if Dalca and I fix things.

My gaze lands on a line in Pa's notes. *The Regia was once two. What was lost when they became one?*

"Vesper?"

I trace the looping line of the watermark to the edge of the page. Beside it is a little notation. The next page's watermark has another.

I loosen the journal's bindings and carefully pull out the pages with watermarks. Each is marked with a faint notation along an edge.

Dalca's chair creaks as he jumps to his feet. His hand rests on the back of my chair as he bends forward, watching over my shoulder. I ignore the way my skin tingles with his closeness.

It takes time to line them all up. Dalca helps, his warmth pressing into my back as he reaches past me. The air trembles with promise.

I hold my breath as I place the last sheet. The watermarks make a beautiful, intricate design, roughly in the shape of a person.

The Regia's mark.

A soft exhale brushes my ear. "That's it."

Dalca traces it, captivated. But then his brow furrows, his elation dimming. "But this is . . . this is no different from the one my mother wears."

"Wait." I clasp his wrist. "There's something here."

One last page, one without watermarks. Its notations place it in the same space as another page, where the center of the Regia's chest would be.

The Storm grows and wanes with the city. When the Great King's soul is balanced and at ease, so shall be the Storm. The Regia's mark is the Regia's mark. But the current Regia is missing something. I believe the key lies with the Storm, that the Storm is more than just the imbalance of the city made physical. There is something within the Storm that must be joined with the mark. A new Regia, the true Regia, cannot be made with only the mark; the other half of the equation lies within the Storm.

I've told her so. She's prepared to do what must be done to discover the last piece of the mark. If she is to be Regia, a true Regia, we must go into the Storm. We will bring back a whole mark, and she will be Regia.

I reread one line over and over. *We must go into the Storm.*

Into the Storm. Into the depths of grotesque writhing things, dark and formless. Into a shadowland of devouring beasts trapped between streaks of violet lightning.

Dalca's pries my hand off his wrist and holds it. "What is it? What does it say?"

I tell him.

I watch as the joy of discovery is chased off his face by dark determination. Dalca draws forth all his strength and resolve, seeming to grow taller, broader. "Then that's what we must do."

"Dalca—" I start, not knowing how I'll finish. "You'll be cursed."

He looks at me with the distant eyes of a king. "I said I would do anything. I should have remembered the Great King listens when we make such promises."

CHAPTER 20

The next few days pass in a whirlwind. The Storm begins to rage as if it's heard our plans, the wall of black cloud roiling like boiling water, an electric taste on the air even here in the relative safety of the palace. It taunts the city with bolts of lightning that streak through purple-black clouds, plunging the city not into darkness, but into a violet twilight. It's a reminder that we can't escape, no matter where we go.

An awareness prickles at the back of my neck: an omen. I dream of Ma and the Storm every night, as if she knows I'm coming, as if she longs for me.

Everyone feels it.

Dalca's a wildfire-in-waiting; inside him, concealed by his careful commands and royal smiles, the Storm feeds a growing mass of dark sulfuric dread. It's in his eyes—a boundless field of tinder, begging for a single spark. It's a dread made more powerful by the hope he carries in equal measure, a war of contrasts with one common enemy.

The Regia's council falls before Dalca's charm, approving what he says is a days-long solo training exercise in the ruins of the old city. Ragno Haveli is the only one that doesn't seem taken in, though I doubt that he has any idea of what Dalca plans.

I note that Dalca doesn't go to the Regia herself.

In Casvian, the Storm stokes a primal fear. He flinches every time a flash of lightning illuminates a massive eye or a flock of winged beasts or the writhing coil of a colossal serpent. I figure him a coward—I am one too—until I realize who his fear is for.

"This is lunacy," Casvian hisses, hurrying to keep pace with Dalca's distance-eating strides, as we speed through the palace toward the entrance to the old city. "This is a new brand of recklessness, even for *you*. Are you listening? I've looked, Dalca—not a single person has ever been recorded coming out of the Storm. Do you understand? Even if you do *what has never been done before*, you'll still be coming out cursed." He grabs Dalca's arm and spins him around, his voice low and even and far more chilling for how he struggles to contain his fear. "Will you let yourself become cursed? Will you live within the ward in a bed next to your father's? I went to them. These people, Dalca, they were our friends, our comrades. Now all they can hope for is a less miserable day than the one that came before. *That* is what you can look forward to. *If you come out at all*."

Dalca fixes his sky-bright eyes on him, but his mouth wears a smile made for war. "You read Vale's journal."

"Yes." Cas's eyes flicker to me. He scowls as if this is all my fault.

"And did you agree with his findings?" Dalca asks.

"Findings? They weren't findings—they were *ideas*." He forces each word through his teeth. "You can't throw away your life on a *guess*."

"I won't let the Regia die, Cas."

Cas's eyes give an answer once Dalca turns his back. *Let her die. Become the new Regia, a better Regia.* Maybe he thinks Pa really is wrong, or maybe he thinks that Dalca can hold on to control of his body by sheer strength of will, unlike every Regia for the past few hundred years.

"Dalca," Cas calls after him, standing still. "You could come back cursed and not know it. The Storm will find its way into you. What if it speaks through you, commands the Wardana through you, takes the throne? Should we not be afraid?"

Dalca's fingers tug at the cord around his wrist. "Is this not what we sought in all those years of studying Vale's work? We knew our search would lead to no easy answer, once we knew Vale would rather die than share it. I'm not saying this is a great plan, Cas. It's our only plan. And that makes it worth trying."

Cas lets out a shaky breath. He doesn't answer.

I bite my lip. Dalca keeps walking. He lets go of the cord, stretching the fingers of his hand wide as if shaking off Cas's doubt, Cas's fear.

He glances at me as my feet slow. "Join me? I'm off to see your father."

I bite my tongue and match his stride as we enter the old city. All the while remembering my last glimpse of Casvian, standing in the middle of the hallway, looking small and terrified and helpless.

Pa can't see the Storm, what with being so far underground, but even here its influence has reached him. His eyes flick to us, hyperaware, nervous.

"I'll leave you be," Dalca murmurs to me, and retreats some fifteen paces. Did he bring me here just so I could say goodbye?

"Pa." I forget what I meant to say. He's so drawn and gaunt. "You and Ma went into the Storm, didn't you?"

He blinks, once, twice, as understanding dawns on him. "You gave him my notebook."

I straighten my back and nod.

Pa deflates. "I told you, Vesper. I told you how important it is."

"I'm sorry, Pa. I really am. It wasn't in me to let you die, not like that, not for no good reason."

"That wasn't for you to decide. You've taken away my freedom to choose." His eyes flit to Dalca. "And you've given away your freedom as well."

I raise my chin. "I'm sorry I acted for you. But if there's a chance of pushing back the Storm . . . Isn't that worth it?"

"Is it?"

"You said the key is in the Storm. Did you go in?"

"No," Pa says. "Your mother did. Alone."

"She didn't find it?"

"She never came out."

"Why?" I ask. *Why did you let her go alone? Why didn't you go after her?*

"I've been trying to understand that for the last twelve years."

"Is there anything else I should know?"

"Vesper—please. Don't go."

Pa sensed what was in me before I voiced it. I clench my burnt fist. "Pa . . . thank you for protecting me all this time. I know it wasn't easy. I'm sorry I never made you proud. And I'm sorry that I have to disobey you one last time."

"You're just like her," Pa whispers with horror in his eyes. "I couldn't save her."

"I'm not like her." I'm not nearly so strong or brave. I'm not a leader. "But maybe that means I'll come back."

Pa holds my gaze, then the words spill from his lips. "All I know is that it is a counterbalance. The Great King bestows upon each Regia one thing—power. Power to order and rule. Strength to fight those who would threaten the city. But there's something missing, something that makes the Regia weak. It's that missing piece."

"A counterbalance? What does that mean?" Dalca asks, stepping up beside me. I wonder how much he heard.

Pa looks at him. "I'm not sure."

"Is it an object? What would it look like?"

"I wish I could tell you more."

"Is there nothing else?"

Pa exhales. "There's an old folktale that gives this warning: 'No matter where you enter the Storm, the Storm is the same. Whatever you take into it will be taken from you. Ready yourself, but no one can meet the Storm prepared to do so. Go as far as you can, as deep as you can, into its heart. I would wish you luck, but luck won't help. You will not return.'"

My heartbeat fills the silence.

"I gave your mother that warning. It didn't help her."

I meet his eyes, the eyes we share.

"Then we're done." Dalca nods at Pa.

"Please," Pa says, voice breaking. "If you must go, go. But don't take my daughter."

My vision blurs. I've never heard Pa beg.

Dalca's voice is quiet. "I would never ask that of her."

I leave before I cry.

But as Dalca steps out beside me, I speak. "It's my choice. It's my city. And I'm going."

He twists the cord around his wrist. "You don't—"

The words stick in his mouth. He's terrified of the Storm. Too terrified to say the noble thing.

In the end, he whispers, "Thank you."

I think about telling him it's not for him. That it's my home I'm protecting. But that's not the whole truth.

I can't stop imagining Ma walking into the Storm. Throwing a smile over her shoulder. Bracing herself—and disappearing.

No one went with her. No one had her back. Pa said he couldn't save her—but how would he have even tried?

I've seen the Storm pick people off, one by one: the stormtouched, neighbors, wanderers who were there one day and gone the next. It's not rational, not based in any sort of pattern that research can detect. Going into the Storm alone is a death sentence. There's no evidence to say that two of us going in will end any better. I know that.

But it gives me hope.

We surface out of the old city to the clamor of stormbells in the Ven. A stormsurge. Dalca shoots me a long, speaking glance, one hand already on his gauntlet's ikondial.

I nod. "Go."

He rises into the dark sky, trailed by a half dozen other Wardana. Shining like a beacon, he speeds toward the lightning-streaked Storm.

The roof of the Ven is cold and windy with the sun gone, but there's no better place to watch for returning Wardana. Pa's notebook lies open on my lap, but I haven't been able to concentrate.

The first few Wardana return, specks of red that grow into folks with faces weary from battle. I search them for a glimpse of Casvian's long pale hair—by far the most distinctive—but there's neither sight of it nor of Izamal's dark mane.

A few more show, gathering in the courtyard, clapping each other on the back, and their weariness transforms into a raucous delight at still being alive.

A lone Wardana arcs down, away from the others. His foot touches earth and without losing momentum, he breaks into a familiar stride: tautly straight-backed, as if straining against a weight and refusing to bend. Dalca. Against the blackness of the Storm and sky, I pick out two others, one with a flash of white hair. I let out a slow breath. They're all heading back. Izamal and Cas are far away and moving slowly, as if they've paused to bicker in midair.

I scramble off the roof, tucking Pa's notebook under my arm, and hurry through the halls, intercepting Dalca just as he reaches the door of the small room that's become our base.

He turns at the sound of my footfalls, and I stifle a gasp. He looks wretched; his hands tremble, and the sun-kissed glow I so envied is gone from his skin.

"You've been hurt," I say, searching him for any wounds. I can't tell what might be blood and what's just the red of his uniform.

"No," he says, stepping back. Even his shoulders are shaking.

I don't know what to say, but my face must show my concern.

"I'm fine. Don't tell the others."

I open the door and set Pa's notebook down. No one was here to turn on the ikonlights, and only the dim gold light from the hall filters in.

Dalca follows me inside.

My voice is soft, the same voice I'd used when comforting one of the stormtouched after a bad night. "What happened?"

Head tilted back against the wall, Dalca breathes in and out. His heartbeat jumps in his neck, fast as butterfly wings. A strange longing makes me look away, and my gaze falls on the view out the window, on the fifth, dark and shadowy. They'll gather soon, as we always did after a stormsurge.

"Nothing. Nothing beyond the usual. Wasn't even a bad surge." He hesitates. "It's just—it struck me, all at once. I'll be fine."

"You don't need to be fine," I say.

In the dark, there's no telling the color of his eyes; only the glint of light caught in them reveals that he's watching me. In the dark, he could be any boy from the fifth.

When Jem needed comfort, I'd wrap my arm around her and let her rest her head on my shoulder. But what would comfort a prince? "I—I'll let you be."

Dalca catches my wrist with a touch soft as a feather's. "Please don't leave."

He lets go, but the ghost of his touch lingers.

"The Storm scares me," I admit. "If my ma tried and couldn't— and she was everything I'm not—"

"You don't have to go."

I glare at him. "Neither do you."

A surprised smile. "Of course I do. In your shoes, anyone else would expect it of me."

"You're going to walk into the Storm just because you think people would expect it of you?"

"People *should* expect things of the Regia. They should expect me to protect them. They should expect me to do whatever it takes to protect them. They should, and they do—they expect me to give up my body for the Great King. Of course they'd expect me to give up the same to save them from the Storm."

"Who's they?"

He tugs at the cord on his wrist. "Anyone. Everyone. It doesn't matter. My point is — no one expects that of you."

My hand goes to my neck. He's right, but it hurts. "You're right. No one expects anything of me." Not even my own father.

"But don't you see? You're free. Don't come tomorrow. Don't throw your life away."

"I'm not free. It's my home, too. I wouldn't face the Storm just because someone expects it of me."

"Then why?"

It's not easy to name. And when I think about it, I hear Pa's voice. *You're making yourself more important than you are. He doesn't need you.*

Out of self-preservation, I silence that voice. My gaze settles again on the view through the window, on the fifth ring. "I'll show you."

"What do you mean?"

"Do you trust me?" It hangs between us for a long moment.

Dalca nods, and a strange and delicate warmth spreads through me.

We hurtle down a passageway, ikonlight rocking back and forth with every footfall, wearing Iz's stowed mosscloth cloaks over clothing that's indistinct enough to pass in the fifth. I catch my breath at the door, returning Dalca's hesitant smile and tugging his hood down an inch to shadow his eyes.

He opens the door, and we step out. The humidity hits me like a wet sponge, soaking into my clothes and hair, letting the cold sink right into my skin. I shiver.

The alley we come out into is furred with moss, and the building to our right has a rotted roof that's been patched with fabric. Dalca steps carefully over the moss-covered rubble that litters the alley, and at once I regret bringing him here. I see everything through the eyes of a high ringer: the damp, the rubbish, the fact that there's nothing clean, nothing dry, nothing in perfect condition.

I wanted to show him what mattered to me, but instead I'm reminding myself of the distance between us.

Dalca taps my arm, startling me out of my thoughts. He squints at a flickering light that grows larger as it nears; a couple walks hand in hand, the shorter figure gripping a palm-sized ikonlight. They pass us by and we follow them. Cupped in my hands is the ikonlight from the passageway, a small globe-shaped one that emits a soft white glow.

We take a turn stormward and come upon a gathering of fifth-ringers. The crowd forms a loose circle, everyone facing inward, holding glimmers of light that illume just the edges of their features and the tips of their fingers. Some hold lanterns powered by ikons, others hold little fires in metal bowls, cupped in hands wrapped with cloth. As more and more people join, the many-colored light grows into a glow that cocoons us in something almost as warm as daylight.

Dalca murmurs into my ear. "What is this?"

"It's what we do after a stormsurge. To remind us . . ." I trail off, embarrassed.

"To remind you?"

My cheeks warm. "Of what matters."

A clear voice rises into the air, a song and a prayer for us to love the little light and the little life we hold. Dalca looks down at me with a question in his eyes.

I offer him the ikonlight.

Instead of taking it, he cups my hands.

Light traces the angles of his face, the curves of his lips, and the pools in his eyes.

The song's last note hangs in the air, but before it can fall, it's joined by warm beats of hands on a drum. The thrum of a sitar joins in, its voice pitched lower than Amma's. The crowd opens up, and three children are the first to dance. A man with long white whiskers pulls a tiny woman to her feet, and she admonishes him as her shawl slips off her head. Lovers and friends, siblings and strangers; they all fall into a dance of interlocking hands and interweaving bodies.

I drop my hands, holding the ikonlight at my side. Dalca's knuckles brush mine.

I steal a glance at him and find furrowed brows over thinking eyes.

What must it look like to him? Folks bundled up to the chin in rags, joining their voices to the music, leaping in a chaotic dance, and wearing expressions of joy that wouldn't be out of place on a child?

Even in the chill, my cheeks grow hot. I can't expect Dalca to understand what makes this precious to me, what makes this worth fighting for. I shouldn't have brought him here.

"Let's go," I say, tugging on his sleeve when he doesn't move.

We've gone two steps when mugs of sundust are pressed into our hands by a cheery woman with a long braid of frizzy gray hair and a gap between her front teeth. Dalca tries to refuse.

"Oh no, love, you're shaking from the cold. Have a little. It's weak, but we have more than enough."

She beams at him until he takes a sip. His expression freezes, and very visibly, he swallows. I hide my smile under my cup.

"My boy was tall like you. Never said when he was cold, too. Stay warm, love. Both of you." She winks at me.

"Thank you," Dalca says with such solemnity that she giggles and pats his cheek before taking her pot of sundust to another cold soul.

I swallow my tea down and take his cup too, stacking them along the wall where there are a few others.

Dalca watches her pour with a funny look on his face.

"First time drinking sundust?"

Dalca blinks at me. "Was that what that was?"

"Fifth ring's finest," I say.

"She didn't know me," he says.

"No, I don't think so."

"That was kind of her," he says, turning to me with a puzzled look.

I resist the urge to roll my eyes. "Okay, I'm sorry, let's go back—"

He cuts me off. "Will you dance with me?"

He holds out a hand.

Mystified, I consider him for a long moment. There's no mockery, no pity in his eyes.

I take his hand. A smile curls his lips as he pulls me into the dance. He's a fast learner, and I'm not much of a dancer myself, but soon we blend in well enough. I catch glimpses of him through a bridge of arms as the dance pulls us apart, and when we come close, he pulls me to him, earning himself a spattering of laughs as the flow of the dance breaks and bends to envelop us.

His breaths puff against my lips, and my skin knows the exact shape of the distance between us.

"I've never met anyone as brave as you," he whispers.

I shake my head. "I'm not—"

"You are. I wanted you to stay, to be safe. But . . ."

"But?"

"I want you by my side more."

His eyes are liquid, aglow with reflected light.

I duck my head. My body is warm all over, and I have a feeling I'm smiling like a fool. It's too much; I don't want anyone to have this kind of power over me.

He follows me as I weave my way through the whirling dancers, out onto the sidelines. He calls after me, quiet. "Vesper?"

I soften at the worry in his eyes. "Sit with me," I say, and pull him down onto an empty stoop, where the shadow of a doorway gives us a little shelter.

I search for something mundane to distract me from the brush of his knee against mine. I touch the leather cord around his wrist. "You're always wearing this. Does it mean something?"

He traces its length with the tip of his finger, and a soft, embarrassed look comes over his face. "When I was small, my father looked after the kinnari birds whose feathers make the Wardana's cloaks. He raised the last one from when it was a hatchling. They were clever birds, but prone to loneliness. Father gave them a bell to ring, for when they wanted him."

My stomach tenses at the vulnerability in his voice.

Dalca's eyes dart away from my face. "I had bad dreams as a child. My grandfather was . . . strict. But he was the Regia. Father gave me a bell on a cord, one that would bring him running, night or day. After his . . . accident, I kept the cord on me."

"That's . . ." I feel like I've walked off the edge of a watchtower and only just noticed that there's nothing but air under my feet.

He groans. "Please don't make fun of me."

I don't think he realizes he's plucking at the cord. I put my hand over his. "I wouldn't."

Dalca looks at me, startled, lips parted. In this low light, mosscloth cloak over his clothes, he could be any other boy. What if he were?

If he were just a boy, would I admit what I feel for him?

His gaze falls to my lips.

Would I lean in and give him the kiss he's hoping for?

Our last was so brief that I remember only the shock. I remember nothing of the feel. His lips are a shade darker than his skin. They don't seem soft. But they might be.

His breath stills.

My body leans forward before my mind catches up. My hand covers his lips, and I press a kiss to the back of it.

"That's as much as I can give." My voice comes out no louder than a whisper. I pull back, pressing my fingers into my tingling palm.

His eyes are soft and a little bemused.

"Don't make fun of me," I say.

His lips part. "I wouldn't."

An electric something hangs in the air between us all the way back through the tunnels—where we leave our mosscloth cloaks—and to the Ven. In the shadow of the main arch, I hesitate, not willing to part ways just yet. I won't be able to sleep, not when I know what tomorrow will demand of me.

Dalca's fingers press against the inside of my wrist, soft as air. "I have something for you."

He strides off, throwing me a look over his shoulder, the dimmed glow from the wall sconces catching in his eyes.

I jog after him, biting back my curiosity. He takes me on a path through the Ven's sandstone halls, past a pair of heavy double doors, into a room I can tell is large by the way our footfalls echo loud and tinny. All the ikonlights are off, save one that dimly casts light across the wide room, onto the racks of weapons and gauntlets that line the walls. The armory.

Dalca beckons me through an archway into another connected room. It's dominated by two large tables with rolls of fabric and strips of leather neatly arranged on their surfaces. One strip of red leather has a needle and thread sticking out of it, as if someone paused in the middle of embroidering an ikon.

"Through here."

A door so small I hadn't noticed it. Through it is a tiny room, where full-length, slightly mottled mirrors have been mounted on the walls. Dalca doesn't follow me in.

I meet my confused eyes in the mirror and turn to him. "Dalca—"

"Ah, here it is." His voice comes from beyond the door. He comes through the doorway carrying a bundle of cloth.

He presses it into my hands. My fingers touch not cloth but leather. Red leather.

"We don't have very many left," he says. "Once we lost the sixth, we lost the ability to make more. So we brought out the old uniforms from the archives—including the ones worn by the great Wardana of old. The mancers have gotten very good at mending them."

I touch the ikons—some embroidered, some etched in the leather—dozens of them overlapping. My fingertips tingle as if the power of the ikons is palpable.

"Here." He takes the jacket from me, and I place the trousers on the floor. He shakes the jacket out and holds it open for me. The inside is a soft black, and ikons embroidered in ivory-thread are studded throughout like stars in a night sky.

Dalca helps me slip it on. Its substantial weight presses my shoulders down, and the sleeves come down past my fingertips.

"I'm not sure it's my size," I say, dryly.

Dalca laughs. "Trust me."

He shows me how to fasten it; the inner layer has slim loops that pull over a row of tiny buttons, and the outer layer laces closed, with a button at the neck.

"Ready?" Dalca asks.

"For what?"

He touches an ikon and I gasp as a tremor runs through the leather. In inch-wide sections, it shrinks and stiffens, as if finding the shape of my body. Another tremor runs through it, and starting from the waist and inching upward, the jacket shrinks to fit me. It stills all at once, and I raise and bend my arms, marveling at how supple and yielding the leather has become. Its weight is no longer knee-buckling—now it's merely comforting, no heavier than a hug.

Dalca's voice is solemn. "Now you're as protected as I can make you."

His words warm my cheeks and have me feeling strangely exposed. I bend to pick up the trousers to hide my face, and Dalca turns his back to give me privacy.

The trousers are embroidered and lined in the same way as the jacket, thick with padding at the thighs and knees. They lace up at the waist, and when I activate the ikon right at my navel, the leather shivers and shrinks to fit.

I meet my reflection's eyes. A Wardana looks back at me. My chin, my nose, my lips. But her shoulders are broader. She stands straighter. And in her gaze glimmers something that's almost like bravery.

I run my hand down my side, tracing the thousandfold protections of the Wardana ikons. I remember what it felt like to look up at the Wardana flying overhead and have longing fill me up to the brim. But it's almost like remembering a dream.

Isn't this what I've always wanted?

Maybe I've changed. Maybe I want more now.

And yet. A slow smile breaks over my face in the mirror.

"Dalca?" I say, and he turns around. I meet his eyes in the mirror. "I'm ready."

When we return to the reading room, we find Izamal and Cas already there. They don't look up when the door opens, focused on poring over a mottled book, heads nearly touching. My eyebrows inch up my forehead; I've never seen them so close without bloodshed or bickering involved.

Izamal looks up first, his eyebrows rising as he takes me in. He smiles. "So. When are we heading out?"

Dalca makes a strange sound. "I've told you, I can't ask you—"

"You didn't ask, though. I didn't hear him ask, Cas, did you?"

Cas flicks a lock of hair over his shoulder. If he noticed my uniform, I can't tell. "No, I don't think he did. Poor manners, really, for a prince."

"Iz, your mother already lost one child. I can't ask—"

"You're not asking, Dalca. I'm telling you. Plus, how much more cursed can I get?"

Dalca turns to Cas, who gives an aristocratic shrug. "I've already packed."

"You could unpack."

"Too much effort."

Dalca's thoughts play out on his body; first an irritated frown, then a settling of his shoulders as he gives in. "Get a good night's sleep. Tomorrow, before dawn, we make our way into the fifth, into the Storm."

The Storm rumbles with thunder so faint it almost sounds like laughter. We've avoided drawing attention, save for a girl sleeping on a patch of moss. She pulls herself upright. I press my finger to my lips.

In her eyes shine the beginnings of the story she'll one day tell about this moment. I've just got to hope that it won't end with *and then they were never seen again.*

If Pa were here, he'd turn to me with a disapproving frown and ask, *You're going into the Storm? Even though you've lived amongst the stormtouched and know what they most regret is touching the Storm? You don't think you've lost enough to it? You're really sure this is a smart idea?*

I shut Pa out from my mind. The golden road leads straight into the black wall of the Storm. I'm as ready as I'll ever get. Every second makes me less ready.

"Did you see the Regia?" I ask Dalca as he contemplates the writhing dark not ten feet before us.

He shakes his head, taking his time putting the words together. "I didn't want to give myself an opportunity to be a coward."

Izamal steps up beside me, absently touching a blue charm tied to his wrist. He catches me looking. "My mother gave it to me."

Dalca stills, the muscles of his neck moving as he swallows.

Izamal rolls his eyes. "If you tell me one more time—"

"I can't ask your family to give up two children—"

Iz groans. "There it is. Twenty-seven times, he's—"

"Iz. I'm serious."

"So am I." Iz meets his gaze, all traces of teasing gone. "I love every corner of this place. The mossy ones especially, sure, but even the absurd places you and Cas call home. Don't tell me I can't defend it."

Dalca exhales, nods. "I understand. I'm sorry for asking—"

"—Twenty-seven times—"

"I don't think it was that many, but I'm sorry. It's your choice. And I respect that. You too, Cas."

"Wait," says Cas. "You're not going to ask me? I've got a whole speech prepared—it's better than his—" He pauses as Iz raises an eyebrow. "Though yours was very nice, Izamal."

Dalca rolls his eyes, catching my gaze.

"I'm going," I say.

Dalca cracks a smile, and something unclenches in me. "Good. Because I'm pretty sure we're all following you." There's a warmth under his words, one that reminds me of last night.

We all match in our Wardana reds. Every time I glimpse my own blood-red uniform out of the corner of my eye, I get a little thrill. Even if our uniforms are designed to protect against casual brushes with the Storm, and not its full might, the gentle weight of the leather is reassuring.

Each of us carries a pack containing food, an ikonlight, and a bedroll. Ikonomancer's tools poke out of Casvian's.

Dalca's gaze meets mine, asking a question.

I take a step toward the Storm and glance back, reaching a hand to him. "You coming?"

His lips stay set in a grim line, but he takes my hand.

Casvian shifts his pack higher on his back. Izamal nods at me, jaw clenched.

I step closer. The taste of copper and spun sugar coats my teeth and my tongue. I swallow it down.

I am small in the face of the Storm's fearsome wrath. In me, the Storm sparks a fear so deep it sinks through my skin, into my blood, through my bones, deep into my marrow. The fear changes me, becomes me. But it's not just fear of being torn apart by the beasts within. I fear the abyss. I fear how the Storm calls to me. This is the Storm that ate Ma. She must have listened to the same siren song that says, *Step into me, and you shall see.*

Everything you want will be yours, if only you dare.

I won't lose myself in it. I pull myself together. I have a purpose.

The Storm watches me.

I take a deep breath and walk in.

CHAPTER 21

I open my eyes.

It's as if I'm underwater, as if I'm seeing through something thicker than air. But the darkness isn't solid. Layers of shadow hang before me, like curtains of dark mist. They part for me as I step forward, each one leaving behind a veil of cold on my skin.

From both near and far comes a sweet song of heartrending longing: the voice of a mother singing her love to her child, the whisper of wind left in the wake of soul mates passing each other by, the muffled weeping of the newly grieving.

The Storm is alive. It sings of its longing.

A hand squeezes my wrist, pulling me back to myself. I follow the hand up to Dalca's eyes, bright as beacons in the dark of the Storm.

Izamal has his hand on my left shoulder, and Casvian is on Dalca's other side. We've all made it in.

"All good?" Dalca asks.

We all make sounds of agreement, though I'm not sure *good* is what I'm feeling. *Unsettled* is more like it. *Like I'm walking to my imminent demise,* even more so.

The air is moist and cold in a way that sinks deep into my bones. There's no sense of time; the light from our golden sun doesn't reach into the Storm. It could be morning, day, or night, but I have the feeling it's none of the above. We're in the belly of a once and future darkness.

Between one blink and the next, a blackened tree appears like a massive gnarled hand, beckoning us. The wrinkles of its ragged bark melt before my eyes, forming faces with howling mouths and agonized eyes. I blink—and there's only bark.

It stands sentinel at the head of a path that rises from the darkness, stretching into the distance.

"Do we take it?" I ask.

They look at me as if they hadn't realized there was another option. But I guess wandering vaguely into the darkness isn't an appealing choice. Izamal breathes a laugh. He's got a look in his eyes that scares me. There's no fear in them, just cold determination.

"Yes," Dalca says, decisive. "If the Storm wishes us on this path, we will take it. *Go as far as you can, as deep as you can, into its heart.* We must not stop until we find the heart of the Storm. No matter what the Storm takes from us."

An echo of Pa's words in his.

He takes the first step, a noble king leading the charge, with his army in tow. And what a scanty army it is: a rebel, a prisoner, and a sycophant.

A black forest rises before us, looming on either side of the path. The trees all have bark of darkest black, but they leak sap that glows molten silver as if the life is being milked out of them. The sap is the only source of light. It's so dim that for the longest time, we don't notice the figures in the woods.

Monstrous beasts, dozens upon dozens of them. My heart skips a beat. But they don't move, don't seem to sense us. I pray they're asleep.

Within the cradle of trees slumber a menagerie of the fanged and furious. To the right rest a family of creatures like those that attacked me in the fifth, when Dalca rescued me. Their chests rise and fall so slowly and evenly that I relax, assured the beasts won't leap at the chance of finishing what they started.

"What is all this?" Izamal asks in a whisper.

No one has an answer.

We walk and walk. The back of my neck prickles with primal awareness—there's a predator in our midst. Its eyes are on me.

I turn my head from side to side, hoping to catch it. The edge of an inky, slippery shadow glimmers in my peripheral vision. Even that barest glimpse gives me vertigo, as if I've found myself teetering on the edge of a precipice, bracing for a fall that'll never end.

"You see it?" Dalca murmurs to me, his eyes carefully aimed straight ahead.

"Just barely."

"We're all seeing it, then?" Izamal exhales. "Thank the Great King."

"What are you seeing, exactly?" Casvian says, his arm outstretched toward something only he can see. My fingers itch to snatch back his hand and keep him from touching the shadow creature.

"A child," Dalca says at the same time I say, "A shadow," and Izamal whispers, "A cat large as a man."

"That's what I thought." Casvian's voice would be smug if it weren't so shaky. He draws his arm back, shoving both his hands into his pockets.

"Neither of you see the boy?" Dalca searches my eyes. "You don't hear him?"

I shake my head. "What's he saying?"

Dalca pauses. "He's laughing."

A shiver runs up my spine. A laughing child, a shadow, a cat. I'm not sure which I'd rather face. At least the massive cat would kill me quickly. Casvian's lips are a thin line. I wonder what he sees, but I'm too afraid to ask.

I catch another glimpse of the shadow. Is this the form a curse takes within the Storm? Is this what will sink into me when I leave the Storm, cursing me?

I smile at my optimism. If we're the first to return from the Storm, perhaps a curse isn't so bad a price to pay.

"The cat is watching us," Izamal says in a measured voice, like he's trying not to spook it. "He has blood on his teeth—massive teeth, like scythes—and his yellow eyes ... they're human eyes. Does it mean something?"

Casvian stares at his own personal demon, a vein in his jaw working. He marshals himself by retreating to the realm of his intellect. "There are two possibilities. One, there's nothing there, and our minds are playing tricks. Two, there *is* something there, and it's concealing its true shape from us."

I bite my lip. Maybe there's a third option: there are four somethings here, each tailor-made.

"What would it want?" I ask. "If there *was* something there?"

"Excellent question, apprentice," Casvian says dryly. "If only we knew more before we undertook this mission."

"Let's keep moving." Dalca's gaze is fixed far ahead. "We may be the first to see this far into the Storm. Who knows more than us?"

I squash down a thought of Ma. How far did she get?

Casvian shoots him an exasperated look. Izamal stares at Dalca, wearing an expression of cold focus. It makes me shiver.

We follow Dalca on the path, our personal specters tagging along, for what seems like miles and miles. Our pace is steady, though frustration shows in tight jaws and clenched fists. At least an hour or two must pass, but as Casvian says, we don't know if time works the same way inside the Storm.

We walk and walk, until we find ourselves standing beside an awfully familiar black tree shaped like a massive, gnarled hand. The path stretches on beyond it, dim and clouded.

"Did we get turned around somewhere?" Izamal asks.

"No," Dalca answers, walking forward. And soon we find he's right.

The forest is gone; instead a lifeless desert fades into existence on either side of the path. I look back at the dark tree. There's no sign of the forest.

The shadow creature follows.

"Still there?" I ask.

"Still there," comes the unenthusiastic chorus.

The desert winds howl, each at a different, miserable pitch, coalescing into a symphony of wails.

"It's gone," Izamal says. I glance back — but my shadow's still there.

Izamal grasps at his wrist.

"Your mother's charm." Dalca understands at once. "Is anyone else missing anything?"

"Yes." Casvian starts. "The Haveli mark." He touches the skin of his chest. It must be some sort of family ikon.

I reach for my collarbone and find nothing. "Ma's locket."

Dalca nods. "Tokens of protection. The deeper we go, the more we'll have to give up."

He examines each of us in turn. His bright eyes ask, *Will you turn back?*

"Let's get on with it, then," Izamal growls.

We walk on and on, the path winding through changing, stark landscapes. But we keep coming back to the tree.

Our third time past the tree, Dalca calls us to a stop. We've all lost our packs, snatched from us without us noticing. Dalca and Izamal have lost their weapons and cloaks, and Casvian's hair no longer reflects like a dull mirror, but is a pale silver not unlike his father's.

I had less to lose, but what I have is gone.

This time around, the path takes us through a land of caverns and stalagmites. Every whisper echoes, but each echo comes back transformed; a whisper becomes a guttural moan, a murmur becomes a keening shriek.

Izamal coughs, and it comes back a scream.

Casvian sets to making an ikon fire. His hands shake, and Izamal puts a calming hand on Cas's shoulder, taking the paper from him. Cas blinks in surprise, cheeks pinkening, and murmurs, "Thank you." Dalca stands beside me, both of us doing nothing useful.

"I think . . ." Dalca puts a hand on my arm, keeping his voice as low as humanly possible. "The little boy—I think he's me."

"He looks like you?"

"He's about the age I was when my mother became the Regia. I think I'm supposed to follow him."

"Okay," I say. "We'll all go."

Dalca hesitates, and I shiver with premonition.

"Dalca," I say. "We'll all go. Together."

"Right. Of course." Dalca smiles at me, a cocky imitation of something genuine. It's not a good reproduction. "You see a shadow?"

He's changing the subject. I pick through my thoughts. "I think mine might be me, too." I've seen a shadow in my dreams ever since the night I slept by the Storm. And the feeling of vertigo I get when I look at it—it's a feeling of falling *within*.

Izamal whoops as a great blaze rises up from the little ikon. His voice echoes back louder, a roar like a thunderclap.

It startles a laugh out of Casvian.

"What do you think they are? The things we see?" I ask Dalca.

Casvian answers. "I think they want to lure us deeper into the Storm." His gaze goes to whatever it is he sees. The look in his eyes is at once incredulous and hungry.

"I don't know," Izamal says. "I don't want to get any closer to mine."

"Vale wrote that the Storm is a catalyst," Casvian says. I startle. I didn't read that. "Whatever we bring into it is what it works with. It's a certain kind of energy, one that's eager to work transformations. It'll take seeds and grow trees—so watch the seeds you've brought with you."

"Like the power that works through an ikon," Izamal says.

"Yes, but the difference is that an ikon represents a perfectly equal exchange. A catalyst introduces additional energy. The Storm is immeasurable. When immeasurable energy is applied to an input, who knows what the output will be? All we know is that it will be something made with untold power."

"And right now . . ." Izamal trails off as it dawns on him.

Dalca finishes the thought. "We're the inputs."

I touch my chest, where Ma's locket would've hung.

Chasing Dalca's shadow, we walk through a land of ice that freezes the soles of our feet and the wetness in our eyes.

We walk through a land of rain with lightning that blinds us and thunder that deafens our hearing.

We walk through a land of vines and overgrown earth that smells of honeysuckle and decay.

The seventh time we pass the blackened tree, a heavy fog descends. I can't see my hand in front of my face, much less any of the others. Which might be a good thing, considering how little any of us have left.

Each time we've gone past, the Storm has taken more. Giving up pieces of myself isn't so hard. But where will it end?

The hunger on Casvian's face, the barely restrained fear on Dalca's, the determination on Izamal's—these things make me worry. The Storm has whittled them to their cores, and now the fog has swallowed them whole.

"Dalca!" Casvian calls. "Izamal?"

"Here." Izamal's voice comes from a few paces away. "Vesper?"

"Here." I reach for him but grasp only air.

"Dalca!" Casvian yells again.

There's no response.

"I'm going after him," Casvian says.

"No—I will," Izamal says, his voice already retreating. "You stay with Vesper."

"Wait!" I tread toward their voices. I don't like the way Izamal's been looking at Dalca.

"He's my responsibility!" Casvian's footsteps fade away.

"Dalca? Izamal?" I shout.

I'm here.

I reach toward Dalca's voice and grasp his wrist.

But it's not his wrist grasped in my fingers. It's the shadow. It so-lidifies into an inscrutable darkness, thickening to the shape of a person, the one visible thing in the fog. And then it turns its featureless face to me.

I can't let go. And from that skin-on-shadow connection, a strange understanding comes to me. It's neither my friend nor my enemy. And yet it's both. Guardian and jailer, protector and executioner, creator and destroyer. It's everything, a wholeness that's indivisible, undefinable.

It's as familiar to me as the formless place that appears when I shut my eyes. The shape of my infinite insides.

"Who are you?" The words disappear into the silence of the Storm, but I know my shadow has heard.

I am your guide. There is no turning back. The Storm is within you now; where you go, it will follow. The only way out is to go further into the Storm, further into you. Down and down you must go, until you descend into the dark heart of the Storm, into the darkest pits of your soul. You must not turn your back on anything that you find. Face it all. Accept it all. Only then may you find what you seek.

"What happens if I can't?"

You must, even if you cannot.

It's not courage that buoys me, but a primal instinct. *Survive.*

My shadow stretches out a hand. I reach for it and keep reaching, my hand touching nothing as I lose my balance.

I fall into the darkness of my shadow, into a darkness that swells as far as the eye can see, through cold wet air that eats my screams, past a hundred other falling girls, each of them twisting toward me, reaching for me, their grasping hands tearing my clothes, their gentle cold kisses stealing the air in my lungs, their teeth biting into my flesh and tearing away the thing that makes the blood beat in my heart. One by one, they pull from me deeper things, memories and dreams and nameless things, until all that is left is my name.

They take that, too.

They set the empty husk that's left on its feet, onto a road made of bones.

Empty of all, the body that was once mine walks on.

There is no sun, no moon, no time. If there's a destination, I don't know it.

Under my feet, the bones turn to sand. It happens so slowly that I don't notice until I stub my toe on a voice. It is a sweet voice, kind and strong and soft and frightened. It is mine.

I pick it up and swallow it.

I find other things. I find faces I once knew. Stories that were once whispered to me. Laughter, promises, a mother's kiss. The blanket my father wrapped around me as he carried me from our home, the day things went so wrong for my parents.

One by one, I pick up the lost pieces of myself. I find dreams, a fistful of seedlings, a wooden doll. My father's chuckle and a golden warmth from before I knew words.

These things fill me up like a sun bursting in my chest; I'm full of light and a weightless warmth.

But there are other things. Things I don't want. A slip of oil that curls around my throat: my terror. A trembling that rattles my bones and tastes of cowardice. And then I come upon a shape I know well. Seven strings that stretch the length of a carved neck, resting on curved rounds. Amma's sitar.

My hand goes to it, but I hesitate.

With just the tips of my fingertips, I touch it. A thrum of pain trembles through me. Sorrow, unending, unyielding.

This I don't want. This I can't take.

You must, even if you cannot.

I take it.

Seven burns meet seven strings. Sorrow crushes me, folds me double.

The faces of those I've let down. Amma and Jem. All the storm-touched who leapt into my life, who I couldn't keep by my side. Their loss hits me over and over again, like waves of an endless sea.

A hundred thousand crystallized tears glitter like diamonds. I pick each and every one up, adding more to their number with every sob.

For a thousand years, I weep, bent double, hand scrambling in the sand to gather my tears.

The end comes slowly, miserably.

I rise, heavier, more real.

And I go on.

I find yet more things. Strange things, unknowable things, vast and boundless secrets from within. I find things that I have never seen, yet I know the shape of them like the ocean knows the shape of the sea-floor. I find mysterious things, a spark of creation and destruction kept deep in the warm dark, and a far stranger thing, a cavernous thing, an inexhaustible and subtle power I can only poorly describe as love. But *love* is such an insufficient word for the potential that purrs within me, an ability to accept and to give and forgive; a transformative power to turn villains into penitents, sufferers into the healed, the abandoned into family. For a second I understand.

I swallow the nameless things — forgetting the wholeness of the understanding as soon as they pass my lips but feeling the shape of them within me.

I become whole. I become me: light and dark and mystery between.

I sink down. The bone-sand rushes over me, and I plug my ears and close my eyes, feeling the earth under me give way and melt into a swamplike sludge. The earth itself swallows me, and I claw my way through, going deeper and deeper, diving through not sand but dark water.

My head breaks the surface of an upside-down pool in a clearing of an ancient forest. I right myself, knowing instinctively that this is as deep as it goes, this is what my father called the heart of the Storm.

Surrounding me is a copse of giant trees; surrounding them is the corpse of a slain serpent. These are trees with trunks so wide it would take a dozen men standing fingertip to fingertip to encircle them. They are old enough to both have earned names and to have earned the right to forget them.

One stands larger than the rest, set apart and forward with its roots dipping into the pool. The greatest tree of all is also a tomb; a woman hangs within a hollow, glasslike core within the wooden trunk, her arms splayed, fixed by branches. A thin branch grows over her mouth.

In the slumbering lines of her face, I see the lines of my own. But she is not me.

I wade through the pool, reaching for her. I tear her from her bindings, wood turning to ash under my fingertips, green glass melting away at my touch.

When the branch falls from her lips, her eyes open with a sudden force, not a blast but a sudden drop. As if her eyelids were shields against the dark: every shadow, every sorrow, every scrap of the nothing between stars.

I flinch at the massive presence within those eyes, half certain my own eyes are going to melt out of my head for daring to look.

"Who are you?"

You know me. Her voice sounds a hundredfold; the trees and the water and the wind lend her their voices.

I meet her gaze, gingerly. It's like looking into a dark mirror. I have her eyes—not the power but the almond shape, the long lashes. The curve of my mouth, the proud length of my nose—both are something like hers. But it can't be. "You're not Ma."

I am. I am the part of her she sacrificed.

"What part?" I ask. Her soft and loving features flicker, like a mask being momentarily lifted. Her face wars with another face, one that's imperious, distant, and far from human. That other face, at once incomprehensibly beautiful and inescapably brutal, is the true face of the Storm.

She gave me her heart. I took the mother. The lover. The wife. All she kept for herself was the conqueror. My chest grows hollow. That means she gave me up. She gave Pa up. I don't say it out loud, but the woman hears.

She gave her heart in exchange for power.

A little voice speaks in my head, a childish, petulant voice, one I thought I'd silenced long ago: *What power could be more important than me?*

She contemplates me at her leisure. *The same power you search for.*

"Can I talk to her?"

The cruel face drops away entirely, features rearranging themselves and stilling into Ma's. The woman reaches out a tentative hand, and I step closer, hoping. She cups my cheek.

"Ma?"

It's a warm and familiar presence that smiles at me through those eyes. I don't know if it's truly Ma, but I want to believe. *"My little darling."* A single voice, Ma's voice, whispers half to the still air, half into my mind.

I have no words—I have too many words. Years and years of words get tangled up in my tongue and stumble before they reach my lips. I cup my hand over hers, soaking in her warmth, her love, the strange foreign-familiar feeling of a mother's touch.

I weep like a baby.

Why did she make such a stupid choice? Why didn't she choose to stay with me?

"You know. You know, my love. I see your heart; you are of my blood. We do not make peace with the great miseries of the world. We do not forgive injustice. We fight. I loved you, but I never could have stayed." It hurts. I was never enough for her. *"You would have made the same choice."*

My insides grow cold. *"I'm not you, Ma."* It's a familiar thought, but for the first time, I don't find the comparison in Ma's favor.

Ma — the shadow of her, at least — grows soft, her lips parting in a bittersweet smile. *"You have my strength at least, and I am glad."*

The childhood stories I spun about Ma fade as I stand before her. I'd imagined someone who would fight for me, who would wrap me in her arms, who'd smell a little like cardamom. I drink in all of Ma, knowing we would have butted heads, knowing nothing would have been simple between us, knowing I would have loved her.

Her smile falls and her eyes tense just like mine do before I cry. *"Vesper . . . I meant to come back to you."*

I crumple. "Ma —" The hand against my cheek turns cold. I let go, knowing that when I look up I'll find Ma replaced by the other face, her features replaced with ones savage and breathtaking.

"Who are you?" I scrub my face dry.

She waits until I meet her eyes, so like Ma's.

I am the Forgotten.

The things she doesn't say echo over and under her words, in a thousand borrowed voices: *I am the moon I am the shadow of the sun I am creation I am destruction I am monstrous I am unknowable.*

The echoes fade, leaving me shivering in the shadow of the giant trees. "What do you want from me?"

She laughs a thousand laughs, some mocking, some joyful. *You have shown strength. With eyes unflinching, you faced yourself and embraced all of what you beheld. You found me bound and chose to free me. For all of this, you may ask of me what you desire.*

For some reason, I find myself thinking of the old temple in the fifth, of the rubble on the ground, the proto-ikon of the tree in concentric circles. I'd assumed that ancient statue was of the Great King's other face, but I was wrong.

"You aren't the Great King. You aren't his other face, either. You're not the King of Wrath."

I am the Forgotten.

"A Great Queen."

Yes. Her voices ring triumphant.

I tremble. "I don't want anything." My mind fills with the hundreds of curses I've witnessed, all of them cruel. If the Storm is hers, I have to assume that whatever I ask from her will be granted with malicious purpose.

Ma's strength was the kind that meant she could sacrifice anything for the power to change the world. She walked into the Storm for that power, met the scattered parts of herself, and took only what she deemed worthy. She took the hard, the strong, and left the soft.

But I'm only made up of soft parts. Would I give up the sorrow that still feels like a kick in the teeth? Or the doubt that dogs every choice I make, that worries I'll never do something right? What of the electric and tentative thing between me and Dalca that makes me strangely conscious and fluttery and unsure?

Or the softest things, the love I hold for Amma, for Pa, for each of the stormtouched who came into my life and left me a little sadder when they left? The love I hold for my home, for the warmth of sundust tea and a smile from under a mosscloth cloak, for the thrill and beauty of ikonomancy, even for the way sunlight glints off the palace and how the Wardana shine against the dark.

I took them, I accepted them, and I'm loath to give them up.

You want nothing? Do not lie. She reaches out a long finger, and with the very tip, she touches my forehead.

Thoughts, naïve and foolish, spill from my mind into hers. *I want to save my Pa I want to save Dalca I want to save his mother I want to save my mother I want to save myself.*

Things that I have no business wanting: *I want to free Izamal of his anger I want to free this place of the Regia's hold I want to free the world of the Storm.*

I want to gather everything and everyone into my heart and protect it all.

I'm embarrassed and angry at being exposed. At being forced to face the truth that, at my core, I'm as soft and idealistic as a child. "You can't use that against me," I stammer, as if I have any power here at all.

You do have power here, a great one. All her voices drop away. She speaks with a single, thoughtful one. *I will give you something.*

"In exchange for what?"

I ask nothing from you but that you accept it. This gift will demand everything of you; if you will master it, you must face it as you have faced yourself.

Vertigo clutches my stomach, the memory of falling into my shadow, of being torn apart, of having to glue myself together again. "What is it?"

It was once called my greatest curse. But with it, what you want may come to be.

"Why give it to me?"

Those who asked for it were not worthy. You, who have not, may yet prove to be.

"But why? You don't owe me anything."

Images come to me, of a man bathed in golden light, the twist of his handsome smile, his hand reaching for an impossibly beautiful woman, their fingers intertwining over the life in her belly, the fire under his skin rising to his fingertips, his red-gold magic wrapping around them in a cocoon made strong by their togetherness, by how they balanced each other, by their love. The Great King and the forgotten Queen.

Perhaps, by your hand, what I desire may come to pass.

I remember the sense of longing I felt when I stepped into the Storm. It was her longing. But this is not the longing of a gentle mother. She is soft and yet hard, loving and cruel, creator and destroyer. She is strong, the strongest woman I'm likely to meet. And yet she misses her King, her love.

She offers me power, the likes of which I've never known. Pa's knowledge is his power; Dalca and Izamal had thought to access it through me. This would be different; this would be power of my own. Power to save Pa, save Dalca, save everyone. My mouth fills with the taste of blood.

The lines of her face harden as she bears down on me. *Will you bear this, greatest of all my curses?*

Yes.

"Yes." I say, repeating myself a thousand times more as it pours into me, prickly and clawing and healing and shining and terrible and wonderful. Every inch of it, I accept. I feel it gather within me. It becomes a stream of darkly iridescent water coursing through me, a torrent that wraps around my core and spreads into a thousand shifting rivers that run under my skin like veins, like a pattern, a mark that shifts and morphs, one that can't be seen, one that can't be drawn.

This is her curse; this is her gift.

Another heartbeat echoes mine, a thrumming in my chest, and I don't understand it. There's something in me, but it doesn't feel like power.

The Queen smiles, but it is monstrous. Her nails grow into claws, and blackness bleeds into the whites of her eyes. She lays a clawed hand on the head of the dead serpent. Expanding like ripples in a still lake, life grows within the snake.

When it is made whole, it blinks its reptilian eyes and unfolds leathery wings.

The time has come for you to return to the world from which you came.

"Not alone," I tell her. "Not without those who came with me."

Her displeasure radiates from her stilled smile.

Only more darkness awaits you in this cage of clouds. Do not tarry.

I grab hold of the winged serpent's scales as darkness seeps into the clearing, and I scrabble for a hold as the serpent leaps into the air, leaving the still pond and the circle of trees far below. But no matter how many layers of darkness the winged serpent puts between me and the Queen, I can't shake the feeling that she's watching me.

CHAPTER 22

The serpent hurtles through layers of darkness; each one we pass is like a breath caressing my face. I squint through the wind, catching glimpses of a hundred of the Storm's guises: a midnight lake that eats the stars from the sky, a desert of black sands, a jungle where vines fall like women's hair.

We fly at breakneck speed, slithering past a dozen nightmares until we find ours. A mountain and its mirror image, stacked on top of each other so from afar they appear to make a great diamond balancing on a single point.

The serpent dips into a nosedive, rushing faster and faster toward the widest part of the diamond, toward a great face carved on its side, with a gaping mouth that stretches into a tunnel.

The tunnel is too small, but the serpent doesn't slow. I wedge my fingers under its scales, desperate to hold on. We're squeezed as we enter, stone scraping my back, until we burst into a wide space and I lose my grip; its scales come free in my hands.

I fall, screaming. Scales plink against the stone walls of the space around me, and a pale something, like a length of fabric, follows me down. The serpent is shedding its skin and *me with it.*

I tumble down into the dark. The snakeskin brushes my hand, and

I grab it and wrap it around me before I hit the ground with a thud. I get to my feet, hurting less than I ought to. The snakeskin gives off a pale silver light, just enough to see by.

I'm in a pit. There's only one way forward: a tunnel carved into the stone, lined with stalagmites that glint like teeth. A dim light comes from the end of the tunnel, and I make my way to it.

A lush garden greets me, full of trees heavy with fruit, lit by fireflies that glow with the colors of dusk. The air is sweet, intoxicating. This is so much gentler than the road of bones the Storm cooked up for me.

Casvian sits on a rock at the edge of a pool, gazing into the deep. Velvet-petaled flowers, white as salt, surround him. He's gotten back his Wardana uniform and his cloak, and the blood-red seems to seep into the white flowers.

He looks like a painting, like he belongs here.

I step closer, sending fireflies flying as grass crunches underfoot. "Casvian?" He doesn't answer, too entranced by what he sees. The sweet, honeyed smell is stronger here. I can't get enough of it. I want to pluck a flower, inhale its scent deep; I want to lie down in this idyllic meadow and dream.

A different sort of danger grows here. I cover my nose and mouth with a sleeve and peer over Casvian's shoulder into the surface of the pool.

Ripples mar the surface. Casvian's reflection is strange. It has broader shoulders, a spattering of pale stubble on a square jaw, a nose that's been broken at least once. It's a Casvian with all the softness pared away, a vision of brutish power. His Wardana uniform melts into one of black and gold, heavily armored as befits a fighter, not an ikonomancer. Ragno Haveli appears in the reflection, and I start, glancing over my shoulder and finding no one. In the reflection, he bequeaths the warrior-Casvian his scythe, the same one he held to Pa's neck not so long ago.

The real Casvian stares down at all this, his eyes wide as a child's. I never thought of him as anything but proud to a fault. Not once did I imagine him wanting to be someone else. But something about this place puts his prickliness in context. Of course he'd want to be someone else. He's pathologically rude, twice as cocky as he has any right to be, incurably and unapologetically classist—speaking kindly, he's a pompous ass of mythic proportions. He's like a half-rotted apple; by the time all the spoiled bits have been cut out, there really isn't much left. I catch myself in the middle of a tirade, feeling the annoyance I have for him growing into something darker. The garden wants the seed of irritation within me to grow into hate.

I get ahold of myself. I think of how he volunteered to follow Dalca into the Storm despite the fear he couldn't quite hide.

I have to see him for who he is. The jerk and the loyal friend both. If I can do that, I can save him. I have to be kind. I have to understand.

"You're an idiot, Casvian Haveli."

Dreamily, Casvian tilts his head toward me, his eyes still locked into the pool. I can't quite bring myself to offer him platitudes like *you're perfect the way you are! Never change, Casvian!*

"What now?" I ask. "You spend the rest of your life staring at this guy?"

"I'll trade places with him," Casvian murmurs in a voice half convinced. I imagine him trapped in the pool, watching from a watery prison as his dreamt-up idea of a perfect son takes his place. He doesn't deserve that. No one does.

"Why would you ever want that?" Yet I already know the answer;

he wants his father to be proud. I begin to make sense of his loyalty to Dalca, who values him for who he is and treats him like a brother.

"Is that too much to ask for?" he says on a breath, not to me but to himself, and as the surface of the water ripples, the warrior-Casvian swings his scythe in a complicated maneuver that showcases his prowess. He falls into a fighting stance, and behind him, a shadow in the depths of the pool mirrors his move. As warrior-Casvian leaps and swings through a series of fighting stances — each flawlessly executed — the figure in the back mimics his moves perfectly, drawing closer with every parry and thrust, until his face resolves into that of Ragno Haveli. They move in a beautiful and exact synchronicity, warrior-Casvian's armor slowly darkening to match the black and gold of his father's.

Poor man. "You're forgetting that Dalca needs you. The you that's a brilliant ikonomancer. The clever you."

If he hears me, he doesn't show it. A hollow certainty takes hold of my heart: if I fail here, if I can't get him to hear me, we won't get out of the Storm in one piece, much less with the Regia's mark.

"Where's your pride, Casvian? That thing isn't better than you."

The two warriors in the reflection fall out of sync, but Ragno corrects warrior-Casvian with a sneer and a prod of the scythe. Warrior-Casvian falls back into line, but his movements are jerky, stilted, like a puppet's — he's invisibly leashed to Ragno, doomed to follow his every move.

I grab his chin and turn his face toward me. His dark pupils eclipse his irises, but some silver returns as he struggles to focus.

"Is that what you want, you foolish boy? Your father already has an army of pawns eager to earn his approval and feed his vanity." His eyes drift toward the pool. I block his view with my body. "There's a reason Dalca chose you, why he trusts you over everyone else—and it has nothing to do with how you twirl a scythe. Casvian, come on. Where's the confident asshole I know and despise?"

His brows furrow, and a little blue comes back into his eyes. But he peers over my shoulder, the reflection proving irresistible.

"How can you admire him, when you can do so much more with just a stub of charcoal?"

Tears of frustration distort my vision.

If I can't even help him, how can I do anything?

Cas draws his dreamy gaze to my face. I hold my breath.

His features pull into the ghost of a familiar scowl, but then something over my shoulder catches his attention. The pool.

In a sudden move, he shoves me behind him. I trip, falling into a bed of flowers.

Casvian stands at the edge of the water, his hands clenched into fists. He's fallen into a fighting stance. I don't know if he can win against what the Storm has in store for him, but the look in his eyes says it's his battle.

The warrior-Casvian touches the water. His hand pushes against the surface, and the water bends like mercury. It holds for a heartbeat.

The reflection's hand breaks through in a scattering of droplets that catch the light like jewels.

Casvian reaches and grips the red-gloved hand, dragging the rest of his perfected self out of the water.

The dream rises in full armor, Ragno Haveli's scythe strapped to his back, wearing an inhuman expression of cold confidence. He reaches for Casvian's throat, his mouth open, speaking in a dozen voices.

I'll live your perfect life, brother. All the things you can only dream, I will become.

In a motion smooth as silk, with the speed and finesse of an expert sitarist, Casvian digs his fingers into the dirt, draws an ikon, and wrenches free a jagged dagger of crystallized earth. With a flick of his wrist, the dagger flies, piercing his dream's heart. "Keep the dreams, brother. I have others."

The slain dream wears a look of fury as he falls, mercury blood spurting in an arc, dousing the water, the flowers, the grass. His head rests on a bed of velvet petals, white becoming silver as they soak up his blood. His body sinks into dark water marbled with pale lines of dream-blood.

The fireflies blink out one by one.

Casvian's dagger floats upon the water, until ghostly hands wrap their fingers around the crystal hilt and reclaim it for the depths.

A strange new light burns in Casvian's eyes as he turns to me. "That's enough dawdling, don't you think?" He reaches out a hand, palm up, not unlike the hand he extended to his dream. I grab it, letting him pull me to my feet. "We'd better find our dear prince. I have a feeling he'll need us."

"Casvian . . ." I trail off, biting back a dozen too-sincere things.

He gives me the tiniest approximation of a smile. "Go on, I'll follow you."

The darkness shrouding the garden gives way before us; an ominous chasm appears. A distant scream sounds from within.

I look back over my shoulder, getting one last glimpse of the garden and its honeyed temptations as the last of the fireflies goes dark. A breeze, soft as a breath, touches the back of my neck.

Do not tarry.

I inhale. I'm about to jump into the chasm when a hand slips into mine. "Thanks," Cas whispers into the dark.

We jump together.

Casvian's hand tightens around mine. His cloak spreads wide be-hind him, slowing his fall. I hold fast, my feet dangling in the air, pray-ing he won't drop me.

My thoughts go to Dalca, to the last time I flew. He'd better be alive.

I gasp as my toes touch solid earth, blinking into the inky dark. Cas's fingertips brush mine as he lets go, and I strain to hear him breath-ing, to reassure myself that the dark hasn't eaten him up. Light flickers to life beside me from within Cas's palm, casting his face in shades of blue.

He holds out his ikonlight, and it glows brighter.

We stand in a cathedral of a cave, so large its edges are lost in shadow. But the ikonlight catches on countless dim golden pinpricks, as if the walls are studded with golden gemstones.

"What is this?" Casvian's voice is pitched low.

I squint at one of the golden things. It blinks back at me.

Eyes. Countless golden eyes.

Casvian draws a breath through his teeth. From all around us come the sounds of beasts: low panting and snarling, the click of claws on stone, the rustling of fur. Golden-eyed monsters, hundreds of them, awake and closing in.

This is a nightmare, and I know whose it is.

"Izamal?"

A whimper. I step toward the sound before realizing it came from no human.

An admonishment comes in growls, screeches, hisses. *Who does she call for? She doesn't call for you. She knows you not.*

I'd braced myself, but the condemnation isn't meant for me.

"Izamal?" Casvian calls. "It's me. Don't fall for it, you hear me?"

I blink at him, at the worry in his voice.

They know not what hungers within you, the thing you have fed with every lie, every moment you set your vengeance aside. Will you show them what you are? Will you show them the writhing dark?

"Stop it!" I shout.

I hear another whimper, and this time I run toward it. "Izamal?"

A shape peels itself off the floor. A beast from storybooks: wildcat from a place I've never seen and a time beyond what I know. Two curved saber teeth glint and gleam from its jaw, as thick and sharp as daggers. Silver fur ripples over limbs thick with muscle. A dream creature with mournful golden eyes. Distressingly human eyes.

Casvian drops to his knees and grabs the beast's head. "Snap out of it, Dazera. *Right now.*"

The fur peels back and reveals Izamal's face, looking wild and terrified. He's gone deeper than Cas did; he looked into himself and got lost. Casvian gasps, and the beast's face folds back over Izamal's.

The monsters press closer, and their beastly voices grow louder.

Never again will you turn back. Never again will you give in to your weakness.

You were born with the gift of power—now you will accept it.

You were taught rage—now you will exercise it.

The beast within you hungers—now you must let it feed.

"Don't listen, Iz," I say, dropping to my knees as Cas throws an arm out, keeping me from getting closer. "Please. What she offers—this power isn't worth it."

I reach for him, and the beast growls, its pupils narrowing to slits, snapping its fangs with enough force to break bone. I jerk away, scrambling back.

At once the creature recoils. "Stay away," Izamal says, surfacing, his voice tapering into a rumble as he disappears once more into the animal, he and it fighting for dominance. "I can't hold it back," he gets out through teeth only half human. "I won't."

"Hold what?" I whisper.

His eyes look out at me from the beast's face, wet with tears.

The Queen's gift beats under my heart, and I taste the darkness within Izamal, a bitter and scorching hatred; all the small injustices he's witnessed and holds in his heart where they crackle like embers; a cruel, oily fury that paints his insides, one that calls him a coward for doing so little; a deep chasm-like loathing for those who have power and don't do more, who hurt those with less, who are responsible for his sister's death. Dalca.

I taste how desperately he wants what the Storm promises, even as he fears it—he aches with yearning for the power to punish, to have his vengeance, to be stronger than the cruel. He wants to become the most fearsome thing of all.

Under all of that is the smallest flicker of something else: he doesn't want to be hurt ever again.

I suck in a breath. "You won't hurt me."

The dagger-toothed creature pounces onto me. My back hits the ground, and the wind is knocked out of me. His clawed paw presses down on my throat, and I can't breathe. I dig my nails into his chest and push with all my effort, and all my strength isn't enough.

"Do you not fear me?" Izamal growls with human lips and slitted eyes, his claw-tipped hands around my throat. "Do you doubt what I can do?"

My vision has started going gray around the corners when Casvian tackles Izamal. I hear them hit the ground as I twist onto my hands and knees, coughing and gasping, filling my lungs with as much air as they'll hold.

The pounding in my ears is drowned out by a thousand inhuman voices, all growling and howling at once. A thousand screams, a thousand horrible things, all overlapping.

NO MORE WILL YOU BE A COWARD NO MORE WILL YOU BE WEAK

Casvian stands between me and Izamal as if protecting me. But Izamal's curled into a shaking ball. He isn't about to attack anyone. I crawl to him, close enough to make out his words over the bestial cacophony.

You let your people die — you gave them knives when they needed a hero — you left them behind — you let them die — you let her die —

Izamal whimpers, clawed hands clasped over his ears. "I didn't — I'm sorry, I'm sorry — she wanted me to — I wanted to do better — I couldn't — I'm not enough — please, oh please . . ."

No longer will you forsake your blood — no longer will her killer walk free —

"Don't listen to them!" I scream. Casvian pulls me back.

"I don't think —" he yells in my ear, but even so he's drowned out.

You did nothing when your father hurt your mother. You did nothing when he killed Nashi —

My voice catches in my throat.

You could have saved them all and you didn't —

All you had to do was take one life —

YOU LET HER SUFFER YOU LET HER DIE YOU GAVE HER NO VENGEANCE

The voices devolve into furious noise.

Izamal screams, one long, furious howl.

The beasts join him. Wisps of dark cloud whirl around him, sinking into him, sharpening his fear, amplifying his hate as he gives in to the Storm.

"I'll rip his throat out and drink his blood," Izamal bellows in a dark voice far more monstrous than all the rest.

Yes, the voices hiss, satisfied. *We see your rage, we see your wrath. Wreak your vengeance. Dig your claws into his heart, tear it from his chest, feel its last beat within your fist. We give you power, we give you fury. You are his reaper.*

Go. Take your justice.

Izamal, half man, half beast, bounds past us, through the thousand-faced darkness. He runs, dogged by his demons, driven by nightmares toward some wicked end.

"We have to save him," I whisper.

"Save him?" Casvian asks with extraordinary calmness. "Or save Dalca from him?"

He doesn't know of Izamal's brave, futile rebellion. He doesn't know Izamal was playing a part. He doesn't know that I believed in Iz, that I still do.

"I won't give up on him," I say. "I'll save him on my own."

Cas's gaze is fixed on the shadows that swallowed Iz. "You're not on your own."

CHAPTER 23

We chase Izamal through passages studded with torn serpent scales. The Queen's curse thrums under my skin like a warning.

Every now and then, we catch a glimpse of Izamal; sometimes he's all beast, sometimes he's a feral meld of monster and man. But he's never all human.

The way slopes ever more steeply downward. The dark presses in on us, squeezing Casvian's ikonlight down till it glows as small and dim as a single blue firefly. The air grows blistering and humid, becoming thick with the smell of smoke and decay. Each half-blind step takes us deeper into the unknown. My courage only takes me so far, and after a while my hope dies too, until all that's keeping me going is bullheaded pride. I haven't come this far to give up now.

Casvian never hesitates. I didn't expect him to: Dalca is Casvian's liege lord and north star. Burn away all his impurities, and the purest, simplest form of Casvian would be his crystallized loyalty to Dalca. What keeps him putting one foot in front of the other as the way grows grimmer is love for his chosen brother.

The Queen's curse hums inside me. It throbs under every heartbeat, and it courses through my veins with my blood. But what is it?

"Why would he turn into a beast?" Casvian interrupts my thoughts.

I'm cautiously glad that Casvian still thinks of Izamal as more than something to be hunted. "Maybe that's the only way he felt he could have the power to make a difference."

"That's absurd."

I bite my tongue, force my anger back.

"I mean, he has power. He's Wardana."

"Wardana enough to sacrifice himself, sure. But not enough for you and Dalca to let him in. He's your token fifth-ringer. Don't you think he knows where he stands?"

"We let him in. He helped us capture your father, if you recall."

"You didn't tell Iz where you kept my father, or even why you wanted him."

"Well, obviously. That was delicate information."

"You never trusted him."

Cas runs his hands through his hair. "With all this, it seems I've got good reason, doesn't it?"

"He fought beside you for years. He walked into the Storm with you. All he wants is to save the fifth-ringers—to help the people who most need it. What more would it take for him to earn your trust?"

Something dark flickers across Cas's eyes. A wisp of the Storm. "He knew who you were when he helped you, didn't he?"

I hesitate, not wanting to get Izamal in worse trouble, but it's answer enough.

Cas laughs low. "You're asking me to trust someone who lied to me."

"If you'd trusted him, maybe he never would've had to lie."

"You can't know that."

I don't answer. The path in front of us grows clear as the haze begins to lift.

Cas's voice comes softly from beside me. "For what it's worth. I . . . if you're right, and maybe you are . . . I'd be sorry. Because . . . I've always admired him."

I glance up at him, surprised. He tilts his head, giving me a sad, crooked smile.

We make our way through the tunnels, and I consider him. I don't know if I'll ever truly forgive the man who threw my plants on the floor—but I'm also getting the feeling that Cas might be changing into a different man, one I might not hate. Or maybe it's me who's changing. I don't know if I like that.

Casvian halts, throwing an arm out.

Izamal stands silhouetted where the tunnel ends, a man drawn in black against a red landscape. His golden eyes reflect the glint of Casvian's ikonlight before he turns and leaps, dropping out of view.

"Izamal!" I shout, sprinting and skidding to a stop at the edge of the tunnel. I brace against a blast of heat.

Before me is a massive hollow space, big enough to fit the entirety of the first ring. A shadow-black lake spans the length of it, red-gold flames licking along its surface.

In the center of the lake is an obsidian pyramid, and at its peak, teetering, is a boulder. A man grips the boulder's sides, dwarfed by its size, single-handedly keeping it from falling down the pyramid's side into the lake of fire.

I don't have to see the man's face to know it's Dalca.

I peer over the edge of the tunnel's mouth. There's a thirty-foot drop down to a crescent of black sand beach that rims the lake. Izamal claws his way down the stone face.

Casvian takes it all in from beside me. He unclips the cloak from his shoulders and throws it over mine. "You can't handle Izamal. Not like this. Pay attention, now. The cloak's kinnari feathers do the hard work of flying. You merely have to activate it—that's a ninety-degree turn clockwise—and you'll have to steer with the dial—that's another turn. Up, down, left, right, it toggles, see? Usually the ikons sewn into the collar would let you steer with a gauntlet, but I'll be needing mine. It's not that hard, anyway."

I clasp the cloak closed and touch the ikondial. The lake seems suddenly impossibly vast.

"I'm trusting you to save him." His eyes bore into mine.

"I'm trusting you, too," I say.

"I know. Ready, apprentice?" He watches me turn the ikondial. The cloak billows out around me, like the feathers can taste the air, like they want to fly.

I take a breath, calming the flutters in my chest. I've always wanted this. "Ready."

Casvian pushes me out of the tunnel, and I scream. The cloak doesn't let me plummet; it rides the air. I grab the dial at my throat and turn it. It pops out, allowing me to toggle it in all directions. I push it up, and dash into the air.

Below, Casvian draws an ikon on his hands and sidles down the rock face. His hands seem to stick to the wall, and he gains quickly on Izamal. I have to trust Casvian to save him, like he's trusting me with Dalca.

I steer myself in starts and jumps toward the pyramid. The lake gives off billows of heat, and I'm thrown off course every time I hit one. They come faster the closer I get to the pyramid. One billow pushes me down toward the black lake, and my toes brush a rising flame.

My stomach dives as I shoot back up. I am not exactly getting the hang of this.

The pyramid looms larger and larger, filling my vision with endless black as I close in.

A gust of air shoves me too close; I'm going to smack right into the glossy black surface.

I twist my body in midair, and my feet hit first. The cloak propels me, and I sprint up the side of the pyramid, screaming.

The top hurtles toward me. I twist the ikondial two turns counter-clockwise, and the cloak dies, but my own momentum carries me forward. My knees bang into the pyramid first, and I begin to slide down until my nails find purchase in a crack. My toes grab hold, and for a moment I'm still and safe.

Under my hands the pyramid's surface is both warm and cold, firm as stone and soft as ash. Wishing I knew an ikon to make my hands stick, I climb up inch by inch, until I reach the tiny plateau where the pyramid's tip flattens out.

A massive boulder, twice as tall as the tallest Wardana, teeters over the edge. Dalca braces it, keeping it from falling—but it dwarfs him so completely that I can't comprehend how he's stopping it. I follow his trembling legs down to where he's dug his feet into precarious foot-holds.

Bulging veins streak along the shaking muscles of his arms. Some-where along the way, he's lost his cloak and outer armor. A vein pulses in his gritted jaw. Sweat drips from his chin, along the ridge of his nose, from a curled lock of hair. He grips the side of the boulder with splayed hands. Streaks of blood paint the stone where his nails have torn away. Blood flows freely from his raw fingertips.

"Dalca," I whisper in horror.

I drag my gaze from Dalca to the boulder, only to notice it isn't just a boulder. On the topside is a miniaturized seven-ringed city in sharp detail, rife with the motion of ant-sized people going about their business, unaware of the giant propping up their world.

The ground is cracked under his reddened feet.

His lower leg shifts, and I see something half hidden by the boulder —a small opening set in the flat top of the pyramid with a narrow set of stairs leading within. It's child-sized; we'd have to bend and squeeze ourselves in.

I get to my feet, gingerly. The plateau is barely three feet across, and most of that is occupied.

If Dalca lets go of the boulder, he can go inside. He's holding on so tightly that it's clear it's not obvious to him—or perhaps even so, he can't let go of this miniature version of our city.

But if I had to give up all of me—my memories, my voice, my dreams—the Storm won't let Dalca hold on to this.

"Dalca!" I shout, inching closer.

He flicks his eyes to me.

I soften my voice. "You have to let go."

"I can't," he grits out. "This is mine. My city. My duty."

"You're going to kill yourself."

The boulder slides an inch, and he roars with the effort of holding it still. His whole body is strung taut, so rigid it could be carved from stone.

"I can do this." It's not bravado speaking. He believes it with the desperation of someone who has no choice but to believe. His muscles tremble like a plucked sitar string. He's going to die like this. He's *willing* to die like this.

Gold blooms at his fingertips, like ink spreading across his skin, forming lines that streak across his hands, up his wrists. The lines surge up his arms, disappearing down into his clothes, slashing up across his neck, curling across his face. The Regia's mark.

Hope rises in me—has he done it? Has he found it?

But the gold is mottled with Storm-black. It wisps into cloud and reforms. This isn't a real ikonmark, but something from Dalca's mind, from his fears. I reach out to touch his arm, as gingerly as I can manage. His skin jerks under my fingers, as if he aborted a flinch. He's burning up.

He makes a sound like a sob.

"Dalca, you have to let it fall."

"I won't be the one who fails."

I swallow, understanding. Dalca sees his place in line amongst the Regias of old, amongst their golden death masks. He's the last in an unbroken chain—and this is the pressure he bears.

"This isn't real."

"If I let this go, what chance does the real thing have?"

"It's a test. You have to let go. You need to go down there, into the pyramid." I say, pointing. "I'll go with you."

Dalca doesn't say a thing. His fingers slide, his grip made slippery with blood and fear. He blinks away sweat and tears, his eyes wide with emotion.

"Do you trust me?"

"I don't know," he answers.

Slowly enough that he sees it coming, I lower my hands over his eyes. I whisper to him. "It's okay. It's not real. We'll protect the real one. I'm with you."

He swallows.

I widen my stance, bracing myself as best I can.

"Come toward me. Let it fall."

He shifts his weight and lets go, his back hitting my chest. Dalca collapses into my arms, and I lower us to the plateau. He cries out as the boulder tilts, then plummets, thudding down the side of the pyramid, breaking apart with each thud, until nothing's left but a thousand shattered pieces that hang in the air like glittering dust.

Dalca takes a shaky breath and pulls himself together. He peers over the edge of the opening, into the dark.

I hold out my hand, and he takes it. He lowers himself down, squeezing my hand once before letting go, and I follow after him. A dozen steps into the depths — far enough to see that there's no reprieve from the dark and just far enough to start having second thoughts — the stairs vanish under our feet.

We fall.

CHAPTER 24

$\mathbf{M}$id-fall, he reaches for me, and our fingertips brush, once, twice; he grabs my hand and pulls me to him. Fighting the wind, I bring my hand to the cloak's clasp and twist the ikondial. The cloak billows wide, catching the wind and slowing our fall.

We hit the ground and throw up a whirlwind of ash.

Dalca unwraps his arms from around me. I peer though the ash, at the opening a hundred feet above us. Red-tinted light falls from the opening in a single column, illuminating a platform raised high above the ground. I squint up at it, but whatever's there can't be seen from below.

Dalca makes for the platform, and I follow him up the stone stairs set into its side. With each step I take, a flurry of ash rises. A speck of ash lands on my palm before it wisps away into stormcloud.

I smother my gasp as I reach the top, a step after Dalca.

A stone coffin, carefully sculpted to resemble the person inside. Dalca wipes the ash from the face. The golden face is cracked, lines spiderwebbing across its eyes and lips. Familiar eyes. Lips I've tasted.

The coffin wears Dalca's death mask.

Dalca stares down at it, wide-eyed. It's not a perfect likeness; the golden mask has a cruel twist to its lips and a deep furrow between its brows. I rub my thumb across sharp golden cheeks, feeling lines carved thinly. Lines that curl across the cheeks, to the corners of the eyes, up the center line of the lower lip. This is Dalca the Regia.

Dalca begins to say something, but I shush him, listening hard.

There. The sound is muffled, but it's one I know well from Amma's. A quiet, secret sobbing.

Dalca shoots me an alarmed look.

Bending over the coffin, I touch my ear to the stone. Dalca mirrors me, his eyes locked with mine as we listen.

The sobbing comes from within; someone's trapped inside.

Dalca rests his bloodied hands on the lid, steeling himself. I hesitate, but he shoves it open, and the stone lid crashes down in a cloud of ash.

A boy, no more than five years old, weeps inside the coffin, curled up so tight that I can't make out his face from under his bird's nest of black hair.

He rubs his eyes, blinking long, dark lashes, and then he tilts his head up at us. His tearstained eyes are painfully blue.

He reaches his tiny hands for us. Dalca nearly leaps back, a strange expression coloring his face.

"It's him. The boy from before." His whispers echo in the silence. "What is this?"

The voice rings out from everywhere, from every speck of dust, from the depths of the earth under our feet, from every dark shadow lurking in the corners of our sight. *This is a test of your worth.*

A serpent of ghostly pale stormcloud slithers out of the shadows. It wraps the long length of its milk-white body around the platform, encircling us once, twice, thrice. The serpent turns to us with ancient and cruel eyes, eyes I met once before at the edge of an upside-down pool. The Queen.

The serpent bends her head toward Dalca.

Tell me, princeling, who are you?

Dalca meets her scrutiny with regal composure. "I am Dalca Zabulon Illusora. I am the son of the Regia. I am the last of the Illusoras, next in line for the throne. The Wardana call me leader."

Is that so?

"Yes."

Dalca says nothing of the boy I know, nothing of the boy who took Pa from me, nothing of the boy who spoke of committing a thousand small evils to do what he must do, nothing of the proud boy who stole a kiss, who swept me up above the clouds, nothing of the boy brave enough to walk into the Storm to save his city.

The serpent flicks her tongue. *What a hollow boy.*

The child in the coffin watches, stifling his sniffles. He scrubs tears away when he catches me looking, fixing me with a scowl that speaks of lonely determination. He's a little older than I was when Ma went into the Storm, but Dalca has at least a year on me. This is Dalca at the moment his mother became Regia, when he lost her, when he learnt what was in his future.

This is when he was last allowed to be afraid, to be just a boy.

The Queen's curse trembles under my skin, unspooling Dalca's heart for me so I may read what is written upon it.

He's being pulled apart by fears. He's terrified of being the weak link in the Illusora chain, of failing the city and his people, of being a poor leader. He's terrified of what it means to be Regia, what it means to give up your soul. There's only one way out: if he saves his mother, if he gives her the power to be a great Regia, then he'll save his city and never see himself enslaved in his own body. I can almost taste the way the Storm stokes his fears, the way something dark grows in his heart.

I reach for him, the grown Dalca, the Dalca I know, and grab his neck so he looks at me, not the serpent, not the child, not the darkness surrounding us.

"Vesper," he breathes.

His skin is hot, and he smells of blood and smoke and sweat. "I know you have to do this. I know you'll ask to save your mother. But please, Dalca. Be careful what you give up. Don't give up your heart." My voice is heavy with unshed tears for Ma, for Izamal. Dalca's not my north star. He doesn't give my life meaning. But I won't lose him.

A dark, sweet expression appears on his face; his eyes soften, but his lips gain a dismissive twist. I brush my thumb across his cheek. He has to hear me.

Dalca presses his forehead against mine. My cheeks grow warm with the heat radiating from him. "What's my heart worth?"

I press my lips to his.

If he can't do it on his own, that's okay. I have enough willpower for the both of us. Let him take what he needs from me. I'll give him the courage to face himself. I'll give him the strength to peel back the claws the Storm has wrapped around his heart.

Dalca pulls back. "Okay," he whispers against my lips. "I'll save it."

Enough, girl.

The serpent strikes, fangs out, and we jump apart. She pushes between us, widening the gap with the bulk of her body. I hold Dalca's gaze as she slithers around me, wrapping me in coils of milk-pale scales and dragging me off the platform, setting me down in the dark.

The serpent slithers forward, separating me and him.

Dalca stands alone atop the platform. The child clambers out of the coffin and reaches for his hand.

"Vesper?"

"I'm not hurt."

The serpent tastes the air with her forked tongue. *Why have you come here, hollow prince?*

"I came to save my city." His voice is loud and clear.

But under it, the child whispers, *"I'm scared. I want my mother back. I don't want to be Regia."*

Dalca jerks away from the child. "No—that's not true. That's not what I'm asking for."

The child's whispers go on in an endless stream of fears. *"I don't want to be alone. I can't fail. I have to be perfect. I have to be the best Wardana. I have to be the best heir. I have to be Regia. I'm scared. I want somebody to love me. I don't want to be Reg—"*

"STOP!" Fury rolls off Dalca in waves. "That's not me."

The serpent laughs, and her tail slinks around the boy, raising him into the air.

The child's little arms grip the serpent's scales, but he's too brave to cry out. With wide blue eyes, he meets Dalca's gaze.

Dalca looks away first.

A dull horror expands in my chest. "No! Dalca—"

The serpent throws the boy in the air and unhitches her jaw, opening wide. She swallows child-Dalca whole and snaps her mouth shut. A lump slides down her throat.

I clap a hand over my mouth as dread makes my stomach sink. Oh, no, no. Oh, Dalca.

The serpent hisses. *You wish to save your city.*

"Yes," Dalca says.

Tell me what ails it.

"My mother—" He stops, tries again. "The Regia is dying. I don't know why. No one does. I need the Regia's mark, the true mark, one that will give her strength."

I have the power to save your mother, the serpent says slyly. *Do you wish this power?*

"What do you want in exchange?"

Her tongue flicks out in a strangely human gesture, as if she's licking her lips. *You have given me much, though you value it not.*

Dalca crosses his arms as if protecting himself.

The serpent laughs, a strange sound in a dozen voices—crows cawing, the crush of a tidal wave, an earthquake rumbling, a rodent's chittering, and underneath it all a woman's soft, charmed laugh.

For the boon of freeing your mother of what plagues her, this is the price. I will keep this piece of your heart, so that what you love you will also fear. Let the dark go with you, let it grow within you, let it become you.

Dalca shakes his head. "Speak plainly."

That will cost you more.

Dalca's face twists in vexation, and for a heartbeat, I think he won't go through it. He'll see it's too high a price. For a heartbeat, I hope.

And then something blots out the light. It lets out a savage howl that echoes in the dark, but it echoes wrong: each repeat grows louder instead of softer, each repeat adds sounds from dark dreams, murderous screeches and nightmare screams.

A berserk Izamal falls onto the serpent. All that's left of his humanity is the hate only a human could nurture. His eyes shine with feverish wildness, and though his body is covered in the bloody evidence of a brutal fight, he pays his wounds no mind. His eyes lock on to Dalca with the force of the inevitable.

On all fours, Izamal bounds toward Dalca. The serpent draws itself back into shadow, as if it would slip away.

"Fine!" Dalca shouts. "I accept!"

Lay this mark upon the Regia, and your mother will be saved.

The serpent bends and touches Dalca's forehead with hers. Like a puff of smoke, something silver passes between them. She rears back into shadow as Izamal races up the steps to the platform. He's grown larger; powerful muscles ripple under his silver coat as he circles Dalca.

Dalca stands with eyes squeezed shut, as if committing something to memory. His eyes open, and Izamal strikes.

I have to stop this. My feet slip in the ash as I sprint toward the stairs, wishing the serpent hadn't dragged me so far from the platform.

Izamal and Dalca grapple on the platform in a flurry of ash, fighting with intent to murder. There's none of the finesse or showmanship of the Wardana practice fights. This is primal.

Izamal's body shifts, fur peeling back to reveal his tear-streaked face, his arms corded with muscle and his fingers tipped with claws.

"Iz?" Dalca falters. "It's me—"

"I know who are, Dalca, I've always known who you are," Izamal growls.

Dalca skitters back, keeping out of Izamal's range. "What's happened to you?"

"You killed my sister," Izamal growls, knocking Dalca off his feet. "I'll kill you for her."

Dalca rolls and springs back up with practiced ease, but behind his raised fists, his expression is dumbstruck. "Iz—that's what you think? That I killed Nashi?"

Izamal springs through Dalca's defense and pins him to the ground.

"I didn't kill her," Dalca grits out, Izamal's arm crushing his windpipe. "I would've done anything to save her."

Izamal roars, and his clawed hands tear into Dalca.

I reach the top of the stairs and hesitate. Maybe they need this—maybe Dalca will get through to him.

"She let go of my arm." Dalca spits the story out between Izamal's attacks. "I told her to hold on. I promise. I never would have let her go. She let go because I was slipping. She didn't want me to fall with her."

"Don't lie to me!"

"She was the best of us."

Izamal roars. Dalca has to fight back to survive, and all those years of practice make him light and strong. Izamal's fury-given strength falters. His rage makes his attacks vicious, but there's no follow-through, no plan.

They have to stop. I search myself briefly for a pen, before taking in the ash. I begin to draw an ikon on the surface of the platform, but the ground shakes and I'm thrown backwards, off the platform stairs.

The breath gets knocked out of me as I hit the ground. I gasp, blinking the blurriness from my vision as something pale moves toward me. A hand touches my shoulder, and Cas's frowning face comes into focus.

The rumbling worsens, and the ground breaks apart under me. An earsplitting crack comes from above, a sound like a thunderclap. Fractures appear all across the pyramid, letting in slashes of red light and sudden jets of black water.

Cas grabs my hand and hauls me to my feet.

He staggers, clutching his side. He looks like he's been thoroughly chewed up and spat out; blood seeps from his side and from a cut over his ear, coloring his hair red. I put an arm around his waist, and he leans on me, trembling against my side.

He murmurs into my shoulder, "I'm s-sorry. I couldn't stop him."

I drag us both through the waist-high water to the base of the platform. Cas drops onto the stairs, catching his breath. Drenched, panting, I climb to the top.

Dalca has a half-human Izamal in a chokehold. He squeezes until Izamal grows limp, then throws him to the ground. "Why can't you hear me?" Dalca's eyes gleam. "I thought of you as a friend. We were, weren't we?"

The water rises to the top of the platform, lapping at Izamal's skin. There's only hate in his golden eyes as he speaks in a purring, gravelly voice. "Oh, Dalca. I hated you from the moment I met you. How could I not? You have all the power in the world—and you only use it to save your skin."

"Iz—" Dalca frowns, shaking his head, disbelieving.

It's the Storm—it has to be—some part of Iz may hate Dalca, but it's not all of him.

Izamal smiles. "No, prince. I was never your friend."

The light leaves Dalca's eyes.

Dalca stands over him like a wrathful god as the black pyramid shatters into apocalyptic light. When he speaks, his words crackle with unforgiving fire. "In honor of the memory of your sister, a far finer Wardana than you could ever be, I spare your life. But from this moment, we part ways. If you manage to find your way out of the Storm on your own, take care not to appear in front of me. I won't show mercy twice."

Izamal spits. "I don't need your mercy."

A coldness I've never seen before comes over Dalca, and he smiles. "Then you shall not receive it."

My body moves before my mind catches up, and I grab Dalca's wrist. He's far, far stronger than I am, but he stills. "Please."

Dalca's gaze bores into me. I search his eyes for the Dalca I know, the one who wouldn't be this cruel. I do know Dalca—don't I?

Dalca breaks eye contact, his gaze darting over my shoulder. I turn, dread sinking my stomach.

Izamal stands, silhouetted against a massive wave of black water. He turns, meeting my gaze. His golden eyes are his own, perfectly human. Some immense emotion swells within them, something I have no hope of naming.

A thousand golden eyes blink open within the darkness of the wave. The wave crashes over Izamal, enveloping him, dragging him into the deep.

"Iz!"

Another sharp crack sounds, and under it comes horrible laughter, echoing in a hundred voices. The top of the pyramid falls, and I leap into the water, out of the way.

I open my eyes underwater, seeing everything in layers of shadow. Pale bubbles rise through the darkness, glossy black hunks of stone sink down into the depths, and through it all winds a ribbon of white. The serpent.

I kick forward. A hand breaks the water's surface between chunks of stone, and I swim toward it, making out the rest of Iz in a slant of red light filtering through the water: wild hair haloing a drawn face, golden eyes open wide but unseeing.

I swim toward Izamal, but the serpent is faster. She slithers through the water like a bullet, opening her jaw wide and swallowing Izamal whole. She dives into the dark, taking with her a man who couldn't escape his hatred, a man who was once my friend. A scream escapes from me in a bubble.

Dread and horror and despair grow into a pit in my throat. I blink away stupid, useless tears. A single thought echoes: *I'm sorry I'm sorry I'm sorry.*

A hand reaches for me out of the dark, and I grab it. A lifeline. I hold on to it with all my strength as the light fades.

A dark and terrible voice fills the water, the voice of the Queen. *I warned you not to tarry.*

Would Cas have left without me? Would Dalca?

Yet you left one behind.

I'll come back for him.

The Great Queen laughs and laughs.

Her curse beats under my skin, in time with her laughter.

A seductive voice calls to me when the blackness grows absolute, when I can no longer tell up from down. It's the voice of the Storm. It promises things lovely, dark, and deep. It says my despair is good, that I should sink deeper into it.

I want to. How I want to.

But the hand squeezes mine. I have promises to keep, a city to save, a father to rescue.

A single spot of white light blossoms, far above. The hand pulls me toward it, but it slows, weakening. With the last of my energy, I push through the dark, grip tight around the hand in mine.

The darkness fades in layers, in fits and spurts. The Storm's call swells.

My head breaks the surface, and the Storm releases us.

I stagger onto a gold-painted stone road, and my legs give out, but the hand won't let me go. It pulls me close.

The fifth ring spreads before us, painted in greens and golds, spotted with pale pink ikonlight. It's too beautiful—it must be another trick.

A shutter bangs open on the second story of a house that looks down onto the golden road. A little girl peeks her head out and gapes at me.

I choke back a sob.

Lips brush my forehead, and I tilt my head back, meeting Dalca's gaze. He wipes away the tears that fall from my eyes.

His other hand grips Casvian's upper arm. I catch Casvian's gaze across Dalca's chest. One of his eyes is swollen nearly shut and blood runs down his neck, and yet he gives me a face-splitting grin.

My tears mingle with a half-wild laugh. We're out of the Storm. I'm pretty sure we're all three cursed, but we made it out.

"Look," Dalca says, and I do. Up the golden road, through the rings, to the palace and the circle of sky above.

The sun rises over the edge of the Storm, pale and solemn.

CHAPTER 25

The Storm is a whisper at my back. I ignore it as I step farther out onto the spongy moss that covers so much of the fifth, sucking in a deep breath. The air is sweet and muggy, rotten wood mingling with a sharp green scent. I've never smelled anything better.

I've come home, but home and I are strangers now.

The Queen's curse courses through me like a dark river, working on me and through me. I have a second shadow, a second heartbeat, and a strange new awareness of Dalca and Casvian, of things tangled inside them. Casvian's face bears no expression, but the Queen's curse whispers that his sorrow echoes mine, that he too hates that Izamal isn't beside us.

My old sorrow is matched with a new one that makes itself known in the weight behind my eyes and the lump in my throat.

Dalca laces his fingers with mine. "I feel light as a feather. I feel I could fly even without my cloak."

His eyes sweep across the path, his eyelashes dark, his lips set in a soft curve. The Storm took more than just the cord from his wrist; it took the furrow from between his brows, the tenseness from his jaw, the weight that his shoulders were always fighting.

He doesn't seem cursed at all. He's a portrait of fearlessness.

The Queen's curse chills my blood as it runs under my skin, as it matches my heart, beat for beat. What is it? What does it want?

It shows me. In the center of Dalca's chest, where his heart would be, is the carved casket. Wisps of stormcloud seep from it and sink deeper into him.

I rub my eyes, and the vision disappears.

Was it only a vision?

"What's this?" Dalca's voice interrupts my thoughts. I follow his narrowed gaze to several fifth-ringers trickling onto the golden road before us, others coming forth to join them. Dalca steps in front of us, hand to his gauntlet.

"Wait." I touch Dalca's arm.

The fifth-ringers jump back as if repelled, clearing the way. Some lower their shawls, revealing wide eyes and mouths agape.

A yellow-haired woman calls to me. "Who are you?" In her voice I hear the echo of a dream.

"I'm Vesper Vale."

A crescendo of murmurs rises from the crowd.

"It's the prince!"

"They truly came from the Storm?"

"Vale's daughter?"

"Look. The Storm could not touch them."

A puff of yellow powder hits my neck, and I jump. Many of the fifth-ringers pull pouches from their belts, fingers pinched around yellow sundust. Clouds of it fall upon us in a blessing that smells like sunbaked clay and spiced honey, like a hug from Amma.

A flurry catches Casvian across the forehead, and he starts like a man waking from a dream. Another handful catches him in the mouth, and he sputters. "What is this?"

"Sundust," I say. "Don't spit it out. It's meant to ward off the Storm's curses."

Dalca smiles, a dash of yellow powder caught in the cupid's bow of his lip.

"That's an absurd superstition." Casvian frowns at a plump-cheeked little girl, and she lowers her dust-filled hand.

I glare at him. "It's all they have, and they're giving it to you. To do what they can to protect you."

He's stunned silent. Blinking, he plasters on a smile that looks like it hurts, and bends low so the little girl can pat sundust into his cheeks. She smiles at him shyly, and Cas thanks her with as much solemnity as if she were the Regia.

When he straightens, his smile is real, soft and with a single dimple. He catches me looking, and the dimple disappears as he turns his smile into a ghost of his usual smugness. "She likes me best."

I roll my eyes, but I like this version of Cas best, too—the one with a child's handprints on his cheeks and sadness in his eyes.

Word must've traveled, because the crowd grows twice as thick as we near the gates to the fourth.

The electric furor in Dalca's eyes is new. There's no fear or fury in them, just jittery excitement. I smile when he beams at me. "We've saved them all."

I push away all thoughts of the Queen's gift, of the locked casket in Dalca's heart. I'm looking for problems. Dalca has the Regia's mark. The Great Queen granted his wish. The Regia—and the city—is as good as saved.

The copper and spun sugar of the Storm still lingers in my mouth, but there's hope to be had. We've done it. We haven't failed. *I* haven't failed. Things will change, because of us. What's Pa going to say? My feet itch to run to him, to tell him everything.

Cas sucks in a breath, his neck craned up. Ragno Haveli flies toward us, descending in style, striding forward as if walking down a long, invisible ramp, until he touches down five feet away. His eyes flick to Casvian before they settle on Dalca. It's not exactly a gesture of fatherly concern, but Cas stands straighter and scrubs the sundust from his cheeks.

"Good to have you back. I didn't realize your training exercise took you into the Storm."

Dalca inclines his head. "Only a few trusted individuals were told."

Their tongues are daggers, even now.

"We go to the Regia."

Ragno bows. "My men will escort you."

We climb under the weight of thousands of wide-eyed gazes.

Ragno's men escort us from ring to ring, through densely packed crowds of increasingly finer dress. Dalca grows more confident the higher we climb. Casvian limps his way across the city, refusing to lean on anyone or have healers come to him. The same electric anticipation that's on their faces quickens my pulse and quiets the part of me that wants to demand we go first to Pa. I'll do this right; I'll see it through.

We go deep into the palace, further than I've ever been. Further than most people have been, I'd wager.

There is nothing personal about the Regia's personal quarters. No hint of coziness could survive under the onslaught of opulence that we walk past; the place is decorated as if in testament to the idea that if something is good, then more of the same must be better. What I can see of the floor reveals shimmering stone laid in an intricate diamond pattern, though most of the elaborate design is obscured by grand carpets that are embroidered so well that I find myself sidestepping for fear of squashing lifelike flowers. In the same vein, some artisan once carefully laid ribbons of gold into the stone walls, only for some other artist to come along and drape the walls in luminous tapestries of ghostlike silk, like veils shrouding doorways to other worlds.

It's as if the finest craftspeople were lured to the palace and trapped in an unending contest of skill.

And yet, even this triumph of mad maximalism seems muted against the intensity of the Storm. The Storm was dark and humid as if pregnant with a hurricane, but this place imitates the opposite: a searingly bright and dry world of air and fire, a world born in the sun, a world you can enter only when the light burns your eyes blind.

This is where the Regia lives.

We come to double doors of pure gold. Engraved with terrible eyes that glower down at us, thin golden rays shooting from irises that glow like twin suns.

Dalca shoves them open.

Casvian and I follow him through the Regia's apartments, past a sitting room packed with courtiers and council members wishing her a quick recovery—and currying for favor—past a herd of black-robed healers, to the Regia's bedchamber. Warm light floods in from the diamond-paned windows and the domed glass ceiling. In all this light, there's no escaping how small and frail the Regia looks against the massive bed, just a dry bag of bones scorched from the inside out.

The air is still and quiet. Dalca stops by her side. The Regia's eyes roll in their sockets, but they burn with life, with the Great King's presence. Her chapped lips part, but though her throat moves, no sound escapes.

Dalca bares his teeth. "We have the true Regia's mark."

With a gasp, he doubles over in pain. The Regia's eyes fix on him, bulging from her ashen face.

"Stop it." The words hang in the air, and it registers that they came from me.

The Regia's eyes turn to me. A crackling burning voice sounds in my mind.

My ancient enemy has chosen this?

A scorching light burns under my eyelids.

A weakling—hardly more than a child!

The voice laughs and laughs and laughs.

All this time, and my enemy has learnt nothing of power.

The voice recedes, and I find myself on my knees, hands sunk into the deeply plush rug. A hand rubs my back and helps me up. Dalca.

The Regia coughs, deep, racking coughs that shake her whole body.

Dalca commands. "Make the preparations. We must adjust the mark as soon as possible."

Casvian nods and barks orders over the head of the healer tending to his wounds.

With one last look at the Regia, Dalca sweeps out.

I follow him through the halls, out of the inner palace, into a hallway studded with wide, grand balconies.

He chooses one and leans against the railing. He unclasps his cloak and unbuttons his blood-red jacket, letting both fall to the balcony's polished stone floor.

The wind runs its fingers through his dark hair, and the sun outlines him in golden light. His face is drawn in shadow, save for the glinting of his eyes.

He hops onto the railing.

"Dalca—" I start.

He spreads his arms wide. "I'm so light. The lightest I've ever been."

The wind whips at his white shirt, flattening it against his body and billowing it out behind him.

"I really think I could do it. I could fly."

"Don't. Please, Dalca." I step closer, heart pounding, terrified of startling him into action.

His eyes mirror the sky above. They're bright with mischief and exhilaration, not a prince's eyes but a boy's, full not of fear and responsibility, but of joy.

My heart clenches at the way his eyes crinkle. I want him to be happy, I do—but I can't shake the jitters under my skin that say *something is wrong.*

A gust of wind shakes him, and he teeters for an endless second, before he finds his balance.

He laughs.

"Vesper, I'm going to be free. Maybe for ten years, maybe twenty."

"Won't you come down?"

"Why?"

"Aren't you afraid?"

He glances over his shoulder at the drop. "I'm not. For the first time in my life, I've nothing to fear."

A portrait of fearlessness. "You're scaring me."

"I don't want that," he whispers. Time slows as he lifts a foot, as a gust of wind catches him unawares, as he tilts back, eyes wide with surprise.

My hand grips his shirt, pulling him down from the railing, onto the balcony floor.

His eyes are warm, his voice wondering. "I've never had anyone to catch me before."

My body vibrates, and I knot my hand tighter in his shirt. "Don't make me do it again."

"Are you still afraid of me?"

"No," I lie.

Dalca closes the distance between us a hairsbreadth at a time, giving me a dozen last chances to pull away.

The first brush of his lips is so soft it could be a passing breeze, a figment, an illusion. The second is a meeting of equals, a kiss like a dance, and I smile against his lips. The third lands like a promise, a kiss meant to be broken, and it already hurts.

From behind comes a delicate cough.

"Prince Dalca, they're ready for you."

CHAPTER 26

Dalca carries the Regia, her too-thin arms dangling, into the Chamber of the Sun. It's a circular room in the heart of the golden inner palace, where the floor, the walls, and the domed ceiling are made of palest marble inlaid with lines of gold. In the dead center is a marble slab like a sacrificial altar.

He lays the Regia on the slab as delicately as if she were made of glass.

An ikonomancer tugs on a long cord, and sunlight streams in through a circular opening. The line of light hits a concealed mirror embedded in the wall, and then another and another, reflecting a dozen times until a cat's cradle of light hangs in the air.

Dalca murmurs to Casvian and another ikonomancer, a man who wears a long ceremonial robe more gilt than cloth. He shows them the mark he got from the Storm.

Tiny pots of molten gold sit beside the Regia, who rests with eyes closed.

There's no place for me here, but as I make to leave, Dalca's fingertips brush my palm. He's finished with the ikonomancer, and he draws me to a low bench to the side, out of the way, as more ikonomancers flood in.

The Regia is soon out of sight, hidden behind their bodies.

I glance at Dalca. I haven't found a moment to tell him about the Great Queen's gift. I haven't even told him the Queen *exists*. But her power thrums in me, like a heartbeat under my own. The things it shows me, the casket in Dalca's heart and the tangle in Cas's — they're curses. I'm almost sure of it. But what kind? What's happening to Dalca?

What's happening to me?

I swallow around the lump in my throat. It's okay if I'm cursed. If that's the price to pay to push back the Storm, I'll pay it. A hundred times over, I'll pay it.

But I can't forget Ma's face. The Queen's thousandfold voice. The serpent and Izamal.

Dalca takes my hand. I trace his calluses and the lighter band of skin around his wrist, where his leather cord was once tied. Maybe this new fearless Dalca no longer needs a token of comfort. Or maybe the cord's comforting presence was what let him admit his fear.

A hush falls. The ikonomancers step away, and Dalca rises.

Standing in a web of golden light is the near-skeletal body of the woman they call Regia. She examines her hands as if seeing them for the first time, and then runs them along her face, her neck, her waist.

She looks up with soft, liquid eyes. I stand. There's no trace of in-human cruelty in them, no evidence of the overwhelming power of the Regia.

"Regia?" Dalca steps toward her with his hand out, as if approaching a wild animal.

"Regia." Though rasping from weakness, her voice is soft, lyrical. "How I wanted the role when I was your age. How I hoped to rise to the challenge. Alas, my child, I am merely your mother."

Dalca's eyes widen, and a smile splits his face. "Mother, I—"

She reaches out with frail, trembling fingers. She brushes Dalca's cheek, and his eyes slip briefly shut. "My son. At last I look upon your face, free to call you what you are. My son. *Dalca.*"

"Mother," Dalca says again as if cherishing the word. "We found it. A better mark. The Great King—"

"The Great King is gone." She takes a step toward him and nearly topples over. He catches her.

A sick chill runs across my skin. The Great Queen's deal with Dalca echoes through my mind. *To free your mother of what plagues her . . .*

Your mother. Not the Regia.

The Great Queen didn't free the Regia from whatever made her weak and allowed the Storm to grow. She didn't save the Regia from a botched mark, or even grant her a different one.

She freed Dalca's mother from what plagued her.

Ice runs down my spine. Dalca's mother bore the Great King's soul in her body, even as the King tore her apart from the inside. That's what she was freed from. The Great Queen played a cruel trick on Dalca— or maybe she gave him exactly what he asked for.

The Great King is gone from her.

I draw closer to mother and son. Casvian moves to my side.

"All my strength he has burnt away," murmurs the woman who was once Regia, as she steadies herself. "For how many years did I hold him? For how many years did I hold the sun in my mouth?"

Dalca shakes his head, a faint smile on his lips. It hasn't hit him that something has gone wrong. "The Great King is gone?"

"We do not have the power to kill a god." Regal authority shines from her, even as she sways on her feet. "And yet you have freed me. You have given me the greatest gift of all, my son."

I glance at Casvian, who looks as lost as I feel. What is it that we have done? Where is the Great King?

I press my thumb to my wrist, feeling my pulse and the Great Queen's curse beating underneath. I'm missing something important, something I need to understand. What's the Great Queen's intent?

A glance out the window shows the Storm as massive as ever. Lightning streaks lazily through its depths, giving no answer.

The woman who was once Regia, the woman who was named Nayeli Azerad Illusora, smiles with all the warmth of a pale sun on a winter's morning. "Take me to my husband. I should like to see him."

"Anything you wish." Dalca offers her his hand as she walks with the slow care of a woman determined not to fall. He glances at her every few seconds, joy and pride warring on his face.

She murmurs to him, an endless stream of words spoken too quietly to make out her meaning, but the cadence of her speech is strange, desperate, broken like that of a creature tortured for too long.

Dalca hangs on every one of her words like he's rolling them around his mouth, savoring them, slotting them away into his memories to save them for later.

Casvian and I follow them, and a handful of ikonomancers and Wardana trail after us.

Our peculiar procession parades through the empty halls of the palace, toward the secret wing where the cursed are hidden. Where Dalca's father lives.

We arrive at the mural, and Dalca presses the poma that opens the secret door and helps his mother across the threshold.

Casvian hesitates, as if waiting for Dalca to give an order. When Dalca doesn't, he turns to us. "All of you, wait here." His eyes narrow and his tone grows dark as he considers. "If any one of you breathes a word of this, I'll have you all strung up."

The ikonomancers and Wardana meekly obey. I move to stand with them, but Casvian stops me. "You don't get to sit this out. Come with me."

He fixes his pale eyes on me. In them I find the fear I expect to see, and something I don't expect at all: trust. Casvian gestures for me to go before him.

The long hallway is empty. In the atrium, a healer ushers someone back into their room, but he pauses when he catches my eye. One of the stormtouched Wardana. I don't remember if I ever got his name.

The Queen's curse rises in me, a pounding throb running through my veins. With it, I sense a tangle within him—not unlike the casket within Dalca—and a thought comes to me: *I could undo this.* Instinctively, I reach out with hands that are not my hands and touch it. A flood of self-loathing and fathoms-deep sorrow bowls me over, and I let go, gasping for breath, clutching my chest.

Those feelings didn't come from me. Something stirs in me, telling me to reach out once more.

But the door shuts behind him, and I don't dare disturb him, not after that.

Only one other door is open, and soft voices sound from within. Silently, I pad closer, and more of the room comes in view: the corner of a headboard, a man lying on a bed, with skin that's mostly stone, the Regia kneeling before him, her head on his unmoving chest, the rest of his blanket-covered body. The curse has inched up his body; even his lower lip is stone.

Dalca stands at the base of the bed, angled away from them, as if he wants to give them privacy but can't bear to be farther away. His hands tremble. I inch closer until I get a view of his face. I stifle a gasp. I expected tears, but instead his eyes are alight with burning intensity.

I back away. Dalca is no fool. So why does he act as if everything is going perfectly? It's as if he can't even conceive that we might've failed.

Casvian touches my elbow, and together we stand with backs pressed against the atrium wall.

The Regia's words still reach my ears. They fall like a torrent, as if she feels she must say everything she has to say in a single breath.

"I love you," she says. "For years and years, I lay awake in some tiny corner of this body, listening to the echo of the love I held for you. The song and shadow of the love we shared. I could never let it go, though I suffered for it. Perhaps, if I had forgotten you, I could have given myself fully to the Great King."

Her voice breaks. I knuckle a tear from my cheek, hoping Casvian hasn't seen. He passes me a handkerchief.

"Can you hear me, my love?"

"He can, Ma, he can," Dalca reassures her, his voice thick.

She begins to weep. There's a rustle, and Dalca emerges from the doorway, shutting the door behind him. He turns to us with an exhilarated expression and comes to stand beside me, tilting his head back to rest against the wall. His eyes close, sealing away that intensity, the muscles of his throat shifting as he swallows.

I touch his wrist, and he takes my hand. Where is his fear? Does he not know what we've done? That one day, his body will be painted with golden lines, and the Great King will look out at me through his eyes? That one day, he'll be trapped in some small corner of his body, alone?

Maybe I'm wrong. I'd pray that I am, but I don't know who would hear my prayer.

The door opens with a click. Nayeli Azerad Illusora stands in the doorway, holding her hand out to Dalca, who flows to her side like river into an ocean.

"Take me to our home." Her voice is thin, swallowed by the underground air. "Make haste, before he wakes."

"Before who wakes?" Dalca asks.

"I feel him, deep inside. Restrained, but even now he burns his bindings. Hurry, my son, please."

I catch Cas's eyes, meeting his troubled expression with my own. Perhaps the mark has to settle—perhaps the Regia will reforge her bond. Perhaps we haven't failed.

Within fifteen minutes, they find a carved palanquin with embroidered veils to conceal the once-Regia for the trip down to the second ring. A handful of Dalca's trusted Wardana help him bear it, not one uttering a single complaint at playing servant. The ikonomancers were left behind, after Casvian swore them to secrecy. He's cautious, unwilling to let the information of the Regia's condition spread too far and wide.

Casvian and I follow the palanquin to the most ornate quarter of the second ring. The air is dry, and the sunlight warms my skin as we walk down wide boulevards, past massive houses with verandas stacked one on top of the other, as if a view of the Storm is one worth having. Sunlight glints from mirrors hidden in the buildings, reflecting onto the path and across our faces. A bench sits under a tree so old it can no longer give fruit, as if there are times these people desire to be in the shade, as if they've had enough sunlight. I take a deep breath and unclench my fists. There'll be time to fix the city, to make Dalca see.

At last we come to the doors of a palatial house, large even by second-ring standards—I count a dozen windows, just on the front.

The walls are inlaid with brass ikons in a diamond-grid pattern, and though the ornately carved front doors are wooden, they show no warping, no water damage, no touch of the Storm.

Dalca calls for them to lower the palanquin, and the Regia descends, taking his arm and making her way to the front doors. Dalca pauses at the threshold, craning his neck.

"He hasn't returned here since he was a child," Casvian says under his breath, for my ears only. "Some minor wing of the family lives here now."

Dalca's shoulders fill the doorway as he steps inside. We follow, his twin shadows.

When Dalca was a child, did he run freely across these polished floors inlaid with opal and pearl? I can't quite picture a child amongst all this cold luxury; would any child be permitted to play on a carpet woven with gold thread, or swim in the lotus-studded pool in the house's central courtyard, or sit and eat at a table made from the massive bones of some long-dead creature?

The Regia clutches Dalca's arm with one hand, and with the other, she runs her fingers along every gilded and carved surface. Dalca glances at all the finery, never touching a thing.

Not a single speck of dust is to be found amongst any of the house's riches, no doubt a feat managed by an army of lower-ring servants. And yet the Regia shakes her head as though she's found this particular treasure chest already plundered.

She pauses at an ornately framed mirror, turning to face it. She sucks in a breath and brings an emaciated hand to her face as if she can't quite believe the image in the mirror. In her mournful eyes and sharp cheekbones are the shadows of a once formidable appeal, one that she shares with Dalca.

"Upon waking from a nightmare, one expects far fewer horrors." Sorrow turns the Regia's features as she looks upon her mirror self. "There is nothing for me here. Take me to a place I can see all of my empire. The highest point. I wish to touch the sky."

My heart aches to watch her. Dalca offers her a hand and wordlessly takes her to the palanquin. As soon as the Regia is ensconced within, I reach for him. "Dalca?"

He blinks at me. "Vesper?" As if remembering who I am, as if waking from a dream.

"What's going on?"

Beaming, he cups my face with both his hands. "I have my mother back, Vesper. My family is together. I'm not . . ." His smile swallows the end of his sentence, but I understand what he's trying to say — he's not alone anymore.

"But what now? Where's the Great King? Do you think the Storm—" I cut myself off. I can't say what I'm thinking. Can't voice my worries that the Great Queen has somehow tricked him.

"You worry so much," he says with a little laugh. "This is a gift. We have done something that hasn't been seen for hundreds of years. How do we know what form this new bond will take? We'll have to see—but you saw her. I have my mother."

Dalca presses a giddy kiss to my cheek, and a smile curls my lips.

"It's all thanks to you," he murmurs against my ear before he lets me go, returning to lift his mother's palanquin.

My stomach sinks. Perhaps he's right. Perhaps I shouldn't question the Queen's generosity. But I do.

Whenever I'm near Dalca, but especially when he touches me, the Queen's curse beats quicker—a tingling in my palms, a sensation both cold and hot, one that swells into the hollow of my chest. I reach out to

Dalca in the same way I reached for the stormtouched Wardana—and there it is in his chest, a darkness in the shape of a sculpted coffin. What would happen if I opened it?

The tallest point in the city is a watchtower in the outer palace. Dalca and the other palanquin bearers lower the Regia, and Dalca helps her out. She breathes in the air, her fingers wrapping around the railing.

All our entourage hangs back. Only Cas and I have the courage—or concern—to step onto the balcony, but even we keep a respectful distance.

Her voice resounds with deep affection and deeper pain. "My city. A lonely city, charged with mighty purpose. It has been far too long since I have looked upon you with eyes my own.

"By the mercy of the Great King, I existed. Cradled within a womb of fire, I could look only within. Yet I have seen a million visions, each more brilliant and brutal than the last. I have watched the birth of the sun and the death of stars. I have seen the creation of this world, and I have seen its fall. I have seen a great and terrible power stirring underneath.

"I have looked deep into my own cowardice. I have seen my essential weakness. That never could I meet the power given to me as an equal. Never could I overthrow the Great King's will and take a breath of cold morning air with my own lungs.

"All these things I've seen while caged in the prison of my own body. No. This is my body no longer. This is one burnt by the King, who loves us not. It's paid its toll to time. This body is fit only to die."

"Mother?" Dalca's eyes shine as she turns to him.

"Perhaps it will not be a sentence for you. Perhaps you have strength I do not. Or perhaps you will suffer as I have, as we Illusoras have since time immaterial. The only blessing we are offered is early death."

"No," Dalca says. "We Illusoras shall not fail. We never have, and we never will. It's our honor to fix what is broken."

She draws him into her arms. "I feel him waking, my son. May you be blessed for giving your mother a chance to die as herself."

"No." Dalca pushes out of her embrace, holding her arms. He wears a soft, puzzled smile. "That is *not* what I have given you. I'm fixing it all. I'm saving you."

"Why?" she whispers, smoothing his hair. "To delay your own pain?"

"Because I love you."

"Oh, sweet child. Perhaps there is one last thing I can do for you."

She wraps her arms around him, and I understand a heartbeat before she leans back and they fall. A shout rips from my throat as I reach for him and grab his arm—my shoulder nearly wrenches from its socket, but I don't let go. I don't let go, pulling with all of myself, the muscles of my stomach and legs straining, pulling with the Great Queen's curse, pulling with hands that are not my hands, and I hold on and *pull*. Inside Dalca, something gives—I tear open the closed casket of his heart, and a deluge of terror rises from him, a sea of fright that crashes wave after wave over us both, a fear so potent it makes me weep, and still I don't let go.

I don't let go, even as I'm pulled to the edge, my hand slipping on smooth stone, my grip failing, my stomach rising to my throat, my thoughts racing—I need a cloak, or an ikon, something, anything, *please*—and a hand grabs mine.

"No!" Dalca screams as Cas yells from above me, "Don't let him fall!"

Below, the woman who was once Regia releases Dalca, slipping through his arms, and falls. She smiles as she plummets, a look of peace upon her face. At the last moment before impact, the Great King wakes, and even from this distance, the reawakened fury in her eyes burns itself into my mind.

But even the Great King is too late to save her.

A shape, too small to possibly be so significant, falls from the highest tower of the palace.

The Regia's body hits the ground with a terrible sound both soft and sharp. The Regia's mark burns gold, then red, then black, and a flood of blinding light bursts from the cracks in her broken body. The light, bright and hot as the sun, surges into the dark sky.

The Storm thunders, a sound of triumph and terror. With no Regia to hold it back, the Storm billows forth, blotting out the circle of sky. My stomach drops, and I swallow back the bile that rises in my throat, focusing on holding on.

Ikonshields flare to life all around the fifth, and I imagine my people screaming, running for the fourth, and I pray that they make it.

A pale rain falls. It's warm, like a summer shower, but it burns where it touches the skin of my cheeks. Hands pull me and Dalca back over the balcony. I touch his face, cupping his jaw, slapping his cheek, anything to thaw the fear that freezes him. He pushes me away, crawling past me without once seeing me, devastation unfolding across his features as he grips the balcony's edge and sees what lies below.

At the base of the tower lies a body that was once the Regia. Now it is merely the body of Nayeli Azerad Illusora, a onetime wife, a onetime mother.

Dalca screams.

It the worst sound I've ever heard, a scream so primal my blood echoes with it. It's a cry of a soul with no hope left.

It's the sound of a boy breaking.

CHAPTER 27

A cold anger comes over me, seeing the ikonshields strain and fail as the Storm advances. How many souls did the Regia condemn? In death, her suffering is multiplied thousandfold; in every fifth-ringer, in every new orphan, in her own son.

How could she love Dalca and do this to him?

The answer comes to me. She didn't choose love. She chose fear.

Cas drags Dalca back into the shelter of the palace, out of the strange warm rain. He staggers, trying to pull him back, and looks to me. "Give me a hand, would you?"

I grab Dalca's other arm, and he turns to me with unseeing eyes, shock and sorrow dimming the light that normally shines in them. My vision blurs, and I blink it away. We get him out of the rain and up on his feet.

Dalca clasps a hand to his temple, agony written across his face. He buckles, and I catch him, lowering him until we're both on our knees.

I know what I've done. The Great Queen gave me the power to undo curses. The curse she laid on him was one that locked away his fear. And now I've undone it. Now his fear is once again his own.

"Dalca?" His gaze meets mine, and I flinch back at what burns in his eyes: a blinding presence like a searing beam of white light. The Great King.

Horror stills my tongue.

Dalca's pupils shrink and grow, as if he's fighting a battle inside.

Casvian doesn't see. He rubs his eyes, wiping away rain or tears or both. He takes a breath and runs a hand through his hair, slicking it back. "You." He points to a Wardana. "Go inform Ragno Haveli of what has happened. You, gather the Regia's council. We meet in the throne room." He gives them all instructions that send them away, until just we three are left.

He grips Dalca's shoulder. "Dalca, please. Come with me."

Words stick in my throat. "He's . . ."

Dalca moans.

Cas helps him up, and we half drag him down the winding stairs, through a maze of bronze and silver hallways, to a room with a large desk and a pair of stuffed chairs by a fireplace.

Cas sits Dalca down in a chair before going to the fireplace and drawing a quick ikon. A merry multicolor fire rises within seconds.

Dalca stares into it.

"Shit," Cas murmurs.

A choked sound of surprise makes its way out of me. "Shit," I agree.

Cas runs his hands through his hair until it becomes a halo of static. He looks like a dandelion.

"Do your thing," he whispers.

"My thing?"

"Comfort him."

"I don't think anything can do that, Cas."

"Do something," he says as a knock sounds, and he rises, going to the door. "I've seen the way he looks at you."

If looking at Dalca would help, I'd stare all day and all night. But how can anything I do make this better? What does the strange, dark, frightening, hopeful thing between us mean in a time like this?

An ikonomancer stands at the door. "Ragno Haveli requests your presence, sir. As well as that of the Regia's heir."

Cas catches my eye before ducking out the door and shutting it with a pointed *click*.

Dalca hasn't moved a finger. My hands are shaking.

I go to him, my feet sinking into plush carpet, and kneel at his side. "Dalca."

He inclines his head toward me, just barely, but it's enough to know he's listening.

But what can I say? I can't touch his sorrow. Part of me thinks the merciful thing is to leave him to grieve however he wants. Every time I close my eyes, in the darkness behind my eyelids, she falls again and again. Over and over, the peaceful expression on her face bleeding into the Great King's scorching fury. If I can't stop replaying the image of her body hitting the ground, what must it be like for him?

The windows rattle, whipped by wind and pale rain. Just last night, he had everything—the promise of a soon-healed Regia, that the Storm would soon be no threat. There was no fear in him when he kissed me, and that made my fears seem small, too, like his confidence buoyed mine.

On the balcony, the Great Queen's curse worked through me. It opened that casket within him and spilled all his fears, all the terror that he'd locked away. Every bit of it echoed in me, as if his fears became mine, as if I could taste every nightmare lurking in the dark of his heart. What was done to him in the Storm, whatever curse he was stricken with, I undid.

"Dalca." I touch the back of his hand with the tips of my fingers. He turns his palm up and interlaces our fingers.

His gaze drops to our hands, watching the firelight flicker across our skin.

"I'm sorry," I whisper, but my words hang loud and useless in the air.

His grip tightens.

"Please, say something."

Some light returns to his eyes.

"Dalca? Maybe we can go to my father, he might know what to—"

Dalca's grip grows unbearably tight, as if he's trying to crush my hand. I try to pry his fingers off, but he grabs that wrist too.

In a voice like silk, he says, "Did you want this?"

His eyes bore into mine. It wasn't light in his eyes, but fire.

Wildfire bleeds out of him, flames in his smile and a flickering in his eyes.

The Regia's death made Dalca—privileged prince and reckless warrior, sorrowful son and reluctant heir, the future Regia and a boy terrified of his future—nothing more than a dry husk, a body holding nothing but the desiccated remains of his dreams and loves and fears and hopes.

All it needed was a spark.

Maybe my words grated on something inside him, like a flint being struck. Or maybe there was something within him all along— maybe under the fear, under the duty, there was this. A fury waiting to be awoken.

The spark was struck. The brittle deadness ignites. The boy is gone.

In his place rages an inferno.

He rises to his feet without letting go of my hand. "Was this your plan all along?"

"Let go of me." I'm three kinds of terrified, but I'm not about to let him intimidate me.

He drags me close, his eyes glinting with a thousand dark emotions and not one lick of reason. "The moment you came, it began. The moment you stepped into the Ven. I thought, let me keep an eye on this one. If she's dangerous, I'd better keep her close."

"Everything I've ever done . . . I wanted to help." I keep my voice soft, hoping to reach him.

His breath puffs against my cheek. "Everything I've ever worked for, destroyed. And it all goes back to you."

"Why would I want the Regia dead?" I push at his chest. "Just *think*, Dalca! It doesn't make any sense."

"Your family killed one Regia, so why wouldn't you kill another? Why wouldn't you kill me?"

"What?" My voice comes out a choked whisper. He knows me better than this. How can he think I'm blindly following in their footsteps? I went against Pa's wishes for him.

With a hand still clamped around my wrist, Dalca drags me into the hall. I've never really noticed his strength before, but now it scares me — even with all my power, I can't pry his fingers off of me.

He drags me through the palace into a dim place lit by only a few ikonlights. As Dalca sweeps through, they flare up and reveal a large room of dusky gold, with tiny mirrors studded into every surface. On a platform stand the gilded bones of some ancient beast, molded into a throne. The Regia's throne.

He pulls me onto the ikon in the middle of the floor. I flinch, but nothing happens.

"No," he whispers, dragging his free hand through his hair. "I forgot. I forgot the Regia needs to power this ikon." He laughs a laugh tinged with madness.

"I'll tell you everything," I say. "But please, stop this. You're frightening me."

He swings me around to face him, his voice uneven with either fear or rage. "Why did you grab me?"

I start, flummoxed. Does he mean up on the balcony? "I—I didn't want you to fall."

"I could have saved her." He gazes into someplace within, his fists clenching at his sides.

"Dalca, you didn't have your cloak."

He pushes me away and paces like a caged beast. "I could have saved her," he says again, his voice low and dangerous. "You did something to me. I felt it. You made her fall."

"No—"

"What deal did you make with the Storm?"

"I didn't—"

"Enough! No more lying, no more playing me for a fool. What did you do to me?"

I flinch at the acid in his voice, at the thing within me. Even now, the Queen's gift—the Queen's curse—simmers in my veins, changing me, giving me a sixth sense of the agony inside him.

His eyes turn knowing, the blackness of his pupils eating away at his irises. "Yes. Tell me the truth."

My voice comes out small. "The Storm gave me something. A curse."

"Go on."

"When I was holding you, I—it saw your curse. And undid it."

He comes close again, like we're two stars locked in orbit. "I wasn't cursed. I'm cursed now."

I take a step back. "You were. Your fear was locked—"

He takes my face in his trembling hands. "Undo it. Please."

His thumbs brush my lower lashes, and I fear him more than I've ever feared a stormbeast. One quick move and he could pluck out my eyes. I squeeze them shut and seek the Queen's gift within me, reaching with phantom hands for Dalca. The gift paints a picture of him for me, one painted in shadows like the inside of the Storm. A black starburst in his heart and his hands is his fury and it's slowly poisoning his head, his eyes, his tongue. His fear is a cold, many-splintered thing in his gut, the shards of which pierce him in the heart, in the lungs, in the throat. It's a portrait of his pain.

There's nothing for me to pull, nothing for me to undo, nothing for me to fix.

I open my eyes, and teardrops crawl down my cheeks. "I can't."

His thumbs dig into my face until my tears drop onto them. Dalca pushes me away as if I've burned him, his face a twist of wrath as he stokes his fury, letting it burn hotter and hotter within him, all the better to melt away his fear, his sorrow, his guilt.

I wipe my tears and stand tall. "I'm with you. I walked into the Storm with you. For you."

His voice is flat, dead. "It wasn't for me, was it? It was for your father."

"For my father, for you, for the city."

Dalca's eyes hold no love, no hope, nothing of the boy who kissed me. There's only something infernal. "What should I have expected from the daughter of traitors? Treachery and murder are in your blood."

He steps toward me.

I run.

The doors slam behind me, and I sprint as fast as my legs will go, fueled by fear, whipping through gilded hallways with no idea where I'm going.

Under the staccato pounding of my heartbeat, under my sharp, noisy gasps, come the thuds of footfalls, speedy and relentless.

How did it come to this? The Regia's dead, Dalca's out for my blood, and Pa's future isn't looking bright, either.

Why did the Queen do this to me? She used me. Why make it sound like I could save the city with her gift? Why make me believe that I could save us all?

I couldn't save Izamal, nor the Regia, nor Pa, nor Dalca.

Dalca tackles me from behind, his arms wrapping around my waist like chains.

I couldn't even save myself.

I say nothing as we return to the old city, as we march through the tunnels, all the way to the fist of rock that holds Pa.

He's slumped over and so still that I fear he's dead, until he lurches up at our footsteps.

Pa gasps in shock. "Vesp? How—you made it back?" He trails off as he keys in to the mood. "What happened?"

"The Regia is dead," Dalca says.

Shock robs Pa of his voice. He looks from Dalca to me.

"The Storm covers the city. Soon I will be marked Regia and all these horrors will be mine. All thanks to your daughter."

Dalca shoves me forward, onto an ikon that glimmers awake under my feet. The rock grows under me, wrapping around my legs, rising up to my torso, then my arms. My own personal stone prison groans to life around me. Darkness pulls at the edges of my vision, and I fight to stay awake, to say something that'll turn Dalca back into the boy I thought I could love. This can't be how it ends.

This can't be.

CHAPTER 28

After all these days with so little sleep, seeing the things I've seen, failing at every challenge put to me, letting every last friend I've made slip through my fingers, losing my very last hope of getting Pa out of this place—after all that, I can't think of anything better than dreamless sleep.

But that's not what I get. The Great Queen thunders into my dreams, guiding them, showing me what she wants me to see.

I dream of Izamal.

He slumbers within the Storm, in a clearing of pale trees. He looks just like he did when I first met him—no claws, no fangs. Flowers like jewels grow around him, and others fall like stars from the sky and settle in his hair. My heart aches to see him claimed by the Storm, adorned like a precious treasure to keep till the end of time.

The dream shifts to a dark sandstorm. A saber-toothed creature pads across inky dunes as tall as mountains. Miles of footprints are slowly erased by the wind. The only color in the sea of black comes from its golden eyes and silver coat.

This too is Izamal.

The dream shows me that there are a thousand miles to go and hundreds of nameless terrors to face. If he can face them all, perhaps one day the creature will find his way to the sleeping boy. That is his quest: to unite himself.

But the Storm tells me that the Izamal I knew is gone. Even if he succeeds, I won't ever see that boy again. Within the womb of the Great Queen, a new Izamal will be forged. If he gets that far.

I whisper a plea to any and all beings who might be listening.

Help him.

The dream unravels into threads of time and space; as if guided by an invisible hand, they knit themselves into visions of the past.

A simple image: a man and a woman sit on a rug by a cozy fire while a child plays between them.

I recognize Pa first. He seems incredibly young, without a single gray hair to his name, though his eyes already have crinkles around the corners. He wears an older design of Casvian's ikonomancer uniform, and his fingers are stained with ink.

The woman looks like me. The same shape eyes, the same nose, the same long limbs. She looks stronger than me, and I don't just mean the muscles. Something glows from her, something fierce and determined. Unyielding, as if she were carved from marble. The face the Storm showed me wasn't Ma; it was only the soft parts of her, the parts of her that she gave up. This is her whole. Soft and hard, capable both of love and violence.

The child must be me, but I don't recognize myself in her giddy happiness. I'm a baby, probably not even a year old. Dribbling all over myself, without a care in the world. Smiling a gross little gummy smile. How did I come from that tiny thing? It's so innocent, so harmless. Words that don't fit me so well anymore.

Pa tucks a piece of Ma's hair behind her ear. She snatches his hand away, rolling her eyes, but then she presses a kiss to his palm. I look away, partly because they're my parents and it's embarrassing. Partly because watching them like this breaks my heart.

This is happiness, what they have. Ma gave this up to be Regia? Did she ever think of fighting to keep this?

It's cruel to show me what once was, when I know it'll never be again.

The color drains from the dream, the background falling away to white, leaving the three of us drawn in gray like statues made of charcoal. The winds of time huff and puff, and the three of us crumble, first Pa's fingers, then Ma's smile, till we all disintegrate into a flurry of ash.

The ash lifts up in a mighty gale, whirling this way and that, toward the future and the past, catching on an eddy and spiraling into a pale rain that falls down, down, into the present, into the waking world I've left behind.

This isn't a dream, is it?

The Queen shows me the present, from the perspective of the Storm.

Several dozen ikonomancers — maybe all the ikonomancers there are — work a shielding ikon to keep the strange rain off the people of the city, thousands of whom have gathered in the open spaces, in the markets and on the bridges, some standing on rooftops and others perched on private verandas, all who have come to bear witness to a massive heap of wood that stands outside the palace, on which lies a pale shroud covering the body of a woman.

The doors of the outer palace swing open. Out walks a boy in a ceremonial outfit of gold, a pale cloak of a thousand and one white feathers flung over his shoulders.

Dalca.

A great and terrible anger awakens within me at the sight of him.

Whatever pity I felt for him, all that nonsense about us being the same, whatever I once felt when I looked in his eyes — I want to stomp on it all and let myself sink into a pure, cleansing hatred.

I tell myself that I barely knew him, that I never liked him, that I only got close to use him. That I'm strong, self-reliant, fearless. That he didn't hurt me.

But in the darkness of my dreams, I can admit this:

Somewhere in the back of my mind, I knew it was happening, and yet I let him worm his way deep, deep into the dark places of my soul. He was never any good for me. I have to let this dream of him go. But what does that mean? Forgetting his rare smiles? Should I forget the way the sun caught on the blue-silver rings in his eyes? I'll let go of the feel of his lips against mine. I'll let go of the one time he admitted his fear, the words *you frighten me*. I'll let go of the way his face tightened but his voice grew proud when he spoke of the Regias of old. I'll let go of the way he looked at me once, as if I were brave and strong and capable. As if I were someone special. Someone profoundly right, made to fit into all the ridges on the edge of his soul, so where he ended I would begin.

I knew he wasn't for me. I knew the blood in our veins would pull us apart. I never wanted to hope. I never wanted it. I know who I am, I know what I want. It has nothing to do with him.

But even without hope, something grew between us. I admit it. I admit he hurt me.

He doesn't deserve to stand by my side. He doesn't deserve my forgiveness.

He deserves my wrath.

Dalca raises a flaming torch. The flames catch on the wetness waiting to fall from his eyes. He holds it over the pyre, but he doesn't let it fall. As though he can't bear to say goodbye. In the firelight lines of gold glint on his fingers, lines that stop at his elbows, incomplete. His transformation to Regia has begun.

A glow grows within the crowds. In a show of solidarity, the people of the city hold paper orbs inked with a pair of ikons. As they're activated, the orbs glow with light. One for each soul bearing witness.

The light spreads like ripples of water. It swells from the first ring outward, the second aglow, the third less so, the fourth with only smatterings of gold. The fifth is dark. My heart clenches. Has the Storm devoured my home ring?

Dalca looks every bit the prince, lit from below by the soft light of a thousand paper lights. And yet I've never seen him look so fragile.

The night was still before, but now it's as though time has stopped. Even the wind quiets its whispers.

All I hear is the crackling of the fire in the torch. But it too is muted. Tender, gentle, like the night around us.

Dalca lowers the torch to the pyre. His arm shakes, just once, and then his tears fall.

The pyre catches alight instantly, fire augmented by ikons. In seconds, the fire stretches tall into the sky. The smoke stretches taller still. Shapes form in the flames, painted in hues of red and blood-orange. They turn into people; a smiling man and woman holding a baby. The Regia's first moments. The flames play out the story of her life. They show her childhood, full of laughter. She grows into a studious, imperious young woman. She meets the man she will love. And then her child is born.

Dalca stands alone as his mother's life plays out. The fire paints his skin, reflecting on the darks of his eyes and the tear tracks lining his cheeks.

It hurts to look at him. Doesn't he deserve this? Shouldn't he suffer? Don't I hate him?

A wash of pale gold shields him from view. The paper orbs, released all at once. A show of light against the total dark of the Storm.

The sky is alight with little suns. It feels overwhelming. It feels holy.

I catch glimpses of Dalca through gaps in the flow of lanterns. His face is tilted toward the sky.

The paper lights rise through the ikonshield, each one blotted out when it meets the Storm.

Darkness falls like a curtain on this not-dream, this vision from the present. The Great Queen whisks me onward.

Something glimmers in the blackness.

In a starless sky, two primordial forces orbit each other, a being like a hundred thousand sparks and another like every hint of darkness. They dance in perfect balance, hanging in this ancient place, pushing and pulling, fear and love, fire and water, air and earth, order and change. They shape bodies for themselves, godly ones, genderless and invulnerable. Equal and opposite. The Great King and the Great Queen.

They do things fearsome and magnificent. The King creates things of structure, walls and kingdoms, words and numbers. A language of power, a precursor to the ikons. The Queen creates things wild and natural, imprecise and beautiful, the dewdrop on a flower and the rot in its roots, planting within people both curiosity and wonder.

The dream draws me through time. They always rule together, the King and the Queen, through human avatars. Sometimes the rulers are siblings, sometimes strangers who grow close, sometimes lovers. Sometimes both men, sometimes women. Sometimes they fight, waging war upon each other until a new balance is found.

The King and Queen choose from among the people, finding those best capable of serving them, bestowing upon them marks of power, ones their vessels must choose to accept. The Great King bestows upon his vessel a mark that appears on the skin, one that gleams like gold and glows with softest light. The Great Queen bestows something else: a mark that lies inside, unseen, but for when it sometimes appears on the skin as if rising from within, in a dancing pattern of ever-changing lines. Hers is not gold but darkly iridescent, like oil over black water.

Those human servants are nothing like the Regia. They retain their minds. They work together with the King and Queen, their aides, not their slaves.

And then the dream takes me to the chasm that happened near three hundred years ago. The Regia Dalcanin fights and kills his brother, and the Queen is set loose. The King intends to leave Dalcanin's body, but cannot. Dalcanin has tattooed over the mark, adding to it, binding the King to him. The Queen bestows her mark upon another, but Dalcanin kills her vessel, and the two others who come after.

Dalcanin, the first Regia of the modern kind, cements his power. His descendants will bind the Great King to themselves, generation after generation.

The Great Queen flees. A simple, ordinary storm had come to thunder and rain upon the city, and she finds refuge in it. It occurs to her that a storm is something that cannot be killed.

She feeds it her power like she once gave power to her vessel, and the storm grows strange, still, undying. She feeds it her anger, her loneliness, her longing.

There is a darkening.

Seeing the Storm on the horizon, Dalcanin scours the city, destroying all evidence of the Queen. He rewrites her story; where her likeness once stood in temples, now stands a king of wrath. He vows that she will be forgotten, that none will challenge his rule by trapping the Queen as he trapped the King.

Time speeds forward. The world becomes unbalanced, as the Storm grows, as the Great King fights back and learns to take control, tyrannizing the minds and souls of those who dared take his mark and keep him imprisoned. The Great Queen is forgotten.

Sorrow and fury, fury and sorrow.

The past slips away, and I'm drawn down, down.

Into a vision of the future.

The golden lines painted on Dalca's fingers now stretch across his body. The ikonomancers have finished; the Regia's mark is complete. Now comes the moment of coronation, where he calls the Great King and gives over his body, where the gold sinks into his skin forevermore.

Dalca—proud and fearful—disappears deep into his body, and the Great King rises forth.

Dalca fights the Storm, and it kills him.

He doesn't look peaceful in death. He looks livid. I picture his glowering death mask, proclaiming to generations to come that here stood not a man but an inferno.

But there aren't generations to come. The Storm takes all.

I reach out to touch his dead face. Is this what we deserve?

"Vesper?"

The dream fades as a familiar voice pulls me somewhere near awake.

My eyelids are heavy, and my voice is a rasp. "Pa?"

A quick inhale. "Oh, thank the King. Vesper, darling—are you hurt?"

I blink awake. It takes a moment for my vision to settle, to make out the lattice of ikons carved into the stone ceiling. A hand touches my elbow as I sit up and find myself on a small cot in a windowless room.

Pa kneels beside me, gaunt and unshaven, worry etched into his forehead.

I swallow the lump in my throat, and it sinks down into my stomach. "I'm sorry, Pa. I should've listened to you."

"Don't cry, Vesper," Pa says as he sits beside me, the cot dipping under his weight.

I knuckle away the tears that fall. "I'm not doing it on purpose."

He lets out a low, slow sigh that hurts as much as if he'd slapped me.

I can't tell where my anger ends and where my misery starts. I bite my lip to keep the trembling at bay. "I'm sorry that I'm a disappointment. I've tried, Pa. I've really tried—"

Pa sits very still, his hands clenching and unclenching on his knees. "Vesper—you're not a disappointment. I've never—I . . . I wanted to protect you from the choices your ma and I made. I thought I'd done enough harm; I removed myself from the world. It scared me that you wouldn't. I could see you following our footsteps . . . and that terrified me." His voice is low, and his words are slow, as if he's drawing them from a locked box deep inside. "It's not something I know how to say. I wasn't raised to say it out loud. But you know, right? You know that I love you."

"No," I whisper. "I don't, Pa."

His eyes are bright and serious before my tears blur his face away. "I do. I always have, even before I met you, when I felt you kick when you were still in your Ma's belly. And when I held you for the first time . . . you grew quiet, as if you knew you were safe in my arms." He looks down at his hands. "But . . . you outgrew them."

"I haven't." I say stubbornly.

He huffs a laugh as if he doesn't believe me.

I put my arm around him. He tenses, then slowly, he puts an arm around my shoulders. I've had better hugs from a stormtouched girl whose body was half turned to wood, but I'll take what I get.

"I'm proud of you," he whispers into my hair.

His words fill me with a strange and gentle warmth that brims over, filling my eyes with tears that I blink away.

"We need to do something," I say. There must be some way to survive the Trials. I didn't face the Storm to fall at Dalca's hands. I won't give him the satisfaction.

"Yes," Pa says. "Something I should have done long ago."

I turn to him, surprised. Somehow, maybe for the first time in my life, I didn't expect Pa to have all the answers. I've gotten used to relying on myself.

It's comforting, in a way, to slip back into the role of being my father's daughter, knowing he's capable and knowledgeable in ways I'm not. It's exactly like slipping into an old, comfortable sweater. But somehow, the sweater feels a little tighter than it once did.

Pa doesn't notice my hesitation. His focus is on the ikons carved into the walls and ceiling. "They've done a good job of nulling this room. Ikons may not work here, but they will work tomorrow. That is what we need to prepare for."

It takes a moment for me to understand.

"I'm going to teach you ikonomancy."

CHAPTER 29

We try to cram learning that would have taken years into the too-short hours of the night. The minutes have a crispness to them, a feeling that these are the most important moments of my life, that these minutes are ones I'll never forget. Even the smallest details are written into my mind: the furrow to his eyebrows, the quick, sharp smile when I memorize a difficult ikon, and every tiny flourish in each new ikon.

He sketches in the dirt a sign like a constellation.

"What many people never understand is that ikonomancy is a language of its own. It's an expression of your will over that which exists. So, you need to express what exists, and then overlay the change you wish to make. And as with language, simple ideas, simple words can be strung into sentences."

I trace his work, drinking in his words, the sight of him. It's a strange time to feel happy, and yet a bit of joy works its way into me. And in the work I recognize the life I used to live; in the geometry of a shielding ikon is the layout of the beds at Amma's, in a slicing ikon the way Pa used to arrange food on a cutting board, in a warming ikon the lattice of beams above my old attic room.

Every ikon he draws on the floor, I draw straight into my memory. But some of them seem to be coming straight out of my memory.

At last, Pa takes a deep breath. "That's enough. Get some rest. We'll have to be sharp tomorrow. You've—" He pauses, and his voice softens. "You've done well. You might've given me a run for my money."

I let my head fall to my pillow, ikons floating in my mind and a smile tucked in my heart. I don't remember falling asleep. When I wake, Pa is gone.

In his place are two women with cold eyes and hands like sandpaper.

"Where is my father?"

They don't answer. Silently, they drag me to another room in the old city, where they strip me and throw bucket after bucket of ice water over my head, scrubbing till my skin glows red.

My head falls forward. Stretching from the soles of my feet is my shadow, my old friend. Does it reach for me, like it did in the Storm? Could I fall into it and swim in my own private darkness?

I toe it, and it's nothing but cold stone.

I shut my eyes and seek out the Queen's gift, reaching out with it. The women are painted in shadows; one is full of hard, slick things, of disgust and frustration, but the other is soft inside, like well-worn linen. She pities me.

I open my eyes. Both women glower, wearing twin grimaces.

Another bucket of ice water is upended over me.

If this is how she shows her pity . . . I shiver. The Queen's gift shows me what people feel inside, not just the cursed. My mind falls on Dalca, on the moment I ended his curse and everything became so much worse.

Maybe he was better off cursed.

One of the women hands me a rough cloth to dry myself, and I've only just wrapped it around my body when the door bangs open.

Casvian pauses in the doorway, averting his eyes. He's in tidy Wardana reds, his pale hair glittering in the light, pulled back from his face in an elaborate braid. I guess he's dressed up for my execution.

Gazing determinedly to the side, he thrusts a bundle of white before him. Clothes.

I take the bundle with trembling hands. "What happens now?"

Casvian turns to answer and flushes, quickly pointing his gaze at the ceiling. "*Please* get dressed."

I turn my back to him and slip on the white overdress and white pants, a slim, flimsy shawl belted across my waist. High-ringer fashion, perhaps, but it seems a rather sacrificial look. "I'm dressed."

"Hold out your hands." He fishes a pair of chains from a bag at his waist and locks them around my wrists. Where does he think I'll run? Casvian ushers me out the door, into the old city. Wardana are posted every fifty paces along the way across a spindly bridge.

I hiss. "What's going to happen?"

He's silent until we pass a short, mean-looking Wardana. "No one can reach Dalca."

Dalca? He wants to talk about Dalca? I huff, though I can't say I'm surprised. "Dalca's fine. I'm the one being led to my death."

"He's gone to some dark place in his mind. It's not like him."

I shake my chained wrists at him. "At the moment I really can't bring myself to care."

Casvian blinks at me as we cross the bridge. "Right. Right."

The dark water glints below, reflecting a city of ghosts. If I jumped, I'd deny Dalca his spectacle. But I'm not ready to accept death, not when Pa and I have a fighting chance.

No one's ever won the Trials, they say. But they also say that no one can come back from the Storm.

We leave the old city behind as Casvian takes me up through a tunnel. The air trembles with a dull roar. The sound of thousands of people packed into one place, dimmed by several feet of rock. The Arvegna arena must be directly above us.

Casvian slows before the end of the tunnel where light peeks around a circular door.

"You're not going to free me, are you?"

Though his face is shadowed, his eyes glint. "Where would you go if I did?"

I've no answer.

He touches my hand, and I try to pull back. Honestly, I don't really want to hold his hand right now. But he holds tight and presses two sticks about the size of my pinky into my palm. Their edges are sharpened to a point. "What is—"

"Shh." He glances down the tunnel.

I tuck the sticks into a fold of the shawl. A grimy residue remains on my palms.

He leans close and whispers. "You'll get through this, Vesper. I know you. You can get through anything."

"For Storm's sake, Cas." I blink away the sudden emotion that blurs my vision.

He tugs once on the chain linking my hands, then steps back and pushes the door open.

Light and sound flood in. He gives me a strained smile. "Prove me right."

My ears pop as I step out into the bright, ikonlit arena.

The Arvegna has changed.

The maze is gone; there's nothing but a flat expanse of pale, scarred stone.

Above, an ikonshield stretches over the visible sky, exactly as I saw it in my dream. It gives off a soft, hazy glow like dreamy, artificial daylight. Beyond it seethes the Storm, a billowing curtain of perfect darkness, punctured by violet lightning.

The bad weather has deterred few; the stands are packed. Maybe they aren't here to watch me die, maybe they believe they'll be safest wherever the new Regia is. But it's hard to believe that when, not fifty feet from me, a potbellied man in a bright orange overdress sells snacks and a gaggle of bejeweled second-ringers clink together glasses of sloshing amber liquid. Even fifth-ringers have shown up to watch—the highest stands are full of people wearing coarse clothes, with their long shawls drawn over their heads as if they don't quite trust the ikonshield.

They're all looking at me. At what I'll have to face.

It comes to this because of all the choices I made: leaving Amma's, giving over Pa's journal, trusting Dalca. I wait for the regret to come, but it doesn't.

I won't regret wanting more, wanting better.

His gaze is already on me when I find him on the Regia's throne. A swell of emotion rises in me as I meet his eyes, a thousand feelings, the crush of them washing over me.

Dalca wears what he wore in my dream of the future, the dream of his death. Ivory armor edged in gold and a cloak of feathers, thousands of them, each a purer white than the last. All that pristine white to mask the darkness inside him.

And here I stand in chains, several dozen feet below him, also wearing white, but the white of a prisoner. It emphasizes the distance between us. Who would think of us as equals, seeing us now?

His gaze changes, and I wonder if I'm seeing him or the Great King.

Dalca looks away first. He rises to his feet with arms outstretched, his cloak unfurling like wings, already the mantle of cold command resting easy on his shoulders. The crowd quiets; their attention is like a weight that lifts from me and falls onto him. Dalca's gold-painted fingertips catch the light. "We are gathered here today in the wake of a great tragedy. Tomorrow the mark will be complete, and you will have a new Regia. We will rebuild. But for us to move forward tomorrow, we must seek justice today."

His voice is all his, no trace of the Great King.

I search Dalca's expression, but my gaze is drawn to the gold lines curling at his neck. Does he dread what awaits him? Thirty, forty years of being trapped in his own body?

Yes. He's a portrait of a man resigned. He should feel at home, charming people with his presence and a dramatic speech. But he's playacting. His voice sounds dead, as if that raging fire swept through him and left only ash in its wake.

"This girl stands accused of engineering the death of the late Regia." Dalca pauses, and some semblance of fire returns to him. "In her veins runs the blood of traitors."

Thousands of eyes turn to look at me, seeing not me but a specter crafted by Dalca's words, someone worthy of their hatred. I'm the focus of his rage and all the pent-up darkness within him. The Storm told me this would happen, in far fewer words, when Dalca let his child self be eaten. If he couldn't face himself then, how can he now? He's left the wounds on his soul to fester. And unable to ease the pain, he turns his misery outward; he inflicts himself on me.

Dalca's gaze bores into me, and I meet it with equal fury. "Today both father and daughter stand Trial, with all of us bearing witness."

Stone grinds against stone, and another hidden door opens in the arena wall beside me. Pa staggers out, squinting up at the light.

"Pa!" I run to him. The chain between my hands catches once, drawing taut, then a link snaps—my hands are free. I'll owe Cas my thanks, if I ever see him again.

"Vesper." Pa gives me a choked little laugh. "Don't fear. We can do this. After all, I suppose this is the family business."

That startles a laugh from me. "What's that, being enemies of the Regia? Getting sentenced to death?"

"The business of changing things. It's always worth being the enemy of a diseased state. I had forgotten that." Despite the dark circles under his eyes, the gauntness in his cheeks, the unkempt beard shadowing his face, he looks *alive* in a way I've never seen him look before.

"The Second Trial," Dalca continues, "is the Trial of Beasts. In ancient times, the accused would have fought monstrous beasts—raptors as tall as three men, serpents as large as houses, great felines with sharp claws and sharper teeth. Fear not, for the ikonomancers have prepared something just as special."

I glance at Pa, who is trying to work his hands free of his shackles. "Vesp, do you remember the ikon?"

I nod. There's a slicing ikon he taught me, one that will cut through metal. I only need something to write with.

"Blood," Pa says.

"I have something better." I pat my shawl, finding the sticks Cas gave me. Pa's eyes light up as he sees them.

"Mancer's charcoal. Where did you—"

"Shh." I focus on drawing the ikon on the widest part of his chains, careful to get it right. I close the loop and wait, holding my breath.

The chain parts in two. All the sounds of the audience die out, and even Dalca pauses.

"Well done," Pa says.

Dalca continues. "If the Beast is destroyed, the accused will stand for the Third Trial. If the accused are killed, the Trials conclude."

He says it so easily. *Killed.*

On the other side of the arena, circular stone doors begin to grind open, as if pulled by unseen hands. Dalca's voice echoes. "May the fates show no mercy. Now . . ." Dalca waits until I raise my gaze to meet his. "Let the Second Trial begin."

He says it to me — not the crowd, not Pa. Eyes fixed on me, he lowers himself onto his throne.

The grinding stops as the circular doors stand open. Whatever the beast is, it's hidden in the darkness.

"Vesper. Remember, follow my lead." Pa runs toward the center and begins laying out ikons on the floor, drawing quickly with Cas's charcoal.

I follow on his heels, drawing out the ikons he taught me. He's done three, linking them with a series of lines and arcs, by the time I've finished my first.

A gasp rises from the crowd. Someone screams. I keep my focus on the ground, on the ikon.

It's only when Pa sucks in a sharp breath that I look up.

A stormbeast.

A four-legged creature the size of Amma's living room, so tall I don't come to its chin. Its body bulges with roiling stormcloud, and its face rapidly melts from a lion's to a horned elk's, to a crocodile's. Every horrible beast out of a fairy book come to life in one body. Its tail swishes back and forth—with each swish going from bushy to scaled to coiled and on and on.

I've never seen a stormbeast struggle like this, as if it's too angry to keep its shape.

Only its claw-tipped paws don't change. Clasped around each of its four ankles are brass shackles inscribed with ikons. That must be how they captured it, how they kept it from returning to the Storm.

"What's the plan?" I hate the way my voice shakes, the way terror turns my palms cold and sweaty.

"Don't die." Pa says, his eyes alight with a fierce sort of delight. He's *enjoying* this.

The beast throws its head back and lets out a roar like a clap of thunder. Its eyes—pinpricks of violet lightning—fix on us, staying the same while the rest of its face morphs.

"Vesper! Go!"

I scramble back twenty feet, dropping to my knees and skidding across stone with the stick of charcoal in hand, and draw the three ikons Pa calls out, linking them together into a shape like a constellation. *Ikonomancy is a language, and as with language, words can be strung into sentences.*

The ikons come easy to my fingers, though I wish Pa had taught me how to keep my hands from shaking.

The stormbeast stomps on Pa's first set of ikons, and they activate; the ground under its feet melts into a gooey puddle of molten marble, and the beast trips into it, splashing bits of rapidly-hardening rock onto its legs. The stone solidifies, stopping the beast in its tracks. It writhes, morphing faster and faster. Pa stumbles away as it loses shape altogether, becoming a swirling black cloud, the four brass shackles glinting in its depths.

It reforms itself outside the bounds of Pa's ikon, landing with a thud on all four shackled feet. It leaps past my first ikon, following Pa.

Pa drops beside me and grabs my hand as I'm about to finish linking them together. He scribbles one more ikon and closes it. "Get back."

We scramble back as the stormbeast treads upon the linked ikons.

The ground rises up in boulders like teeth, jutting fifteen feet tall and clamping shut around the beast. It's sealed inside a rough, ridged mound of stone.

Pa holds his arm out, stopping me. My heart pounds in my ears; the crowd is silent.

The rock holds.

"What now?" I ask.

Dalca watches from above. A vein jumps in his jaw, and I give him a grim smile. Pa and I'll get through this, we'll beat the Trials and then —

Something tickles my skin, making the Queen's curse throb within me. The stormbeast prowls inside its stone cage, leaping from one edge to the other, expanding in a twisting, gusting tornado, pressing on the stone from within. It's a vortex of anger and heartrending sorrow, and it suffers to be separated from the Storm. But then I sense a moment of dark glee as it builds pressure, finding weak points in the stone and pushing.

"Pa! It's going to break out!"

His brows furrow at me in doubt. With my eyes open, the stone mound looks solid — but the Queen's curse tells me the beast is moments from breaking free.

A sharp crack rings out in the air, followed by a loud hiss. Another crack, then another hiss. Fractures spiderweb across the surface of the stone, wisps of dark cloud eking their way out in ominous spirals.

The stone cage shatters.

The stormbeast roars with a dozen serpentine heads, lightning streaking between its fangs. Its body is that of a massive hound, and somehow those ikon-inscribed shackles are still around its ankles.

It sprints toward us, its many eyes agleam, and I stagger back. A rippling wall of gray stone rises before me, nearly clipping my toes as it stretches ten, fifteen, twenty-five feet in the air. Pa lifts his stub of charcoal from the ground. The wall he created spans the width of the arena, sealing us in a small section, maybe a fourth of the arena, while the stormbeast has full rein over the rest.

"Let's just stay here," I say.

Pa barks a surprised laugh. "I once read about a Trial that went on for days. The accused couldn't kill the beast, so she hid. She drew water from the air and lived on that for as long as she could."

"Thank you, Pa, real uplifting."

He gives me a thin-lipped smile and gestures for me to throw him my stick of charcoal. Mine's still a good three inches long, but Pa's used his up to a small stub. We'll run out soon. I glance down, seeing how my veins jump in my wrists, and I know what my backup plan will be.

He begins to draw ikons on the ground. I press my ear to the stone wall and close my eyes. The stormbeast prowls, aching. I exhale long and slow, and slip into the spiraling whorls of its body, its emotions becoming mine: *I want to go back, I want to go home, to a soft, sweet embrace, to where I belong, but these things on my feet keep me here, burning me, and it hurts, it hurts—*

"Vesper!"

I blink back to myself. Pa throws me the stub of charcoal.

"We're going to try again. The beast was trapped; it just found cracks in the stone. We can create a tighter seal this time, one that'll slowly squeeze it."

"What if we free it?"

"What?"

"If we take its shackles off. I think it'll go back to the Storm."

He shakes his head. "Stormbeasts want to destroy. It'll only go back once it's been thoroughly beaten. Like any stormbeast."

"But, Pa—"

"How 'bout you follow my lead on this?"

I squash down the feeling that rises in me, one that says I'm no longer just a child he needs to protect. "Sure, Pa. Let's do it."

He directs me to draw variations on the same three ikons as before, in spaces he's left open in a complex, overarching ikon.

I get to work, but the hairs on the back of my neck rise. I glance up, meeting Dalca's eyes.

Pa follows my gaze. "We need to talk about your taste in men."

I don't say anything. I guess he has a point.

As I finish up the last my ikon, I feel the presence of the Queen's gift, like a whisper in the back of my mind.

I'd told Pa about the Storm briefly last night, in between him teaching me. But his face had crumpled as I'd started to tell him about Ma, and I couldn't go on. We'd spoken of the curse, of the Queen, and he'd grown excited in a thoughtful, scholarly way.

I want to ask him what he thinks of it, but now there's no time left.

"Ready?" I ask.

He nods and squeezes my hand.

I take a deep breath, and he connects the last lines of the ikon on the wall. The right half of it dissolves.

The beast bounds in, led by the opening right to the ikon. I hold my breath as it tromps on it.

As another cage of rock snaps shut over the stormbeast, Pa dissolves the rest of the stone wall and we put some distance between us and the beast. The next set of ikons goes into action: the rock cage heats up, its outer layer becomes molten, melting in sections and becoming smooth. I throw my arms up over my face as the blast of heat reaches me, squinting through my fingers.

The air ripples with heat. The outer layer of the stone cage shines like glass—no cracks, no weak spots for the stormbeast to exploit.

I crane my neck up. I ignore the roar of the audience—they don't matter, not right now. Through the heat haze, Dalca draws his gaze from the glinting, glasslike mound to meet my eyes. There's no hate in his expression, no fury, just a strangely blank, intent expression.

I inch closer to the stone cage, reaching out with the Storm's gift. "Don't touch it," Pa calls. "Or the ikon will start working upon you."

I nod and stop twenty feet away. The beast inside is frenzied, expanding in a volatile whirlwind of stormcloud, seeking a crack and finding nothing.

Pa motions me aside as the heat begins to dissipate. "Now the hard part."

He begins drawing ikons to shrink the stone cage, to destroy the beast.

My heart pounds in time with the Queen's curse.

Something is wrong.

The cage explodes, shards of glass-smooth stone flying. The crowd screams as some of them are pelted. One comes to a rest inches from my feet.

Pa stands, arms hovering at his sides.

He staggers back, just one step. Sucks in a halting breath. Blood drips to the sand below him.

Oh, no, no, no. No.

The beast rises from the debris, glaring at Pa.

I call to it, thrusting myself into the curse and pulling. The beast's head—now just a single leonine one—swivels to me. I tell it: *Come*.

It pads forward, away from Pa.

Pa takes a stumbling turn to face me. His front is coated in shards, his white overdress spotted with red, as if flower petals have fallen on him.

I force my hands steady. It's okay. He taught me a healing ikon. Two, actually. He must know hundreds. I blink back hot tears, focusing on the stormbeast. It opens its jaw, unhinging it like a serpent, lightning streaking down its throat.

Kneel.

It hesitates, and I sense its confusion. It recognizes something in me, some part of the Storm that it calls home, but it also sees that I'm a girl of flesh and blood, not cloud and lightning.

"*Kneel,*" I whisper.

It steps closer, close enough that it could take a single leap and wrap its teeth around my neck.

The ground under me rumbles, shaking me, testing my balance, and a stone wall rises between me and the beast.

Pa. He's on all fours, charcoal gripped in his hand, a completed ikon on the ground before him.

I run to him, shock bleeding into terror.

"No," he says as I drop to my knees beside him. "Don't touch."

Some dozen shards pierce his overdress. His skin glints like glass around the shards, visible through rips in the cloth. I suck in a breath—it doesn't look good. This is the kind of thing that trained healers are for.

"Pa . . ."

An ache spreads inside me. The Queen's power calls to me, not in words but in tears, telling me that my tears are her tears, that all the tears in the city can be mine to drink, to drown in—before me, my shadow grows long, and it opens its mouth, whispering.

"Takes . . . more than that," Pa says, rising to his knees. I get a good look at an inch-long shard in his forearm, the skin glassy around the point of impact. Drops of blood hang unspilt, like teardrop rubies.

"The glass—it's stopping the bleeding," I breathe. "Does that mean . . . you'll be okay?"

Pa's lips curl in something between a smile and a grimace. "I'll be fine. You won't get rid of me so soon." He says it to make me laugh, to comfort me. But he's not a good liar. His eyes say he can't see me break down, not here, not like this.

"It's just a scratch," I say, trying to do the same for him. "Don't be so dramatic." I duck my head and scrub my eyes, once, quick, so he can't see.

He gets to his feet, and I hover beside him, offering a hand that he never takes. His eyes are fixed on the jagged wall that encircles the beast. Already a wisp of smoke curls over the top edge. "You were doing something to it."

"Yes," I say. "I feel it, somehow, as though I can talk to it. Not with words but with something else."

"The Queen's curse," Pa says, fixing his gray eyes on me, the eyes we share.

I nod.

He sighs, a deep, bone-rattling sigh. He tilts his head up, blinking at where the circle of sky would normally be, where now there's only the Storm. His lashes are wet, and my eyes tear up again.

I follow his gaze up, and then I find Dalca. He sits hunched over, elbows on his knees, his head bowed. As if he feels my gaze, he looks up at me. There's no triumph, no glee, no nothing on his face.

"Let's try freeing it."

I start, eyes wide.

"Yes, Vesper," Pa says with a soft smile, "We're doing it your way. Now, your first ikon still stands — what was it, a sticking ikon?"

I glance back at where I'd drawn an ikon beside Pa's ground-melting one. His was used up; mine is still intact. "Yes."

He staggers to it on stiff legs. "Lead it here if you can. Keep it still and bound as long as you can, and I'll handle the ikoncuffs."

The charcoal crushes to dust before he's finished with the first ikon. He pulls out a shard, but his blood spills in crystalline droplets that clink as they hit the ground. I fish the stub from my sash and toss it to him.

"That's for the beast," I say.

I grab a sharp-looking rock — not one of the glass shards — from the ground and cut my arm. Blood wells up, and I use it to finish the ikon for him.

The beast pounces over the edge of its stone enclosure. It now has a ridged back and a squat body, snapping two lizard-like heads.

I focus on the Queen's power within me, reaching for the beast. It pads toward me, mesmerized.

Its front legs touch down upon the sticking ikon, and it gets stuck. A thunderclap breaks from its throat.

Pa gets in close and scribbles quick on its left hind leg. The brass falls. The roar from the audience grows deafening, and I tune them out.

The beast shifts from leg to leg, roaring. Its newly freed leg changes shape, growing talons as it struggles against the sticking ikon.

It jerks its front legs free, leaving wisps of cloud like paw prints.

Be calm. It turns its heads to me, smoke breaking apart and melding back into a face like a panther's. A face like Izamal's. I exhale through my teeth.

Pa gets another leg free.

The beast's focus goes to the man under it, and I leap forward, putting my hand to its muzzle.

Pa sucks in a breath as if he would shout at me to get back. I shake my head without looking at him.

I stare into the stormbeast's lightning eyes. *Go back to her. Go back to the Storm.*

Pa frees another leg.

It huffs a breath against my palm, black clouds curling around my fingers.

Pa frees its last leg.

Go.

It dissolves into stormcloud and rushes toward me, enveloping me, gusting past me and through me. For a moment, I'm back in the Storm, with Ma, with the Queen, with my shadow, with Dalca, before everything went wrong.

The stormcloud frees me. It rises up and returns to the Storm.

"We did it," I say, something almost like joy rising in my chest. I drop to my knees before Pa, but as I get a good look at him, the joy dies.

Pa stays kneeling on the ground. The glass has inched up Pa's neck. After the glass punctured him, it didn't stop spreading.

"Vesper." A tear rolls down his cheek and drops to the ground with a tinkle, rolling to a stop.

"Pa?"

He reaches a hand to my cheek. He moves so, so slowly, each movement accompanied by the sound of grinding crystal. His hand stops before it touches my skin.

"Pa? You'll be fine, right?" My voice breaks. "We did it, we beat the Trial."

His eyes burn with fierce love and determination. "You've shown them, love. You're stronger than them all."

The glass freezes his expression as it takes him over.

"Pa?"

He falls back and the glass that was my father shatters into hundred thousand pieces of glinting dust, catching on the wind, rising up in the wake of the stormbeast.

I scream and scream and scream.

CHAPTER 30

Something comes loose within me.

A flood. Part sick horror like moth wings beating in my lungs, part black misery like an icy oil slick sliding down the back of my throat and pooling in my gut, part dark fury that turns my blood into shards of glass that tear my veins raw. This deluge tastes like fate; all my choices brought me here to drown in something I can only call pain, but it's a sick, hungry thing that feeds upon itself, devouring, aching.

The ikonshield flickers, telling us all that the ceiling of the world has been made dark and low. The Storm bears down from above on the city, and the whisper of the Queen's power—her curse—thrashes me from within. A wrathful tornado, remaking my insides in its image. As it batters the city, it batters me, flooding me with its pain even as it draws upon mine. We feed each other, growing stronger.

The Queen's curse is a conduit, tying me to the Storm and the Storm to me. I taste the Storm on my lips, salt-sweet, the flavor of tears.

The Queen can cry, but my eyes are dry. I'll cry when I'm dead.

"Is that all you've got?" I scream at Dalca on his spotless throne, at the watchers in the stands, to the Great Queen hiding, haunted, within the Storm. "That's it?"

My blood is aflame.

"Let us begin the Third Trial." Dalca's voice echoes, punctuated only by thunder, as he stands with his white feather cloak billowing behind him. He steps off the edge of the platform, falling. His cloak catches the wind and spreads wide in an arc of stark white made blinding against the black sky. None of the thousands of people watching us matter. It's just him and me.

My heart pounds in my ears.

The air is thick and simmering with the echo of another moment, another descent. I meet his gaze. This time, I have nothing to hide. Let him see every dark thought. Let him see what he has done to me. Let him see that I come to make war.

In his eyes lives a matching tornado. He's prepared for battle. The tightness in his jaw, the downwards curl to his lips, the red rimming his once-bright eyes — this is his war paint.

My heartbeat, a thunder crash.

Only one of us is walking out of this. I don't care if I survive. I only care that I make him pay.

Dalca touches down, holding my gaze. Not a speck of dust on him, just gleaming white and gold. All the glory of the sun, all light, no darkness.

What a disguise.

Out of the corner of my eye, I catch flashes of black and blood-red, as several Wardana and Regia's Guard form a loose, wide circle around me. Two heads of pale hair are among them—Cas and Ragno both stand sentinel as if to ensure a fair fight. All lies.

Gray-robed attendants approach me with armor and a sword. An awful laugh rises in my throat. What am I supposed to do with a sword?

"Do you mock our mercy?" Dalca asks.

"What mercy?" I struggle to lift the sword, my arm trembling with the weight of it. "This is an execution."

"What an honor this is, then," he says, flinging his arms wide. "Your Regia himself comes to carry out your sentence."

"You're not the Regia. Not yet."

"No." Dalca lifts his eyes to mine, and there's no trace of the Great King's blinding presence. "Not yet."

So this is his choice. His last choice. I'm honored. A wretched amusement blends with the anger in my blood. "Your last act as a free man is to kill me."

He looks at me with a dark smile in his eyes, one that says *I was never free.* "This is what happens to traitors." He swings at me, and I heave my sword up just in time — the blow hits the sword instead of me, but I'm still knocked back. The metal rings in my hands, sending vibrations all the way to my teeth.

I drop the tip of the sword to the ground, where Pa stood a moment ago. "Would you have fought Pa yourself?"

Dalca pauses. "I would've fought Alcanar, yes."

"Don't say his name."

Dalca circles around me, and I turn to keep him in sight. "Why not? I'll dance on his grave if I want to. He *killed my grandfather.* Finally, I, last of the Illusoras, have avenged the wrongs done to us. All but one." He raises his sword to point at my heart.

Was he always like this? Did I just never see? Was I too afraid to look close, to look beyond the good to what lay underneath?

"He . . . was my father," I say in the end, through gritted teeth.

His eyes are hard as flint, but there's understanding in them. "The Regia was my mother."

He lunges. The sword's too heavy — I can't get it up in time — and the blow hits and I fall, sprawled on the ground. The taste of blood fills my mouth.

But he didn't cut me; he hit me with the side of his sword. He's toying with me.

"You know it wasn't me who killed her," I say. "*You* gave them the mark."

"Get up!" Dalca bellows, taking a menacing step forward. But I saw it — the briefest flinch. My words hit.

I get to my knees and lean on the sword to push myself up.

I've barely made it to my feet when his sword smacks me again. I fall; my knees crunch in the sand. It doesn't hurt as much as the humiliation of not being able to fight back.

Dalca steps in front of me, his blue eyes electric. "You took everything from me."

"I came to save my father." My voice shakes. "I came because *you* came into my home. Because of you, I lost everything. My family, my home." I bite back the pain, the tears that want to come with my words.

"No," Dalca says. "You lost everything because your parents were traitors."

My ears start to ring. My blood pounds like a drumbeat and, under it, the Queen's curse.

Dalca continues, a terrible smile on his lips. "You did what you had to do. I understand. But so must I. And what I have to do is cut down all people like you."

He lets me get to my feet, but the sword falls from my numb hands. "People like me," I repeat, recoiling at the casual way he says it, as if we're now from two different species.

"Liars, traitors. Killers."

"Who have *I* killed?"

"You don't deny the lying?"

I laugh. "Wasn't it you who lied to me? Didn't you promise to pardon my father? You lied to get his work, to have me walk into the Storm with you, and then you threw me away! You played with my life! You played with my father's life! What a prince! What a Regia you'll be!"

Everything is his fault. He took Pa. He designed the Trials. He killed Pa. He imprisoned me. He kissed me, he used me. And he got in; he wormed his way into my heart. I let him. I let him hurt me.

No more.

The flood of rage, that thing within me, the Queen's curse—it snaps taut, a line to the Storm above, like a beacon drawing it in. I'm in two places at once, half in my body, half in the heart of the stormclouds above.

Above, beyond the straining ikonshield, the clouds fold back into the Great Queen's face, one that looks like Ma. She fixes her infinite void eyes upon me.

I hear her like a thrum inside me, a voice that understands me better than I understand myself. She promises me love; she promises me power. She promises to punish all who have hurt me, swearing I'll never be hurt again.

She promises retribution.

Her curse comes alive under my skin. But I know now what it is; some part of me knew the moment she sent me the dream of the past Regias. She didn't give me a curse; she gave me her mark.

Let me in.

I suck in a breath.

Take the power you so desire.

On the ground, I open my eyes, taking in Dalca anew. "People like me?" My voice is strange; it's strong, brutal. "It's people like *you* that this city would be better without."

Become my vessel.

"What are you doing?" Dalca staggers back as the Storm sings in lightning and thunder.

Let me in, and take your vengeance, she says straight into my heart, her words rattling in my chest. *Wreak your darkness upon this world. Become a god of wrath. Punish them for what they have done to us.*

My fists clench. I want it. I want payment for every one of the smiles Amma would've given had she lived. I want blood for every second I'm forced to live in a world where Pa's gone.

You will become a creature of revenge. A darkening fury. You will see that your pain is reflected in the world, on every face that jeers down from the stands.

Why shouldn't I accept her power?

Why shouldn't I let her in?

She sends me a vision: a new Regia sits upon the throne, one who wears a shifting mark of darkly iridescent lines. Her face is proud, fearless — and mine.

Why shouldn't she rule?

Why shouldn't I?

My attention narrows to the boy before me. His eyes are wide with fear.

Dalca is a dark, twisted thing inside, his pain written in his veins. I see all of him, with Queen-given eyes. The dark has eaten him up, save for a small bit of light at his core. So small I could snuff it out between my fingertips.

The Queen whispers into my heart. *Take a taste of what I offer.*

My shadow rises from the ground, a perfect silhouette, a dark echo of me. It peels itself from the faintly sparkling stone, looming large over me, growing bloated as it feeds on my pain, eating up the knot in my throat, the prickling behind my eyes. It trembles with the grief I can't face, not right now.

I faced it once. I accepted it then. It reaches for me, arms out as if it would embrace me. But now . . . I can't bear it.

It doesn't slow, showing me no pity, no mercy. All I can do is endure its embrace and brace myself against the sorrow it reflects back onto me.

I can't break down. But I *can* turn my sorrow to fury.

With my shadow's arms wrapped around my torso, I turn to Dalca. "I pitied you, you know. All this burden you had on your shoulders. Unwilling to share it."

His eyes show fear. Fear of me.

It makes me powerful.

"I thought, what must it be like to grow up like that?"

"I don't need your sympathy."

"No, you don't. You're a cruel boy. Selfish. You've crafted this image of the valiant Wardana, the dutiful prince, all to conceal what you really are. But I see you."

"Pick up your sword." Dalca's voice shakes.

"Some part of me hates you and will always hate what you've done." The Queen's power crackles through my veins, electric and coursing under my skin.

Dalca raises his sword and points it at my chest. His gaze darts between me and my shadow.

My shadow laces its fingers with mine, and together we reach for him. The skin of his throat flexes under my fingers. The cord of his wind-pipe is so fragile. I could end it; I could snip the thin thread of his life.

Why shouldn't I?

I press. Dalca shuts his eyes, his lashes wet with unshed tears.

This is power. This is what the Queen offers.

The Storm whispers again, that same siren song, but this time I hear it for what it is. In each thunderclap is the echo of weeping, sobs like those I cried for Amma, under the wind is a scream, one just like the scream that tore itself from me when Pa—

A scream like the scream Dalca made when his mother fell.

The salt-sweet raindrops on my lips are tears.

The Storm. The Queen found a vessel in a storm, but as she lent it her power and her fury, it became what it is. And it poisoned her, feed-ing her back what she gave it. It isn't her wrath.

It's her pain.

The Queen shrinks back inside me, but she shows me images of how the Storm grew large and strong and violent with the pain of all the children who lost their parents, the suffocation and self-loathing of high ringers in their gilded cage, the low ringers who grew up second-class, their burdens, their miseries, the pain in all of their hearts. The Storm took it all.

My pain lives in it, too. The Storm's tears—some of them are mine.

Who knows where it began. Pa's choices killed Dalca's grandfather. Mine killed Dalca's mother. Dalca's killed Pa.

And now, I could kill him.

Dalca's eyes open, boring into mine as he claws at my shadow's hands wrapped around his neck. His summer-sky eyes shutter, his pu-pils dilating. His mouth opens, his lungs fighting for one last breath.

Who'll come to kill me?

The Storm feeds on him, on his pain. On mine. On that of the people in the stands, of Cas and Ragno and their soldiers.

It will grow strong and endless with our pain. It will blanket the land to the horizon. It will bleed into the sky. It will spread until there's nothing left but the Storm.

I know what I must do. My shadow's hands release Dalca, and he staggers, stricken and uncomprehending.

The Storm must end. Without the Great Queen fueling it, it will. All its beasts and all its curses—all will end.

I turn my face up to the Storm.

Come, I tell her. *I accept.*

The ikonshield shatters. Ikons snap like strings drawn too taut, and the remnant wisps of blue light fall and fade into thin air. The pale burning rain singes my skin, but I hardly notice.

There is no sky above. Only dark clouds, streaked with lightning. A spiral grows, clouds rotating around a central point, claws and teeth and glittering eyes within them, spinning faster and faster, spooling into a funnel that shoots toward me.

I hold my breath, bracing myself. The Queen's mark rises, burning through me, moving outward, rising through layers of bone and muscle and flesh to my skin, appearing on my body in shifting lines.

It hits like a whisper.

Hands of shadow and cloud caress my face, Ma's hands, the Queen's hands. She holds my face still.

The lines of her mark shimmer across my skin; the mark is a door, and she opens it, opens me.

Her power pours into me so fast and so full that I'm drowning with it; my mouth floods with the taste of midnight rain and copper, my lungs fill with ozone, my chest is squeezed with immense pressure—

I scream.

It's too much—It's been too long, she's forgotten how to fold herself into a body—

I wrap my arms around myself and pull—

—the crushing flow stutters to a stop. I gasp for air, coming back to myself, coming out of myself. I am a ghost, half out of my skin—and yet my skin is newly raw, goose bumps as significant as mountains, the tingling in my fingers like earthquakes.

The Great Queen hovers over me in a shifting form of intertwined shadows; she has only poured a drop of herself into me, but her mark binds us close. Something has drawn her attention—her awareness is fixed up above, beyond the Storm blotting out the sky.

He has come. Her monstrous overlapping voice echoes in my ears and rattles my bones. *From the time he was freed, he has waited, pooling his power. He thinks me diverted; he comes for war.*

A blinding shard of light cuts through the clouds. It craters into the ground with an explosion of stone and crackling air that stings my teeth.

The billow of dust obscures all but a halo of radiance, beams cutting through the dust as if the sun has come to the ground. An impression of a prism, sharp as cut glass, casting and fracturing light.

The Great King. Unbound and vengeful, too dazzling to behold.

Thunder rumbles from the Storm.

I have longed for this, the Great Queen hisses. *I am stronger than I ever was, and he is weak from centuries in a cage.*

I take a step back as heat scorches my face, blinking away the green afterimage of a sharp, thin face—all edges, no softness, no mercy.

The tether between the Queen and me grows taut as she draws back into the Storm, pooling her power.

My heart stutters. The city won't survive a battle between gods. Thousands of people in the stands, dozens of Wardana and Regia's Guard on the arena floor—all at risk. None who can do a thing. And I'm alone.

The Storm is one roiling mass of lightning and shifting beasts, worse than ever before.

Have I brought this upon us all? Am just I following in Ma's foot-steps—dreaming big, leaving more pain in my wake?

No. I won't let this happen.

I close my eyes. Deep inside, the Queen's power runs through me, a heartbeat under my heartbeat, a river of shadows under my veins. I reach for it the same way I reached for the curse in Dalca—and I pull.

The Queen—a wave of roiling shadows and clouds—roars. *Do not interfere in our war.*

The air crackles in warning. The Great King raises a hand, and a scorching light hits me, scalding my skin and deeper, as if it would burn out all my shadows. As if it would burn out the Queen and all hope of ending the Storm.

A body comes between me and him; a dark silhouette against the King's blinding radiance. I squint against the glare. A bird's nest of black hair, a cloak of white feathers.

Dalca stands between me and the King with hands outstretched. The light catches on the gold lines inked upon his fingers.

He throws me a speaking glance over his shoulder—and a thou-sand things war in his eyes. *I'm sorry* and *forgive me* and a promise: *I'm with you. I'll hold him, whatever it takes.*

He turns to the King and says the one thing I'd never imagined him brave enough to say:

"I am your vessel. Let us be bound."

The air crackles with the Great King's laugh. *Nevermore shall I be bound.*

Dalca squares his shoulders and steps forward, reaching for the King with his bare hands. The lines of his unfinished mark flare with light as he holds the King still.

The King's voice booms. *You are not worthy.*

A piercing cry. The smell of burning skin fills the air as the Great King begins to burn the mark from Dalca's skin.

Dalca bites back his scream, planting his feet as if he would push the King back. Dalca's incomplete mark lets him engage with the King—but he'll never become his vessel, not like this.

He's stalling—for me.

My heart thuds in my chest. It's as if time slows to a stop.

Dalca means his promise, but in the end, he's a boy against a god. The Great King will blot him out to get to the Queen.

A thread of shadows connects me to the Great Queen. The Storm stretches wide above us all, a mouth waiting to bite down.

The stands are full of people whose faces are masks of terror. Fights have broken out everywhere I turn.

The Wardana have formed a circle around Dalca and me; they are locked in combat with the Regia's Guard. Cas fights his father, his spear against the blade of Ragno's scythe, teeth gritted, a streak of blood in his pale hair.

The Great King claws for the Queen.

Dark infernos in all their hearts.

And the Storm drinks it all in.

"Is your hate worth so much?" I whisper to the Queen.

In the stillness, her attention falls upon me, sharp as lightning. A howl of a thousand overlapping voices. Fury and other things.

The silent moment ends; a crush of noise, and time breaks upon us.

I whisper, "Let's end it."

She yields. I breathe her into my lungs, I swallow her down, I pull her through my tear ducts, bind her to me. Jagged pain follows in her wake as my bones shatter, my skin tears, my veins burst. Her power heals me instantly so I can break all over again — she's too much —

But I can't stop, I have to take all of her. If I do this, it all ends. The Storm ends, the pain ends —

For the chance that something else will come, something better —

For the chance of breaking this cycle of vengeance —

For even the smallest glimmer of hope —

Don't hold back, I tell the Great Queen. *I can take it. I can hold all of you.*

She speaks with just one voice, Ma's voice: *You will shatter.*

I can take it.

This time I don't scream. Pain swallows me whole.

And beyond the pain — a moment of perfect stillness. I unravel past myself, into land and sky and earth. Through stone and wood, air and dirt, flesh and bone, in all directions, a whisper on a ghostly wind, catching snippets of voices from countless conversations, screams and sobbing and a newborn's wail; slipping through the slimmest gap between two lovers protecting each other with nothing but their arms; tasting the sundust falling from a little girl's cupped hands as she runs from the Storm's edge; and going deeper, tasting of each heart and finding a hundred thousand exhilarations, yearnings, terrors, each a starburst, a firework; and rising higher, into billows of curling stormcloud, each band of lightning separating into thousandfold color; slicing through black into a lost world, sliding through what were once farms and through forests of trees gnarled and strange, flowing through the figures of countless cursed, tasting their hearts and finding one familiar; and then sinking into the ground, into the old city, brushing against the watery barrier to the city of dead and hearing the chatter of ghosts; and further, seconds unspooling into centuries and faces and names losing meaning; the stars darkening one by one—

And a face, immense and terrible and beautiful, that presses through the dark and presses a kiss to my forehead, and all the infinite dark tucks itself within me.

I become it all; it becomes me.

My eyes open in a fractured body. Blood wets my lips. The Great Queen is within me—a dark heartbeat, a simmering presence—and she holds my shattered edges together.

A blinding light. Dalca wrenches back from the King, cupping his burnt hands against his chest.

The Great King turns his radiance upon me, but he cannot touch me, not with the Queen brimming under my skin. The air shimmers with heat as he shoots into the sky, a shard of light streaking toward the first ring.

My legs won't hold me.

I fall.

Arms wrap around me, lowering me to the ground. My cheek rests against a warm chest; I'm held tight in hands covered in burn-darkened lines.

"Look," Dalca says, voice gruff.

I do. The clouds are bright and soft, aglimmer with iridescent light.

Behind them is unbroken blue. A sky so impossibly big.

Distant bells clang, joined by others, a song I've never heard.

The Queen's curse upon us all is broken.

His voice trembles. "Can you see it?"

The Storm is gone.

Something slips out of me with every breath, and I think I'm leaving, I'm slipping away. I don't want to die; I wanted to live, and I wanted to protect them all, everyone I've loved and everyone else, those I might've loved, with a little more time.

A hand finds mine, holding tight. Dalca's eyes shine, and he won't let go, not until the end, but the end is here.

"Vesper . . ." He brushes the hair from my face. I look up, past him.

A different darkness closes in at the edges of my vision.

I want to gaze upon it one last time, before I go.

An endless sky.

EPILOGUE

The city holds its breath.

And then, slowly, carefully, as if approaching a skittish creature, the city embraces a fragile joy. Giddy laughter mixes with weeping and the pealing of bells.

The Storm is gone, and in its wake all is illuminated.

Everywhere are upturned faces. On some, the smiles are soft, astonished, smiles belonging to those who only knew the warmth of sunlight from stories. The sixth and seventh rings are found stranger than when they were lost, farms and forests of odd creatures and odder plants. Under shimmering branches, people rise as if waking from a dream, bearing curses as badges of their time in the Storm.

And in the third, in the arms of a weeping prince, Vesper Vale slips into a land between that of the living and that of the dead.

The prince tells her a thousand things. A promise: *All will know your name and what you have done for us.*

A plan: *I'll find a way. The mancers must know—I'll find a way to wake you.*

But most of all, he pleads:

Come back to me.

ACKNOWLEDGMENTS

A toast—

To you, who, by reading, have made this dream your own.

To those who beheld my story and, like a magic trick, transformed it into the book you now hold: editors and champions Nicole Sclama and Emilia Rhodes; designers Alice Wang and Samira Iravani; artist Peter Strain; those who pull the strings behind the scenes: Taylor McBroom, Emma Grant, Anna Ravenelle, Elizabeth Agyemang, and Cat Onder; to the incredible team across the pond at Hodder & Stoughton, Molly Powell, Kate Keehan, Callie Robertson, Sarah Clay; to Christabel McKinley; and to Tracey and Josh and all those at Adams Literary who went to bat first.

To those who read this story in older and stranger forms—and who gave wise counsel (some of which got through my thick head): Alita, Maria, Ellen, Graham, Jules, Penny, and Adalyn. And to Jake, who listened and whose sage words unlocked doors.

To those whose support came in other ways: to Acho, who models balance and quiet tenacity; to Laura, whose eyes were made to find beauty; and to my aunts, uncles, and cousins.

To Kobe, who, after reading one line of this story, offered me my first writing job. I hope to one day be worthy of that faith.

To my mother and father, who showed me how to fight for a dream.

To my grandparents, to my Ammamma, who taught me when to lower my fists.

And most of all, to my sidekick, who already knows why.